Immortal Love

Ludmilla Petrushevskaya

mmortal Love

Translated from the Russian
by Sally Laird

Pantheon Books
New York

*Sally Laird would like to thank Natalya Perova,
Svetlana Carston, Layla Alexander Garrett,
and Galina Antipenko for commenting on drafts
of this translation.*

Translation copyright © 1995 by Sally Laird

All rights reserved under International and Pan-American
Copyright Conventions. Published in the United States by
Pantheon Books, a division of Random House, Inc., New York.
Originally published in Russia in 1988. Copyright © 1988 by
Ludmilla Petrushevskaya. This translation first published in
Great Britain by Virago Press, London, in 1995.

Library of Congress Cataloging-in-Publication Data

Petrushevskaia, Liudmila.
Immortal love / Ludmilla Petrushevskaya; translated
from the Russian by Sally Laird.
p. cm.
ISBN 0-679-42257-9
1. Petrushevskaia, Liudmila—Translations into English.
I. Laird, Sally. II. Title.
PG3485.E724I48 1996
891.73'44—dc20 95-42673 CIP

Manufactured in the United States of America

First American Edition

2 4 6 8 9 7 5 3 1

Contents

Histories

Monologues

Histories

The Storyteller

You could get her to tell you anything and everything about herself if you only cared to ask her. She set no store at all by the sorts of things that other people hide or, on the contrary, tell you with great bitterness and self-pity or with muted sorrow. She gave the impression that she didn't even understand why concealment might sometimes be necessary, why there are certain things you tell only your nearest and dearest – and even then regret telling afterwards. She'd even embark on the story of her life to a colleague on the bus who'd asked idly 'how's life?', just for the sake of passing the time.

She'd reply quite cheerfully that things were pretty bad at the moment. Mum had been put in hospital, she'd say, and her father had had to get time off work to look after her. 'What, is your mother's condition that bad?' Yes, her condition was moderately serious, she'd reply, but if her father had got leave it must mean the end was near. 'What do you mean, the end?' Well, the usual thing. 'So what does your mother have?' Cancer, she'd say, in a perfectly normal tone of voice. 'Has she had it long?' the colleague would ask, so absorbed in the story she'd lost all sense of where she was. 'Eight years,' our storyteller would answer, and carry on answering all the questions that followed one after the other, so that when they arrived at her stop and the storyteller got out, her colleague would be left standing there in the bus quite overwhelmed, flushed from the sudden rush of blood to her head and adjusting the little silk scarf that had worked itself loose on her neck.

The girl who had just got out was twenty years old, tall, extremely tall in fact, but sufficiently plump that she didn't look out of proportion. All the same, people were apt all of a sudden to notice that she had enormously long calves. And if they happened to remark on the fact she'd just glance down, lift up her leg and say with total simplicity that during the last year she'd grown a good three inches and was quite sure now that she'd be just like her Mum. If anyone enquired further she'd say that her mother was pretty fat, especially in the tummy – it sagged as if she were nine months' pregnant. 'And it's absolutely covered in scars, but every three months she goes and has another operation just the same and they cut open her stomach all over again. It's been going on eight years now.' She's still alive, our storyteller would say, the doctors have all given up on her long ago, but she keeps staying alive and walking from room to room. And father's completely demented by now, every so often he throws a fit and starts pummelling the table. He gets especially mad and suspicious when his own conscience isn't clear – then there's no real need, she explained, for her to come home again after the movies, he wouldn't believe her anyway if she said she'd just been at the cinema rather than God knows where else. During these periods he and her mother took away her every last scrap of clothing, all her dresses and tops, all the things they'd bought her or that she'd managed to buy herself out of her own wages, and they'd lock up all these bits and pieces in the wardrobe in their room and then hand them out to her only one at a time, until finally all the things had migrated back again.

Or else she'd tell you how her father beat her up the whole time, ever since she was a child, especially if she stayed late at a girlfriend's house after school. Her father might go for her with a chair on these occasions, although other times for no particular reason she'd get away with it. She'd got used to distinguishing between these moods of her father's and guessing whether her father had anyone on the go at that moment or not. As for her mother, she'd become quite indifferent to these affairs of his, after all she knew there was no chance of her getting out and about with that stomach of hers, and she didn't have any special training in anything. So she baked pies and sewed her husband's collars on and pottered round the house doing this and that. But her father didn't want to admit that anything was ever going to change or that he could no longer look people honestly in the eye, even though no one reproached him and, on the contrary, everyone kept urging him to make a break for it and do something to improve his life. But her father stubbornly made sure his behaviour was such that no one would ever dream there was anything amiss, and just for that reason he was over-assiduous in suspecting Galya, making clear by this means his own impeccable honesty. But still, Galya would say, why, even in the old days – when her mother's health was still good and everything was fine in the family – why did he used to suspect Galya even then and come and fetch her from school, or else suddenly, late in the evening, when she'd already been put to bed and the light turned out, come into her room, catch her unawares by turning the light on, and then pretend that he was searching for something in the desk – an eraser or indelible pencil or whatever?

She'd relate all these things one after the other, so long as you went on asking questions. And she never gave the impression that she was embarrassed or reluctant to answer some particular question, but had just decided on the spur of the moment to go on answering because what did it matter anyway. No, she'd unpack with an air of complete equanimity everything that was in her soul. For example, on a winter's evening at the bus stop she might explain that she had a boyfriend, an architect, but he'd been talking about having to part with her for a month while he went on holiday; it would give him a chance to take stock of things, he'd said, so in a month's time he'd be able to see her again and finally decide how things stood. And when asked whether she loved him, Galya calmly replied that of course she did, but the question was what would come of it all. He had an elderly mother, and he himself was nearly forty years old, and he couldn't make up his mind even to picture what it would be like to have, not just one woman ruling the roost in their two little rooms, but his own young wife as well; he couldn't begin to think how complicated it would all be, with him working so hard and being an artist into the bargain. For the time being he would invite her to visit him at their home, he and his mother would sit her down in an armchair and wait on her and meanwhile cautiously exchange glances, as if asking themselves how on earth they'd all fit into those two little rooms? He had painted Galya's portrait and would sometimes ask if no one had ever told her how much she resembled a Greek goddess with that hair of hers, and those eyes, and that nose and mouth and chin and neck and ears?

And then a new boyfriend turned up in Galya's life,

and it was just the same story as with the architect, and everyone got to know all about this new one, the engineer, as well. Indeed, in the office where Galya worked her colleagues made a kind of game out of wringing every last drop of information out of her, right down to the bottom, the final details, the things Galya herself didn't really understand but that all the others, experienced men and women, would understand a great deal better than she did. All the more so since at the present stage there was no need to start from the very beginning, everything was a continuation of what had gone before. For example there was no need to find out whether she was a virgin or not, she'd already said she was a virgin and there was absolutely no reason to doubt that she was telling the truth. In fact she was so utterly guileless that one sometimes felt a bit uncomfortable or ashamed to go on probing her. There were certain things she just didn't understand, certain shameful women's secrets; she didn't know the art of self-defence, the tactics of the mollusc which slams shut its shell before anyone's had a chance to glance in and find out what else is concealed in there, although everyone in fact knows perfectly well what sort of things might be hidden inside. But it's as if things that have never actually been named don't really exist in nature, so all you can do is guess, and no one knows about them for sure. That's what real bashfulness, real modesty means.

But with Galya, no, Galya for example would tell you that every evening her father used to ask her how the day had gone and then he'd check up on her, ring up the teacher and her various friends, so that Galya willy-nilly had to tell him the whole truth. But that wasn't enough for him either. He'd question her about her thoughts, about her experiences, whether or not she had cried and if so where, when the teacher had made her stand outside the class for chatting too much with the girls at the desk in front. And what had they in fact been chatting about, her father would ask, his hand clasping the back of the chair beside him where Galya was sitting, and she knew that at any moment he was liable to shout 'you're lying!' and start to beat her, so that she would turn her whole self inside out straight away; and if in fact she hadn't been thinking or talking about anything particular at the moment in question, the moment that her father had been asking about, she didn't even try to invent some appropriate thoughts, because her father could sense very precisely when she started making things up. Instead she'd sit there trying to remember, and in the end she'd report that they'd been talking about the fact that she'd asked the girls in front to give back the eraser she'd lent them the previous lesson.

So with Galya there was no need to start questioning her from the very beginning, you could just take up the story where you'd left off the last time. For example, you could ask how her mother was feeling. And she'd answer that for the moment she was feeling pretty bad, her father's leave had come to an end, he'd been sitting there at the hospital with her mother every day, so that the whole hospital knew him and respected him now, and the ladies at the cloakroom would just take his overcoat and hang it up without asking for his visitor's pass, and give him an overall to wear, and now he didn't know what to do, after all you had to force her to eat, on her own she mightn't take anything at all or just a spoonful of broth, while come what may he'd boil up some chicken for her and take the broth in a wide-necked thermos flask to the hospital. But now her grandmother, her father's mother, had arrived on the scene and she was going to the hospital now, and her father didn't even ask her grandmother how things were going, because he knew that when anything happened he'd be the first to be informed at work, he'd left his telephone number under the glass on the little table where the nurse on duty sat.

And when she related these things she didn't even cry, although everyone else's eyes would mist over when they got to hear the story, one after the other. Somehow it never happened that Galya would tell everyone the story at once – it wasn't as if she were delivering a report so that everyone had to meet up to hear it. So everyone would ask her about it in turn in the corridor or in the canteen or standing by the mirror. In passing she might also answer a question about the engineer, her new boyfriend, and relate that he was a very good man, eight years older than her, and that he'd already introduced her to his family on his mother's birthday and that she'd liked everyone very much. 'Don't count your chickens' almost all the women without exception had said, but she'd just brushed that aside and said what on earth did they mean.

Then Galya disappeared for a long time from the office, took official leave in her turn to sit with her mother in the hospital. At this point everyone immediately forgot about her, only now and then someone would say 'We ought to give her a ring and find out how things are', but that was always the end of the matter, until her leave of absence ran out and she was supposed to turn up for work but was missing the whole day. The boss came out of his room into the general office together with the head of personnel, and they asked if anyone had heard when Galya was going to turn up, because her leave had run out, but if there were any extenuating documents, certificates or suchlike, she should have brought them in in advance. At which point there was a phone call, and a male voice informed them that Galya's mother had died and that in connection with this she would be coming to work on Thursday, and would bring the application for an extension of leave with her then, and she'd asked them kindly to backdate it for her.

And then Galya turned up to work as if nothing had happened, exactly the same as she'd always been, and no paler than usual. And at this point everything went into reverse. On the contrary now no one asked her anything, they'd communicate with her only about things relating to work or the weather, but no one was prepared to question her at all. Something had happened in the souls of all of them, a sort of total reversal, so that no one wanted to hear about the funeral or how Galya's father was doing now, and whether he was planning to marry again, or how things were going with Galya's boyfriend, the engineer.

But then a month or two went by, and out of sheer inertia one of the women asked Galya a question after all, just as a joke – the sort of question no normal girl would have answered: 'So when's the wedding going to be?' To which Galya, not the least put out, replied for all to hear that the wedding ceremony had been fixed for two months hence, on the seventeenth, a Friday.

For a start no one had expected such a precise answer from her, nor could anyone care less, Galya's wedding was of absolutely no interest to anyone. Besides, if only from motives of simple self-defence, no girl in her right mind would have started notifying all and sundry of her wedding two months in advance: a great deal could happen in the course of those two months, and why anyway did every Tom, Dick and Harry have to know about this profoundly personal and intimate event?

Everyone was completely taken aback. No one had expected this of Galya, especially since the department was being reorganised and in the course of the reorganisation Galya was going to be made redundant, so that by the time Galya was due to get married she'd no longer be part of the office team anyway, which was all the more reason why this deeply personal event in her life would be of absolutely no interest to anyone. But for the moment Galya didn't know anything at all about her forthcoming redundancy. Later, it's true, she did find out, she was summoned to see the head of personnel who informed her of it, adding that they would try and get her employment elsewhere since the head of department had good connections.

But by that time Galya had already made a great mistake: she'd invited the whole office to come to her wedding and had even given them the address of the café where the reception was going to be held in a month's time. She began bringing in various things to the office – the material for her wedding dress, which everyone had to brace themselves to look at, knowing very well as they all did that Galya was going to be made redundant, while she herself at that stage wasn't aware of the fact at the time. Then Galya brought in the pearly collar and cuffs that were to go with the dress and drew a picture of the design for everyone who cared to see. But there was none of the old element in these stories now – with other people asking all the questions, and Galya just answering. No,

now Galya herself started volunteering her story un-
prompted, frantically almost, as if she were afraid no
one would hear her out. And people started pointing
out that there were other things one was supposed
to do during working hours, for instance do the work
one was paid to do. At which point Galya would
immediately shut up and put away all the drawings
and cuffs and whatnot, but the following day the same
business would start all over again.

When Galya came back from seeing the head of
personnel, from whom she'd finally learned that she
was to be made redundant, she said quite unperturbed
that she'd be expecting everyone at the wedding reception in the café just the same and would be sending
them all proper invitations. And everyone was unpleasantly taken aback, especially since Friday was such a
precious day for them all, the end of the week, the day
you went off to the country or looked after some other
private business of your own. But she failed to pick up
the slightest hint on this score, and when she was saying
farewell to everyone on her last day she repeated yet
again: 'So, we're all going to have a great time at my
wedding, don't forget, it's a week on Friday.'

Besides it turned out that far from being out of work
she'd got a good new job in an archive, on a higher
salary than she'd got in the office. So she had no reason
to feel put out at all, the head of department had taken
care and gone to a lot of trouble on her account.

And everyone would have forgotten all about Galya
and her wedding, except that the day before the
wedding, on the Thursday, she rang the office and
caught literally everyone unawares. People would
come up to the phone, because she called each and
every one of them in turn and said 'You haven't

forgotten, I'm expecting you tomorrow evening at the café on Semenovskaya Street? You got the invitation all right, didn't you?' And absolutely each and every one replied that they'd received the invitation, and thank you very much, but unfortunately they weren't able to come. At which point, believe it or not, she in turn started asking – over the telephone, down the wires, without even seeing them, like a blindwoman – asking why they couldn't come. Such things are just not done. And if you do go as far as to ask people such things it absolutely must be face to face, when you can see your interlocutor and understand what's what from his face and decide on that basis whether it's worth maintaining friendly relations, after he's done something so utterly base as to refuse to come to your wedding. But this Galya, it was as if she didn't understand anything at all, she kept asking and asking everyone in the office why they weren't going to come to her wedding. And she didn't have a single person in the office that she could have relied on, not a single girlfriend who out of concern for her would have zealously organised a rota for people to come to the telephone. And indeed what girlfriends could Galya have had there, when she was only twenty years old, and the only other people of that age in the office were the typist and the courier, but they both sat in the little room next to the cloakroom, in the dispatch office. Those were the only girlfriends she might have made.

And everyone in the office tried to wriggle out of it as best they could. One woman didn't even come to the telephone but asked someone else to say that she wasn't there, that she'd had to go off to fetch supplies. Another promised over the phone that she'd come, but everyone realised how much this promise was worth, knowing that she always found some way at the last moment to get out of any unpleasant situation, and that it would be as simple as anything when the wedding was over and done with to explain then why she hadn't been able to come. Galya wasn't even working in the office any more and was hardly likely to turn up after the wedding to find out the excellent reasons why people hadn't turned up for the reception. One young man of thirty or so, very intelligent and completely unable to bear it when anyone put psychological pressure on him, trying to organise his personal life, gave her a very clever answer on the phone: 'Galya dear, you're still young, you have your whole life before you. Whereas I've been invited just this very Friday to the home of a dear old lady I know who's celebrating her seventieth birthday just that evening. So you understand I'm sure, and I wish you all the happiness in the world from the bottom of my heart. You deserve it. Be a good girl and don't drink too much at the wedding. So once again all the very best. Take care.' At which point he put down the receiver, having successfully relieved the situation for everyone else in the office.

But the worst thing happened just five minutes later, when the boss came out of his room into the general office and said, cheerfully rubbing his hands, 'So, shall we organise a special outing to Galya's wedding then?' Everyone exchanged glances and realised at once that Galya must have slyly phoned him direct and he'd accepted – being completely out of touch with all the affairs of the office, seeing them only through the fantastic, unreal world of memos, pronouncements and occasional tête-à-têtes with one or other of the staff in his office.

Everyone began awkwardly explaining that they couldn't go to the wedding and why. Some of them, like the young man, simply kept quiet and didn't explain a thing. In the end the union rep bestirred herself and said that she was planning to go too and that she'd organise the outing, and later, when the boss had disappeared again behind the doors of his office, the union rep darted off to the dispatch room and in a twinkling organised the girls – the typist and the courier – and rang up the office photographer, so that the next day they all set off to the wedding in a Volga sedan and on Monday morning had endless funny tales to tell about the wedding. About how Galya, with typical *naïveté*, had asked them 'So what do you think of my husband?' and showed them the shoes she was wearing under her long dress – 'What do you think of these shoes?' And about the terrible shortage of food, so that the girls from the dispatch room had simply been sent off to the other tables to reconnoitre and had carried off and brought back a dish with aspic and two plates of salami, one cooked, one smoked. And their table had been the rowdiest of all, although all the guests had been pretty riotous, all hundred of them. And how the boss had been in stitches and had shouted along with the rest of them 'Life is bitter, make it sweet!' And how they'd been overcome by a kind of acquisitive mania, they'd gone straight up to the other tables and started grabbing things, bottles of vodka and bouquets of flowers. And how the girls from despatch had run off with a huge bouquet of white lilies from the neighbouring table when it was already time to leave, because the boss had said to them slyly, like a little kid: 'Help yourselves girls, when'll you get another chance like this to let your hair down at a wedding?' – so they'd grabbed this huge

15

bouquet of white lilies straight from the vase as they were on the point of leaving. And on the way out they'd gone into the toilet to tidy their hair and powder their noses, because they were all pretty drunk by then. And there they'd run into Galya, felt terribly embarrassed, and proffered her the ill-starred bouquet of lilies, saying absolutely idiotically 'These are for you'. And Galya in her long dress down to her heels had taken off her bridal veil and her gloves and was standing there in floods of tears in the dirty café toilet.

That was the thing they kept recounting, this appallingly idiotic incident, when right at the end of the wedding they'd suddenly gone and handed the bride this bouquet of white lilies there in the dirty toilet, and how she'd had to clutch it and her gloves together in both hands, quite at a loss as to what to do with the flowers.

A Case of Virgin Birth

Both mother and son were having love affairs con-
currently, and one Sunday morning after breakfast the
son revealed that his girlfriend was called Natasha
Kandaurova. His mother burst out laughing, because
her sailor's surname began with 'Kan' as well; she told
him the whole name. But her son forgot it immediately.
He couldn't understand why he'd suddenly said
'Natasha Kandaurova' out loud. He tried to join in his
mother's laughter over the coincidence, but in fact
felt terribly threatened. And when his mother started
laughingly telling him something about her sailor, he
got up and went into the kitchen. She carried on talking in the other room, smiling at her own story, but he
couldn't take any of it in and stood there frozen over
the sink. At last his mother fell silent, as if expecting
him to tell her his own story now about Natasha
Kandaurova. And you could sense in her silence that
she felt somehow sated, as if she had got just what she
wanted and was poised and waiting to take him under
her wing, console him with her greater experience of
life and in turn receive consolation. And there was something idiotic, female, over-excited in her glee at how
the two of them – in a little family plot – would join
forces now against the two 'Kans'. It was as if she were
overjoyed at a sudden unexpected victory – overjoyed
that he'd finally grown up and could understand her
life and let her understand his life too.

He stood on the two bricks in front of the sink,

cleaning his teeth and pausing now and then to stare fixedly at a point in front of him; then he removed the towel from his neck, hung it on the nail and carefully stepped along the plank that led over the newly-painted floor to the outside door. The plank bent under his weight, and he started rocking on it absent-mindedly. He realised that he'd given away Natasha Kandaurova's name just out of the desire to say it out loud: 'Natasha Kandaurova'. In his mind he was talking to her the whole time, but it turned out that wasn't enough. It turned out that he needed to pronounce the name out loud, in a kind of blind bragging, a sort of oblivion. 'Kandaurova,' he said out loud again, testing himself, testing to see if he could manage to feel even more overwhelmed. He didn't say the whole word, 'Kandaurova', but instead sang 'Ka . . . a' to himself – and went out onto the stairs humming. His mother, no doubt, understood this 'Ka . . . a', but didn't shout out anything after him; calm now, she just sat in the room, over the dirty cups and plates.

He'd many times suffered these torments from her; when she was washing him in the tub as a child, for instance, she'd tell him that certain boys indulged in silly things, but that was very bad, you could land up in hospital and have to have injections. And when he was a bit older she'd suddenly started telling him what terrible agonies she'd been through giving birth to him – she was only eighteen years old and her case was one in a million, a case of virgin birth, she said laughing: she'd been a virgin when she lay down in the labour room but the doctor hadn't wanted to interfere surgically, so it was her son who'd made her a woman . . . She told him all this in the dark as he lay there on his folding bed, the blanket tucked in all around; she'd put on her nightie and crawled over to her own bed on her knees, and now lay rubbing her feet together with a dry, rasping sound. He lay there staring up at the ceiling and clenching his teeth in horror. Virgin, birth – he'd only just started looking up words like that in dictionaries and encyclopaedias, there was something unbearably forbidden in them, secret, essential, something that shouldn't be destroyed but should have accumulated in him gradually, so he'd eventually be able to reconcile himself to it all. But his mother had no pity. It was as if she pined for her own family, the family she hadn't had for ages now, and couldn't wait for her son to grow up a bit so that she could get even closer to him, explaining to him how much he belonged to her, how much he was hers. And because of this he couldn't bear even quite harmless recollections about what it was like when he was little, how when she lived in the hostel she wasn't allowed to hang up the nappies to dry in the daytime – she could only hang them up at night in the communal kitchen; or how, when she was still pregnant, she'd made some lace to trim the edges of his little bed-clothes, to protect his face from the flies but still allow him to breathe. And how she loathed the smell of her husband Stepanov's body – for some reason she felt he smelled of acrid dirty hair – and how she wouldn't let this Stepanov get near her, and all the girls in the hostel used to guard her when she lay in bed, feeling sick at the mere thought that Stepanov might come within shooting distance of her.

And he was forced to remember all this and keep it inside him and feel shame at the mere mention of the words 'birth' or 'virgin', because they were quite different for him than for all the other kids in the class.

19

And when the other kids sat around on the old desks behind the school, relating various incidents to each other and saying what meant what, he'd force himself to laugh along with the rest so that no one would notice anything, because he had a dreadful secret – the words 'virgin' and 'birth' were words about him, he had played a shameful part in all this himself.

And he didn't have any close friend with whom he might have discussed it all, cleared up the whole story and finally confessed that it was he who had made his mother a woman in the course of his own birth.

Later, when he'd grown up and begun to look at his mother with condescension – and he found a certain unexpected support in this, support for his budding sense of dignity – he ceased to remember the reason for his childish shame, although now and then for no particular reason he felt terribly sad. But he quickly suppressed this sadness in himself. And his mother didn't know how to approach him now; she was afraid of being hurt afresh, of reopening old wounds by trying to get closer, while every time he calmly moved away and became yet more aloof. Sometimes, it's true, he'd chat to her for a while about this and that, mainly about the books he'd been reading. And every time she became so immersed in these conversations, entered into them so eagerly, latched on so keenly to his every word that he began to feel stifled and uncomfortable in his role of adored son and would distance himself again, moving off and leaving her perplexed and afraid of herself.

Once, it's true, she stopped paying attention to how he was behaving towards her and asked him straight out to accompany her to hospital. She had been upset since the morning, when he was getting ready for school; instead of making him scrambled eggs as usual, she just lay there drowsy-eyed looking out of the window. When he got back from school he felt a bit piqued because he sensed that she no longer felt burdened by his superiority, she had some grown-up business of her own which he wasn't yet old enough to deal with. And that in general he knew very little about her, and that there were other things in her life besides him.

Obediently he went along with her, admittedly not wanting her to lean on him, because he felt there was a certain pretence in that; if he hadn't been there she would have just walked there by herself without leaning on anyone. But she didn't sense his thoughts, even though she normally sensed everything that he was feeling. She leaned on his shoulder, and he took her to the bus stop. It was a deserted summer evening, there was no one about. And there was no one round the hospital either. When they went up the stone steps his mother rang the bell and just waited there, without turning round. Then she turned and hastily, as if preoccupied, kissed him on the forehead. She was met at the door by a fat nurse.

He was left alone and wandered about the stone steps outside, reading the notice stuck up on the other side of the glass door: 'Maternity Reception: Side Entrance'. The word 'maternity' made him feel terribly uncomfortable, but he smiled ironically in an effort to suppress his childish chagrin. Soon the door opened slightly; on the far side a nurse was working away, pulling the handle towards her without looking at him. In the same way, without looking at him, she handed him a string bag containing a fat package wrapped in newspaper, holding it out through the gap in the half-open door. He turned and left with the ridiculous string bag, his mother's underwear wrapped inside, and the nurse quickly shut the door and again started tugging at the handle to close it.

He was left quite alone with just the money his mother had given him. It was nearly the end of term, and many of the kids at school – those who had already taken their exams – were mucking around and creating a riot during lessons. He read through all the lessons and felt an unprecedented sense of lightness and freedom. During the last drawing lesson, when he was waiting with his drawing book for the teacher, Nikola, to summon him, the headmaster's secretary Zoya Alekseevna suddenly interrupted the class and loudly called out his name. For some reason it gave him an unpleasant fright. He got up and followed the secretary. The telephone was lying off the hook on the table on the ground floor. 'It's for you' said Zoya Alekseevna significantly, 'Your mother ringing from the hospital'. He took the receiver and said importantly: 'Speaking', but couldn't hear anything in reply, only a vague crackling. Then he heard his mother's faraway voice: 'Can you hear me? Is that you?' 'Speaking!' he said significantly again. He wasn't very sure how you were supposed to speak on the telephone. 'How are you doing?' his mother asked. Zoya Alekseevna stood over the table sorting out various papers. She was obviously annoyed at having a pupil use the telephone so long. 'Are you eating properly?' his mother asked in a strained voice. 'Yes, yes!' he said, both trying to answer his mother yet failing to hear anything down the line. From far away his mother shouted: 'Maybe you could come and visit me. Everyone here has . . .' she didn't manage to finish, but just seemed to fade away. 'Yes, yes, of course, of course,' he answered after a moment's pause. 'I've got to go, bye for now . . . We're doing our end-of-term exams,' he added. 'I've already had the operation,' she said hastily, 'I lost a lot of blood, you know, but everything's OK! Everything's OK!' she shouted, and then it was as if a sudden dryness choked his throat, he had to strain every nerve not to burst into tears. 'Everything will be all right!' he said, 'Everything will be OK,' he repeated heatedly, saying goodbye to his mother. 'I'll come and fetch you and get you out of that hell-hole.' He put down the receiver and quickly turned to go, avoiding Zoya Alekseevna's glance. He felt quite shaken, perhaps by his own goodness.

For a long time afterwards he felt a kind of lightness and tenderness, he wouldn't allow his mother to get up and once went to the chemist himself to buy her cotton wool for dressings, as well as doing the regular shopping each day. She didn't pester him with her usual endearments and confessions – that period had already passed, she had learned her lesson. She lay there quietly, on her stomach or on her back, turning her face towards him. She followed him with her eyes, watching whatever he was doing in the room, and only from time to time lifted her hand to smooth the hair back over her ears.

Then she recovered and began to bustle about again, so that he'd at least be able to go to the second session of summer camp, but he said he wouldn't dream of going anyway. So she stopped bustling and started quietly going out in the evenings, snapping her handbag shut as she stood at the door. She always checked she had her keys on her before going out.

Nowadays she no longer chatted idly of this and that, as she used to do. But sometimes she'd suddenly seem to forget everything, her customary tension evaporated, and he'd hear her singing in the kitchen in her breathless, nasal voice: 'And only . . . then . . . on the far . . . shore . . . when you meet . . . an . . . other . . .'

It usually happened when the weather was fine and the sun was shining on a Sunday morning. She'd strip the curtains off the windows and the sheets and pillow slips off the beds and set off to wash them all, tilting her face to one side as she carried the whole heap. And on these occasions, giving in to the new impulse inside him, he'd get down barefoot to wash the floor, awkwardly wringing out the cloth.

But on that particular Sunday he didn't wash the floor – it had just been painted, and he and his mother had just spent the whole day in any case scrubbing and cleaning up after the painters. But that wasn't the real reason why he didn't wash the floor. Even if it had been dirty and unpainted he wouldn't have washed it on that accursed Sunday, when he'd let himself be crushed, saying out loud the name Natasha Kandaurova. He would have leapt down the stairs just the same, with open mouth, singing 'Na . . . a', but mentally still drawing out that same sound 'Ka . . . a . . .' . . .

His mother stayed there sitting over the dirty dishes, not because she was disturbed or grieved by hearing that her son had a girl called Natasha Kandaurova. The name didn't mean anything in itself. Years back when she used to fetch him on Saturdays from the kindergarten where he boarded in the week, she'd ask him who he was friends with these days, and every time he'd reply seriously: Svetlana Yagodinina and Lena Perova: she remembered them to this day, these names that she used to hear every week. They meant absolutely nothing to her. She was simply happy that her son had friends, that he wasn't alone and lonesome when he went to bed in the dormitory with twenty-five other children or sat down to eat in the canteen. And every time she'd check that her son was still friends with Svetlana and Lena.

But every time he'd cling to her just the same when she said goodbye at the kindergarten and left him there. Sometimes she managed to slip off without his noticing, and the teachers would tell her later – though sometimes they forgot, because a whole week had passed since – that he'd looked for her behind the cupboards and in the teachers' toilet, because once he'd seen her go off to the teachers' toilet and lock the door with the little hook, and he'd been terribly scared and started desperately tugging at the door, holding on to a nail that was sticking out – he couldn't reach the handle. And many times afterwards he'd stand patiently outside the teachers' toilet waiting for her to unfasten the hook. Or the night nurses would tell her that he'd stood weeping by his bed again at night, determined not to get in and lie down.

But once, on a parents' day in summer, when he felt specially stunned by her sky blue dress and the box of candy she'd given him – three different sorts in layers – he'd lost all self-control and simply hung on to the edge of her dress, even when he was still sitting there in her lap. He seemed to her particularly pale and listless that day, barely able to eat his salami sandwich, and he suddenly turned round in her lap and said, 'I've been thinking about you, Mummy'. With his other hand he clung on to her dress, and his mouth glistened with butter.

And when the bell rang for dinner and all the parents crowded round the steps, watching the children go inside with their various gifts, he understood what it meant and gagged on the sandwich. She calmed him down, held him tight and rocked him on her knees, and he believed then that she wouldn't go away. But the teacher had already gathered all the children in the washroom, and the dinner had been carried past the pavilion outside in a pail covered with fresh gauze, and the other parents were blowing kisses outside the washroom window and hurrying away past the pavilion, and that's when she resorted to playing a trick on him. 'You haven't picked flowers for Mummy for ages,' she said. He nodded, let go of her dress and walked out of the pavilion. 'Don't pick any of the planted flowers, just the wild ones,' she shouted after him. She never missed an opportunity to try and educate him, it was only a shame that they spent so little time together, and he never listened to her properly, he spent all the time they had just trying to be with her. Even at night he'd get up, stand there hesitating beside his folding bed, then quickly run over to her bed, clamber over the blanket and stay there breathing timidly until she told him to go away. But he'd climb in beside her all the same, and she'd tuck the blanket round him and watch over him all night, so that she didn't get a wink of sleep and by morning was often scrunched up at the foot of the bed, bent double so that he could sleep in comfort. In her sleepy state she didn't stop to reason but simply did what she had to to make him comfortable. Once awake she realised that she ought to do what was right, not just what made him happy. And now he'd walked off over the grass and disappeared behind a bush, and she quickly got up from the bench, ran to the gates and set off heavy-hearted to the station. She didn't wait behind the fence to watch him come back to the pavilion, step wordlessly on to the wooden floor, then rush back to the house and stand outside the teachers' toilet, tugging at the nail . . .

And by the time she came next, this time to fetch him for good and take him to a different kindergarten, a month had already passed since the incident with the flowers. And she had already forgotten about it, as he no doubt had too. But he showed no joy on seeing her. He stood there patiently while she did up his buttons and his shoelaces and tied on his hat. She kissed him and his cheek was cold, compliant. He flashed a glance at his mother, and his eyes looked weary, as if he could hardly bear the weight of his eyelids.

But what could she do! She was still so young then. If it had been now she would have gone to any length, laid herself out to manage, but not played that trick on him with the flowers or tried to push him away when he came to her at night when he was afraid. Oddly enough, though, he had no recollection of the incident with the flowers. It seemed to have been erased from his memory straightaway, as if it had never been. He never brought it up at all, and she never told him about it, although she was naturally so communicative and open-hearted. She never mentioned the incident at all. She only remembered it over and over again, and punished herself for it.

Vanya the Goat

Once upon a time there lived a great writer – or quite possibly a bad one – who left on earth no memorial to himself save a son, an overgrown idler and mummy's boy, and a daughter, also grown-up, who knew no boundaries or moral obligations in life. Oh, and he also left a wife. But it's not in the form of a wife that the memory of a man resides, but in the form of his offspring, in this case the son and the daughter. Those other sons and daughters of his, the only ones that should have remained to represent him – the plays and novels he wrote, in other words – had got mislaid for the most part, little by little, God knows how, in the turmoil of the post-war years; at all events, when the family moved to a new apartment, the manuscripts formed no part of the luggage conveyed. True, it was possible that the elderly widow had concealed the manuscripts in mattresses or sewn them into pillows, and in this form borne them from place to place. But why? Why, for what reason, for what possible future to come would the sombre widow have sought to preserve these worthless scribbles, these manuscripts that no one had ever read? At all events, when the phone call came from that southern university town and a male voice delivered the information that he, a postgraduate named Blagov, was engaged in a study of the writer N, the widow was quite unable to tell him anything worthwhile. And she was equally unable to tell him anything in a personal interview, when Blagov came to Moscow and suggested that they meet and have a chat. The interview, moreover, took place not in her home but at the home of Blagov's cousin, a room in a communal apartment where Blagov was staying, and during the interview the cousin kept coming in and out of the room, getting dressed and undressed, went off to the baker's and in general behaved like an untamed bird, showing no concern whatsoever for her cousin's affairs, not even for the fact that he had brought God knows whom back to her room, some relative of Pushkin's for all she knew, to inspect the stains on her wallpaper and the window that hadn't been cleaned since autumn.

The widow, in her daughter's presence, churned out all sorts of drivel about her war-time youth and about her present life as a toiler in the field of librarianship, about the difficulties of being head of department and about the readers' conferences she ran, one of which Blagov was invited to attend.

This encounter took place in someone else's house, rather than the writer's own, because no stranger could set foot in the latter's home – for the writer's son Kolya, a forty-year-old catatonic who'd given up the use of water, soap or razor and pissed only in a bottle, had locked himself up in one of his father's rooms. Kolya had stained the walls of this room particularly badly in certain favourite places; he'd reached out to touch these chosen spots on the wall thousands of times over as he lay in the room, smoked, cracked the dirt off his nails, whispered away to himself or worked himself up to loud cries. It would have been shameful to let anyone else see how they lived, the widow and her young daughter, who was, after all, the writer's daughter too. But no shame, on the other hand, was actually involved, for no one ever set foot beyond the lobby of their apartment. Evening began in Kolya's room according to the laws of natural light; for ages now he'd had no other light in the room. In the winter the radiator dripped through the lagging into a jar, and the wallpaper was torn in places, although each time he walked the perimeter of his room Kolya fastidiously stuck back the dangling shreds of paper; they'd got filthy from the constant touch of Kolya's thin, almost transparent fingers; the shreds had curled like fleece. Kolya had disappeared from the world at the age of twenty – scared off by his stint in the army, though the formal reason given was a particularly severe bout of flu. Kolya's sole occupation during daylight hours was chess – playing chess and reading chess journals. And when his fame as an inventor of games flew round the whole world and a young Swede started coming to the house and trying to get in and see him, Kolya's mother wouldn't even let him into the lobby, and Kolya himself in a state of terrible agitation stood behind the door and listened to his mother sourly answering the translator, trying to push both visitors further down the corridor where the oppressive stench of Kolya's lair would not reach them.

In any case, Blagov got no joy out of them on that occasion, but the next time he came to Moscow, two years later, N's family had moved to a new apartment, where nothing so far had managed to fall to bits and where Kolya was leading a new life with electric light and a floor coated with varnish.

Thus Blagov was received into this home where, for the time being, everything shone and sparkled, including the dinner service and the crystal on the table, for although the widow had lived in poverty in the old apartment, the poverty was only external, for show, and it was evident she must have kept the best crystal and the Sèvres porcelain wrapped in rags and stowed in boxes in hope of better times. The better times came, and the best day of all those better days turned out to be the one when Blagov came to visit, for the apartment was gleaming like a new pin, and the furniture, crystal and china were all antiques, and God knows what poor Blagov might have thought (indeed, undoubtedly did think) in relation to the main object of his life – the manuscripts of the writer N, which amid such prosperity must certainly have been preserved.

The widow, however, was fiercely on guard, for at any minute Kolya might come out of his room shouting, 'Don't give up on me!' The fact was that during those years of intense suffering the widow had accumulated a great many illnesses, among them a new one which had not yet been diagnosed, but ever more insistently demanded diagnosis, becoming daily more apparent. Several times a day the widow would press her palm to the place that hurt, and her eyes would fill with tears. She said nothing out loud, however, because there was no one to complain to – at the library her young deputy caught her out in an error every so often and was obviously on the lookout to take her place, since the widow was already past pensionable age. The situation at home was as already described, though in fact only half-described, since the writer's daughter Elsa has not yet appeared on the scene. But in her worst nightmare the widow could not have imagined staying at home with Elsa, since the latter brought her nothing but trouble. You couldn't rely on Elsa for anything. That was precisely what that unfortunate composer of chess games, Kolya, had had in mind, feeling all that last week the threat hanging over him, so that he kept bursting out into his mother's territory and shouting: 'Don't give up on me!' For indeed whom could the widow leave Kolya with – Kolya and his bottle of urine – if she were to go to hospital for tests, and in due course depart still further? Not with Elsa for sure – Elsa who stayed away from home for days on end, so that only the gradual disappearance of her garments indicated that she visited the apartment during working hours, and took her bits and pieces off somewhere else, and was generally alive and living somewhere or other.

As for Blagov, Blagov sat at the table and showered them with compliments. He liked everything in the house: the writer's sweetly venomous widow, who kept bustling about while her thoughts, quite obviously, had wandered elsewhere (to the room next door, we can safely surmise), and the writer's daughter Elsa, who slapped the wine into wine glasses and didn't eat anything as she drank and altogether led an autonomous existence, never once joining in the conversation. It was with her that Blagov decided to have a talk about the main thing, the manuscripts.

'May I just have a quick word?' murmured Blagov, when the mother had disappeared off to the kitchen or somewhere else, 'You were very young, weren't you, when your father died?'

'Yes,' said Elsa, 'if I was even born.'

'I see,' said Blagov, and a heavy silence ensued. He wasn't sure what Elsa had meant – whether she meant she was born after her father died and had nothing whatsoever to do with him, or rather that she was in doubt whether she'd been born at all and was not perhaps merely dreaming.

'You look like him,' Blagov said, rejecting thereby

both the first and second interpretations of Elsa's answer. 'I have a portrait of him. He was a very handsome man.'

Elsa had not in fact intended either meaning in her reply; she simply didn't want Blagov to know her age.

'I never knew him,' she said.

'Would you like a photo of him? I've got a spare one.'

'Thanks,' said Elsa, at which moment a crash of broken glass resounded from the other room and someone was heard running. 'We haven't got any pictures of him. He left my mother, you see.'

'Oh! – so that's why she seems so pained at everything . . . Did she suffer very much?'

'I don't know, I wasn't around then,' said the stubborn Elsa, although at the time in question she'd been five years old.

'You know, the more writers' lives I go into, the more I see there's always something wrong. Strange lives that leave other people crippled – as if the human race went on living and living and then suddenly fell to bits, all because a writer had appeared and started wreaking havoc. You're lucky having the mother you do . . .'

'Yes, Mum's a good sort,' said Elsa.

'I suppose she must have kept a few of your father's things?'

'What things? There was a cap of his. A leather coat . . .'

'By things I mean of course his works.'

'No, I would have known if she had. When I was a child I used to rummage around in all her stuff.'

'So where did it all go?'

'How should I know? What was there anyway?'

'Well there was a big novel and several novellas and lots of stories, two volumes at least . . .'

'"Vanya the Goat", d'you mean?'

'What's "Vanya the Goat"?'

'My brother told me the story – he'd read it.'

'Your brother? Do you think I could get to meet him?'

'Here's Mum now.'

The widow came in, flushed and out of breath, her hands red from cleaning up, and met the question head on: could he meet Kolya?

'No of course not, that's out of the question. And if you'd excuse me now, I've been feeling very tired these last few days . . .'

And the widow put her hand on her stomach and her eyes filled with tears.

Blagov stood up and Elsa stood up too, seizing an uncorked bottle of wine.

'Where are you off to now?' the widow asked.

'I'll see him out,' said Elsa.

Need one explain further that Elsa then proposed the two of them drink the bottle of wine down in the entrance of the block, whereupon Blagov felt obliged to invite Elsa out to a café, so they sat for a while in the café, and then the whole thing came to a head back in the hallway of the block, where Elsa and Blagov, having got to know one another pretty well after chasing around for two hours, drank the bottle between them and, to Blagov's even greater astonishment, began to kiss.

Blagov, incidentally, never did get what he was after, but since his dissertation was based on the lives of four writers (new findings and research), he decided, if not without regret, that he could make do with a dissertation based on the lives of just three.

Cycle

Nadya Romanova had gone to an old school friend of hers to spend a completely empty evening. Her friend had been taking a bath; she emerged in her dressing-gown and started combing out her wet hair. She was tired after spending her Sunday on chores and absolutely refused to go anywhere that evening, as Nadya Romanova suggested, irked by the fact that she was just sitting twiddling her thumbs and couldn't, for her part, get down to anything. In actual fact there were only two other places they could go – either to the cinema or to their other old school friend, Larisa, who unlike them had her own family already. But the friend whose couch Nadya Romanova was now sitting on had been just recently to visit Larisa and didn't want to go and see her again straight away, especially as there was no particular reason to do so. The friend, whose name was Tatyana, said: 'No, no, it's out of the question. How can I go anywhere in this state anyhow. I've still got to curl my hair for tomorrow and do all this ironing.' The friend was already living through the next day, Monday, while Nadya Romanova spread out on the sofa, still going through the motions of trying to talk Tatyana into spending an empty Sunday evening together.

Tatyana, not in the least embarrassed by her failure to provide any entertainment for her guest, went and fetched the ironing-board from the kitchen and methodically set about her ironing. And Nadya

Romanova reached up from where she was sitting to the bookcase, on top of which lay a packet of 9×12 photographs.

'What are these?' Nadya Romanova asked her friend, sifting through the photos.

'You know,' Tatyana answered, 'They're from when we went canoeing, up on the White River.'

'When was that?' Nadya Romanova asked again, sensing that her friend had withdrawn and wasn't much inclined to talk, indeed was slightly irritated.

'What on earth does it matter?' her friend said. 'Why should you care? What's it to you whether it was this month or that month or this year or whenever? Think about it.'

Nadya Romanova quite liked even this quality in her friend – the fact that she always said exactly what she felt, without embarrassment or self-justification, without even a trace of fear, and – this was the main thing – gave the impression in doing so that she was preoccupied with something much more important. And her irritation seemed quite appropriate and justified, so that at such moments Nadya Romanova always felt herself a whole head smaller than her friend.

'You're being engaged, may I tell you, in conversation,' Nadya Romanova began jokingly, still looking through the photographs. 'If I were you I'd receive my guest like a queen – make some coffee, put on a spot of Mozart.'

'You know what . . .' Tatyana replied, and Nadya Romanova felt suddenly quite afraid: what was Tatyana going to say? – 'You know what, I really couldn't care less.'

Nadya Romanova went on looking through the photos, but more mechanically now, in silence, although in other circumstances she would certainly have asked the identity of those good-looking muscular guys in the pictures and started joking – quite inoffensively, of course – that it was high time she got herself a lover too. But Tatyana was not the least disposed to get into that sort of jokey conversation, especially since on more than one such occasion already she'd stopped Nadya Romanova short, saying she couldn't bear that kind of girly chit-chat, the endless spinning out of the same old boring themes with the same old friends, whose views on everything you always knew word-for-word in advance. Although Tatyana herself, when she was in the mood, was quite capable of talking, for example, about how good it is to have a little no-risk affair with a man who owns a car and can take you out for drives in the autumn woods, and you sit there alongside him taking a swig on the quiet now and then from a bottle of nice dry wine, while he doesn't drink at all – he wouldn't dream of drinking at the wheel for fear of being stopped by the police: you think you're safe in the country, but they always turn up when you're least expecting them. And how this particular man – the one with the car – had said with a smirk that she had nothing to fear from him, he'd been rendered quite useless by a dose of radiation. 'Ha ha!' interjected Nadya Romanova at this point, 'Of course he meant just the opposite – there was every reason to be scared stiff.'

'So,' said Nadya Romanova, pulling herself together and with an effort straightening up from the back of the couch. 'So, Tatyana, how's it going with that man of yours, the owner of the car?'

'You're a regular interrogator,' came Tatyana's reply, 'You never let a person open herself out naturally, it's always a case of "Well?" or "So?" or "Go on" with you. That's why I can't bear telling you anything.'

That's what she was like, Tatyana, and there was nothing Nadya Romanova could do about it, you had to take Tatyana as she was, because at their age it was already pretty late to start finding yourself new friends – new friends could suddenly turn out to have new and potentially dangerous qualities; and then again new friends tended to be found at work, and that was another reason it wasn't safe to trust them.

Now Tatyana would have to be kindled if she was to warm up and start talking properly, not in the way she'd been talking up till now.

Nadya Romanova knew two methods for doing this. The first was to start a conversation about some mutual friend of theirs, and to express views about her quite contrary to the ones Tatyana held. Then Tatyana would be genuinely put out, and keep presenting more and more new facts in evidence, all of which, it's true, would already be quite familiar to Nadya Romanova. And Nadya Romanova, as if polemically, as if quite convinced by the force of Tatyana's arguments, would agree to consider the facts advanced and would say 'You may be right, of course' – and avert her gaze, as if a bit chagrined that she'd been proved wrong. From here the conversation would proceed smoothly forward, and seeing Nadya Romanova upset, Tatyana would even become slightly ingratiating and say the first thing that came into her head – for in her heart of hearts she was really quite kind.

But unfortunately this first method didn't always come off, and sometimes there seemed no point in even trying it, since after all both of them had long since left school, and the various people who might have been recollected from two opposing points of view were as good as dead now, frozen at the particular age and in the particular circumstances in which they'd been left when school ended. Both Nadya Romanova and Tatyana had already staged this recollection of events many times over, and Tatyana always managed to win her friend over by introducing various impressive facts, which she always knew better, because she'd been closer to the people in question and would defend them with agonised passion, so that there was no choice for Nadya Romanova but to lay down her arms and surrender. But all of this happened over and over, and Tatyana started to complain about the repetition of thoughts and feelings, complained of having the sensation that she'd been pushed into a cramped cage and forced to pace up and down inside. She complained of having to twist and turn forever within the same circle of associations and the same circle of faces. And yet every time the conversation turned to events from their schooldays Tatyana was unable to let the matter rest until she had induced the right attitude in Nadya Romanova and got her in thrall over this particular question too.

The second method was that of embarking on various confessions oneself; here Nadya Romanova would be forced by Tatyana's total indifference to start relating, if not the total truth about her own feelings, at least that part of the truth that wouldn't be too hard for Tatyana to swallow, the part that was not too miserable and indeed humanly quite interesting, although for Nadya Romanova herself it might involve a matter of intense suffering, suffering that defied description. But as time went by this method of communicating with Tatyana became more and more complicated for Nadya

Romanova, because it meant avoiding those details that Tatyana had known nothing about at the beginning, and which now constituted Nadya Romanova's only real possession, her last refuge, as she herself realised full well.

The story in question was that Nadya Romanova was in love with the man who lived with her best friend at work – not the friend's husband, but precisely her 'cohabitant', as the friend herself called him. And this designation – 'cohabitant' – only aggravated the drama for Nadya Romanova, for having herself gone through the horror of being an abandoned wife, she couldn't be the instigator of the same drama in her friend's life, indeed one that was even worse: worse because the friend wouldn't even have known the happiness of being a lawful wife, and the long years of torment with this 'cohabitant' would be left just hanging in the air, never having come to a lawful conclusion.

But in fact that wasn't the main reason why Nadya Romanova shrank from getting too close to the man in question. The fact that her friend sat opposite her from nine to five every day and chose to confide all her sufferings precisely to her, Nadya Romanova, may have played a certain role as well, for Nadya Romanova couldn't bear to bring upon herself the fearful hatred of her friend if what she desired were in fact to come to pass. The friend moreover enjoyed a good deal of authority at work, she was a strong character, strong that is in everything except her relationship with this 'cohabitant', with whom she was a complete weakling – in fact she simply lost her head where he was concerned and behaved quite foolishly. Nadya Romanova indeed had to admit to herself that she didn't love this man as deeply as did her unfortunate friend. What's more, somewhere in the depths of her soul Nadya Romanova had to admit that she had fallen in love with this man only because the stories of her unhappy friend, who had lost her head over the man even though she was generally such a strong person, had so excited her interest. Nadya Romanova had for a very long time now been informed of this man's every movement of the heart, she knew everything about him that one single person could possibly know about any other, every word and action of his, and even precisely how he'd behave in this or that situation, and how he had a blown-up portrait of Nadya Romanova's friend hanging up in his room. And Nadya Romanova couldn't avoid running into him from time to time in the canteen or on the stairs; several times he'd given way to her as they came in by the swing door, saying 'after you' in a significant tone of voice – and Nadya Romanova knew everything about him, every little trifle. But all of these things were just trivia, will-o'-the-wisps, and Nadya Romanova had to distance herself from them in her stories to Tatyana, construct some proper conclusion from them, fret and grieve over them and know every last detail about them – precisely what had happened and exactly when.

And although Tatyana had long since got bored hearing all these details, she'd invariably swallow the bait again and heatedly start telling Nadya Romanova to live her own life and stop thinking about other people's, stop building castles in the air that required no real action but left you free to indulge in endless talk and fantasy. Tatyana maintained that other people could perfectly well take care of themselves, to which Nadya Romanova replied sadly that she couldn't overcome this inhibition, she'd been bewitched and simply couldn't make a move. And on these occasions Tatyana was wont to exclaim: 'Say what you like, but it's good to have a man with a car.' And thus warmed to her theme she would go on to tell all about him – how he earned so much that he never had to worry what time of the month it was in relation to pay day; or if he realised that his suit was a bit worn he'd simply stroll into a shop, change into a new one on the spot and casually drop the old one – carefully wrapped and tied up in the shop – straight into the bin.

Sitting there on Tatyana's couch, Nadya Romanova wanted to say that she felt quite painfully miserable today, but she kept herself in check, realising that Tatyana might consider this an unwarranted liberty, taken only because one evening prior to this she had admitted to Nadya Romanova that she had got herself a lover – indeed the very same man, the one with the car – whom she didn't really love at all; she'd done it despite herself. And on that occasion Nadya Romanova had exclaimed with genuine enthusiasm 'Good for you! Brilliant! Congratulations!' At which Tatyana had immediately dried up; and yet not to go on, just to stop there was somehow pointless, stupid, a pity even from her point of view, not to mention Nadya Romanova's, endlessly sitting and waiting there on the couch. So Tatyana had gone on and related how the whole thing had come about, with all the same details that Nadya Romanova's colleague at work would reveal as well.

But this time, on that Sunday evening, Nadya Romanova kept quiet and looked dejected, sitting there on the couch, while Tatyana kept methodically ironing at the ironing-board. Finally, Tatyana said thoughtfully:

'Honestly, what a nerve I've got!'

Nadya Romanova glanced up from the photos as if she were waiting quite indifferently, indeed wasn't waiting at all for Tatyana to go on.

'Yesterday,' Tatyana went on, 'I somehow contrived to switch lovers in the space of a single day.'

'Good for you! Brilliant!' Nadya Romanova exclaimed.

'Just imagine, that car-owner of mine thought I was his for the asking just because I slept with him once. He just turned up here first thing yesterday morning. It's all plain sailing for them once they've done it the first time. OK. So he lies down right next to me and starts talking. Thinks now it's happened I'm bound to be interested in everything about him – his intimate thoughts, his Japanese knick-knacks, his views on what he's going to do on Sunday, and his wife and his daughter and his garage, and how he can fix everything with his little repairs and his little tools, and how he'd never spend his foreign currency on rubbishy foreign trinkets but uses it to travel and look around and eat and drink and have a good time. I was so fed up all of a sudden, I simply got up and scooped everything up in a trice and told him forget it, forget I live here, never set foot here again.'

'What did he say?'

'He was so taken aback. He said he had the feeling I looked down on him and didn't take proper account of him at all. But I'd come to my senses, he said, and then it would be too late. And then he left. And I rushed to the telephone and started leafing through my old address book. And I came across this number, d'you remember I told you about that guy whose bathroom I got locked in once and I had to sit there the whole night on the bathroom stool and even tried to go to sleep in the bathtub?'

'Of course I remember. I remember the whole lot perfectly.'

'So there's no need to tell you, that was the guy I rang up.'

'So go on, what did you say?'

'I said: "I want to see you."'

'And what did he say?'

'"What a pleasant surprise. Are you serious?" I said: "I'm here waiting."'

'And he came?'

'He did. With flowers and a bottle. Nadya Romanova, how I laughed at myself when he left that night! How I laughed at the whole damn lot of them! How free I felt!'

'Good for you! You're brilliant. I could never ever have made up my mind to do that, never. I feel I'm in thrall . . .'

'And he kept saying: "You're not just pulling my leg, are you? You're not going to turn me out? Did you really want me to come, or are you just making fun of me?"'

'So which of them's better?'

Nadya Romanova couldn't restrain herself from asking the question, though she knew very well she shouldn't, because it was so revealing of her relationship with Tatyana, her true relationship to her, and Tatyana sensed this herself, although she was quite unable to stop and carried on relating this and that. The cycle of the evening was complete.

The Adventures of Vera

Vera, a young girl, fell in love, very understandably all things considered; but it didn't happen straight away, because when you start work at a new place you don't see everything clearly straight away; you have to settle in for a while before you start remembering everyone's names.

Vera got her new job through her father, who could easily have got her employment long before when Vera had just started out on her working life in her capacity as assistant salesgirl. But Vera's father hadn't wanted to get her a job in his own place of work; he was afraid Vera would behave too unpredictably, and his fears proved justified literally one month after Vera started her new job and when she had just started learning everyone's names.

Of course her father had worried beforehand that Vera would lose her head working in a place where she'd be surrounded by men. And when all's said and done this was understandable, since for the past four years Vera had been working behind a counter in the sterile atmosphere of mutual inspection, searching questions and answers, and the endless chit-chat of the older saleswomen. A different person might not have been affected; but if there was one thing her father had learned by now, it was that Vera was ready to trust any man except him. Her father kept telling her that she shouldn't show such blind trust in men, that as a young girl she should at least have a bit of pride, shouldn't let go of herself, weeping her eyes out to the point of hysteria every couple of months – and all this beginning when she was just sixteen years old.

Vera's father could long ago have had her sent to reform school, and indeed had threatened day in day out to do so, though he never actually took measures, and by and by Vera turned eighteen and came of age. But it must be said that at the age of fourteen, indeed twelve, even ten, Vera was as physically developed, more or less, as an eighteen-year-old, way beyond her years, although her mental capacities, in the opinion of her teachers, lagged far behind her physical development. One of her teachers, who greatly respected Vera's father, told him that she couldn't imagine what would become of Vera when she turned fourteen, but Vera did turn fourteen, and eventually sixteen, and at this point she chucked in the whole stupid rigmarole and set herself up independently as an apprentice salesgirl.

And there behind the counter Vera for four years led a life that on the surface seemed to everyone perfectly straightforward, although from the inside it was just as complicated and inexplicable as everyone else's. Outwardly it all looked very simple, and that's what struck each and every person, and on the basis of appearances Vera was judged, although you could have found thousands of other girls in the exact same outward circumstances – and every girl, after all, is essentially quite different from every other.

But this in no way served to justify Vera in the eyes of others; and only those friends who found themselves trapped within the same outward circumstances, all of whom – whatever their apparent similarities – were by nature absolutely different: only these various friends, each of whom had found her own solution to the problems meted out by life – only these friends understood Vera and regarded her as a creature not of this world, an ideal being; and would often say, clapping her on the shoulder: 'What a sweet little ninny you are'. On these occasions the subject of the conversation was invariably love, because what else can girls of eighteen talk of amongst themselves! Of course they can talk about films, and sport, and books, and the weather, and their mothers, and money, and about the awful things that happen out there on the street, and about the hatefulness of injustice and treachery; and about childhood, and how tired they get, and how their legs ache and how stuffy it is, and about the shady goings-on at work. In fact, whatever others find to talk about, they do too; and there's no concealing that girls of eighteen are just the same as other people. They differ only in one respect – that they talk a great deal about love and relationships, interrupting, analysing, using their intuition or shutting their eyes to things, confiding and weeping, and, finally, acquiring through these conversations a certain toughness in life, which in due course seals their mouths and leaves them alone with themselves, somehow or other to fight their lone solitary fight.

But Vera's father would have none of this; he wouldn't accept or take into account the genuine fondness and affection that Vera's friends felt for her; he took all this to be a kind of collective corruption, and thus, when Vera decided she wanted to leave the shop, he fully endorsed her decision and resolved to get her a job in his own establishment, where she'd be right next door and it would be easy to obtain regular information about her behaviour, allowing for a margin of two or three days.

Of course he had to reckon with the fact that Vera, who until now had observed life only from behind a shop counter, had to all intents and purposes not yet lived in the real world at all; she was, in that sense, no better off than a novice straight out of a convent or a young delinquent newly-released from reform school, with all the consequences that this entailed. But Vera's father had great faith in himself, allotting himself a very significant role in Vera's future life, a role that was, of course, immensely exaggerated, based as it was, once again, on the control of certain purely outward circumstances.

The fallacious logic of this system soon became evident, because although he knew everything, Vera's father could change nothing, for nothing that was strictly illegal occurred. Soon after Vera started work, her father received information that she was behaving, not exactly improperly, but with peculiarly cheerful abandon; already, when she had barely had a chance to look round, and didn't yet properly know who was who, she was engaging in long conversations on the internal telephone and in the corridors, and generally behaving as if she were at a party, testimony to which was the excessive make-up which the silly nitwit kept plastering on her face. And from her expression it was already quite evident that she was just waiting to hurl herself into an abyss of voluptuous pleasure with whoever might turn up, for it was very natural, after her long stint behind the counter, that every man should appear to her a demi-god, with an unrealised potential for love locked within him.

With a lapse of only a day or two, for example, Vera's father, to his horror, found out that Vera had tapped out a letter to someone on her typewriter and with an air of great triumph had borne it off to the mail room. The letter, as her father went on to learn, was addressed to a certain I.E. Drach; in it Vera thanked him for returning the sum of five roubles and said that she could not supply Tatyana's address, firstly because Tatyana had given her no authority to do so, and secondly because she was, in any case, ignorant of the address in question. 'With greatest respect, and thanking you once again for the five roubles, yours, Vera' – thus the letter ended. Gradually Vera's father calmed down, calculating after some thought that the letter represented no more than a faint echo from the fortnight's holiday that Vera had taken recently at a local resort.

Subsequently Vera's father learned that Vera had been trying persistently to wangle a meeting with one of her colleagues, a balding, sporty-looking type, in connection with the fact that, ever since the two of them had taken a joint trip in his car after work one day, the colleague in question had been avoiding Vera, and through a friend of hers had given her to understand that 'this was a bad moment'; and in fact there had been a frightful row, with the colleague's ballerina wife kicking up a great scene when she found out the whole story, although the bald fellow had taken Vera to some out-of-the-way spot, avoiding anywhere that they might run into anyone they knew.

Vera herself, of course, remained in ignorance of much of this; in a sense, indeed, she learned nothing of it at all; and for a long time afterwards the memory of that evening drive to the accompaniment of jazz continued to haunt her, representing for her the epitome of unattainable happiness and vanished love; and for a whole month Vera walked around in a state of deep melancholia, ready to love that distant image her whole life long.

Her father, it's true, endeavoured to open Vera's eyes to the truth, to the full absurdity of her love and her suffering, but he was quite unable to do so, just as he'd been unable to send Vera to reform school; and in the meantime the following event occurred. One evening Vera stayed behind at work to take some letters from dictation, at the request of a talented young colleague of hers, an ace at his job, who had romantically sued for divorce on the grounds of 'absence of children'; and indeed he had no children and was, moreover, the owner of a whole apartment all to himself.

The following day Vera went to work deeply moved, radiant, expectant, with a chaste sorrow in her heart and a deep conviction that there wasn't another in the world like him and that this was the greatest success of her life, even if nothing further were to come of it. That it was rare indeed to find someone like him, someone who doesn't insist on anything the first evening, merely asks you not to abandon him there in solitary confinement, especially after traversing so great a distance to visit his private apartment – and who allows himself finally to embrace you with utmost tenderness, but goes not a step further.

Anyway, all this came to nothing in the end, since this comparatively young colleague of Vera's seemed to take fright as well and started avoiding her the very next day, even avoided looking at her, for all the world as if he were afraid that she'd remind him of something unpleasant, something he didn't want to know or hear anything more about. And the words of this young man, said in reply to a woman who'd remarked that dear little Vera was crying and was threatening to quit her job, reached Vera's father in their full and unadulterated form: 'If she can produce a certificate from the doctor saying she's free of disease then by all means, no problem.' These words being spoken right in front of everyone, and causing great merriment all round.

But Vera still failed to understand a thing and chose to believe that he'd somehow found out about her excursion in the car, and was planning to reassure him, if only she could catch him, that nothing had really happened, it had all been a mistake and he wasn't to take it to heart; of course she'd had her misfortunes in life, but none of them had been her fault, and so on and so forth; indeed she was quite ready to set out her entire biography before him, though neither he nor anyone else required any such thing of her.

Her father, for his part, was meaning to explain everything to Vera, but he didn't have the heart to admit that he knew the whole lot, for he wasn't too sure how Vera would react to that – she might get up to some dreadful mischief; and the fact was it no longer made sense to go over the entire story, in circumstantial detail, once Vera fell prey to the purest, most radiant love of all.

This situation went on for some considerable time, during which Vera mechanically fulfilled all her duties, ate only the skimpiest of lunches in the canteen, went to bed early every night and got volumes of poetry out of the library. At the age of twenty, indeed, she showed every sign of having lost all taste for life, and to her girlfriends at work she complained of feeling like an old, old woman.

But before she was gripped by the decisive, central love of this period of her life, Vera experienced a pleasant, melancholy attraction to yet another colleague in her department, a man of short stature, who took great pains to address her with great formality, was forever bantering and teasing her, called her by her full name and patronymic, 'Vera Sergeevna', and now and then permitted himself to steal a kiss when they were alone, or do something else in that spirit. Alone with Vera he became quite animated, told her interesting stories from the intimate life of humankind, and sometimes brought her some old – very old – books about love, of the kind you can only read from the sliding drawer of your desk, in case anyone should happen to come by.

Vera became quite used to this strange man, who was quite different, alone with her, from his normal self in the office – not nearly so energetic, so vehemently determined in his struggle for truth, so implacable on questions of duty, so unwilling to make the slightest compromise even where others' peace of mind was concerned. With Vera he was immediately softer, more unbuttoned; he abandoned his severe standards and business-like approach, and in Vera's presence he'd even take pleasure, now and then, in swearing at the world, often in quite unbridled fashion; in short he unburdened himself to her. It was from Vera's little cubby-hole that he made his most intimately private phone calls, taking pleasure in not concealing anything from her, saying every single word out loud and deriving great amusement from her embarrassment and her efforts to pretend that she did not want to listen to such things.

But this flutter, too, ended in a rather strange fashion, even though Vera had grown used to the little man and sometimes would even put a hand on his shoulder and say: 'So how's it all going, my friend? . . .' On this occasion their rapport came to an end because the little fellow had asked Vera to make use of her former trade connections and get him a coat, since he found it impossible to get one the right size himself. And Vera moved heaven and earth to do so, sought out all her old acquaintances, till at last the hour and the day were named when the little man should go and collect his imported overcoat.

But on that particular day the little man was unaccountably absent, and Vera, not wanting to go through the trauma of going to his department herself, started periodically ringing up and asking when he would be in; and when asked in turn what message to pass on, she monotonously requested him to call Vera Sergeevna regarding the coat. Finally, after a number of phone calls, new voices, choking with laughter, started answering the phone; the receiver would be left for ages on the desk, as if someone had gone to look for him, then, unexpectedly softly and gently, replaced on the hook.

And when next day the little man eventually turned up at Vera's office, he gave her a brief but angry lecture on proper conduct in the workplace, and the correct mode for conversing over the telephone, and this put an end to his sessions sitting on Vera's desk, and telling her stories, and educating her, as he liked to put it.

Strangely enough even this small episode shook Vera with extraordinary force, as if she'd been rejected by a man who truly loved her, someone she'd learned to adapt to, got used to, whose charm she'd discovered, although there'd been nothing of the kind in this case, but something quite different, something she found very hard to name.

Her father was equally shaken when, two days later, he learned of the festive and jubilant atmosphere that had reigned in the department when Vera's voice on the phone had come ringing through, and how everyone had congratulated each other on discovering that even this little colleague of theirs had had his turn with Vera; and how, when the little fellow himself turned up, he'd been hounded to death by stories of the coat and the phone calls. And then the balding colleague had seized the opportunity to volunteer his own views on the subject, speaking of Vera with a disgust bordering on fury, though smiling all the while like everybody else; and so had the romantic young man – though in a softer, more emollient way, with a due degree of forgiving irony, restraining himself from expressing his views with full force out of respect for the women in the room. No allowance at all was made for the fact that the coat might actually have been needed; everyone simply felt sorry for the little man for having fallen victim to Vera, and in the end even he gave in and chuckled quietly and said a few words, strictly for male ears, which resulted in a veritable uproar, everyone laughing till they wept.

Then, finally, the most significant period of all began in that brief epoch of Vera's life, when, to her great misfortune, she fell deeply in love with the head of her department, who had just returned from abroad, and who spent a long time dictating to her a report on his trip, meanwhile relating all sorts of funny stories on the side – strictly for her ears only, as to a trusted colleague – about all the things that had actually taken place, and the real reasons why so-and-so behaved in such-and-such a way, and deeply lamenting that things hadn't gone quite as they should or worked out more effectively.

For several days following this indiscreet conversation Vera wandered round distracted, lost to the world, literally not knowing what was happening to her. Nobody knew anything about the state she was in, or about the way the head of department had treated her, for the rest of the department could only guess at what went on in the soul of their boss, and why he sometimes went into a rage, and at other times simply dumbfounded everyone with his completely unfounded faith in people – idealistic, old-fashioned, touching, mad. Equally the boss himself had no access to information of that kind about the various upheavals among his staff.

If Vera had simply stayed in her office, absorbing the atmosphere of the group – nosy and sarcastic but quite good-humoured for all that – she might have avoided a lot of mistakes in life; though on the other hand the poison of love for her boss would have seeped in all the more quickly, for the spirit of that man, his great individuality, hovered over everyone in the group. Everyone was transfixed by his persona, his habits, his likes and dislikes, his various eccentricities and the pompous pronouncements he came up with when he spoke at meetings.

This wasn't common or garden passion; it would have been absurd to imagine any such thing of the men and women who worked in that office. But at the same time they showed all the signs of being in love – joyful and agitated whenever the boss appeared, always hoping for a tête-à-tête with him, their hearts missing a beat when he glanced at them; and they attributed a quite unwarranted significance to any chance deed of his or to words that, on the face of it, were quite insignificant. It was somehow assumed in advance that nothing he did was accidental; there was nothing simple in him at all, nor could there be – nothing that did not in some way illuminate some higher goal of his; and his faults, which everyone knew inside out, were precisely of the kind that cause only pain when revealed in the beloved. Sometimes, indeed, they were disappointed in him, hated him even, got into fights with him – but again, exactly in the way that people do when disappointed in a person they have at one time loved.

Little Vera suspected none of this, and at staff meetings – the only occasions on which she came out of her seclusion and might have absorbed the sweet poison in the general staff relationship to the boss, the watchful, jealous attention they showed him, she remained untouched by that atmosphere. She was unfamiliar with that form of devotion: when she worked at the shop all of them, the salesgirls, had a friendly scorn for the boss, and at the slightest provocation they got straight down to the point and told him to his face exactly what they thought of him. Behind all this was an unpardonably flippant and indifferent attitude on their part to their jobs; they couldn't care less where they worked. 'We can't sink any lower,' the salesgirls would joke when they gathered in the café over lunch.

So it would be true to say that this was the first time in Vera's life that she had experienced, so incredibly fully, such trust on the part of an older person, such straightforward trust, directed at her, without ulterior motive – trust that sprang straight from a fleeting mood of the heart, that demanded a kind of reverence, without the slightest misgiving that such reverence might prove exaggeratedly sincere, and involve a great many ulterior motives. With Vera and her boss it was simply a case of two souls meeting on the same plane of simplicity, with no hidden agenda of any kind. Trust and reverence conducted their tender duet, as the boss dictated, and Vera typed away.

A relationship of such simplicity, a flight into so pure a union of souls, could not but have consequences for poor Vera and her boss. At some point the boss broke off his routine dictation to engage Vera in a bet on who played the lead role in some film or other – an 'American' bet, whereby the person who loses has to carry out the wish of the person who wins, whatever that wish may be.

This was the most ancient of ruses, familiar to the boss ever since the days of his youth as a working man, and to little Vera from the routines of summer camp, where she went every year till she reached the unhappy age of sixteen. Vera lost the bet and grew subdued, genuinely saddened. It would be hard to convey the mixed emotions she felt: the longing, the sense of self-sacrifice, the regret that things were moving too fast, the frantic joy and expectation of something supreme; in short, the mixed feelings experienced since time immemorial by a woman in love – in this case little Vera, who had made up her mind, as the saying goes, to stop at nothing.

To cut a long story short, Vera said that, since she had lost, she was ready to carry out a single wish. The boss said that in this instance an 'American' bet meant the winner got three wishes. To which Vera agreed; if he said three, so be it, three it was.

But then the matter was left dangling. The boss rapidly finished his dictation and went hastily into his office, to emerge presently with his briefcase and overcoat and promptly disappear.

And in vain did Vera, ever paler and colder, wait in the months that followed for at least some sign, if only some brief message or a telephone call at least. At last, after a sleepless night, Vera made up her mind to call her boss during the lunch hour from a public telephone and ask if she could see him – which was sufficiently odd in itself to put the boss on his guard, since he had arranged things so that his staff could always come and see him without any prior announcement. However, he gave her a specific appointment at the end of the working day, and asked her moreover to knock at the door of his office three times separately. Vera went boldly to this unusual appointment and stayed a long time in her boss's office, barely letting him get a word in edgeways; as if a dam had burst she just went on and on, telling him the entire story of her life. The boss listened attentively and even made the odd remark now and then – comments such as 'This is all extremely interesting, extremely interesting, you can't imagine. I'd love to make a case study of you.' In the end the boss agreed to meet her, choosing a rather late hour, nine o'clock in the evening, and telling her that they should leave the building separately, for it would look very odd to everyone if the two of them left together; even at that late stage in the day all sorts of incidents might occur.

As might have been expected, and as Vera's father would certainly have predicted, though on this occasion he knew nothing about the affair, Vera waited one and a half hours in vain, freezing to death by a tram stop on a cobbled street in some godforsaken place – a spot evidently well-frequented by the boss ever since the days of his working man's youth. At last Vera set off at a run, just to warm up a bit and stop her teeth chattering, and it was a good thing that she had in fact got another rendez-vous, an hour later, with her boyfriend, and a good thing too that he'd waited patiently for her, so that in the end Vera's evening really went off quite well.

The Violin

She would lie unrestrainedly, muddle up her own stories, forget what she'd said just the day before and so on. It was a typical, easily recognisable case, fibbing to make oneself look important, presenting all one's actions as being somehow frightfully significant, of enormous consequence, bound to result in something momentous happening; but in fact nothing did happen; she went on trailing to and fro through the ward with the same self-important expression on her face, holding slightly aloft a certain pale blue envelope, containing God only knows what message; but she carried it down the ward with tremendous dignity, demonstrating with her entire being the utmost urgency of having this letter despatched. All the women in the ward were more or less familiar with the contents of the letter – although of course what they were familiar with was only the intention behind it, not the particular words in which this obvious intention had been couched, nor the particular form in which the author had chosen to hide all her longings, those pathetic, clear-as-daylight long-ings of hers, nor the particular lies she'd told this time in addressing her heart's elect, a certain engineer called Valery who lived in another city.

None of this however meant that she was particularly chatty, this Lena, or that she was over-eager to enter into explanations of her present situation. On the contrary, she was rather taciturn, apt, if anything, to be over-ceremonious; and this tendency to stand on ceremony came to the fore especially when the consultant was making his rounds; for the consultant liked to sit and chat with Lena when he came on a Monday to see all his patients. With a fatherly frown he'd tell Lena that everything was going to form and if everything continued to do so our little student would soon be better and be able to get out and about again before it was time for the big event; and there was no reason to be afraid of going out, he'd say, forestalling Lena's objections; on the contrary fresh air and strolls in the park were just what were needed, just what were needed to build up your strength before giving birth. 'And what about those hands of yours?' he'd ask Lena. 'Don't violinists' hands get out of practice if they don't keep at the old strings and bow? It's a well-known fact. How many hours a day are you supposed to practise, you budding musicians?' 'Four, sometimes five,' Lena answered without a hint of a blush. 'And before exams you're supposed to practise all the hours you can short of actually pulling a tendon – it's a question of sheer stamina then.'

Then the consultant would move on and finally vanish from the ward, leaving everyone to get on with their own affairs; and Lena, conscientious Lena, would sit down again with her notepaper and write and write and write, until it was time to seal up all these writings and triumphantly bear them down the entire ward to the exit. Or she'd go to make a phone call and in a low voice conduct long conversations with a certain person, obviously on some practical business of the utmost seriousness: from her expression it was evident that she needed to explain something of decisive importance to her; and it was the same thing each day with these telephone calls: the same preoccupied face, the same hushed voice, the same vague, incomprehensible questions.

61

But despite all these immensely serious conversations on the phone, and the fact that there was evidently someone-or-other who was supposed to be doing something-or-other for Lena, nobody ever actually came to see her, and consequently there was nothing at all on her bedside cupboard but an empty glass covered with a paper napkin.

After her first few days in hospital, when she lay in bed in silence – she was not allowed to walk about; it was the rule in the hospital that no one was allowed to get up if there was the slightest hint of complications developing – after those first few days of compulsory bed rest, Lena was at last allowed to get up, and she set off somewhere out of the ward, taking with her the latest letter in its standard blue envelope. She began walking to and fro, engaging the nurses and orderlies in endless whispered, meaningful exchanges – though what all these furtive discussions amounted to, and quite why she had to engage all the nurses in them, was not entirely clear, since they never seemed to bring any concrete results: just as before not a soul came to see her, and just as before the clean glass yawned emptily on her bedside cupboard, and from time to time she'd take it off and get a drink of water. And still Lena busied herself with her letters, or went to the mirror in the hall to do her hair, or modestly ate up her hospital dinner. And all these activities, it must be said, she imbued with a lofty and quite impenetrable significance.

And the only channel through which at least a certain amount of information on Lena filtered out were her talks with the consultant on his Monday rounds, when, newly made-up, she lay back on the tall, stacked pillows and in her quiet voice answered all the consultant's questions, although the latter must by now have known everything there was to know about the history of her illness.

But the consultant asked his questions anyway, and Lena answered, and from these brief, quiet answers of hers the other patients in the hushed ward learned, for instance, that Lena had fainted in the street one day and that her friend had had to phone for an ambulance. In response to further queries from the consultant Lena said that she now felt extremely weak and dizzy, and that she sometimes had pains in the small of her back. 'You must rest up, rest here with us,' the consultant would say at the end of these conversations, turning to the next bed on his rounds.

And every Monday, as these brief conversations were resumed, Lena monotonously made the same complaint, of a certain dizziness and a certain weakness, although, as these same conversations revealed, all the results of her tests were just fine, and there was absolutely no problem with her heart; and then one fine day, on one of these Mondays, the consultant recommended that she be discharged, advising her to be as active as possible to overcome any weakness resulting from her rest in hospital, and to be a good girl and do her exercises and prepare herself properly for the birth so she'd be nice and strong and be able to take it all in her stride. The consultant jested that she ought to let him take care of her here at the hospital when the time came, and asked her for the hundredth time when she was going to send him the tickets to her solo concert, and then he vanished once more whence he'd come.

By that time, by that Monday, Lena had made herself at home in the ward and gradually told everyone about her husband Valery, an engineer who lived in another city and wasn't able to come and see her right now. And she told them all how she'd spent New Year's Eve at his parents' house and how welcome they'd made her feel, and so on and so forth.

And she still kept conscientiously writing those letters, and processing down the ward to the far doors with the same triumphant gait, and holding those secret conversations with the nurses; and she went on ringing up her friend and conversing in hushed tones with her over the phone – and all to no effect.

Meanwhile, however, it must be said that her bedside cupboard was no longer empty, but had started filling up with all sorts of fruits and vegetables and things to eat. And this development had occurred rather quickly, in fact as soon as the other women began to guess the real state of affairs. At first rather timidly and self-consciously, but ever more calmly and straight-forwardly, they began putting their spare provisions in Lena's little cupboard, and Lena too began rather timidly and self-consciously, but gradually more freely to avail herself of these gifts: she was forever eating, nibbling away; she'd trail up to the washroom to wash a plateful of fruit and then set to and eat again. She ate apples, salad, cheese and sausage and chocolates and once even half a head of raw cabbage, which someone or other had brought in for a woman suffering from stomach problems.

And the nurses, too, started bringing Lena extra large portions and sometimes, when there was nothing else on offer, simply gave her a second bowl of soup – after they'd already served the dessert. And Lena, nodding her assent with great dignity, accepted these second helpings, calmly ate them up, then went off to comb her hair or sat down and wrote the next letter. The envelopes she used for this purpose, incidentally, were no longer hers, for, as it emerged, there had been some delay in her husband's transferring her money, and her friend was unable to come. This friend of hers, it must be said, kept on not coming and not coming, and indeed, during the whole month that Lena spent in the hospital, the friend never showed up at all; she put in an appearance only at the very last, culminating moment, when Lena was leaving the hospital.

It's true that, before Lena left, the women in her ward had negotiated with the doctors to try and have Lena kept in the hospital for another two months, right up to the birth, but evidently this was quite impossible, and so Monday duly arrived, and the consultant sat down for his usual chat with Lena about the difficulties of studying at the conservatory, by that time well aware that there was no such conservatory, nor any trace, indeed, of a violin. However, this conversation was conducted with the utmost propriety, and soon afterwards Lena left the ward for good, taking with her the yellow comb that had become such a familiar sight over the last month.

Lena left the ward unmasked, so to speak, completely dethroned, but without for a moment losing her majestic poise, her mysteriousness – even after the whole ward, right in front of Lena, had started quite seriously discussing what she was going to do with her future child, and whether she could count on any help at all from that engineer, the one whom Lena claimed to be her husband – all these problems immediately rising to the surface the minute Lena started to say goodbye. She left the ward to a chorus of advice, one and all telling her to put the baby in a children's home, at least for a year, and during that year to somehow or other get herself on her feet, to find herself a job and somewhere to live so that she'd be able to fetch the child back and give it a proper home. Lena nodded grandly, sitting on the edge of her bed, and then just the same said farewell to everyone all over again and set off with her great belly before her, and then half an hour later she could be seen again, through the window, majestically sailing off into the distance in a crumpled yellow raincoat, on the arm of the famous friend, and it was quite clear to everyone then that the fainting fit in the street had quite simply been staged, and that in a while the two of them, out there on the street, would manage to think up another ruse – so long, of course, as Lena didn't actually faint before they'd managed between them to work out all the details.

A Dark Fate

An unmarried woman of thirty-something, that's who she was; and she kept trying to persuade her mother, kept begging her to go off somewhere for just one night; and her mother, strangely enough, acquiesced and took herself off; and she, the daughter, brought home a man.

He was old, balding and overweight, embroiled in complex relations with both his wife and his mother, living on and off neither here nor there, disgruntled and peevish about his situation at work, though sometimes he'd pronounce with great self-confidence that he was bound, wouldn't you think, to become head of the lab? What do you think, he'd exclaim suddenly, will they make me head of the lab? – naïve 42-year-old boy that he was, a finished man, dragged down by his family, his adolescent daughter who'd grown up for no good reason into a great big female, fourteen years old and rather pleased with herself, and the other girls in the yard were all set to beat her up over some boy or other . . . and so on and so forth. His approach to this adventure was thoroughly business-like; on the way to her apartment they stopped to purchase a cake – he was notorious at work for his partiality to cakes, wine, good food, quality cigarettes, and whenever there was a party he'd scoff everything in sight; and it was his diabetes that was responsible for it all, his insatiable need for food and drink that stood in the way of his career and always had. He looked awful, that was the sum and substance of it. His jacket and collar unbuttoned, his chest pale and hairless. Dandruff on his shoulders. Bald. Thick-lensed glasses. This was the treasure that this woman brought home to her one-roomed apartment, this woman who'd decided once and for all to put an end to her loneliness and get it over and done with – not, however, in a practical, business-like fashion, but rather with a black despair in her soul that manifested itself on the surface as overwhelming human love, a love expressed in claims, reproaches, prodding and persuasion, to all of which he replied: 'OK, all right, I agree.' Altogether, there was nothing good about the way they set off home, and duly arrived, and the way she shook as she turned the key in the lock, trembling with fear lest her mother should be there; but everything went according to plan. They put on the kettle, uncorked the wine, sliced the cake, ate part of it, drank the wine. He sprawled in the armchair and gazed at the cake, wondering whether to eat just a bit more, but fearing his stomach wouldn't allow it. He gazed and gazed and finally plucked a green rose from the middle, lifted it safely to his mouth, ate it, and licked up a little crumb with his tongue, like a dog.

Then he looked at his watch, took it off, put it on the chair, and undressed completely down to his underwear. The underwear turned out to be unexpectedly white. A nice clean child, plump and cosseted, he sat on the edge of the sofa in his vest and pants, took off his socks and dusted his feet with them. Finally he took off his glasses. He lay down next to her on the clean, white sheets and did his thing; then they had a little talk, and as he was saying goodbye he insisted again: what did she think, would they make him head of the lab? And there on the threshold, already in his overcoat, he got chatting again, came back in, set to on the cake and ate another big chunk straight off the knife.

She didn't even offer to see him to the station, and he didn't seem to notice; he gave her a kiss on the forehead, kind and friendly, then grabbed his briefcase, counted out his money on the doorstep, sighed and asked if she could change a fiver, got no reply and took himself off with his fat tummy, his child's mind and the smell of his clean, cosseted, stranger's body, and the thought never even occurred to him that he'd been shown the door forever, that he had lost out, taken a false step, and that he'd never have a chance of scoring here again. He didn't understand any of this, but slipped away down the lift together with his change, his bank notes and his handkerchief.

Fortunately they worked in different departments. The next day she didn't go to the general canteen, and frittered away the whole lunch hour sitting there at her desk. Ahead, that evening, lay the prospect of seeing her mother; in the evening that other, real life of hers would begin again; and suddenly she surprised herself by asking a colleague of hers, out of the blue: 'So have you gone and found yourself a new feller?' 'No,' the colleague answered, rather stiffly, for her husband had recently abandoned her and she was suffering her humiliation alone; she wouldn't let any of her friends come and see her in her deserted apartment or communicate any news of her life to anyone. 'No, what about you?' the colleague asked. 'I have, yes,' the other answered with tears of joy in her eyes, and suddenly understood that there was no turning back now, she too was condemned forever, henceforward forever now she'd be smashed up and shaken, and would hang around in public telephone booths, not knowing where to phone – his wife's place, his mother's, his office; her suitor didn't work fixed hours, so he might very well be neither one place nor the other. That was what awaited her; what awaited her too was the shame of being the one who kept phoning him in vain in the same familiar voice, adding to all those other voices who'd already phoned him in vain, for no doubt he was beloved of many women, this slippery man; no doubt he took fright and ran away from all of them, and no doubt he asked all of them, in the same situation, exactly the same thing: was he going to be made head of the lab?

Everything was quite clear in his case, for her suitor was quite transparent, stupid, not subtle at all, and thus a dark fate awaited her, and there were tears of joy in her eyes.

Manya

Let's start by saying that, although Manya wasn't beautiful, she had marvellous ash-blonde hair and the lovely figure of those tall, perhaps even slightly over-tall women of the north.

But the marvellous ash-blonde curls weren't all, they weren't enough, though not in the sense that you have to have something else besides curls. No, they weren't enough because there's nothing good what-soever in natural curls as such, they're the hardest thing in the world to deal with; it's very difficult to do anything with them at all, even with big curls like Manya had, and these curls of Manya's in fact did her looks no service. Many curly-haired women – it's a well-known fact – go to tiresome lengths to get their hair stretched and straightened at the hairdresser's, but even there you have to know a proper stylist, you have to be able to picture the look you want, plan it properly and set about it in the right way to get the desired results.

In fact it must be said that in this artificial day and age the natural beauty of Manya's hair was if anything a disadvantage when it came to comparing Manya with other girls who had lovely hairstyles, not to mention assets of other kinds. And in fact, try as she might in these artificial times of ours, Manya with her wonderful ash-blonde curls couldn't deal with them at all and went around just as she was, with great twisted tendrils, when the least she could have done was get them straightened out at the front, instead of having that great bush of curls all over her forehead.

As far as artificial straightening went, several people advised Manya to go for it and even gave her the names of stylists they knew, but Manya didn't do anything with the names and addresses they gave her. The reason for this, it has to be said, was that there was something naturally inert about Manya, a sort of absent-mindedness, a tendency always to put things off till tomorrow or, to put it more simply, a lack of any obvious incentive to do anything for any purpose whatsoever. For it was pretty clear to everyone around her that Manya couldn't see much point in straightening her hair, seeing as, at the age of thirty-something, Manya didn't expect anything much from this life at all.

But even when the necessity did arise to make something of herself, when Manya fell in love with a long-time colleague of hers, everything went on just as before, as if Manya had somehow got frozen in her tracks and was quite unable to make any move for the better, even though that was quite clearly what was needed. And you could bet your life on it that this wasn't any sort of principled position, a deliberate decision to leave everything as it was so that she'd be attractive, just as she was, to this or that particular person. No, things were much more simple and banal in Manya's case; she would have been happy to do something, but she sort of lost her head, or that's how it seemed, and at crucial moments, when she went indoors, she simply kept her fur hat on, which of course looked a bit strange. However the hat suited Manya better than her own hair, so everyone more or less reconciled themselves to it, and so the whole winter of her love Manya went round in a hat.

Now as far as this love of hers went: everything there was also absolutely clear from the start, but no one tried to warn Manya off, point out some rather obvious facts or open her eyes to what was going on in reality. No, somehow or other everyone seemed to avoid the theme, managed not to talk about it, and the only thing they permitted themselves from time to time was some discussion of Manya's qualities as a person. They said that she was a very good, conscientious girl, devoted and loyal even to excess, and this particular characteristic of hers – loyalty – was the one they mentioned most often in conversation. They said she was absolutely healthy and normal too, a fact of great significance in the relations of this couple, as will become apparent when we get round to speaking of the other side of the coin, namely the colleague that Manya had fallen in love with.

People also used to say of Manya that it was very odd she should be overlooked, such a nice girl after all; it was an accepted fact that she really was very nice, the favourite of the whole department; by any serious reckoning, they agreed, you couldn't wish for a nicer girl. It was enough to glance in at Manya during working hours, or spend just half an hour with her in the office,to realise that her colleagues treated her with special affection, almost tenderness. Indeed it was they who'd invented the name Manya for her – her real name was Marina, but her colleagues in the department had all started calling her Manya and the name caught on, everyone was united in the same impulse to call Marina Manya. It was a nice, kind, human impulse, almost like saying a password; just to pronounce the name was to enter an atmosphere of special intimacy, a family atmosphere almost, with tender nicknames and all that sort of thing.

To cut a long story short, no one said anything to Manya about her behaviour, and no one attempted to direct her gaze, mournful enough as it was already, at certain bleak and glaringly obvious truths. She was made welcome wherever she went – whether in the room where her colleague, Yura, worked, or even in the corridor outside his door, where she sometimes hung around with her girlfriend, waiting for him to come out so she could have a word with him, make some arrangement – as if there were no time for this outside working hours, as if they hadn't a free evening between them, as if neither Manya nor Yura had a telephone on their desks. Be that as it may, Manya was often to be seen in the corridor outside his room, and Yura, who was always very busy, would pop out to see her just for a minute – and it was transparently obvious to everyone that this was what was going on, with Manya hanging about in the corridor and Yura rushing out just for a minute to discuss whatever urgent business it was that Manya had come to see him about.

It was obvious to everyone, and yet there was really nothing to see; it was enough to glance in passing at the two of them – watch them, for example, going up the stairs together when they'd just come to work at 8.30 in the morning, she with her hat and handbag, he with his briefcase, and hear him talking so loudly and cheerfully while she, mounting the stairs beside him, kept so quiet and hung her head! There was no reason to suppose, looking at the two of them, that they'd arrived at work together; and absolutely no reason to suppose that they had just travelled together that morning from one and the same place. And even if that were the case, Manya with her entire being seemed to refute the fact, so utterly downcast was her expression, and so terribly timid at the same time.

And nobody ever scolded her for spoiling the whole thing just by her funereal looks; no one ever said to her that it's precisely your bearing, your behaviour, your pride that very often prove decisive in these cases, that come what may you have to go round looking proud and cheerful, and when things aren't going too well there's all the more reason to keep up appearances, dress well and do your hair nicely. None of this seemed to apply to Manya's case, for with Manya everything was so nakedly obvious and banal: Manya was absolutely transparent and Yura was absolutely transparent. Nobody placed great hopes in Yura; the only possible motive for the affair on his side, presumably, was his passionate desire to have a child by a healthy woman. Yura's ex-wife had been a sick woman, unable to have children herself; Yura had spent many tormented years with her before finally making up his mind to separate, and everyone knew of his desire to have a child if only because Yura had cited it as the reason for his wishing to divorce.

That was precisely why Manya's colleagues paid a good deal of attention to how Manya was feeling, whether she was eating well and how she was looking generally. Once Manya mentioned naively that she kept feeling unaccountably sick, terribly sick. On top of this Manya seemed rather confused, possibly because she really wasn't feeling well; and indeed she did look a bit off-colour. According to certain sources, it's true, Manya must simply have been suffering from food poisoning or some other routine tummy upset; there could be no other explanation. Manya herself had apparently told a friend of hers, not realising that the latter moved in the same circles as some of her colleagues, that the thing that most touched her about Yura was simply that he always talked to her very nicely, that there was never any hidden agenda, his conversations were never just a means to an end. She'd been struck by him precisely because he demanded nothing of her; his courtship of her was, in the most genuine sense, quite beautiful; he never took liberties, indeed he behaved almost protectively towards her. It was a beautiful romance, Manya had told her friend, with all the trimmings – roses in December and so forth; and the friend passed all this on to her various acquaintances and thereby, though she didn't realise this herself, to Manya's colleagues, which was the reason why many of them regarded with some scepticism Manya's admission that she was feeling sick.

Month followed month, and nothing seemed to change; Manya was as timid as ever; she still wore her hat indoors, embarrassed by her curls; and Yura, just as before, would pop out of his office, right in front of everyone, to chat with Manya for a minute when she came for one of her absurd rendez-vous in the middle of the corridor.

It might have been assumed from all this that Manya had simply lost her head; except that she behaved exactly as she had always done, nothing seemed to change – that was what was so strange. What was strange was that everything continued on exactly the same note as it had begun, there was no crescendo or diminuendo. Here, of course, you had to take into account Yura's own character. Yura, right from the beginning, had made his romance with Manya a little too concrete, too binding, too elevated. With Yura this was par for the course; without meaning any harm he always tended to exaggerate things, just slightly, right from the start. Whenever there was a row in the office he immediately got terribly heated; that was just the way he was. And then he always went a bit over the top in any friendship he made, he was ready to give away his all to a new friend, only to become – as anyone could have predicted – bitterly disenchanted later. That was why the instant friendships he struck up on business trips were always so strong. When they visited head office from time to time, the friends Yura had made round the country always got everything they wanted from him straight away, everything he could offer, he was such an immensely generous and hospitable character.

And that was what happened with Manya; the whole affair was given impetus at the start by the fact that the two of them were sent on a business trip together, and Yura, on these business trips, was literally irrepressible; he immediately revealed all the hidden sides of his character and made a quite unforgettable impression. Those roses in December were also, incidentally, the result of a business trip.

All Yura's boundless kindness of heart, his insatiable desire to make a fuss of people, take them under his wing – all this Yura unleashed straight away on Manya, together with his astonishing capacity to talk. Yura, when he was enjoying himself, when there was nothing to stop him, was capable of talking for hours on end. He was a magnificent raconteur, just like a writer – his plots seemed to come ready-made, all with unexpected twists and the sorts of little details that only a truly talented man would observe and store away in his memory.

The end result wasn't hard to guess. Almost as soon as he'd arrived back Yura took Manya to his parents' home, where everybody liked her very much. Indeed it would have been impossible not to like Manya; there wasn't a soul on earth who wouldn't have taken a liking to her. Then Yura took Manya to meet all his various friends, and they all liked her too. Yura literally didn't let slip a single opportunity to introduce Manya around, and he more or less called her his fiancée outright. When they visited friends that had families already the women sometimes started congratulating Yura and wishing him fine healthy children, to which Yura would reply 'It won't be long, old girl'. In short you could have sworn there were wedding bells in the air, but Manya still went round looking lost, in the eternal fur hat, and the look of her alone was enough to discourage anyone.

So the story dragged on with no clear end in sight, and everyone had predicted things would turn out this way, though no one could tell exactly what the outcome would be, what final chord the whole story would end on. In fact it ended very simply: Yura was promoted and moved to a different place of work, indeed got a very significant promotion considering he was so young, and Manya, along with her girlfriend, came for the last time to the door of his office to say goodbye, and there in front of everyone he held out his hand to her, and then to her friend, and said farewell, and invited them both to come and visit him at his new place of work, and their parting could not have been more calm, quite unlike what usually happens in such cases, with the women weeping, the men morose and silent, and all the rest of it.

So everything came to an end exactly as everyone

had foreseen, but to such an extent, so exactly and unswervingly as they'd predicted, without any deviation whatsoever, that everyone was left with a strange feeling of incompleteness, a vague sort of expectation of something further. But nothing further happened.

Another Land

Who can say what life is like for a quiet woman addicted to drink, who lives hidden away from everyone in a one-room apartment with her child? Who knows what it's like for her, night after night, no matter how drunk, to gather up all the little things her daughter needs for kindergarten, so they should all be to hand in the morning?

She still has traces of beauty in her face – arched brows, a slender nose, but her daughter's all listless, pale and fat; she doesn't even resemble her father, for her father has bright blonde hair and bright red lips. Usually the little girl sits and plays quietly on the floor while her mother drinks, sitting at the table or lying on the divan. Then they both go to bed and turn out the light, and in the morning get up as if nothing had happened and run through the frost and the dark to the kindergarten.

Several times a year mother and daughter take themselves off to visit friends, and they sit at the table, and the mother brightens up, starts talking loudly, props her chin on her hand and turns this way and that, pretending, in other words, to feel quite at home. And indeed she used to be quite at home here, so long as she had the blonde fellow for a husband; but then everything fell apart for her – all her former life, her former circle of friends. And now she has to pick the right home and the right day, to make sure the fellow with the bright blonde hair doesn't turn up with his new wife, a woman of tough outlook, so people say, who wouldn't give way to anyone on anything.

And so the mother, whose daughter the blonde fellow fathered, cautiously rings up to congratulate this or that friend on their birthday, then somehow strings the conversation out, murmurs, procrastinates, asks how life's shaping up, but won't say finally if she's coming or not. She waits. She'll wait till everything's been decided, there at the other end of the telephone line, before finally putting down the receiver and running off to the store for her routine bottle, and then to the kindergarten to fetch her daughter.

In the old days she wouldn't have dreamt of opening the bottle before her daughter fell asleep, but later the whole thing became much simpler, everything took its natural course, because what did it matter to the little girl, after all, whether her mother was drinking tea or medicine.

And the little girl really doesn't mind at all; she sits on the floor playing with her old toys, and there's not a soul in the world who knows how the two of them live, how the mother keeps calculating over and over, and decides in the end there's no harm done if the money that should have been spent on dinner goes instead on a bottle of wine – the little girl gets fed at the kindergarten, and she herself can make do without.

So they economise, switch off the lights and go to bed at nine o'clock in the evening, and nobody knows what divine dreams they dream, mother and daughter at night in bed, nobody knows how they both fall asleep the minute their heads touch the pillow, to return once again to that other land, whence in the early morning they'll both come back, in order to run, who knows why, who knows where, down the dark, frosty street – when in truth they'd do better never to wake at all.

Clarissa's Story

In its initial stages Clarissa's story was the exact replica
of Cinderella or The Ugly Duckling. Indeed until the age
of seventeen Clarissa, a schoolgirl in glasses, never
aroused the slightest interest, let alone enthusiasm, in
anyone she met – and that included not just the boys in
her class but the girls as well, they being especially
sensitive to beauty, on the lookout for it wherever
they happened to be and apt to give each other a dig in
the ribs whenever they happened to spot it. Clarissa
herself was not especially sensitive to beauty; in fact she
was rather a primitive creature who paid no attention to
anyone, so it seemed, least of all to herself. Heaven
knows what filled her thoughts all day long. She was
inattentive in class, her gaze permanently directed at
something unimportant. She'd watch open-mouthed
as the chalk was wiped from the blackboard, the sight
of it sending her into some deep meditation, but God
only knows what she was thinking of at such moments,
sitting there gazing at the blackboard.

One day, already a grown-up girl in her last year in
school, Clarissa happened to get into a fight with a boy;
the fight, however, arising for no other reason than that
Clarissa, as a matter of honour, had slapped her classmate in the face for uttering a word that struck her as
insulting, though he had said it to no one in particular
but just like that, by chance, straight into the air. And the
classmate, rather than explain at length that Clarissa
was neither here nor there, that the insulting word

had nothing whatsoever to do with her, that in general he couldn't care less about her and she was making a big fuss about nothing – instead of this, he gave her as good as he'd got.

This incident bore witness to the major shift which occurred in Clarissa's inner being at this period of her life, towards a heightened awareness of her position in life, of her position as a girl who in future would have to stand up for herself and make her solitary way through a hostile world, reckoning and dealing with all life's developments herself.

As we shall see, however, this tendency was later eclipsed, though under other circumstances it might well have grown. But circumstances developed in such a way that, only six months after leaving school, Clarissa, by then a college student, began leading a completely different life; she took a trip to another town during the winter holidays, got married in a flash, and returned in a quite different capacity as the wife of a man who lived in another city, a role which imposed on her certain obligations.

No one knows what exactly went on in Clarissa's heart during these six months; all one could go on were the external indications of certain inner changes: Clarissa's former, almost aggressive attitude towards the hostile outer world was replaced by a quite different outlook, that of a dull-witted, rather weak-willed girl, apparently at a loss to understand where circumstances were leading her, and succumbing to these circumstances without a hint of reflection. And meanwhile, though she was still just the same girl in glasses, Clarissa was transformed into a fully-fledged beauty with golden curls and delicately sculpted fingers.

As might have been predicted, Clarissa, with her

weakness of will and inability to see beyond the end of her nose, didn't last long in her role as the wife of a man who lived in another city; and when people asked about her husband she'd say she hadn't a clue what he was up to and was sick of the whole thing anyway.

In a trice, however, she was married again, this time to a doctor working in Casualty, a big man with a powerful chest and thick hands who smelled of tobacco. This marriage proved a downright tragedy for Clarissa, because as soon as their first child was born the husband started messing with other women, took to drink and sometimes beat her up.

During this new period of her life, initiated by the new state of relations between herself and her husband, certain marked changes occurred in Clarissa's manner and behaviour. She carried on her quarrel with her husband incessantly, never let up, insisting on her rightness and her point of view even when she was nowhere near her husband, when she was at work, for instance, or out visiting friends, in short in all the most inappropriate places. She conducted this monologue on a single sustained note of protest, with burning cheeks and always close to tears. It was quite beyond her, it seemed, to bear with dignity the scorn and indifference her husband inflicted on her, nor did she recover her one-time schoolgirl's ability to defend herself from insult with a slap in the face. Throughout those years she seemed to live without rudder or sails, thrown this way and that, from one blow to the next, with the sensibility of an amoeba that shifts from place to place with the single primitive aim of avoiding collision. During this period of her life Clarissa seemed completely unable to define her role, grow into it and adopt any dignified course of action. She was barely able just to withstand the blows of fate, as represented by her intemperate, utterly shameless husband who led his gross, clumsy life alongside her in the single room he shared with Clarissa and her child.

Finally it ended with the greatest blow of all – the husband walked out on Clarissa and went back to his parents, taking their child, a boy, with him. Clarissa then did the only thing her bedimmed consciousness prompted her to do; she started pounding on the door of her in-laws' apartment, pounding in vain, for the old people had departed and were renting a dacha in some unknown location, as Clarissa learned from their neighbour when he glanced out at the landing to see what was going on.

Clarissa had no alternative but to return to her ravaged nest with nothing at all to show for her pains. All the actions she then proceeded to take were thoroughly illogical and hopeless. For example, on three occasions she took a train to a station out of town and walked at random among the dacha allotments, hoping somewhere to catch sight of her son's little yellow straw hat. Clarissa also phoned various of her husband's friends, serious men, men preoccupied with their work, and asked for their help in stealing the child back. None of these efforts yielded any result; the only result in fact was that one evening a doctor, whom she certainly hadn't summoned herself, turned up at her door with a nurse; and the doctor questioned her solicitously about how she was sleeping, and whether she had any enemies, anyone who was persecuting her, and whether she wouldn't like to spend a bit of time in a sanatorium, where she'd at least be given the chance to sleep for a good solid week. Clarissa then enquired who was going to give her sick leave to do this, but both doctor and nurse assured her with one accord that this was the last thing she need worry about. 'He sent you to see me, didn't he,' Clarissa replied, 'I realised straight away.' The doctor and nurse then made ready to leave, reminding Clarissa once again at the door that the chance of a good rest was available to her; but Clarissa was no longer listening. She sat, cheeks aflame, at the table, quite lost in thought.

At this point the curtain falls on the scene, for now Clarissa, ever so quietly, underwent yet another transformation, and again six months later, who knows by what means, she once more rose to the surface of life, this time in her capacity as a divorced woman, left with a child in her care, and alimony once a month, and the usual problem of how to dispose of the child each day. In this new capacity of hers Clarissa became much like everyone else and in her own short-sighted way proved to be quite clever. She didn't try to plan too far ahead, because there was another complicating factor in the picture, namely that the boy was terribly attached to his father and the father's parents, who gave him plenty of good, loving care and the kind of upbringing that Clarissa herself was unable to provide, living as she was in the singular now. So Clarissa didn't try and look too far into the future, or plan her life with her son too far ahead, understanding only too well that her rights in the matter might well prove transient; instead, she concentrated all her attention on the problems of here and now, problems which accumulated one after the other.

Clarissa laboriously calculated the time it would take her to get from the kindergarten to her work, dashed round the shops in her lunch hour and treated her professional duties as obligations of secondary importance in her life, which given her situation was no doubt quite understandable.

So it was a great event for Clarissa when, for the first time in her life, she took a holiday in the south completely on her own, leaving the child as a boarder in a kindergarten out of town. Having arrived on the south coast, Clarissa was unable at first to discard all her recent anxieties as a preoccupied single mother, and was conscience-stricken at the sight of the sea, the sunshine, and the abundance of fruit, recalling the poor child she'd abandoned up north in the pouring rain. Thus at first she had no stomach for pleasure at all, and would spend the better part of each day standing in the long queues at the inter-city telephone exchange in order to ring the kindergarten and find out how the boy was doing and whether, indeed, he was still there at all. She wished passionately that she could have him there with her at the seaside, as all the other mothers around her had their children, but the deed was done, and thus she spent the first half of her summer holiday.

But the sea and the sunshine and the southern fruits, which Clarissa bought because they were so cheap, began to exert their influence, and a secondary metamorphosis occurred in Clarissa's appearance. She was now a mature woman of twenty-five, looking out through her glasses with a certain gentle estrangement, and it was in this capacity that a civil aviation pilot, spending a day between flights on the city beach, fell deeply in love with her. The pilot was embarrassed to approach Clarissa, since he was sitting on the beach not in the swimming trunks that befitted the occasion but in ordinary satin drawers. He simply gazed at Clarissa from afar, watching as she rootled about in her bag like a pecking chicken and eventually fished out a touchingly tiny hankie, with which she proceeded to wipe her spectacles.

Two days later the pilot was once more on the beach, this time in the late afternoon. On this occasion he'd prepared himself for his visit to the seaside, dressing appropriately so that he'd be able to go up to Clarissa. Clarissa was unpleasantly startled, got all hot and bothered, tried to find an excuse to leave and finally, with pounding heart and premature revulsion, simply ran away before the pilot's astonished gaze.

But everything turned out well after all, for by the day after next Clarissa was already able to squeeze out a few phrases in conversation with the pilot, although she spent the whole of the next morning queueing up to make her inter-city call, receiving the news that her son was well and running about and that the weather up there was fine.

It all ended, three months after her summer holiday, with Clarissa moving to join her new husband in his three-roomed apartment, and thus began a new era in the life of our heroine. The boy in due course started school, and another little girl was born, and all in all it would be fair to say that everything settled down and flowed smoothly into a natural, healthy maturity, into the normal course of winters and holidays and purchases and a sense of the fullness of life, if it were not for the fact that, on the days her husband was due to fly, Clarissa, left alone, was apt to spend hours phoning the airport and nagging them into giving her some information about the flight, and when Valery Petrovich came back he'd get all sorts of remarks from his colleagues about his wife's phone calls. And that was really the only thing that darkened the bright horizons of life for Valery Petrovich and Clarissa, really the only thing.

Xenia's Daughter

From time immemorial, whenever literature has seized its pen to describe the life of prostitutes, it's always and everywhere sprung to their defence. Indeed it would be absurd to imagine an author undertaking to describe a prostitute just in order to cast slurs upon her. The task of literature, it seems, is precisely to present, as people worthy of respect and pity, all those who in life are commonly despised. Thus authors adopt a rather lofty position in relation to the rest of the world, taking upon themselves the role of sole defenders of the aforesaid despised, assuming the role of judges, defence and prosecution rolled into one, and undertaking the hard task of educating the masses and purveying great ideas.

And indeed whose heart – even in those most steeped in prejudice – would not be wrung with pity at the sight of a whore, one who in Russian cries out to be called *prostushka* – a simple soul, a poor bareheaded creature. Mind you, this one does have a scarf of sorts on her head, a crude rough thing like an old felt boot, pushed to the back of her head so all her hair draggles down. That's what you'd have to call her – a *prostushka*: a bit on the fat side, a wee bit short, no Madame Universe, unlike some of those women – thoroughbred champions with great broad shoulders and withers and narrow waists and legs plump in the calf and tapering at the ankles.

So yes, a *prostushka*, a simple soul, because that's the

word that sits alongside 'prostitute', and a prostitute's precisely what she is. No wrestler, it's true, arms bulging like doughnuts. No, she's just a *prostushka*, that's all there is to her. And no great femininity about her either, for how can you be feminine when you're lank-haired, short and fat; not that she's gross, no, she just holds her own, blending indistinguishably into the crowd as she presses her way forward among the women standing there, women just like her. But a whore's what she is; and now, in one of the defining, unforgettable moments in her life she stands there and says:

'I just want to give her these fags, look, and biscuits.'

'Go on then, go on,' say the women in the crowd. 'She's over there with the policeman, look, maybe they'll allow it.'

'It's just a few fags and a pack of biscuits.'

'Course it is, off you go now.' As if she'd only just now been arrested, as if this were her first day and she needed the fags that badly – it's tough giving up all at once, right away. And yet our defendant's had three months in prison, and plenty of packs of biscuits and fags . . .

But now, this dark evening, amid the crowd outside the courtroom, this unforgettable scene unfolds, with the prostitute Xenia leading the waltz, pushing forward in the crowd to hand over her gift, her pathetic little gift – and to whom? To her daughter, her convicted daughter – a whore just like her. She's been sentenced to one year, and now, in just a moment, they'll lead her out of the basement, in a moment we'll see her white face appear, there in the dark doorway, with the policeman behind, or maybe just in front, and who knows what he'll be like, this particular one, what expression he'll wear on his face as he marches forward, in front of the convicted woman or perhaps just behind, marches forward to put her in the waiting vehicle.

What kind of expression is he supposed to wear anyway? Maybe he's already got used to escorting them in and out, into the hall and out into the yard, into the car and up to that crowd round the doors, the crowd that's gathered to watch them led out. But even so, even if he's completely used to it by now, there'll still be a special look on his face. And they all watch eagerly and feast on this great misfortune (not in the sense that they 'enjoy' it, no, although there's a bit of that too, somewhere they're glad to witness this unique spectacle, so natural, so true-to-life it sends a shiver down your spine, with all the details no one could have invented, the mother-prostitute rushing up to the daughter-prostitute, right on cue with the cigarettes and the biscuits, because the daughter's had nothing to eat since lunch) – and they'll feast their eyes, too, on the look on that policeman's face, that unimaginable look, like nothing else on earth, such as only a police-man could wear, only a policeman in that precise situation – though it's hard, it's impossible to predict that expression – just what kind of expression is it going to be? What will we learn from that face of his, what will we learn from the look of her, whore and whore's daughter, nineteen years old, with her white face, about to appear in the doorway now, right now, look, as her mother moves through the sparse crowd saying, 'Here you are love, just a few fags.'

They all know her here, they all know Xenia, and there's the twelve-year-old who used to visit them in their little den; he gave the young one some fancy underwear once. There he is standing like a grown-up

with the other grown men, in his fancy raincoat with
the waist and raglan sleeves, a Lilliputian alongside
those two great fellows – and what are they doing
there, standing next to him? What do he and they have
in common, you wonder? They're just standing there,
not leaning towards him especially but talking in the
direction of the entrance, and now and then he utters
a few brief words too, addressed, again, not to them
but to the crowd, the crowd at the entrance, where
any minute now we'll see, emerging from that dark
martyrs' basement, the whiter-than-white face of that
twelve-year-old's nineteen-year-old bride, for being a
whore means you can't despise anyone, old or young
or plagued with pox; a whore can't turn a soul away –
she can't, she's not allowed, perhaps doesn't wish to
– how turn away someone who's come bearing gifts?
Who's come, not just anyhow, but with something for
her, a bottle or money or fancy underwear; someone
who – gift or no gift – wouldn't dream of going elsewhere, wouldn't deign to look at anyone else; so
elsewhere the doors get closed and locked and the
dust and cobwebs are left to gather.

While here they come often, though God knows
why. What on earth is it brings them? What need
have they for this bought love, when all around – in
ladlefuls – there's ordinary love to be had, requiring no
payment, just warmth and attention, just a few little
words and the presence of someone, someone who'll
accept this waiting, unselfish love and who'll give in
return, not something costly either, but the simplest of
things – a mere nothing, a trifle – and yet, in doing so,
will celebrate his own need; do what he has to, yet give
happiness too.

But no, it's precisely there that they go, there they

went once, to that little room, with that simple-souled mother and that daughter of hers, who's only just, just grown into her adult's body, only just, just grown out of ugly, pimply adolescence and yet looks stale and used up already; already, in some way, as ordinary as they come, without a secret, simplicity itself. There's nothing here, you'd think, of that aura of mystery, the eternal mystery surrounding sin. There's just what you see, nothing special at all, nothing but the most naked simplicity – perhaps just a faint dash of coquetry in the gestures, but such simple, essential, unmysterious coquetry, just a shade of teasing, a shade of playfulness. The playfulness of a good-hearted woman with no tricks up her sleeve, redolent only of pleasures in store, pleasures guaranteed to ensue, from the laughter and teasing of a woman undressing.

And yet even she can turn out to deceive, chuck the bottle at you and throw you out the door. But that, in its way, deserves respect too; these are just moods that you have to give in to; they have nothing to do with the person concerned, the one who just happens to get hit by the bottle; they're simply the product of melancholy and caprice, the caprice of a person in her own right, one who has no desire to humiliate others, but is seized by plain, terrible melancholia, the kind that demands respect, demands that you just give way; because this isn't a game, it's simply the way things have turned out this time, simply the way things have happened to turn out.

And nobody's afraid of them, these moods – you just have to kiss the lock on the door and go along home, not take it as an insult, just a case of desire frustrated, love unconsummated, sadness at the chance of a holiday missed – just that. And it's not at all like missing out on the party when music is blaring in the street and everyone else is enjoying themselves, and you alone have been left uninvited. No, it's not like that, it's completely different here – no one's having a party today, it's been put off, everyone's in their everyday clothes, there are no bright lights and warmth to be had today. There'll be warmth and light in plenty the next time around, but then everyone will start gathering round again, and the serious twelve-year-old will turn up, the one everyone respects for the dignity he showed, giving his gift of fancy underwear; he's not an outcast or a reject in the world of that room, where mother and daughter live side by side, both of them schooled long since in mutual conflict.

For after all it isn't as simple as it might appear at first glance for a whore to bring up another whore. No doubt the mother, once upon a time, had other intentions; no doubt she didn't welcome straight off the fact that her daughter had chosen the path of sin – it isn't hard to guess that the mother, as a mother, would forgive herself her own failings, but not her daughter's; that she'd want to see her daughter succeed where she had failed – see her daughter, for example, get a proper education. But it's easy enough to imagine, too, that the daughter would grow up wanting to prove herself, and no matter that when she was little she got bullied in the yard and used to bite the other children out of spite – or so people said, and indeed that's what happened. She was the skinniest thing when she was a child, there wasn't an ounce of flesh on her ribs, she was mean and rude to everyone she ran into; even grown-ups she'd tell to mind their own business. Then all of a sudden she blossomed out, acquired some curves, got some meat on her bones, growing up in that atmosphere of permanent feasting, in the little room with the laden table; and suddenly her mother took to weeping, not because her daughter, in response to being scolded for her bad marks and rudeness, would kick her in the most painful spot on the shins – no, the mother now started weeping and smoking, swollen-eyed all the time because everything, but everything was over now, all her hopes had come crashing down, and there was her daughter bringing yet another one home, and yet another, and now all the petitioners tramping along to that room no longer related to her daughter as a daughter, no longer offered her a sweetie before her mother put her out of the door and left her in the kitchen. No, from now on their mutual relations would be quite different, and the mother would reconcile herself to them as any simple person would – oh well, she'd say, that's it, that's it, that's it.

And so everything took its natural course, and bit by bit the daughter, spoiled by all her nice new friends, began to simplify her life, quit any pretence and started doing exactly what she felt like, because she was so thoroughly cosseted, so petted, so completely approved of; and because, after all, she was so needed – imagine it, and for money too – even by that twelve-year-old, which was a pretty rare thing, and could only be regarded as an extraordinary manifestation of the general love and respect which that little fellow had earned out there in the yard. She was so spoiled that it couldn't but end in tears, and in a routine fit of depression she chucked a bottle at the head of a policeman who just happened to have dropped in to check up on things, and that was how her adventure ended, because here after all was a policeman and a representative of the law, the law which took no account of anyone's whims, or anyone's natural depression or words such as 'Go to hell' – and this, in turn, was all bound to end as it did, with that courtroom in the basement, and her emerging, one dark evening, out on to the street to face the crowd, and with the public appearance, right in front of that crowd, of all those people who had an interest in the case, who had seen Xenia's daughter, not in her torn school stockings, biting the other children she fought with in the yard, but in some quite other guise: though in what guise, exactly, is another question entirely.

Father and Mother

Where do you live now, cheerful, light-hearted Tanya, stranger to all doubts and hesitations, innocent of night terrors and of horror at what lies in store? Where are you now, in what apartment with flimsy little curtains have you built your nest, to live surrounded by children and, fleet and light, accomplish everything and even more?

But what matters most is the dark despair from which this sliver of morning radiance struggled into the world, grew up and took shape – this agile girl, agile as only the eldest daughter in a big family can be. For it was in just such a family that Tanya was the eldest, Tanya whose story we're going to hear.

She had numerous little sisters and one little brother, the youngest of all; her mother carried him round on her breast all through the last stage of her married life, ran after her husband when he set off to work with the little boy in her arms – ran to stop him escaping to his accursed work, where all he did was engage in debauchery, outright debauchery. Tanya's mother ran after him pretty well every morning, well nigh every morning she was overcome by despair, despair that yet again she was letting her husband escape through her fingers, escape to that loathsome, free and easy, time-wasting life of his at work; she'd run till she dropped with the little boy in her arms, run down the street to catch up with her husband, at least grab the cap off his head with her one free hand as he dashed headlong to work – yes, scenes like these were nothing new in their street, where all the residents were military families. Tanya's mother burned with hatred for her husband, the sharp, painful hatred that a suffering woman feels for a drone, a spendthrift, a man who lets his whole family down, even though the father returned every evening to the bosom of his family and scooped up the latest baby in his arms. But the mother thought even this a dirty ruse, something a guilty male does just for show, and they'd end up virtually tearing the baby in half – the father wresting him away from his furious mother, and the mother struggling to stop him showing off, playing his downright dishonest game, aping the family man when he hadn't a leg to stand on. In fact all the mother seemed to see in her children was the material proof, face after face, of her life's effort, her superhuman work, her indisputable yet daily disputed value in the face of her dog of a husband, who trembled and shook like a jelly every time she raised her voice – terrified that the neighbours would find them out, though there was nothing the neighbours didn't know anyway, she'd told everything to everybody everywhere, and the women would comfort her and call her Mrs P. and advise her to go and see the deputy, it was really disgraceful, they said.

Somehow or other, despite all this, the father held his ground in the family, and it's hard to say what his reasons were for trying every evening to come home in a peaceable frame of mind, with an expression that was either embarrassed or deliberately indifferent or something quite else, but at any rate not his own, as if he'd just got it ready and hadn't grown into it yet, rather than with the natural expression, glowering, full of hatred, that under the circumstances you would have expected.

But no, it seemed beyond him to come home looking resentful, he kept trying on new faces, to create the best possible image, coming home every evening at 11 pm. He didn't want to come home any earlier, he'd never wanted to in his life, and this in fact was what lay at the bottom of it all; so every evening, wearing this expression or that, he'd turn up at home at 11 o'clock, and every time he'd come upon the same scene at home, with not one of the children asleep and his wife sitting in tears with the little one on the bed. And if the father then tried, on his own initiative, with his usual emollient manner to put the little girls to bed, the mother would tear the children away from him and start shouting that if that's the way it was they'd best get no sleep at all, any of them, but just take a look at their depraved father, fresh out of someone else's bed with the flush still on his cheeks, their father who'd just been kissing God knows who with his stinking gob, that filthy crater of his, and now came thrusting his slobbering lips at his clean little girls that he'd no doubt be happy to go to bed with as well – and so on and so forth.

Besides all this the poverty of the household defied description, since the mother didn't have a job and pretty much let the housework go, waiting only for eleven o'clock to strike, and then midnight and even later, so that the children quite often dropped off as they waited for the great moment, the culmination of the whole day, and it was quite impossible to rouse them in the morning. The mother went further and further in her righteous fury, she was quite capable of turning up at the officers' mess to find him and start kicking him right there on the spot, still clutching the baby in her arms; it was as if she were protesting against the received opinion that you'll never get anything out of a man that way, you'll just scare him away and turn him off for good; it was as if she were issuing a challenge to fate and everyone around her, leaving her other children to starve while she set off just with her little boy into the open steppe surrounding the base, or shouted dreadful things about Tanya getting pregnant by her father and having a miscarriage, she'd found some bloody rags stuffed into a chink in the wall.

It wasn't clear, to be sure, what Tanya's mother was aiming to achieve; perhaps she just felt the need to destroy the lie, the deceitful picture that the father, with his emollient look and false expressions was trying to create, above all in front of the children; for the thing he cared most about was creating this illusion of peaceful family life. The mother seemed to feel she'd been caught in a trap, that she was surrounded on all sides by disgust and disdain, while everyone, she felt, meanwhile pitied her husband and tried to guard him from her – for example, once when she went on the eve of Women's Day to a shop where she knew her husband would be buying her and her daughters some little gifts, someone managed to get into the shop before her and get her husband out through the back door before she'd managed to push her way through the crowd to the counter.

And yet in the midst of this utter mess, virtually every year, the little girls kept being born and the last in the family, the boy, was only six months old when the father finally left. How it all happened, what brought about these marital couplings, what led up to their mutual embraces and made them even possible nobody knew, and even Tanya, who possessed the clearest mind in the family and kept a vigilant eye on both her mother and father, had never seen it happen.

And with every step, seeking to disgrace her husband, the mother sank deeper and deeper into shame herself, and there seemed no end in sight to it all, since the husband stubbornly insisted on keeping up appearances and denying his wife any pretext for presenting him in the light she sought to. But in the end these two stubborn beings reached that extreme where suddenly one of the partners at least finds there's nothing left in the game for them, nothing that matters any more, when they cease to care what happens – and this moment lies in wait precisely for the most stubborn adversary, the most insistent, who, in response to some gesture of indifference, utters a cry of victory, greeted with equal indifference by the other partner – the partner now vanishing into the distance; and yet that cry of victory's so powerful that it's audible all round the neighbourhood, and willy-nilly the neighbourhood echoes it back.

And so it came about that Tanya's father departed from the family and indeed from the garrison: he was transferred to another unit, and this worked to his benefit, because now he had every justification never again to show his face in the home of his long-suffering family, and every chance to live in peace with the new woman he'd found there, reportedly a simple soul, much simpler than Mrs P.

Tanya, incidentally, didn't linger long in the family after her father's departure; she stayed just a year, until she was seventeen years old, whereupon she caught the eye of one Victor, an electrician who'd come to the base on a work assignment. Victor was much older and more experienced than Tanya and realised straight away what a treasure he'd stumbled on at the garrison club in the form of this alert, easy-going girl, so he immediately took matters into his own experienced 24-year-old hands. That very evening on her way home from the club Tanya consented to run away with him, and by morning she was gone, despite the fact that her mother told her absolutely openly that she wouldn't be able to cope without her and that the children were bound to suffer.

'Enough's enough,' Tanya must have said to herself, 'I've done all I can', and she wagged her tail and off she went, and thereafter lived a happy life with the shrewd and tenacious Victor, and nothing bothered her: not the fact that they had nowhere proper to live, and come every March their landlady would try and hang herself, so that every March her son would take leave and come and hide the rope; nor the fact that they had just one bed and two forks and a penknife, because there was nothing at all in the old woman's ménage, she lived the whole year round on buttermilk. Everything she encountered thereafter Tanya took in her stride, everything she accepted with happiness, she tripped about with her quick light step, and not a shadow of doubt or despair ever visited her again – ever at all.

A Clap of Thunder

The chain of events which led up to the close relationship between Marina and Zubov was really quite
mysterious and incomprehensible, because all the
events which took place during the course of their
eight-year acquaintance were of a completely official
character and in no sense could have led to what they
did in fact lead to; they gave no grounds at all for such
a close relationship. Indeed no grounds existed for this
relationship between Marina and Zubov at all, granted
they were such different people, even in terms of age,
although Zubov looked ten years younger than he was
and in that sense could be considered well-matched
with Marina; and yet it was this very circumstance, the
fact that Zubov looked ten years younger than he was,
while Marina's appearance exactly corresponded to her
age – it was this very circumstance that divided Marina
and Zubov more than anything else, although they had,
despite everything, such a close relationship.

The events of an official nature which preceded this
relationship between Marina and Zubov were of the
following kind: Marina had on many occasions proved
useful to Zubov, since for several years she had worked
in the enquiries office, and equally Zubov, during
those years, had sought in so far as he was able to make
himself pleasant and useful to Marina – he had given
her gifts of various kinds and knew all the details of her
married life, which Marina had presented him with on
each occasion, in the course of the regular conversations

that took place between them during those years. In turn Marina knew all the details of Zubov's life as a solitary old bachelor who, despite his age, looked like a young man and had kept every hair on his head.

However none of this could have brought the two of them together; what brought them together in fact was something else, something unfathomable, beyond human reason, something which went on alongside their official conversations in the enquiries office, conversations whose contents related rather to work, which arose from work and had consequences only in terms of work – at all events, it was only when Marina had left her job in the enquiries office and was working in a completely different place and could no longer be in any way useful to Zubov, that he suddenly rang Marina up and said that since they were close neighbours now he would be most appreciative if she would care to drop in and admire his chandelier.

Marina lost no time in calling round and found him in a completely empty apartment, in which an electrician had indeed just hung a chandelier of extraordinary proportions, an antique chandelier, made of porcelain, with forty-eight bulbs and numerous tender little petals and pendants.

Zubov himself was not much interested in the fixing of the chandelier; he gave Marina a conducted tour of the empty apartment, but it was obvious that he was restless and eager to get away, and that his thoughts were elsewhere; and it was in this frame of mind, this state of distraction that he remained virtually throughout the time that Marina stood about under the chandelier, studying the delicate craftsmanship that had gone into it and chatting to the electrician who was screwing something into the centre of the chandelier. From then on this peculiar relationship proceeded to develop on some quite other and mysterious basis, since the pretext of Zubov's move was soon exhausted, as were other circumstances such as the death of Zubov's old mother, whose funeral Marina attended on her own initiative; and no further events of any great substance occurred; that's to say, both Marina and Zubov had their reasons, but these belonged to some quite different plane, not connected in any way with Marina's relationship with her former husband or with the question of obtaining furniture for Zubov's apartment.

Nevertheless Marina continued to come to Zubov's apartment. And the apartment remained empty, and in the apartment they continued to talk about the principles of interior design and Marina's erstwhile married life, talked just as unconstrainedly as they used to when they'd chatted in Marina's enquiries office, amidst all the files and books of clippings.

Zubov, for example, loosening up, would tell Marina that one of these days the woman in her would awaken and she'd feel the desire to love and be loved, but she'd have no luck at all, no one would pay any attention to her. 'Above all,' Zubov said, 'you need to fix up your hands and do something about your hair.' And then, Zubov said, you need to get rid of all this stuff you're wearing and everything underneath it, change your whole style. 'Couldn't you buy,' Zubov asked, 'couldn't you at least buy a nice pair of shoes?' None of this need cost more, he said, than the things you're wearing now. 'Show at least an ounce of taste,' he said.

Marina would leave and come back again on this same Zubov's invitation, and Zubov would bring her into the dining-room, warning that he had guests, and these guests every one of them were pretty young girls,

106

Zubov's new floozies, and a general conversation would arise among them. The girls called Zubov by his first name, and Marina was particularly struck by one of them, who informed the company in all seriousness that French people called Paris 'Paree'.

Marina would listen in to Zubov's telephone conversations too, and one such conversation especially caught her attention. Zubov was talking about some girl or other and said in conclusion, 'The girl knows how to love'. When Marina enquired whether Zubov had in mind the soul of this girl or just her technique, Zubov said he was referring exclusively to her technique. Whereupon Marina said that she'd been reading some American book, not yet translated, about hippies who lived in communes and for educational purposes studied Indian and Swedish literature on the technical aspects of sex, and that she herself didn't understand if you really could learn anything about sex techniques from books and indeed whether it was necessary to do so. Zubov, animated, started asking Marina where she'd got hold of this book, and Marina said she'd read it in some publishing house, but the book didn't contain any descriptions of the techniques as such. Zubov then brought the conversation to a close, and everything ended as it always did, with Marina going to the door, and the chandelier tinkling, and Zubov closing the door behind her.

And then Zubov would ring Marina, or Marina would ring Zubov for no particular reason, to ask him how things were going or to tell him some snippet of news from her own rather straightforward life as a woman and mother. And this relationship carried on, outwardly unchanged, right to the very end, to an end which somehow happened twice over. It happened the first time during a trivial telephone conversation, in the course of which Zubov started complaining about his co-author, and Marina tried logically to explain to Zubov the situation and feelings of this co-author, and then advised him not to take the matter to court.

All of a sudden, at the end of this conversation, when Marina had already uttered her final sentences, a powerful woman's voice came on to the line, rang out like a clap of thunder, saying that there was absolutely no call to keep a man talking on the phone for a good quarter hour about his own affairs, which he was perfectly capable of sorting out himself. In a state of shock, completely bewildered, Marina quietly put the phone down and decided that she wouldn't ring again.

On the second occasion Marina was more careful, having already learned something about this new female resident of Zubov's apartment, a thoroughly uncouth character, educated but with a great penchant for swearing.

At the very start of this second and last conversation Marina asked Zubov whether he was freely able to talk, despite the fact that there was another extension in the apartment. Zubov answered in the positive, saying that he was quite alone, that, yes, he wasn't busy and so on, and they embarked on their usual telephone conversation, which ended this time with Zubov relating to Marina two episodes from his own life which offered material proof for his contention that there was great virtue in self-control: and Zubov related these two episodes, one after the other, in response to Marina's informing him that she wasn't sleeping at all at night, and that for some unknown reason her son kept choking and quite distinctly complaining, despite being only two and a half years old.

Zubov promised Marina to summon a first-rate doctor for the little fellow, and the conversation, on Zubov's initiative, then turned to quite other matters: Zubov started complaining about some dreadful woman in his life, and complained at some considerable length, and the conversation concluded with these complaints, since Zubov said that he had to go off and work. And at this point the woman's voice once more rang out loud and clear, like a burst of thunder in Marina's ears, saying there was no call to be ringing so late, she was sick and tired of it.

Marina put the receiver back on the hook, mentally saying farewell to Zubov and to the eight years of her life in which she'd known him; then she rang up a friend of hers, who also knew Zubov, and told her everything she thought about him, and her friend supported her on every count, and then excused herself, saying that she couldn't talk long, and they both hung up; and for a long time afterwards Marina sat frozen on the chair in her office at eleven o'clock at night, when what she should have done there and then was get up and urgently go home.

That Delightful Young Lady

It was the most lamentable story, it really was, when you considered both the principal characters involved and the utmost banality of the story itself. And just for that reason it was perhaps surprising that in its rehearsal and performance it so accurately followed every note of the score, right from the beginning – so apparently harmless, so comically insidious – to the very end, where everything seemed literally to have been mapped out in advance, right down to the squeezing of hands, so very innocent on the surface, and to all those despairing glances; and the only piquant factor in it all was that it was a man of sixty-odd years who cast the final despairing glance, from the window of a taxi, smiling broadly all the while and waving to the people he was leaving behind, among them a young woman of twenty-odd years; and it was indeed to her that he threw his last, despairing grimace of a smile – from somewhere down below, from the seat of the car, already hermetically sealed and ready to go.

We thus have an outline sketch of the two principal characters in our story, and a sketch is quite sufficient; for it was precisely the difference in their ages that played the key role in the story of these two, since in every other respect they were quite perfectly matched, and in other circumstances, given some other configuration of ages, a classic romance might have developed between them, doubtless involving a great many other characters – the heroine's husband, for example, or the hero's wife, a lady no longer in her prime; indeed a full-blown tragedy might well have arisen, and goodness knows what else besides.

As it was, however, she was born just a little bit too late; that's to say, the Earth and the stars had revolved an irreparable number of times before she deigned to appear in the world, while he had been around for a good long time already. Aside from these revolutions of the Earth and the stars there was simply no other reason, no other reason at all to explain that despairing grimace of his, as he sat in the taxi and prepared to depart for ever and a day, all the while repeating that there was no need for all these farewells, since he'd be back again just the day after tomorrow, he had so many odds and ends to do down here in the country.

It was incidentally quite possible that he had made a few optimistic plans, counting and calculating and carving out a little extra time in the future, so that he'd be able to carry on those idle conversations with his new flame, his delightful young lady, who was now going to stay the rest of the week in the country for the sake of her small child – and who now kept nodding in response to his assurance that he would soon be back, nodding in the careless conviction that this would indeed be the case.

Quite possibly he was convinced of it himself as he prepared to leave, hermetically sealed up in the car – and quite possibly what prevented him returning was not, after all, the sublime consideration of all those fruitless revolutions of the Earth and stars throughout the time that he had lived without her, without his delightful young lady, since she had not yet appeared in the world; quite possibly his failure to return had nothing to do with the consideration that the game was up, irrevocably spoiled by her late arrival on Earth, her excessively, unwarrantedly late arrival. Quite possibly such reflections had not even occurred to him, and he was thinking only of the muddled affairs that awaited his return to town, where grim, ordinary, every-day life would start all over again, so different from his carefree holiday life in the country, with all those little chats in the sunshine and walks in the evening mist. It was perfectly possible, indeed, that city life simply swallowed him up without trace, when, after days of sweet country air, he plunged straight back into the atmosphere of the city, leaning back in the rear seat of that low-slung, decrepit taxi.

On the other hand it's quite conceivable, too, that all those sublime considerations came crashing down on top of him the minute he sank down on the low back seat of the taxi and, crouched under its roof, began waving and smiling to that delightful young lady of his.

He was accompanied in the taxi by his wife, and she too smiled and made that despairing grimace; indeed they both wore one and the same identical smile; it had appeared on the wife's face the moment her husband had introduced the delightful young lady to her – his neighbour down there in the country, his companion on so many walks. His wife, it's true, had arrived quite unexpectedly, like a midsummer snowfall, although she had no reason to feel threatened; she'd arrived just like that, out of the blue, taken time off work and come down for no reason at all. The three of them spent some ten to fifteen minutes together, and at first, of course, it had been a little awkward, since the wife, with that despairing smile of hers, looked the delightful young lady over and finally declared that she was mentally calculating the difference in age. 'Not all that big,' the young lady joked, and the conversation then wandered on to mindless things, like the packet soups her husband was obliged to consume down here, and the nature of ready-made soups in general. No doubt the wife felt extremely agitated throughout this conversation, and a sudden pause arose; but the woman who owned the dacha happened to be present and embarked on an independent conversation with the wife at this point, so that finally the other two were able to have another talk, a final talk, this time in distinctly dangerous circumstances. And they began talking all sorts of nonsense, literally interrupting one another and truly forgetting about everything else in the world.

And then the taxi came – they'd ordered it in advance – and that put an end to everything; and the problem of her too late, or his too early arrival on Earth vanished too – everything vanished, lost in the great revolution of the stars, as if nothing whatsoever had happened.

The Ball of the Last Man

You can say time in time out he's a finished man, an alcoholic, and that does just about sum him up, but not quite. He's dependent on hand-outs from his sick, house-bound mother, which is why he always tries to leave before half past midnight, before the metro closes down – because he never has the money for a taxi. And if in the end he does get marooned, somewhere out at the back of beyond, then he goes home on foot or by some other means – at all events come morning he always turns out to be home, though it's a complete mystery how he makes it back. And it's not because he's saving the money his sick old mother gives him, it's just that he's spent it all, he doesn't have any, and that's that.

But somehow or other, no matter where he sets out from, he always does seem to make it back home. And I can't help thinking how his mother must love him, love him unfathomably, beyond imagination.

You'll tell me, I know, he's a spiritual bankrupt, there's nothing sacred in his life any more; he's spent a whole year translating Tennyson – who needs Tennyson, for heaven's sake? – and the last straw, you'll say, is that he's just twenty-three years old. And yet that doesn't quite get to the nub of it either. And you'll go on about how, once upon a time, you'd thought of having a child by him, and then realised that would make no difference, because the child would turn out to be a thing in itself, an independent thing, with no desire to influence matters at all.

And now, finally, in the semi-darkness of your room, he's sitting there with the others at your table, and you sit at a distance from him, self-possessed, not thinking of yourself one bit, not a bit – that's the loveliest thing about you – you sit, as always, perfectly serene. He's quite full of himself, with his gentle ribbing and his courteous manners – a real gentleman with a devilish look on his face, suddenly laughing in a much higher voice than his own. Everything's going smoothly; everyone's eating a spot of fish with dry little pancakes quickly rustled up by your sister, and everyone's pouring out the vodka, best Moscow Stolichnaya or Polish Wyborowa. And he tops up the glass of the woman sitting next to him, who wears subtle make-up and smokes a bit ineptly; God knows how she got here but who cares anyway. And you sit there squinting at the company and laughing so heartily, without a hint of self-consciousness, without for a minute comparing yourself to anyone else in the room . . .

It's all terrific fun, sitting round the table in the semi-darkness with 'Bye bye, mon amour' playing on the gramophone; there's no great flirtation, no hanky-panky, none of the usual fuss over age or hierarchy at work. 'Fish, fish, fish in a dish' – the cries ring out in the semi-darkness.

He downs one glass after another, completely sober, nibbles his fish and makes witty remarks, offers his neighbour a light and refills her glass, and all this appears completely commonplace. The conversation keeps going on reminiscences about mutual friends and the place where all of them work off and on – but there's nothing here of that wonderful talk that sometimes gets spun from a trifle, nothing of that at all. Bit by bit the bottles empty, and then something very simple happens: your sister brings in a phial of pure spirit, 200 grams worth, and plonks it right in the middle of the table. She's a biochemist, your sister; she gets the spirit at work for extracting higher molecular organic compounds, for separating acidities from the cellular wall, for spectrophotometry of antibiotics, and for sterilising her work table and vessels.

No one is shocked by the arrival of the spirit; some refuse to drink it neat and dilute it down, but he carefully pours himself a full glass with a drop of water to drink on the side, and then offers his neighbour the same, and she unexpectedly agrees.

Here you can see his famous charm at work, though she starts explaining in an undertone that she's agreed to the spirit only to distract attention from the fact that he's been helping himself twice as often as everybody else. By way of reply he puts on his most courtly look and proposes that they at least clink glasses, and everyone else looks away, distracted; and you alone, with simple-hearted concern, keep an eye on the two of them as she boldly downs the spirit, all in one go, and without pausing for breath – that's what he's taught her, never pause for breath – swallows the water straight off and assumes an air of total indifference; and everyone exclaims at how suddenly doleful she looks.

At this point several of the guests get up and take their leave, it's twenty to midnight and they've things to do at home. And now our hero, who's name incidentally is Ivan, gets up and leaves the room, leaving his neighbour downcast and disappointed. Someone gingerly picks up the phial by the neck and shakes it, discovering thereby that all the spirit is gone. 'Aha!' they exclaim, and you look towards the door. Ivan reappears behind your sister the biochemist. He calmly returns to his corner and sits down with his erstwhile neighbour from the table, who for lack of other occupation has been leafing through a book in the semi-darkness. She carries on reading, laughing soundlessly from time to time, and he sits there patiently staring in front of him, propped with one hand on the edge of the table and puffing away at a cigarette. The conversation gets going again, with his neighbour reading out loud some funny titles from the book. Then your biochemist sister comes in again, holding a brimming glass in her wet fingers. Ivan, awestruck, rises to his feet, reverentially swallows the glassful, then washes it down with water and sits down again with his neighbour, who proceeds to ask him 'And what about me?'

After a while he starts looking restless, leaves the room and comes back with the biochemist in train, her expression by now a mixture of vexation and involuntary mirth. An inseparable pair, they go to and fro, have words in the corridor and finally return to the room, and at this point he delicately shuts the door behind him.

Agitated by these comings and goings, Ivan's neighbour from the table gets up too, goes into the kitchen and stands there foolishly leaning on the fridge and smoking in total darkness, while bursts of female laughter drift in from the other room.

At last footsteps are heard and Ivan enters the dark kitchen, followed by the chemist whom he's leading by the hand. Ivan's neighbour slips out of the dark kitchen, leaving the two of them alone, and comes back into the room, where a pretty young lad is dancing all by himself, and she with exaggerated rhythm starts dancing opposite, while you with the silliest of laughs get out of your chair and kick off your shoes and start dancing too.

Meanwhile Ivan and the chemist come in and out, enter the room or file one after the other into the corridor and pull the door to. And with each new turn Ivan looks more and more distraught and the chemist, ever more vexed, keeps shrugging her shoulders, because for reasons of her own she won't give Ivan his spirit. And you laugh and laugh, dancing just in your stockings on the dirty floor, until there's a sudden terrible loud cry from the kitchen, 'But it wouldn't cost you anything!' and something shatters on the kitchen floor. 'Is he often like this?' Ivan's neighbour asks when the chemist returns. 'Every single bloody time,' she replies.

'Yes, yes, yes,' you say, 'he's completely done for, hopelessly addicted.' And the pretty youth puts 'Bye bye, mon amour' once more on the gramophone, and everyone starts dancing again, and the chemist says, 'I can't cope, you go, he keeps rootling around in there trying to find it.' 'You shouldn't have brought that whole glass just for him, that was a mistake,' says someone.

Ivan comes into the room, straight away grabs his former neighbour and pulls her over to dance with him, but he dances somehow lamely and awkwardly, completely out of sync with the beat of the music, and his neighbour feels obliged to adapt to his sudden jumps and soon starts jumping every second step herself. And in a shrill voice he says, 'Take a look now, the ball of the last man'.

But he soon abandons her and takes the chemist once more by the arm, rousing her half-dead from the corner where she seems to have dropped off to sleep, and so the process carries on endlessly, till finally Ivan's neighbour leaves the room herself and begins the long rigmarole of dressing for the winter streets – first the suede boots, then the heavy cardigan, the big scarf, the fur hat. And then Ivan, who's standing there with the chemist, suddenly rushes up to his former neighbour and says, wild-eyed, 'Just give me fifteen minutes, OK? Just fifteen, twenty minutes, no more, all right? I'll come with you, I can't let you go just like that.' And he seizes his former neighbour by the arms and pushes her back into the half-dark room, but stays put himself with the chemist in the corridor.

And you sit on your divan, your legs tucked up, and laugh away happily: 'I keep seeing things in four dimensions, it's fantastic, fantastic.'

And Ivan's neighbour, seizing the moment when Ivan's gone by with his chemist, who keeps involuntarily snorting with laughter – the neighbour slips out of the door, puts on her fur coat and runs down the stairs.

And you understand everything, everything and sit there smiling on the divan, just in your stockings, and it's three in the morning, and you know that Ivan will have to go home on foot.

La Bohème

From the opera *La Bohème* we learn that once upon a time someone loved somebody, and lived somehow or other, and then chucked her in or was chucked in himself, but in Claudia's case it was all much simpler. Though she deserved just as much to be called 'La Bohème', since she hadn't a bean or a home to call her own, and for the eighth year running she'd been an extra-mural student at some institute of librarianship, ate only three days out of seven and just staggered about from house to house in the company of others like her, rogues and rascals the lot, and there wasn't a single one of them she hadn't had an affair with; but she was the only woman in this little bohemian circle, the most bohemian in town, because they really hadn't a thing, neither a roof over their heads nor clothes to wear in winter, they walked about hatless or just in their raincoats; and in summer Claudia's bare heels were an embarrassment to decent people, yet a young woman endlessly walking the streets was bound to have dirty bare heels like that, and legs like that and hair and face like that; that's how a bohemian was bound to be, silent, modest, laying claim to nothing, for she had nowhere to stay but was always off and away, sleeping and eating God knows where. She was always writing, poems or novels, even gave readings in her little circle, no worse than other poetesses in other circles at other times and places; and in the summer the lot of them would suddenly go wild and escape up

north, find themselves a shelter of sorts, live in huts and
gather folk-songs or go and sing at weddings themselves; Claudia at any rate travelled a lot that summer,
hitching lifts on passing lorries down heaven knows
what roads, roads where she bounced in the back
of trucks, alternately banging her head on the roof or
hitting the floor with those same bare heels, and it was
then that something completely inexplicable happened
to our bohemian Claudia: she developed a terrible
stomach complaint. But she had to keep moving, that
was the rule once they'd got on the road; she and her
companions just had to keep going, keep going on and
on and on – wait by muddy roadsides, in marshy
woods, hang about in haylofts, squat behind bushes or
in backyards; and Claudia by this time no longer
needed food. She started fading away right in front
of people's eyes, if anyone that is had had eyes to look
at her, but no one had, for Claudia's two travelling
companions had decided to up and leave, and leave
they did, and Claudia couldn't see herself and didn't
know what was wrong with her. But in any case she
made her way to a port, and managed somehow to get
aboard a steamer among the fourth-class passengers, in
a pit deep under the water where it smelled of exhaust
fumes; once the ticket inspectors even came to bother
her, but luckily retreated, distracted by the loud cries
of some non-Russian passengers shouting something
about tickets. When the steamer arrived, Claudia, semi-
comatose, emerged into the light of day, got herself on
to a local train, still with the pain in her stomach, and
stayed on board till she found herself once more on the
familiar platform of her native N. Here in N she was
discovered lying in the garden by her mother, and here
in N she moved into a clean bed, into a clean bed at

last after all her long travels; and here, going out one early morning to have a pee, she suddenly let forth a stream of blood beneath the sweetbriar, and everything then fell into place, for there was the foetus, already quite large. Her mother, who'd helped her into the garden, said the baby was a boy, and later on Claudia was wont to tell people how she'd been going to have a boy baby – how it was due in so many months, or, as time went by, so many months ago: she'd count out her months like a real mother, although she'd add in passing that it had all happened by chance and she hadn't even suspected it beforehand. But everyone accepted her stories and calculations, feeling as they listened a little strange, and responded with a companionable silence, as if unsure what to do with the information. And so after a while Claudia fell silent; and only her mother, spending a great deal of money, for some reason had the privy moved to a new place in the garden, and in the old place, now filled up and covered, she planted a birch and a rowan tree.

Two Souls

In summertime two lofty souls – a man and a woman – may sometimes be found queuing up at the counter of the greengrocer's.

In winter, for some reason, you almost never see them. Sometimes you catch a brief glimpse of the man, of his proud, febrile gaze; but she seems to evaporate in winter, disappear, as if she's flown away to warmer climes; though one assumes she must spend the winter searching for food, traipsing this place and that with her bag over her shoulder, always with the same tragic expression on her face. But she's not to be seen in wintertime, and no one knows what kind of fur she wears, though it must, one presumes, be a very expensive kind. And yet for some reason she never appears in it, so vanity, one would have to conclude, is something quite foreign to her, at least in relation to our neighbourhood, the neighbourhood where, since the death of her husband, she's been obliged to live out her solitary existence.

And in summertime it can't be from vanity that she wears those crazy, black and gold outfits of hers, the black and gold headscarf and that huge bag over her shoulder which gives her the air of being an eternal wanderer.

Altogether she doesn't really seem to notice our neighbourhood, as if it didn't exist for her as a genuine category or even as some form of abstract power, surrounding her just at the moment of purchasing the bread, vegetables or sausage required to sustain life.

But still, how does she sustain life in the winter, how does she manage to obtain that bread, those vegetables, that sausage? She doesn't surely just sit in her burrow starving, staring melancholy through the window at the winter landscape outside? No, obviously not, she doesn't die of hunger, for as soon as the warm days begin again she's there same as ever, in her black silk with her bare, veined hands and her bare legs, just as she always was, as if the long winter had never been, as if another year hadn't passed since the death of her husband.

As a matter of fact it was precisely this story of her husband's death that somehow revealed her, legitimised her, laid her bare as an absolutely comprehensible being, even though a great many other details of her life had long since been known, for nothing in the end gets hidden from people, one way and another everything comes to light through the walls of houses or seeps through the skin and skull of a given person, fully defended though they might seem to be, guaranteed by the walls of their homes or the thickness of their skulls. Once upon a time, though, she'd been well-hidden and protected, despite the fact that everyone knew everything about her, about the fact that her husband, a prominent man, neglected her and led his own, quite independent existence. She seemed defended and protected nonetheless: for example, sometimes they'd come out of the house together and get into the car to go off on some joint excursion, or their young son would come to see them with his wife, and on such occasions there could be no doubt how well defended she was, how well protected. Her defencelessness, indeed, was no more than a myth in those days, a beautiful detail from a fairy-tale, finding no external expression, but hovering like a halo over her image in the eyes of others.

Her defencelessness, in this sense, existed somehow quite apart from her, independently of her. From her outward appearance you could never have guessed she was vulnerable. People often said, it's true, that she had extraordinarily tragic eyes, and that her taste in clothes was quite abominable, as if she were overwhelmed by choice and never quite knew how to adorn herself further in order to restore some past state of affairs. Then she underwent plastic surgery . . . Indeed, on the surface everything she did seemed to coincide with the state of mind generally attributed to a neglected wife. It is quite possible, however, that all this did not in fact coincide with her real state of mind at all, and that all attempts on the part of others to judge her frame of mind purely on the basis of certain external details were neither here nor there: for example, it might have been quite incorrect at that stage to say that the reason she made such efforts to retain her former beauty was that she wished in some way to reinstate the past. It might well have turned out that this was not her main concern at all, and that she didn't really believe that her outward appearance could change anything. Quite possibly she had resorted to cosmetic surgery for some other, completely unknown reason.

Whatever the case may be, she did resort to surgery and everything in her behaviour did seem to confirm the general view of what must be happening in her heart – and so it went on right up to her husband's death, which occurred unexpectedly, as a result of a stroke.

That was the only occasion on which she acted as if she truly, indisputably had been left quite defence-less: she immediately started begging not to be evicted from her spacious official apartment. Her husband's body was not yet cold before she started urgently demonstrating her rights to the apartment, although at that stage it had not even occurred to anyone to question whether the apartment might be too large for the widow. Even to hint at such a thing at the time would have been blasphemous, but as if possessed she made haste to bring it up with all and sundry, and with her obsessive, crazed persistence and stubbornness managed to alienate a number of people who till then had been complete strangers; she also made a very unfavourable impression on her husband's friends. She thus displayed herself in her full colours, and as a result was now completely alone, deprived of all the support that undoubtedly would have been offered her, as it is generally offered a woman left alone by the death of her husband.

This seemed, however, to cause her little concern, for in the end, after pleading her case at length, she found she was able, after all, to hold on to her official apartment; and that was when her subsequent existence began, when bit by bit she began to appear in public, her tastes and habits making her, to passersby, a highly distinctive figure in her eternal black silk dresses, sticking out absurdly in every queue – the more absurdly because she was so much taller than the mass of housewives who crowded into the shops each morning. She stood out, upright and incongruous, squeezed and hemmed in by the queue, and always maintaining under these circumstances the same superciliously mournful air.

And it was there, in one of these queues, as she stood

in her melancholy pre-eminence with her silk turban, the
curls dangling beneath it in a fashion so inappropriate
to her age – it was there that he, the second protagonist
in our story, sought her out with his gaze.

This gaze of his, it must be said, was well-nigh insatiable, permanently trained on everyone about him.
The expression 'to devour with one's eyes' seemed
invented for him as he approached the shop, dressed
as for the height of summer in his yellowed linen suit
and canvas shoes. It wasn't merely that he contemplated
others with idle curiosity; no, with frenzied impatience
he fastened his gaze on every passerby – even on
children, especially on children indeed.

He was quite capable of stopping in his tracks some
naughty little creature who'd crashed into his knees in
the course of a game – but not in the patronising way
that most adults do; no, he'd grab the child and engage
him in furious argument, doing all the talking himself
from beginning to end since the unfortunate child was
quite likely unable to answer him back.

Indeed, this cantankerous old man – for he was a
cantankerous old man – had no pity even for those of
the tenderest age, and was once found berating a child
of two who was quite incapable yet of stringing two
sensible words together.

Permanently on the lookout, this old man one day
came slowly and surely wending his way towards a
queue for spring cherries. Straight way, of course, he
embarked on a quarrel with the salesgirl, and the
agitated crowd was soon in an uproar. Unable to resist,
he then turned to address the crowd, among whom our
widow rose up like a pillar in her black and gold garb,
her turban and the curls which fell in tendrils right to
her eyes.

Suddenly, interrupting his lengthy indictment, the old man shouted out to her:

'Your name, please!'

She shrugged her shoulders and answered in a proud, clear voice.

The crowd, as if nothing had happened, resumed its usual exchanges, the salesgirl weighed out the cherries, while these two stood still as if struck by lightning. He shouted to the widow:

'I know, I read about it. A terrible death. They couldn't save him.'

She bent her head with the curls and he, jerking his chin, suddenly marched past in his yellowed suit, inexpressibly happy, leaving behind him the queue, in which the widow with her black turban was slowly inching towards the spring cherries, having just lived through, perhaps, the greatest experience that she was fated to have, for encompassed within it was the whole of her former life, long since vanished and now vindicated at last.

Youth

Where does it all go, where does it get to, where does it vanish, that fabled charm of youth, its notorious freshness, the softness of features still undefined, hidden till the time is ripe by taut, elastic, all-covering skin? One minute it's there, this soft, diffused charm, and suddenly it seems to vanish, as everything vanishes in good time, including life itself, and then everything turns clear-cut and well-defined, everything gets exposed, and so it goes on till the last component parts are bared, until the final disintegration, the distillation of everything from everything else.

And suddenly it seems that only youth itself *is* life, life in its full incarnation, in its most unconscious florescence and development and unrestrained growth, and all the rest, all that philosophising and glancing back, the apprehending and acceptance of everything that's been and everything that is to come – all that is a different matter entirely.

It was, for instance, to this condition – the full, all-forgiving, optimistic understanding of all her past adventures – that a certain Nina had attained; now a mature woman, she was just as plump as in her youth, but her long, luxuriant curls had been replaced by a more modest, shorter haircut now, and she no longer attracted any particular attention.

Yet there'd been a time, once upon a time, when Nina with her rough, husky voice, so natural in a creature as young as she then was, had held everyone's attention and fully deserved it, fully deserved those constant looks she got: in the first place with her thick, unruly, luxuriant hair, and then with those lazy, animal habits of hers – her way of stretching out on the ground when they went for a stroll in the country, her sleepy, yawning gestures, and that total forgetfulness of time, place and circumstance that often seemed to overcome her and appeared, in her, so extraordinarily natural. Thus, for example, when she set off into the country with a group of colleagues to clear the ground for summer allotments, she was found, soon after they'd started work, stretched out on a patch of newly-grown grass, just basking in all the fresh air and sunshine, and looking the very embodiment of turbulent, blossoming youth, which seems only to await the right moment to burst forth, and until that moment lies hidden in ambush.

And the key moment came when everyone threw down their rakes and brooms and gathered in the bushes to eat and drink; it was then that the real explosion came, as Nina burst into song in her unbelievably husky voice. She sang some rough street songs, and everyone rolled about laughing and reached out to clink glasses with her, and by that time Nina was already lying with her head in somebody's lap; but by and by the party wound up, and after her outburst, when these bacchanalia with her colleagues were over, Nina ended the day riding home on a city bus, clutching only the empty bag that had held her sandwiches.

Thus Nina made extravagant use of the gifts of youth, plundering them without a thought for the future. Indeed, she started to overdo it a bit, exhibiting these gifts of hers, exaggeratedly trumpeting the tale of her conquests to all and sundry and fluffing up her hair into a veritable lion's mane, so that little by little, beneath the surface, a certain impatience on her part became evident, a frenzied expectation of certain mysterious rewards, even a downright exactingness towards the rest of the world, as if the world were in some way guilty or ill-disposed towards her, when in fact the world hadn't changed at all, it was just as it always had been, and would have responded just as eagerly to Nina's reckless, uproarious outbursts of joy; but Nina herself had changed, and there was a certain sorrow, even anguish in the way she performed all her showpieces now. She seemed dogged now by a determination to smash and destroy something, a determination to express herself in the filthiest language and engage in outright pillaging at the table, sometimes whipping off the tablecloth or slapping somebody in the face.

Strange as it may seem, though, this period of turmoil passed too, although one might have imagined that with time, and the advent of fresh losses and failures, the trouble would only have intensified further. But that wasn't what happened. Obviously this was due in some way to the fact that Nina herself had changed in external appearance, and as a result the external circumstances surrounding her changed too; she could no longer walk down the street in the same way as she was wont to do before, and she could no longer sing or talk in the same way either, bearing in mind her completely altered appearance; and the scandalous scenes she used to create might well have attracted no attention now at all. So that's how she began to live, no longer drawing attention to herself; and in keeping with this new state of affairs she cut her hair short and gradually turned into the most ordinary of women, living alone with her little routines, and even her husky voice bore witness only to firm principles and strength of character – and nothing about her now recalled the young girl she used to be, so that friends, reminiscing about old times, involuntarily shook their heads and felt a bit sorry, never suspecting how simple and purified their Nina felt now, or what new era of her life had now dawned.

Immortal Love

So what became of the heroes of our romance? It must be said that after Ivanov's departure everything remained in place, just as it had been before. For life itself doesn't move on just because a single person has moved, any more than the roof caves in on a whole institution, and all the people in it, just because of his departure. So that the fact that the roof had, figuratively speaking, caved in on Lena, and that life had definitely moved on for her, didn't mean anything for anyone else, and the world remained just as it was when Ivanov was there, regardless of the fact that Ivanov had gone, leaving in his wake only a gaping hole.

So Lena was forced to go on working just where Ivanov had left his gaping hole, and where only a week ago Lena herself, as if in jest, had sunk to her knees before Ivanov's desk. She knelt there as if in prayer, her hands clasped and her eyes closed, literally a couple of yards from where Ivanov, seated at his desk, was calmly putting his papers in order and laughing good-naturedly, as if unaware of the condition into which Lena had sunk. Right up to the moment when Ivanov had started tidying his desk she had evidently kept hoping that something would happen, a reprieve of some kind, for it couldn't be over just like that, it couldn't have all come to nothing; and when Ivanov began tidying his desk prior to his departure she fell to her knees as if senseless with grief. She knelt there for ten whole minutes, and for the duration of these ten minutes everyone went about their business as usual, a trifle embarrassed but quite composed; they took it all in their stride, never batting an eyelid, as if over the years they'd seen a good many scenes like this. Everyone took it as a form of hysterical behaviour which merited neither attention nor intervention, nor any indication of belief in the genuine existence of the grief and despair that such hysterical behaviour generally suggests.

And Lena herself knelt there quite calmly, without any noisy demonstrations of feeling; and thus the two or three people present in the room at the time were forced to acknowledge that the only thing left to a person in these circumstances was precisely the right to kneel, and that there was a sweetness in that very act of kneeling.

Finally Ivanov departed, and Lena was left behind, and it was clear as daylight that Lena would go after him, by some means or other and notwithstanding the fact that here in her native city she had obligations towards her mother, her son and her husband.

Lena never discussed her plans for the future with anyone and went on working as usual; she did, how-ever, befriend the librarian, and this was an indication that she planned to escape. For the librarian, Tonya, a sweet and mournful blonde, was herself a wanderer, adventuress and escapee. Just like Lena, Tonya had a home where she lived with her child, a little girl; but from time to time she abdicated her maternal responsi-bilities, made arrangements at work and, leaving the child in her parents' care, set off for another town to see the man she loved, the object of her desire; and moreover she set off unasked, uninvited, slept at the railway station, hid out on the stairs and so forth, all in the hope of catching a glimpse of her beloved.

Lena made friends with Tonya and spent her lunch hours with her in various snack bars and coffee shops, and after work they'd walk together to the tram stop, afterwards going their separate ways on different trams, Tonya to pick up her daughter from kindergarten, and Lena to her apartment, where her duties towards her mother, her son and her husband awaited her.

As later emerged, however, none of these duties absolutely had to be fulfilled, for in the end Lena left in any case for the town where Ivanov now worked, and returned only many years later, seven years to be precise; returned with her mind bedimmed, full of paranoid fears; returned because her husband, Albert, had brought her home.

Here, however, some clarification is in order concerning the nature of Lena's duties towards her mother, her son and her husband.

It all began with the arrival of Lena's son, to whom Lena gave birth in unbelievable torment, though without uttering a single cry. The child itself had evidently been through similar torments, for it suffered a brain haemorrhage during its birth, and three months afterwards the doctor informed Lena that her little son would never, in all likelihood, be able to speak, let alone walk.

Lena spent a year looking after the child, and then it was time for her to go back to work, and she went back to work, finding a childminder for her son. Her mother was unable to give her any assistance, for she took leave of her senses three months after the boy was born, obviously from despair at the sight of the motionless little creature; although, as the psychiatrist said at the hospital, the cause of madness should be sought within, rather than without; and other, quite insignificant circumstances might just as well have served to trigger her illness; at all events, a trigger there undoubtedly was.

That spring, when Ivanov went away, Lena was preoccupied with purely practical affairs: she had rented a dacha on the edge of town, where her son, by now seven years old, was to live with his minder, herself and Albert. Lena organised the move to the dacha and lived there for two months; but in July of that year she picked herself up, left the dacha and their apartment in town and her friend the escapee Tonya. She left on the pretext that she had enrolled at a college, supposedly departing for no great length of time, but in fact, as it turned out, for seven years.

She did indeed enrol, for the second time in her life, at a college of some kind, and three years later was borne away from the college hostel in an ambulance, which took her to a psychiatric hospital in a state of the blackest spiritual despair, though precisely what circumstances had served in this instance to trigger the illness will never now be known.

And now let us see what became of Ivanov. Strangely enough, despite his brilliant start in life, he too sank into gloom and desolation, though not quite so rapidly as Lena.

But things weren't so complicated in Ivanov's case; everything was much simpler and cruder with him, and could be explained solely by his partiality to alcohol. Over the course of the years Ivanov dug his own grave, and in the end, following an almighty row, was relegated to the humblest of posts, humble at least by comparison with his former status; he found himself head of a department consisting of just two persons – the sort of post occupied by someone at the start of his career.

So this was the end of that romance which, to everyone else, had seemed to end with Ivanov's departure – though to this day it isn't clear whether it did in fact end at all.

But now it's the figure of Albert, Lena's husband, that comes, in all his titanic greatness, to tower over the story, Albert who throughout those years bore everything that Lena was unable to bear, indeed bore more; it was he, after all, who, seven years after she had vanished, set off to fetch her, knowing everything there was to know, and brought her home, whether because in some unfathomable way he needed her, or because he felt compassion for her, sitting in her hospital bed in a godforsaken district of some strange city, deprived of absolutely everything except that bed, buried alive in her deep vault as Ivanov was in his.

Strictly speaking it was Lena and Ivanov who experienced that unquenchable, immortal love which turns out, on examination, to be just the unfulfilled, unrealised desire to propagate the species, unrealised for different reasons in different cases, but in this case for the simple reason that Lena had once given birth to a motionless child, and thus had reason to doubt her ability to give birth to healthy children at all. But whatever the case may be, whatever the real reason for Ivanov's abandoning Lena, the fact remains: the instinct to propagate the species remained unfulfilled, and quite possibly that was all there was to it.

And yet in this story, whose every detail has now been clarified, it's Albert who should provoke the greatest astonishment; Albert who after seven years came to fetch home his wife, with whom he'd long since lost all contact. What feelings inspired him to do it? – that's the mystery. You could explain it all in terms of that same immortal love, but not everything can be explained so simply. And so the figure of Albert continues, in its titanic greatness, to tower over this otherwise simple, human story.

The Flu

On the face of it the flu was to blame for the whole story, though some insist on a different view of the matter, maintaining that everything was just as simple as it looked at first glance, after the wife first told her story, and that in this instance there was no need to go searching for hidden depths or underlying causes or an interweaving of various different factors; and that it was especially absurd to go making the flu the main culprit, that strange illness that afflicts everybody so differently that one can't even speak of a concrete illness, but rather of a general predisposition towards various maladies, of a universal weakening in people's systems, affecting them all at one and the same time during the coldest months of the year.

But the various possible explanations were put forward and compared, and almost willy-nilly a kind of post-mortem, involving a fair number of people, got underway; it began even at the cremation, when various acquaintances met unexpectedly, people who'd never suspected beforehand that they shared an additional link in their acquaintance with the deceased. There were a great many people present, and that was excluding those women who didn't go because they knew only too well their own propensity to go into hysterics at a dreadful scene like this; but those who did go maintained admirable composure, with the exception of the wife, who never ceased weeping throughout.

But there was no reason to go searching for complex, underlying motives behind her weeping either – there wasn't a hint of posing or histrionics in it. She wasn't pretending – what reason had she to pretend to play the role of a suffering woman when that was precisely what she was; though it's true her situation was not exactly the same as that of a woman left widowed in normal circumstances. Everything in her position was indeed horribly entangled, dreadful even, somehow inhumanely dreadful, and that was why the terrified weeping which filled the entire vault of the crematorium was very understandable.

Everyone felt sorry for her, of course, but again their pity was not of the usual kind – decent, proper, but not very profound, not penetrating to the essence of things – no, they genuinely pitied her. Everyone, seeing her, felt quite at a loss, because she was the one who had suffered the most – and whether deservedly or not wasn't clear. And at the end of the day none of them had any final guarantee that such a thing wouldn't happen to them, apart from the unlikeliness of all these chance circumstances coinciding – the flu, the hunger, a quarrel between husband and wife, appalling cold, the lack of a telephone and the heightened susceptibility that arises from all this – for most of the time, after all, people part quite easily, even after they've been married many years, when they get to the stage where everything's lost, all feelings gone, and every quarrel turns out exactly the same – the quarrel of any two people who've once let anger flare up between them.

So in this case, too, everything might have happened quite calmly, for it was no secret to anyone that for some time now the two of them, husband and wife, had been getting on badly. They were no longer embarrassed by the presence of strangers, never mind their own daughter. People rarely came to see them, not wishing to become chance witnesses to some distressing, unbearable scene, but this didn't stop him from maintaining friendly relations with a good many people, and the same went for her. Their family affairs were of no concern to anyone; they weren't considered worthy of attention. He was a fine, tender, feeling man, prone to tears, with a sensitive conscience and excellent taste. He spoke three languages, was a fine specialist in his field and so on – all the good things you could say of a man were said over his coffin at the cremation, and throughout these speeches his terrified wife kept weeping; and in fact it would have been appropriate right then to say a few nice things about her as well, since the whole thing was beginning to look like a criminal trial – and yet she, after all, was a good person too. But like it or not everything good that was said about him turned into an indirect accusation against her, even though no one intended anything of the sort. And in the final analysis it was she who might just as well have been lying unrecognisable in the coffin; the whole thing was a matter of chance, at least if you overlooked the fact that she was a woman and that it would have been very difficult to imagine her in a state of such complete helplessness as he descended to in the course of those five days. Tenacious, like all mothers, she at least would have found some way out of the situation, she wouldn't have tried to eat the dry tea-leaves out of the teapot or the cornflour straight out of the tin. She would have thought of something, found some way out, opened the door of her apartment for instance and lain down on the doormat, even if she lacked the strength to go out, so that someone at least would have seen her. After all, even after those five days, he did have some strength left, he was still capable after all of climbing up on to the windowsill! She would have found a way out, because she had a daughter, and that means a great deal, not in the sense that the daughter would have looked after her, for her daughter was still too small; no, the daughter would doubtless have caught the flu too, and it would have been precisely her mother, feverish, raving and semi-unconscious who would have been forced to go out to the shops and the pharmacy, make something to eat and sweep round the apartment with a damp cloth so that her child would be able to breathe. So it would have been more difficult to imagine the wife landing up in the coffin for so small and trivial a reason as a marital quarrel. Still, all sorts of things happen in life, and women after all are involved in cases of suicide just as often as men, if not more so; the only exception being mothers. Maybe everything that happened to the husband would have happened to the wife too, if she hadn't had a daughter and been obliged, come what may, to go on living.

But still, even the child – and it's always the child that a woman puts forward as the main argument for her existence – in this case even the child didn't really come into it. After all no one had dreamt of blaming the wife for remaining alive, and there was no need to adduce extenuating circumstances such as her being a mother. She stood accused only of one small thing – and, as always happens in such cases, this was the thing that no one could understand and everybody shook their heads over. Or rather, there were two things, and it was the first especially that seemed incomprehensible. No one blamed the wife for not coming to look after her husband for five whole days, while he lay there completely alone and without any food or medicine. The pair of them had quarrelled, that's all there was to it; and the wife had gathered up the child and walked out of the house just as she was, taking not a thing with her and regardless of the fearful cold – in itself a pretty sure indication that she was not in her right mind. And it was quite understandable that she didn't want to come back, although she had nothing with her but the clothes she was standing in. No doubt she wanted to stay away as long as she could, her husband knowing very well, as she couldn't but realise, that sooner or later she'd have to come back to fetch her suitcases and other things. The fact that she'd sooner or later be forced to return, and that her husband could rest arrogantly assured that she couldn't really go anywhere and would come back in the end, notwithstanding her vow never again to set foot across their threshold – all this could well have kept the wife away far longer than five days. Just knowing that your vows are sneered at, treated as mere histrionics, not for a minute actually believed – just that knowledge can incite a person actually to carry out those vows, though the sneering may just be a form of blackmail, an incitement to do just what you'd sworn you would.

All this, of course, is rather too superficial fully to explain the wife's state of mind when she did in the end come back to fetch her things, but doubtless she was mortified that she'd been forced to come back and that her vow never to return, pronounced in tears and fury, had after all been proved mere histrionics, an empty phrase.

And so the wife, without so much as a glance at her husband, who was lying on the couch, started rapidly gathering up all her essentials, especially her daughter's textbooks and all the bits and pieces she needed for school. She tried, most likely, to pay no attention to her husband at all, though she couldn't help noticing – as she related afterwards – that he looked pretty grimy and unkempt and extremely thin; but she was determined not to investigate this impression further, stubbornly busying herself about her work. Then she noticed the various empty packets and tins strewn about the floor in a pool of spilled water. She made some scathing remark to this effect when she came back into the room, which set off one of their regular quarrels again, a completely routine quarrel; and, when he burst into tears, the wife went to the closet and started gathering up her clothes. She turned round only when she felt a stream of freezing air come into the room. Her husband was standing on the windowsill. And this is the main thing that people blame her for now: that instead of rushing to pull him back off the windowsill, she abruptly and demonstratively turned her back on him and continued to sort out her clothes. This was intended, no doubt, to show her husband that she didn't believe him, just as he hadn't believed her, and that she considered his gesture mere posing, caprice, histrionics, an attempt to play on her feelings or what have you. But in the light of what happened, the fact that she just turned back to the closet could be regarded as a direct incitement to suicide. That's what people blame her for in the first place.

In the second place, when he threw himself head-first out of the sixth-floor window, she didn't run down straight away; she came down only after the ambulance had long since carried him off. She maintains that all that time she was sorting out her things. How long was she there? Probably almost an hour, by the time they'd called the ambulance and everything. So that's the second thing they blame her for.

Anyway, in the place he used to work they often say how they only had four and a half people working there to start with, and of these one went and threw himself out of a sixth-floor window; it sounds like a joke, but that really is what happened.

The Wall

People always make extreme, extraordinarily exaggerated demands of anyone who's said to embody perfection. Confronted with such a person, indeed, they well-nigh boil over with indignation, won't for a minute believe the claims made for them, and go searching and searching for dark spots on the sun. In Anya's case, at all events, everyone said that she was a total nonentity; there was nothing to her, you could see straight through her. In fact, people said, she was like a brick wall, you could see straight through her, and oddly enough this absurd expression didn't sound like a deliberate witticism when applied to Anya. It was just a straightforward mistake, a failure to consider what the words really meant, and over the years the phrase kept cropping up in discussions of Anya. Obviously the expression 'banging your head against a brick wall' had somehow got muddled up in it, as different expressions often get muddled in everyday speech, creating absurd images that everyone understands just the same.

Be that as it may, when she was still barely eighteen and a simple young creature, quite unformed, Anya was declared to be perfection itself. She was pronounced perfection by a bunch of raw young students, the boys in her group at college; and this first sign of the impression she made is worth bearing in mind. It's a well-known fact that people's tastes don't really change with age, people's real tastes, that is, the ones that don't apply to ordinary life but evidently constitute one's ideals. At any rate one day these raw, callow youths in her group at college, with the ideals that they'd acquired once and for all in life, decided to amuse themselves by awarding marks to all the girls in the group, and came to a surprising conclusion; they suddenly hit upon something they'd never thought about before, never called by its proper name, never defined so clearly and in that sense never given free rein to emerge and exist in the world; their conclusion was that, of all the girls, Anya constituted perfection. Anya was awarded B+ only for her slightly plump legs; in due course, however, as we shall see, Anya managed to overcome even this shortcoming, which was really quite a miracle. But that's what happened, and in their subsequent evaluations of Anya no one even remarked on her plump legs, such was the overall harmony of her appearance.

And yet Anya, at the age of eighteen, was a total nobody. The only noteworthy point about her, the only feature one might have seized on to provide at least some indication of her character, was her surprising attachment to another girl, Tamara, with whom Anya on the face of it had absolutely nothing in common, apart from the fact that they always sat side by side in the same corner during lectures. Their friendship – decorous, ceremonious – was striking precisely because it was so obviously a matter of form alone; it had all the outer form of friendship – sitting side by side, going together to the canteen and so on – without the inner content. The usual, inner stuff of friendship – the trust, the shared tastes and interests, the long conversations – was entirely missing. No one had ever seen Tamara confiding in Anya, entrusting her secrets to her. And yet, despite the rather sceptical and

knowing attitude that others took towards it, the friendship carried on in its formal and ceremonious way,
weathering the course even when subjected to the test
of experience, and surviving unchanged right up to the
time when fate parted Anya and Tamara for good.

The aforesaid test was of the following kind:
Tamara, as we've already mentioned, never confided
any of her secrets to Anya, who was the chastest of
girls in every sense of the word. But at one point a
scandal broke out at the college, occasioned by the fact
that Tamara had gone to some party or other and got
involved in a rather ugly affair. While this affair was
being sorted out, Tamara stayed aloof from everyone,
associating only with Anya, and Anya went on uphold-
ing this wordless, ceremonious friendship, unchanged
in her behaviour towards Tamara and showing no sign
of devoting more marked attention to her, as she might
have done if she'd felt that Tamara were somehow at
fault and considered herself to be her only defender in
the face of a hostile world. No, Anya, being the chaste
girl she was, simply didn't believe a word of the story
and carried on not believing, no matter what people
said about Tamara; in her own way she got quite angry
and shunned all those who, out of some partiality
towards her personally, attempted to apprise her of
what was going on. And it was only many years later
that Anya, as if admitting that she'd known the whole
story all along, let slip that Tamara had been back,
come on a visit from the town where she now lived
and worked, and that Tamara hadn't wanted to see any
of her former friends and even with Anya had declined
to meet up a second time or bother to come and visit
her in her new apartment.

So throughout this first stage of her life all that others

knew of Anya was the side of her character that she'd shown in her friendship with Tamara, an insignificant character, just glimpsed in passing before life in the provinces swallowed her up, along with all the sufferings and unavenged insults of her late teenage years. And yet it wasn't as if Anya carefully hid all the other sides of her character, as if she were a mysterious, closed personality who deliberately hid her light under a bushel. No, Anya responded quite easily when engaged in conversation, answering in some detail the questions put to her; yet she manifestly failed to express any real part of herself in doing so, and the conversation would dry up immediately, run into a complete brick wall, as soon as the questioner stopped posing his questions; and everyone complained that she was somehow lifeless, unreal, dead-seeming. And the result was that Anya lived somehow apart, lived her life at one remove from everyone else; or rather, she didn't live any real life at all, her whole life consisting only in the schedules and timetables that for others constitute just the outer casing of life. Anya was obliged to make do with a schedule of activities, and her existence was limited exclusively to this.

We should, however, bear in mind that during this period of her life Anya was seen by others only externally, only in her material being. It's quite possible that whole cataclysms were taking place in Anya's soul at the time; that, far from sleeping, her soul was in turmoil. At all events, Anya sometimes made efforts to break out of the simple round of activities that were common to all, and establish her own separate identity. One such effort was her purchase of a fur coat, a foolish purchase of a rather small, childishly cheap and cheap-looking coat made of synthetic, woolly, reddish-brown fur. Anya bought this coat for herself, despite the fact that she had every opportunity to wangle a good one from her parents, who looked after her solicitously – especially her mother, a beautiful woman, still young, who had excellent dress sense herself. Anya, however, bought the little fur coat with her own money, selling her old winter coat and a few other things rather than borrow from her parents. And she went on wearing it for many years afterwards, long after she was a fully grown woman, always looking a bit pathetic in it, childishly cheap; but she would never admit the fact and behaved as if there were nothing awkward or mortifying about it – exactly as she'd behaved once upon a time in relation to Tamara.

Another of Anya's efforts to break out, this time extremely significant, was her decision to spend New Year's Eve one year at the Student Union party; a pathetic and desperate decision, risible because it was so obviously an attempt to buy for money, through the purchase of a ticket, all the pleasures of an ordinary student get-together, whose charm consists precisely in the fact that one's participation in them can't be bought for cash.

Anya bought her ticket to the New Year party in good faith, never suspecting that the only people going would be loners like her, the ones who'd been excluded from the real student parties. Thus, for example, when she learned that champagne was going to be on sale at the buffet she put aside some money to buy herself a glassful to drink when the clock struck midnight.

As things turned out, however, Anya didn't in the end go to the New Year party; some relatives of hers invited her to a wedding instead. So she was spared that particular trial, though it's quite possible she would have survived it with honour, as she survived with honour all the trials that befell her subsequently.

But it's time now we spoke of Anya's steadfastness and determination, because it was precisely these qualities which began, very discreetly and imperceptibly, yet steadily and inexorably to emerge through the colourless picture of Anya's soul that hitherto had formed in people's minds.

And yet no one could be quite certain how this process occurred, for it took place over a long period of time, throughout those long, difficult years of her life in which Anya would from time to time disappear into obscurity, only to re-emerge into people's field of vision – always the same, unchanging, friendly, predictable, and yet ever more distinct and well-defined.

Here one could appropriately speak of sheer force of circumstance – the circumstances that Anya was forced to endure and overcome and which revealed her for what she truly was to those around her; for it's only circumstances themselves which illuminate a person's character for others, and every circumstance casts light on some new facet, throws into relief some different side of them; and in due course, after many turnabouts and corroborations and recapitulations, an image of the person at last gets forged, an image that leaves less and less room for doubt, less and less room for illusion, and to which others in the end may reconcile themselves, coming to rest on this image alone in their search for the definitive truth.

With hindsight, through the prism of all the years gone by, we can now definitively establish that this steadfastness and determination on Anya's part emerged for the first time clearly in her choice of a husband. For now, years later, it's clear that Anya chose her husband very early on: she'd made her choice long before any-one else, least of all Anya herself, suspected that this would be the boy she'd marry; she chose him blindly and unconditionally, without ever revealing the fact in any way; and all of this in due course bore fruit; in retrospect one can see that her success was due in part to the fact that she gave no sign of her choice, although in fact she was quite unable to do so, so that there was no deliberate method in her approach.

The boy in question didn't stand out in any way among the other male students; in fact he was a com-pletely uninteresting fellow of average height, average appearance, average abilities and not too much charm: not in the sense that he had no charm at all, or very little, but in the sense simply that his charm did not exceed the limits; he was not without charm but he had, precisely, not too much of it. And in this regard it was very telling that he was befriended – admittedly through no initiative on his part – by an extraordinarily striking girl, virtually a star, who'd chosen him herself, just as Anya had; but this friendship was entirely harmless and on the whole one-sided; more a case of friendship on the part of the girl, the young star, than on Oleg's; friendship for the sake of having company and exchang-ing ideas. But from the outside it was a friendship like any other; the two of them went round in a pair and were always to be seen together.

And it wasn't that Anya, somehow letting this friend-ship escape her consciousness and failing to consider what Oleg's life consisted of, simply spread out her nets and waited and waited for her hour to strike – no, it wasn't like that at all. Anya lived just as she always had; she didn't turn prettier overnight or appear of a sudden brilliant, gorgeous and impassioned, as sometimes happens with girls. Nor on the other hand did she seem oppressed and tormented; she appeared just as she always had been; but one fine day, with mind-boggling speed, they were brought together – Anya and Oleg; no one could understand this dizzyingly precipitous union, and they themselves barely understood what was happening to them until, in a burst of thunder, Anya's parents banished her from their home, and she moved into Oleg's room, to live with him and his parents and await the birth of her child.

She was still to be seen at college; the two of them would come in a pair to their pre-finals tutorials, both of them quiet, not very tall; and Anya, with her small, neat, pregnant belly would wait for Oleg at the door so that they could go home together. It was during this period that the first signs of martyrdom appeared on her face, the first signs of physical suffering – but it wasn't as if she'd dissimulated before; she'd never been one to control her feelings, or argue that you should keep your sufferings to yourself; you could never have said that she hid them away. That was the very essence of the trick, indeed – without hiding anything, she somehow left others with the sense that there was nothing to her; she was just like a brick wall that you could see straight through.

And then the long years stretched out, the years in which Anya worked modestly and quietly at the various humble jobs she took on after her child was born, jobs well below her level of education; in which she lived in one room with her husband, her husband's parents and her son, and turned up at work each day as she'd always done, friendly, equable, predictable, and got called 'Anya, dear' by all her colleagues. Her composure was such that she gave no sign of living the life that all women live – washing, cleaning, cooking, doing the round of the shops, coping with her child and somehow, on top of that, sharing a single room with her parents-in-law. But this was how it was, despite the fact that, outwardly, Anya's behaviour reflected it not at all. Here we have simply named the circumstances in which Anya existed, in which she was obliged to solve the vital problems of her life; just to name them, however, is to say a great deal. But no one knew anything about the way Anya lived during this period of her life; and a few years on various changes came about: a new apartment was found, and Anya was promoted to a well-paid post. Thus was Anya's virtue rewarded. And yet it must be said that, to a certain extent, all this was simply the result of a schedule fulfilled; and it was no coincidence that the phrase 'she's like a brick wall, you can see straight through her' is sometimes still used in relation to Anya; the description has accompanied her throughout her life, from the time she was a plump-legged simpleton of just eighteen to the present moment, when all doubts as to her flawless figure have long since been erased, and her flawless beauty remains poised in florescence, arousing in all who see her an unaccountable sense, a sense of something no one dare name, though once upon a time its name was spoken out loud by a group of raw college youths.

Elegy

No one at all would have staked a bet on it – that the whole thing would finally end in tears. They might perhaps have said that she so swamped him in love that he had no escape: no matter where he went, she ran after him, to check things out on the spot and create just the same scenario there as elsewhere. It got to the point where you had to laugh; she'd run off with her daughters to see him at work – holding one by the hand, the other in her arms; they'd come on a visit to see Pavel in his office, come to look at what Daddy was up to. The little girls would sit down at the typewriters, and Pavel's wife, always very cheery, would chat away with his colleague opposite, telling her all about the difficulties of their present life and the apartment they'd rented. Everything looked absolutely natural and proper, so long as you ignored the basic outrage of the whole family turning up, like a troupe of gypsies, at such a respectable institution.

The visit paid, Pavel's family would bestir themselves and set off home again. The little girls loved it at Daddy's work, and every time they happened to be walking in the vicinity, which happened pretty often, they'd beg their mother to take them in to see him; and so they'd all turn up again, as if it were the most natural thing in the world, and Pavel would take the whole troupe along to the canteen, where the little girls ate a proper staff dinner and their mother, resting from her chores, sat alongside her husband; and there again they looked like a tribe of tinkers, so closely bound to one another, so loftily heedless of the usual proprieties that they gave not a damn for the customary routines of the working day.

Especially striking in this regard was the wife: even if the little girls didn't or couldn't understand how inappropriate it was to go chasing down the office corridor, the wife at least might have given some thought to the complex feelings that Pavel, her mild and easy-going husband, was likely to experience when his entire brood set off from home and appeared, in their full complement, at his place of work!

To his great credit it must be said that he never showed the slightest irritation or alarm at the sight of his emaciated wife and the two pale, fair-haired little girls who, as if to give him a nice surprise, would hide a long time in the doorway and then laugh happily when their father came and discovered them. Pavel took it all very lightly, as if it never occurred to him to worry at the possible consequences of his having the whole family to dine in the staff canteen, or of conducting the sort of conversations married couples tend to have right there at the cheap little table, in full view of the advancing queue.

At first the explanation seemed to be that Pavel's family had no proper lodgings and no real home life, because they'd only recently returned from the town where Pavel had been sent to work after graduating. There they'd acquired nothing apart from two children, and returned just as they'd left, with their suitcases and no furniture; and in the meantime Pavel's mother, at the age of fifty, had upped and got married, so that Pavel and his family had to get an apartment of their own and find money for the rent, on top of everything else, out of the small salary Pavel got at his new place of work. So that was the obvious reason why Pavel's wife brought the whole brood along to eat in the cheap canteen with its flimsy tables, a place where grown-up people would go only because they had to and were in a hurry, not one that you'd grandly bring your children to as you might to a restaurant for a special treat, to celebrate properly without all the hassle of doing the shopping and cooking yourself.

Yet during the time they were living away from home you might have thought Pavel's wife could have learned at least some elementary cooking and got to grips with her basic responsibilities as a housewife and mother! Surely she didn't have to dress like that, all in black, as if to present, by her whole appearance, the living embodiment of honest poverty. Though poverty of course there was, since out of his meagre salary Pavel in addition had to pay alimony for the child from his first marriage. For yes, Pavel had had a first, botched marriage and God knows what else besides, and must have well nigh acquired a gypsy's imperturbability to have got to the stage of feeding his children double rations in broad daylight in the staff canteen, where all the women serving knew the heart-rending story of this poor family and did their best to try to feed them up.

This imperturbability on the part of Pavel and his wife, and the look of unruffled peace in the eyes of those little girls, whom no one had ever yet rebuked for their pranks, had evidently exerted their magic on the management too; they knew all Pavel's financial and domestic difficulties inside out, and so no one lifted a finger to put a stop to this strange family tradition, especially since Pavel was a very promising worker, gifted indeed, and devoted himself wholeheartedly to his work.

It's true that voices could be heard now and then complaining that the whole thing smacked a bit of child exploitation; other people, it was said, could just as well have brought their children along to be paraded, but they would have had more scruples about dragging them in for the sake of a bit extra and feeding them up the way Pavel's wife did.

Yet no one tried to prevent these regular visits by the girls and their mother. The little girls always looked the same, perfectly all right, and nothing seemed to make them ill, not even canteen dinners that would have damaged many an adult constitution; for Pavel's family enjoyed the healthy appetites common to all poor folk and every waif and stray. Somehow or other the two little girls always looked clean and scrubbed, somehow or other their mother must have got the washing done, although whenever you glanced into the yard at Pavel's work the two little girls could be seen playing there, first in the winter and then in the spring, and Pavel's wife with the same old handbag was always wandering about down there as well, in her black coat and her black shoes, for as everyone knows, black is the cheapest colour, the most economical, and doesn't show the dirt.

But time went by and the summer drew on and in due course Pavel and his wife were given a room by the management, nothing to write home about but a room at least, one that had formerly belonged to the stoker. And that, one would have thought, should have put an end to the family visitations; now Pavel himself could rush home in the lunch hour to the bosom of his family; true, they had just an electric ring, but still the wife could have cooked him something to eat. But not a bit of it; the children turned up just as regularly as ever and sat down at their little table while their mother and father queued up, and so the whole family went on camping out for dinner. All in all there was no great change in their life, no real improvement, though they'd now been relieved of the rent for a private apartment and in principle there should have been more money around than there had been. But evidently no amount of money would do; it was just a drop in the ocean considering the sheer poverty that reigned in the former stoker's lair.

With the management's permission Pavel furnished the room with office furniture, a few chairs, a desk and an office cupboard with lots of shelves. Pavel's wife even threw a house-warming party and without batting an eyelid invited all Pavel's colleagues and the bosses, and everyone turned up in a friendly crowd and had a whale of a time, it took them all back to student days, parties in hostel rooms with hostel furniture, glasses borrowed from the student canteen and great hunks of bread spread out on newspaper. Everyone enjoyed themselves hugely, Pavel played the guitar and they sat by candlelight and everything was nice and cosy. For their house-warming the young couple were given a number of basic household items, Pavel's colleagues having drawn up a list of essentials after heated arguments as to what they needed most. The management contributed a record player and a few records, so that the girls would be able to listen to music, but the music stayed unlistened to, for the children carried on messing about in the yard, and Pavel's wife apparently never deigned to touch all the saucepans and plates they'd been given, but just went on bringing the girls to dine in the canteen.

These student ways of theirs were enough to bewilder anyone, and convince them that Pavel and his wife still had their whole lives before them, that everything lay open still, they could choose any path they liked, and in due course everything would fall into place as it did for everyone else, the children would grow up and come to know the peace and warmth of life round the family hearth, not just their camp beds and cheap canteen tables. Meanwhile they could live like the birds of the air if they wanted, why not? – let them live like that if they liked meantime, frolicking about, completely unencumbered by possessions or worries, even the worry of bringing up children, who in that family grew up all by themselves, just like grass in the meadows. Many people envied Pavel's wife's ability to set things up so she'd have no burdens at all, everything would go smoothly all by itself, all the washing and ironing; quite often the women in Pavel's department would drop in on her for a chat, for the sight of another's happiness, their calm well-being and total freedom has a wonderfully purifying effect on the soul, and that was true above all of the happiness to be found with Pavel's family, when the two girls, quiet, inconspicuous, mischievous within reason, like all well-brought-up children, sat drawing at the office desk, drawing with quite some talent, and Pavel and his wife paid no more heed to them than to the grass growing in the meadows. And Pavel, perfectly composed, whistling now and then, might be quietly assembling a television from a bunch of spare parts, and his wife would be doing the laundry and hospitably offer you a battered office chair – and all this produced an unforgettable impression of freedom and simplicity, such as none of the women who visited enjoyed themselves, burdened as they were by lives as yet unresolved, or so completely resolved as to leave them shackled, with no room for manoeuvre at all.

Sometimes these encounters took place at the office in the evenings, when for instance Pavel was finishing some urgent work with his colleagues, and his wife, having put the children to bed, came and sat with everyone else and did a bit of pasting or retyping. The women in Pavel's department guessed that Pavel had nowhere to go in the evenings but home, and that his apparent conscientiousness in this sense couldn't quite be classified as conscientiousness about work; it was more a case of shirking, getting away from the family nest and domestic routine, no matter how free a routine that might be. Pavel also took to spending his evenings doing technical translations or working in the library, and there his wife was unable to follow him, chained as she was to the twins, who had to be put to bed and, in the case of the younger, weaker one, be given a foot massage every night.

So all the women wholeheartedly took the wife's side and blamed Pavel for the frivolous, altogether thoughtless way that he disregarded the family's interests, light-heartedly going off on business trips, for example, when this was more than his wife could bear, even though it brought in extra money; on these occasions Pavel's wife didn't even bring the girls to the canteen, and dropped in on Pavel's office only to phone her husband long-distance in the city to which he'd flown.

At the same time a few people suddenly began to register that Pavel really was working very hard, to the benefit both of his work and his own family, who else; and meanwhile his wife's behaviour was such that everyone came slowly to appreciate Pavel's side of the story; as if hemmed in on every side, he couldn't set foot outside the yard without his wife and the two girls coming after him; sometimes, it's true, the two girls stayed in the yard and only the wife ran to catch up with him and walk alongside him, even if he was only going to see the management, which indeed he mostly was.

But wherever he went she was bound to follow, and Pavel must have felt himself perpetually surrounded; all of which was bound to have its consequences. Thus when Pavel's wife received a telegram summoning her to her sick mother's bedside, and she finally flew off together with the girls – flew off herself for a change instead of him – Pavel almost went out of his mind; like a caged lunatic he paced up and down his little room every evening, and it was a blessing it all lasted only four days, for on the fifth day his wife and children unexpectedly returned – and whether this was because her mother had swiftly recovered, or just because Pavel's wife couldn't bear the separation and had come home to her husband leaving her mother still ailing, at all events Pavel was still getting the letters his wife had sent three days after she'd returned.

So the sum and substance of it was that Pavel's wife had thoroughly entangled him, depriving him of his own means of self-defence, his instinct for self-preservation, for he was quite unable to exist and survive without her, and straightway perished on the first occasion that he found himself at risk: one evening he slipped and fell from the icy roof where he'd climbed up to install an aerial for his home-made television. The television might well have been the first indication of their having, in the near future, a life of greater comfort and convenience, no longer a stoker's life but something different – a more stable existence, more like other people's. As such the television took on a symbolic role, though it's true that everything that precedes anyone's death tends in retrospect to look symbolic. In Pavel's case it was also symbolic that, having stumbled on the roof, he was unable to steady himself and slipped right off. That, at any rate, was how the accident was subsequently explained; but establishing the truth of what happened could do nothing to alter the subsequent course of events. Pavel's wife and their two children simply vanished from the city, declining all invitations to stay put where they were; and thus the story of this family remains unfinished, and no one now will ever know what this family were really like or what end awaited them; for sure, everyone had thought that something was bound to befall them, that he was bound to leave them in the end, unable to withstand so great a love; and leave them he did, but not in that way at all.

The Lookout Point

He'd stroke his girlfriends' hair and, taking off his cap, would ask them to stroke his too. This generally took place at the lookout point on the Lenin Hills in front of Moscow University. Below, on the far side of the river, stretched the panorama of Luzhniki Park, and beyond that the panorama of Moscow with its great tall buildings. And he would go through the exact same procedure with all of them, literally every single one: either our hero had no idea where else to lodge himself, other than at this lookout point, or else every time, with each new love, he really did experience some sense of spiritual exaltation that demanded space, wind, and majestic panoramas. And perhaps, too, he hadn't entirely lost a certain provincial enthusiasm for the capital, the sheer thrill of it, the feeling of victory over the mighty city that both lay at his feet and stood guard securely behind his back, in the form of the university's gigantic wall.

An integral part of this feeling of victory over the city was a sense of his innumerable minor victories over the men and women inhabiting it – or so at least one assumes. We can't expect to understand much at this stage, even if we add to the aforesaid that these victories were to a certain extent unwished for and that the victor himself, in the depths of his soul, evidently yearned to be vanquished. Yet every time it was he who proved victorious. What exactly happened each time, what happened with him and with all the people he conquered – women, old ladies, old men, colleagues, bosses, passing acquaintances – and why all of them so willingly agreed to be conquered, why they never resisted but apparently submitted, each time with a feeling of total surrender and defeat, and whether they had the sense at the time that their defeat was just a temporary, one-off thing, and that they had but to give a wave of the hand for normal life, free from all these horrors, to resume its natural course – all this is hard to say, impossible to fathom. The only thing beyond doubt was this: the conqueror yearned to be conquered himself and was setting the scene for his own defeat – or that's certainly how it seemed, for he acted carelessly, worked pretty crudely, was slipshod in everything, all his constructions. It was all quite transparent; he advanced directly, as if there were no obstacle in sight, as if, for him, this weren't the main thing at all – the business to which he happened to be devoting his energy right now – but as if what really mattered was some thought which he kept probing from every possible angle, as if testing it out: now what would happen if we tried this or that? What would happen if I posed this question or rang a certain person and said this, that or the other (as if he were forever thinking, not of the business at hand, but of some other problem apparent to him alone).

It was this, presumably, that accounted for his air of permanent distraction, of being preoccupied not with whatever he was engaged in at that particular minute – as if he weren't engaged in that at all but in something quite else, and was anxious on account of that other thing, the main thing – even though, one might have thought, there was nothing behind all this that warranted any great anxiety. But the anxiety was certainly there; it was as if he were trying to speed up events in the present so they'd be over as quickly as possible and would make way for something else – only what?

So he went from victory to victory and from phone call to phone call and all in tremendous haste, helter-skelter, never for a moment forgetting this other problem of his, the main one, whatever it was. But on the surface, the way it looked, you might just think he was being cunning – the natural conqueror, swiftly taking one position after the next. And so he took his latest girlfriend up to the university.

And when you think about it, where else could he – this Andrei – have taken her, his latest beloved, when to all appearances his soul demanded something individual, uniquely his, and was poised on the threshold of supreme happiness? Not to a restaurant, surely; for restaurants all too often serve as a kind of payment, a bribe, a little sweetener and recompense for forthcoming sensual delights – so that some girls refuse to go to restaurants at all with men they hardly know, well aware that good money doesn't just get spent for nothing and presupposes, as a matter of course, some response and repayment, and a failure to respond and make proper repayment will be regarded as a form of petty theft: what, have a bite to eat and a couple of drinks, enjoy the music, take a good look round and get looked at yourself, eat and drink a bit more, and all this without protest, without a murmur of complaint, with apparent enjoyment indeed – and then clear off without paying? The girl herself is well aware of that subtly developed atmosphere whereby minor concessions, like a few little kisses in the back of a taxi, can come to look like an even greater swindle, an even grosser villainy – tantamount to having eaten and drunk

166

even more, at even greater expense. That's at any rate the adult view, the view of people who've had a bit of experience, and Andrei was an adult and might well have been familiar with his point of view, though he had apparently abandoned it at some earlier stage of his development.

This form of seduction by way of a restaurant assumed, as a given, that without the restaurant things might not work out, and Andrei, as we've said, went straight for victory come what may. So insofar as he took his girlfriends up to the lookout point, he did so purely for his own sake, for the sake of tenderness, to make his own soul soar; or perhaps it was just that he'd established a certain tradition, dear to his heart, and a once-attained happiness had acquired by now a fixed, immutable form. And indeed, if you think about it, it's quiet up there at the lookout point, a soft breeze blows, snowflakes whirl over the black ice, and down below the myriad lights of the city wink and glimmer so invitingly. It's quiet, there's no one around at all, you're unlikely to come across other admirers of precisely this night-time cityscape; some might even say that it's here that a certain overwhelming, colossal architectural idea comes into its own, a superhuman surge of desire, beside which even the Cheops pyramid, as it's generally pictured by those who've never set eyes on it, looks homely and unthreatening, just a nice little upward-sloping, well-proportioned hill.

So there's no one else up there at the lookout point, the city lies at one's feet winking peacefully, entirely at one's disposal, offering hospitality at every point, completely open to its conqueror, and he, done now with marauding, can begin loading up the whole place by the wagonful – absorb the lot, the whole lot, or that's how it seems. But if you look closely you'll see that it's not so much that the city's slowly disappearing into him – on the contrary, it's Andrei who spreads himself further and further out over the city. The process of absorption occurs of its own accord, while the mind remains quite free; and the desire for happiness can no longer be satisfied by the simple act of devouring more and more streets, more and more alleyways – the dainty titbits, for instance, around elegant Kropotkin Street. Now that desire moves one step higher, requiring not just that you live here, not just that you conquer one thing after another: opponents, rivals, blatherers, wrongdoers, the lofty and the lowly, brothers and friends and girls and mature women whose breasts, for example, surpass all possible bounds; quivering breasts that set you a-quiver at the very thought that this mature matron, a mother of children, wife of a bigwig – she who drives round in her very own car, drives off to receptions at the Bulgarian embassy, lives in a world of comfort and convenience, and spends her whole time fussing over these comforts – at the very thought that she might just offer herself without even being asked, suddenly unbutton her fur coat and . . . my God! But again all this is purely external, all that we've ascribed above to Andrei, purportedly in the form of his own oblique-sounding monologue – for he wouldn't have dreamed of delivering such a monologue himself, his own style of thinking was completely different, pre-occupied as he was with his own main idea; and it simply turned out that his behaviour was such-and-such, leading everyone to believe that his thoughts must be such-and-such, granted he was behaving in this or that way. If this is how things stand then this or that follows: that's what everyone supposed Andrei to be thinking. But what he himself thought we can't possibly know.

But let's return to that oblique monologue and pursue the line of thought therein: yes, the quest for happiness is not limited to this, and that matron with her indescribably voluminous breasts, her fears and desires, her naïve awareness of the value of those breasts, which she thereby devalues completely – this matron floats into Andrei and gets absorbed by him, along with her five-room apartment, her husband, a passionate motorist and member of the automobile association, and her children, among whom the youngest daughter especially, a virtual Lolita at the age of five, falls in love with Andrei and crawls straight into his arms, thereby evoking laughter all round: 'Andrei the lady-killer!' – while the little girl just stays firmly put, gazing distractedly around. This remarkable little girl gets absorbed as well, floating into Andrei, and the little house too glimmers somewhere inside him, its inviting windows glowing faintly within; you can see the roomy armchairs, the delicious food, the cosiness and warmth; perhaps only the hostess sits a little too stiffly, holds her back too straight as she walks and bends down, always keeping, within her field of vision, her magnificent bust – her bulwark, her enduring treasure.

But the matron is no longer just a matron: her name is Sonya, and she now comes to light as an unloved wife, a wife whose husband has calmly ceased to live with her, absenting himself for a number of years now; for this imperturbable motorist has made other arrangements, not entirely proper, one has reason to suspect, for he seems to have various research assistants on the go, his students and followers – fans of this crude, jolly fellow who lives so serenely, idiotically full of his car and his private garage. Oh Lord, why is the world constructed thus? – with not an ounce of pure literature in it, nothing that can be read just once, from one single point of view? For everything's susceptible to some deeper reading, and ever greater abysses open up before you, and plunging deep into them, seeking the very bottom, the truth itself, a person loses a great deal on the way, paying no heed in passing to truths no worse than that which awaits him at the very last. But people always want to get to the bottom of things, and afterwards (just like Andrei in our case) have a good laugh and say that the world is full of wankers and queers and women are all either whores or lesbians or masturbators or old maids. 'But what about Sonya?' enquired the typists to whom Andrei delivered this very speech – Sonya, as we recall, was after all a matron. But Andrei cunningly gave his typists no answer.

And incidentally there was real bile in Andrei's voice when he delivered this cynical maxim of his, the one beginning 'The world is full . . . ' So it stands to reason that Andrei wasn't totally and solely absorbed in himself, he wasn't just fretting and stewing over his own inner themes, to the exclusion of everything else – for he had made known to the world his bitter grudge against the filth of it, the filth of a world where everything had become entangled and there was no honour nor, on the other hand, any genuineness either, everything had been crushed and scared off and driven into hiding, and manifestations of real masculinity and femininity were rare and evoked a curiosity that bordered on indignation; and what options had a poor man in the midst of all this? Either eunuch or priest or one of the types designated above, in a manner so offensive to the ears of the typists addressed (and we should note that the poor typists, upon whose heads this speech of Andrei's had been unleashed, had attempted, with their hint about Sonya, to make Andrei understand that there *is* something else in the world, something else does exist; but Andrei, of course, had cunningly kept silent).

So everything in the world had been crushed, and Andrei himself, a normal person with no perversions (else why all these accusatory speeches against every form of perversion, why this desire to lash out and abuse, why this extraordinary bundle of feelings – from laughter and scorn to grief and sorrow and the utter bewilderment of a soul betrayed?) – so Andrei himself, a man in a million, walked round eternally as if poisoned by his own reputation; for rumour preceded his appearance everywhere, and girls swooned on the spot, unable to resist the fate that awaited them in the week to come – a week being the longest Andrei could stand it before losing his patience and breaking it off. And because of this even the opening moves, the ritual of standing at the lookout point and surveying the city, lost some of its original grandeur and tenderness.

And yet at first Andrei couldn't help himself; each new attachment made him softer and kinder, instilled in him the hope of God only knows what. But this bright period was not to be trusted, for it was quickly replaced by a period of boredom, ending finally in exhaustion and ennui. And yet, as he took off his cap and said gravely 'stroke my hair', our Andrei would recklessly disregard what was bound to befall him in the wake of the hair-stroking, after only a week – and more often than not it was less than a week before the unpleasantness set in. It set in, that's to say, immediately after the lady's first visit to him; immediately after Andrei, having made a single movement with his entire body, carefully detached himself from the visiting partner, who's position was now horizontal, and asked: 'Are you staying or are you going home?'

The unpleasantness in question involved the inevitable comment that he fulfilled his masculine obligations in too business-like a fashion; but what after all does business-like mean? God only knows; there could be all sorts of possible interpretations, including even the possibility that Andrei had perceived his own actions as a pure waste of time, a waste of energy, a disgraceful act of charity, a way of just squandering himself on someone else – while in the meantime (let's imagine this possibility too) his main concern was at a standstill, not moving, not developing; everything had come to a halt, nothing was happening, as if life itself had been forcibly stopped in its tracks; and Andrei might well have suspected his partner of being just plain greedy, wishing to hitch a free ride at someone else's expense, using someone else's energy for motives of pure personal profit. This no doubt accounted for the economic style, the lack of spiritual animation, the reserve which became a generally recognised fact with regard to Andrei, and which represent, indeed, the empirical cornerstone of the present narrative. The ladies, however, perceived this economy of style as simple haste and an overly business-like approach.

And Andrei himself was grieved (this too is an established fact) that he was unable to seize the bird of happiness by the tail, that he was unable to forget himself, unable to get into the swing of things. He himself admitted his defeat every time and would say, on these occasions: 'Call me a bastard if you like, but we won't be seeing each other again.'

And yet every time the whole thing was meant to happen in the best possible way. Take for example Tanya (the same Tanya that was destined to hear that cruel question – 'Are you staying or are you going home?)' – Tanya who was so unattainably charming and sweet, completely dotty, adored by all the boys, childishly innocent, not yet subject to categorisation (or subject to it, of course, but as yet only vaguely, half-consciously). Tanya who played so hard to get suddenly allowed herself to be got; she rang up and said that, since he was ill, she'd come right over and bring a chicken. There were no two ways about it in his case: in a total reversal of nature, the chicken was found running after the rooster! Andrei opened the door to Tanya, Tanya behaved with awkward familiarity, adopting the manners of a good old chum but mean-while shaking from cold; she immediately jumped at the offer of tea and shivered over her cup and under the rug – and this shivering of hers was so transparent, such a cliché, and it didn't go away even when Tanya was cosily ensconced with her feet up on the couch, listening to music (some fashionable pop-opera, a hundred-rouble record), tucked up under his rug, in his house, listening to his record, munching the nuts that he'd bought for himself – and still, on top of that, awaiting great pleasures with pounding heart, awaiting some payment for services rendered! And he started going through all the necessary motions, performing his duty, meanwhile racked with fever and chills and not feeling up to the whole thing at all, while Tanya felt very much up to it herself, and thus the whole thing proceeded. And the incongruous thing about it was that Andrei – the very essence of whose character was his total rejection of any sense of obligation towards anyone whatsoever – nevertheless didn't fail, on this first occasion, to perform his duty: that was just how it had to be.

Thus, as we've said, the whole thing proceeded: with Tanya, on the one hand, ever more feverish and Andrei, on the other, ever more feverish in an entirely different sense, so that at the grand climax of events he even remembered to take his own pulse, and had got as far as releasing one hand to grasp the other by the wrist, when Tanya, interpreting this as some new nuance, almost a perversion, forcibly detached the second hand from the first and cried 'What on earth are you doing?'

What did they all want from him? How was he supposed to serve both them and the world at large? What did the world out there lack if it needed him so badly? – These were the questions that inevitably arose every time that Andrei refused to invest anything more than a business-like efficiency in the execution of his mission. Manifestly he refused to invest his whole self, refused to waste and expend himself; after all, he still had other prospects ahead, prospects of something important, some great resolution; hence the conclusion that he performed what was required of him simply and economically, since no one but he could carry out the task in hand, and his services were therefore needed. The only thing that he was unable to provide to the eagerly-waiting world out there was – one supposes – emotion. For it seemed the sole emotions that fired him – nothing else comes to mind – were those he experienced at the sound of the wind gently whistling on the lookout point, and the sight of the lit-up city below, with the great bulk of the university towering over it all. And indeed, when you weigh the matter carefully, it was only here that the possession of a woman would have had any real meaning or sanctity for Andrei – on condition, however (if we may add our own comment) that Andrei himself grew to gigantic proportions, so that he wouldn't look too diminished beneath the balustrade of the lookout point, but would tower over the scene and fill everything with himself. And, this being the case, a woman alone would not really do; he'd need the whole body of the city, its whole gigantic organism, its soul – a soul not yet wholly dependent on him – he'd need all the secret little alleyways off Kropotkin Street, its noble mansions, its grand embassy houses, and all its little girls walking their dogs, and its little shops and old ladies, unimaginably gentle and grand, who walk round in lace the colour of tea-roses, in their drooping skirts and slightly twisted stockings, carrying ephemeral net bags containing just a modest roll and a bit of cheese for tea. And just imagine the things these old ladies have at home, what splendid porcelain on the table, what magnificent linen in napkin rings, what silver tongs and sugar bowls – what a life, in short!

What a life indeed, a painstakingly measured, emaciated life, half portions of cheese for dinner and for breakfast next day, and once a month a visit from the old lady's niece and the niece's husband and a certain Alexandra whom nobody knows, including us, and on the wall a portrait of the lady of the house by Serov, and what else, what else: perhaps her late brother's doll collection, and the odd water colour by Nesterov, and furniture reupholstered by her mother in 1904.

Oh! all of this could have been appropriated, the old lady too could have been absorbed, swallowed up, so that sooner or later she wouldn't have been able to survive a day without a phone call from one of us; nor would it have presented any special problem to absorb the niece and the mysterious Alexandra as well; and finally the furniture, too, could all have been appropriated, swallowed up and absorbed. Something, however, restrained us from doing this, stayed our hands, for, once appropriated, the old lady would have become just a lonesome, solitary old lady, demanding this and that, medicine and chats; and the silver sugar bowl, relocated to our table, would have meant immeasurably less there than it did before it was absorbed, before it lost its pride of place on the old lady's table at her monthly teas, when the mysterious Alexandra would come to visit, and the niece, a plain, plump individual with a silver brooch and a tear in her eye, would sit there too and eat the pastries she'd brought herself.

This niece had a great many surprising qualities, among which one should mention her unfathomable, punctilious loyalty to this old lady, a loyalty manifested in her regular monthly visits, and in her uncomplaining, unloving, decent and honourable ability to sit it out at table, and in her performing similar services for her numerous other aunts and uncles. The apotheosis of it all was her niece's own birthday, when the whole gang came together for its annual gathering, took stock of its numbers, and brought extraordinarily valuable gifts – gems, precious stones, earrings and the like – a sapphire in a bow, for instance, or platinum encrusted with diamonds. And most noteworthy of all was the fact that the niece, in turn, presented such gifts, on birthdays and weddings, to her own nieces and godchildren, and that she visited the old lady not for mercenary reasons

at all, and not out of love, and not in the hope of
acquiring the Serov portrait and all the other antique
junk – for the niece had the same kind of junk herself,
and where on earth would she put it all? That's why
people on the lookout for booty, people in the know,
are always amazed to run across Biedermeier armchairs
and Empire furniture from the reign of Paul and other
such valuables in cheap secondhand shops at the local
market, mindlessly dumped there like so much old junk;
such things, after all, are what others go hunting for,
year after year, searching and searching, keeping a
weather eye out for a sale, or a death, or one of the
owners coming on hard times; they keep their eyes
skinned, breathlessly anticipating the moment when
they'll bring the beloved object home, when they'll
strip it, restore it, cover it with Edelwax polish – and
then what? Then comes another hitch, in the form of
possession, for one distinguished *objet* mixed up with a
load of other distinguished *objets* constitutes at best
a collection of furniture, but who collects furniture in
this day and age? Who's going to start collecting it for
show, complete with conducted tours and a pointer?
But without the conducted tours and the pointer
you won't be able to gather much of a crowd; by itself
no amount of furniture is going to ensure those regular,
dreary tea-parties, or attract the kind of loyalty and
devotion that are guaranteed on both sides by the
observance of tradition.

At best you're guaranteed a one-off visit and a one-
off expression of admiration; but one has heard of
cases where a fully furnished, equipped and prepared
apartment has succeeded only in scaring guests away.
And then, of course, no special traditions have evolved
around this furniture, whereas the old, pre-furniture

traditions have all remained: the old squabbles with relatives, the reluctance to entertain those guests from out of town, and the essential rigmaroles of going to the laundry and making jam for winter. And it must be said that Andrei himself, while remaining an amiable and punctilious attender of the Sunday teas, was himself painfully devoid of tradition. He steered well clear of it, in fact; he didn't take his sheets to the laundry on any set day, but slept on them till they'd truly had it; and he couldn't stand visits from relatives, and never so much as mentioned his mother. His mother was a plain country woman, and he'd dumped and rejected the entire family, abandoning the whole bunch to their life in the village – and it was out of the question that he was going to start instituting traditional teas with all these relatives, with napkins and sugar tongs and a plump little sugar bowl covered in medallions – no, it was unimaginable! What relatives of that sort needed was just a barrel of pickles and a row of camp beds.

To be sure, there were things Andrei was fond of – the majestic lookout point already mentioned, and one other thing, a certain family whose 'mama' he'd adopted: he'd always refer to them as 'my friend's parents and my adopted mama and papa', and sometimes he'd call them long-distance when out of town. Evidently they had the same sort of tradition-filled lifestyle as the old ladies on Kropoktin Street: one can imagine the warm, cosy, orderly life they led, right down to the theatre tickets in the glass-fronted bookcase, propped up as a reminder for all to see, and one can imagine the innumerable guests, even guests from the country, who'd never be turned away: a camp bed would always be kept for them in reserve – and how jolly it can be, after all, to sit round the family table, laden with aspic, preserves, mushrooms, bacon and smoked ham! And the man of the house doesn't bother a soul, and once a week – on Tuesdays, say – irons his white shirts on the dinner table, never trusting this manly business to his wife! What can one say, a home like this would be dear to anyone, and once upon a time, indeed, the home in question was dear to the author; whence our detailed knowledge of the whole set-up, where the most striking thing of all is that bunch of theatre tickets, standing in a little sheaf behind the glass in the bookcase. But that particular house no longer exists; the man of the house has to cook for himself now, while his wife runs a separate household for herself and their son and suffers from endless bouts of eczema; and the daughter has upped and left altogether and lives in a private apartment now, and apparently leads a make-shift, solitary existence with not a hint of theatre tickets, for the purchase of theatre tickets requires a good deal of effort and self-love and attention, whereas what the soul craves above all is peace.

We have strayed somewhat from our central theme, but this digression will shortly prove useful to us in that part of the narrative which deals with a certain Artemis, tall, beautiful and young, whose mother was a professor and whose stepfather a lecturer; the daughter had grown up in solitude and neglect in a three-roomed apartment where (let's imagine) the mother locked herself up in one room, and the stepfather read proofs in another, and Artemis sewed herself a dress in the third (a dress cut out by her mother, for her mother understood such things, she was a professor in all departments) – so Artemis sewed away in the third room, finding it rather uncomfortable, for this was the common room, the sitting-room, the one with the television, and everyone kept barging in and being 'pestiferous' – there's another nice, tender, funny picture of someone else's home for you, central to which is the word 'pestiferous', just as one of the attractions in the home described above was that the daughter there, too, had her various pet words. We know already what happened in that earlier case, and later we'll see how events will unfold in this other household that Andrei was so fond of – unfold, as it turns out, rather strangely and sadly. But that comes later; in the meantime, bearing in mind what we shall shortly be hearing of Artemis and her home, let's merely observe that we'll be dealing here too with Andrei's patriarchal ambitions, his taste for tradition and his longing for decency – decency, precisely, and loyalty to duty; his taste for everything that wasn't deliberately created, that hadn't just arisen on the spur of the moment, that seemed simply to live, acquiring solidity over the years – his taste for things that endured, didn't fade or die out, but lived their own life – just like a city, seen from outside, that we come upon ready-made: the older it is, the more we believe in it, and the key thing is that it hasn't just been created right in front of our eyes. A city such as this we'll drink in deeply, we'll inhale its beauty – a beauty that appears not created by human hand; whereas we'll never breathe in or drink deep of something that was set up deliberately, created just now. And in the young Artemis one sensed, precisely, good blood, the fusion of her parents' long, enduring love; in short one felt in her a certain stability, of the kind Andrei had always yearned after; and it was here, apparently, that this internal Theme of his came to the fore, seeking contact (and battle) with the inner Theme of another. Or so we may surmise.

It's here, when we come to deal with this young Artemis – one of Andrei's failures – that we'll discuss the attraction exerted on him by another's patriarchal traditions; but in the meantime let us turn to Lidka: agile, featherlight, gentle, slender, plain thin-haired Lidka; Lidka, forever flying, tummy out, like a little sailing boat; ardent, compassionate, meek, unmalicious Lidka, who had so many admirers and a red-faced husband, to whom she was loyal, though she argued with him in her good-natured way whenever he announced, for the nth time, that he was going off to marry elsewhere in view of the child about to be born elsewhere; and Lidka had two children of her own.

Depriving someone of their pride – something which Andrei would never have tolerated in relation to the affectionate old lady from Kropotkin Street, and which could, in her case, have been accomplished quite easily, but would have brought nothing but extra trouble – depriving a person of their pride was precisely what Andrei, to all appearances, wouldn't tolerate in his relations with women and girls and the beautiful young Artemis in particular: Artemis who seemed so out of the ordinary; she swore like a trooper and dressed with indescribable elegance, wearing only things that she'd made herself (the only thing she didn't sew herself were her boots) and who maintained relations with a millionaire artist so that she wouldn't be dependent on her chaotic mother, the professor, whose money flowed like water and went for the most part to her two married daughters. Artemis herself did not need much, and her artist friend gave her only objects of great value, and loved her into the bargain and phoned her at the office and picked her up after work in his dark blue Mercedes.

Andrei couldn't stand objects that had been deprived of their value, whereas objects that possessed this quality he was determined to acquire for himself. But in the course of appropriating them he was evidently unable to keep within the necessary bounds, and as a result the objects in question got broken. Thus, for example, he ruined all the furniture (putting a hot kettle down all over the place) in his colleague's apartment, his colleague having departed for Africa for two years and left all his possessions in Andrei's care, including his collection of Alpine violets. The flowers, being weak and dependent creatures, were abandoned by Andrei the first time he went away on a business trip, and only the aloe, a hundred-year-old plant, proved capable of weathering all the storms of life with Andrei, the floods that took place during his periodic invasions and the droughts that could last up to six weeks at a stretch. During such periods the aloe seemed to draw in its claws; it shrank, curled up its leaves, and began to soften, which in its case was a sign of imminent demise. However, Andrei would return and douse the aloe with a kettleful of tap-water which, despite its toxicity, had long since become the aloe's natural means of existence, its natural element, so that the aloe became a chlorinated aloe and an anti-corrosive aloe, long since incapable of rusting, just like a water pipe. And the fact that the lady of the house used once upon a time to let the tap-water sit and settle for several days had long since been forgotten by the unfortunate aloe, which now grew only upwards and stuck out of the pot in the manner of an aspen stake. To a certain extent the aloe demonstrated what a creature could turn into if it was both dependent on Andrei yet in itself resistant, that's to say, forced to endure for a great period of time, in this case one hundred years. The aloe, so to speak, managed to keep standing, but standing on its knees, spending water with an old woman's stinginess just as, apparently, Andrei's mother spent her pension down there in the village, surviving on potatoes, cabbage and mushrooms.

To conclude this extended introduction to the story of Lidka, we can't refrain from adding that people of Andrei's ilk are quite incapable of hanging on to anything – cats, dogs, their parents' graves, let alone Alpine violets, which require the most devoted attention, and on a regular basis at that. Consequently the owner of the apartment, returning on leave after a year away, was astonished and grieved at the sight of the wallpaper, the dry flowerpots, the furniture, the floor in the front hall, and the aloe, which had come to look like a phallic symbol. And consequently Andrei shrugged his shoulders and found himself another apartment, while the apartment's owner spent three days clearing out the dirt and was obliged, furthermore, to give his returning spouse an explanation as to the peeled finish on the furniture and the little circle-marks that covered everything.

Andrei, it must be said, was a man of no apartment. He was officially registered as living in a hostel, a form of existence to which he was organically ill-suited. He could have married a dozen times over and acquired ready-made living quarters or bought himself an apartment, but he didn't do so and wouldn't get married since – one assumes – he considered that this would be a far greater sacrifice on his part; he couldn't give up his freedom, and he couldn't acquire anything without immediately spoiling and ruining it, and he was a man much devoted to comfort and convenience; he loved, as we've already mentioned, getting plenty of sleep and placing the kettle wherever he chose. And let's remember the aloe, transformed from a slender shrub into a gnarled phallic symbol, with only the barest hint of foliage, and let's imagine how unpleasant it is for a man to be constantly confronted by his own destructive, fatal influence. Who'd want to be a despot, who'd fancy listening all day long to justified reproaches of amorality? – Well stop getting at me then, he'd doubtless feel, don't get yourself burned, I'll survive perfectly all right by myself and make my own way in life, for there' s still something out there waiting for me – this, or roughly this, is what Andrei might have thought at the sight of that gnarled stick growing in its flowerpot. Time and again he kept blindly believing in happiness, as he had on the one and only occasion he did get married; however, he left his wife the morning after and never saw her again – although word reached him that she still loved him and was waiting for him faithfully, like a mother.

But we've digressed from the theme that we earlier designated, somewhat clumsily, as 'depriving someone of their pride', though, as it turns out, we've merely developed it, taking different examples, whereas we'd begun with Lidka, a creature so soft and nimble and light as a feather that her colleagues loved to grab her and lift her up in their arms, though she'd get angry and say 'lay off, you bastards' – she being, after all, a serious woman.

Once upon a time she'd been a champion skater, and sports leave their mark above all on the way a person moves – gymnasts, for instance, have a special springiness and precision in their walk, like a ticking pendulum, whereas Lidka, who went in for long-distance races, moved like a pointer on a map, darting elusively over great distances and appearing to touch the ground only now and then. In Lidka's case, even comparison with a ballerina wouldn't do, for a ballerina's gait is the opposite of aerial, and what can compare with the lightness of a pointer flitting over the map?

That was how Lidka flitted about; she did everything amazingly quickly and deftly, everything in her home sparkled, and her neighbours in the communal apartment would give up their rooms for Lidka's guests, so her children could sleep peacefully in their own beds; thus on festive occasions Lidka's neighbours, who all simply adored Lidka despite the difference in age, were lumbered with all her visitors in their rooms. Lidka's husband, it's true, begrudged his wife's popularity and got his own back by having endless affairs; he didn't hesitate, moreover, to bring his lady loves straight home, which upset Lidka, of course, but somehow not unduly. 'Ah well!' she'd say with a dismissive wave of the hand – a hand that looked burdened enough, by the way, by all her duties as housewife and mother. 'Ah well! He can go to hell!'

But her husband's parents would come on a visit from Lithuania and (morally speaking) he'd get down on his knees, and during one of these visits Lidka upped and went on holiday, for two whole weeks – leaving somehow rather quickly, hastily and secretly, saying only 'Andrei's such a strange person'. Evidently the circumstance already mentioned had here come into play: namely, the impossibility of determining what really occupied Andrei's thoughts when he was engaged in this or that action – actions carried out in great haste, but somehow as if in passing, as if he had in mind some other, more important business, something that lay in the future, something that was still to come. Hence Lidka's description of him as 'a strange person'. I personally would add that even the behaviour of a cat or a dog can seem strange and incomprehensible; who knows, for example, what a dog may be thinking of as he runs down the street or dashes into a yard and bolts straight out again, or for what precise purpose he chooses suddenly to sit down in the middle of the street – but you only have to look at him to see he does have a purpose; he looks precisely as if he's just sat down for a moment, awaiting something strange and important that no one else is aware of.

There was also a certain Edik, a colleague in the same department, who worried a great deal about Lidka and the other girls in the office who'd got afflicted with Andrei. It was Edik, himself almost a woman, the sort of man who notices when someone's underwear is showing or she's got a ladder in her stocking – Edik, who loved Lidka like his best friend and kept crying: 'Lidka, when will you surrender to me at last?' – It was Edik who watched on jealously, waiting for Andrei to pounce on Lidka. And unfortunately it was precisely to Edik, as to her closest girlfriend, that Lidka kept repeating, as she hurriedly sorted out her affairs before setting off on holiday, 'Andrei's such a strange person, such a strange person'.

And Andrei – this was an odd coincidence – just happened to be heading off, on a business trip, in exactly the same direction as Lidka, and Lidka – now this really was very odd – hadn't even bought a ticket for her trip to the nature reserve where she was spending her holidays. 'Have you bought your ticket?' her 'girl-friend' Edik enquired. 'I haven't bought it, it's been bought for me,' Lidka – generally a rather secretive and reticent person – answered mysteriously. 'Lidka,' Edik implored her, 'Who bought you the ticket?' 'A certain strange person', Lidka answered thoughtfully, quickly scooping up some papers and fastening them with a paper clip.

And now begins that part of our narrative which departs from the foregoing in so far as what follows is an account of Andrei's actual, real actions, his service record, so to speak. And if in the first part of our story a good deal of space was devoted to conjecture and guesswork and attempts to draw conclusions, it's now high time we looked truth in the eye and examined the life Andrei actually lived, and how it was seen from the outside by his various colleagues. In the second part, therefore, we will encounter various episodic characters to whom we should pay close attention, for, as we know, man is the product of his environment, and everything that will happen to Andrei in the end will be attributable precisely to the influence of that environment.

So anyway the point is they departed – Lidka and Andrei, that is – and Edik was the first to decide, upon their return, that he was going to take no notice at all of how the pair of them looked: bronzed, well-fed, both simply gorgeous, like twins whose lips were stamped with an identical seal. Lidka, everyone's favourite, looked even more mysterious than usual; her glowering husband came to meet her a couple of times after work and was obviously depressed, for he'd again announced his intention to marry, this time right in front of his parents. His new amour even turned up at Lidka's house and in front of the parents and Lidka kept staring at her own tummy, scarcely two weeks gone (if you reckoned from the start of

Lidka's holidays). It's hard to say what happened after that. Lidka maintained a humble silence while Edik, walking on thin ice, kept raging about Andrei behaving yet again like a total bastard. 'Where've you been, Andrei?' Edik kept asking, 'You've got such a nice sun tan.' 'Oh, among the pines, among the pines in the great wild woods,' Andrei replied, for some unknown reason revealing his hand. (We might recall, in this regard, Andrei's tendency – mentioned in the first part of our narrative – constantly to venture out on thin ice as if determined to tempt fate itself.)

What happened next was that Edik – in response to Andrei's request in the latter's capacity as supervisor (albeit a minor one), that Edik immediately write a report – announced hysterically that he was sick and tired of slaving away for everyone else. 'I'm tired too,' said Andrei, 'I've been slaving away as well and I haven't had a vacation all this year,' he said, just itching to get into battle; and he got his battle, and proved a quite unequal opponent, a powerful logical machine; except that he flung himself into it all with no great enthusiasm, as if forced into entering the fray, reluctantly, dragging his feet.

In this connection – just to make a further slight digression – it's of some interest to recall the means by which Andrei had achieved his minor promotion; and it was no simple story.

The previous supervisor, Borya, had asked to take unpaid leave, and everyone knew that he was going off to play the part of a scuba diver in a film and was going to make a heap of money. The boss, V.D, being extremely lax, was ready to sign the necessary form, but Andrei, in a secret fury – he was going to have to cover for the scuba diver for the whole month – simply went on strike. Andrei accurately calculated the temptation clouding Borya's mind (the filming was supposed to take place in Bulgaria), knowing, moreover, that Borya would be unable to find work anywhere else without a reference from his present place of work. Andrei had some influence over V.D, who in any case had no time for grand airs and scuba diving, and the soil had already been heated to volcanic temperatures in any case, since Borya had a whole history of making inappropriate trips to scuba-diving contests, rallies, gatherings and filmings of all kinds. So V.D, without mincing his words, told Borya: apply for transfer to the post of senior engineer, or else. Up against the wall this time, Borya wrote the application and left. And Andrei himself became the supervisor and received, by way of a gift, the neurotic Edik, who with his sick gaze followed every one of his former colleague's demonstrations of power and will. Still perceptible throughout all this, incidentally, was Andrei's unswerving determination to get somewhere else, somewhere far away, somewhere that lay in some quite other direction; and in the light of this any episode, even Andrei's acquisition of power appeared accidental, inessential, whereas the essential, non-accidental thing was something quite else, something that was yet to emerge at some point in the future.

The next move in the whole course of events was bound to be the sacking of Edik, and let's see how this took place. Thus:

'I'm tired too and I haven't had a vacation this year,' said Andrei provocatively, though with no great enthusiasm.

'Haven't you?' said Edik, dumbfounded.

'No,' said Andrei, needling him further.

'And who just went to a nature reserve?' enquired

Edik, losing his wits out of sheer rage. 'Who just went sunbathing with somebody else?' he asked, completely forgetting Lidka, poor Lidka, whose husband meanwhile was just waiting to lay his hands on hard evidence to use in his duel with his parents.

'You'll pay for this calumny,' said Andrei, and the next day the whole group, convened by V.D, met to debate this emergency in their intimate family circle – Edik's slander, his moral downfall, not to mention his lack of punctuality. V.D was especially furious; he didn't like Edik for being so unpunctual and for making friends with one of the guards, a lady, who never recorded Edik's late arrival but warned him not to get caught on the next shift, where the guard was not exactly mean, but was annoyed with Edik for having befriended the guard on the first shift.

Under these complex circumstances Edik apologised to Andrei in front of everyone (he didn't have to apologise to Lidka: out of solidarity they'd decided not even to mention her name; the issue here was Andrei, whose papers from his business trip were in perfect order), and it was clear, moreover, that V.D had got furious above all from motives that he himself didn't really understand, from a sense of having been coerced, forced into being a mere pawn in the game – and the unexpected finale of the whole thing was that Edik was asked to hand in his resignation. 'It's either him or me, but I'll take him to court for slander,' Andrei apparently said, knowing full well that the fastidious Edik would never bring himself to utter Lidka's sacred name. 'Go to hell, Edik,' said V.D, and Edik spent the rest of the day writing his resignation and was afraid even to look at Lidka, who had assumed an enigmatic air and was busy typing away with one finger.

So Edik vanished, disappeared in a puff of smoke, and Edik had a wife, a son and a mother, and this was the second time he had lost his job.

And Lidka, that unfathomable woman, refused – oh joy! – to give in to Andrei. And she maintained her secretive air, although everybody knew that her husband had come back to her, since the information concerning the forthcoming baby turned out to be premature, and the husband's parents took a dim view of the would-be bride, who had since thinned out again, and they departed after reconciling the two spouses.

At first sight it might have appeared that the affair with Lidka represented a model of that long-dreamed-of union with an independent woman who didn't lose her pride. It all came to naught, however, since Lidka wasn't prepared to leave her husband, and Andrei, it goes without saying, wasn't planning to take her and her two children off to goodness knows where. Andrei's path, at the end of the day, apparently lay elsewhere; and there must have been something not quite right about the whole thing in any case, since it all came to an end just like that – not in shame or suffering or death, but just like that. The absurdity of their union didn't intensify their feelings or fan them into a mutual flame – they didn't fling themselves about or weep that they had no future, and even, in a strange way, seemed quite content at their success in deceiving Lidka's red-faced husband. In short the whole thing just fizzled out – if, that is, you leave Edik out of account: Edik, the sole victim in the affair, who kept phoning Lidka and cursing Andrei, slinging mud at him and blackening his name – all to no purpose, poor thing, had he but known it, since the whole affair was by now a thing of the past. Which was rather funny in itself.

Lidka, however – still unconquered, still unbroken, quick, tender, ardent and knowing very well what's what in life – has been kept in reserve and will reappear right at the end of our narrative; and we'll also bid farewell to Edik before we're done. He eventually departed from the scene, and it's well that he did, since Lidka, after all, was not his only girlfriend: there were two girls that he adored in the laboratory – Lidka and Artemis, the young professor's daughter, a young, lissom, fresh and willowy creature, but a real tearaway too, a girl of rare skills and plenty of spunk, who once walked round almost an entire day with a nail in her boot and was covered in blood as a result, because she had no other shoes to change into and the nail refused to be hammered in. So anyway this Artemis, who always came late to work and ran in with her little face still pink and sleepy, and never ate more than a sandwich for lunch – this Artemis worked as a typist in the lab, but everyone knew that she just hadn't bothered to go to university after graduating from the English school, and that the wages she earned in the lab were just pin-money for her, and that her mother and the millionaire artist formed a solid wall around their Artemis and wouldn't let a speck of dust fall on her. Her mother cut out all her clothes for her, and the millionaire drove her around in his car, and she didn't eat much: so answer this simple puzzle: how much did she spend on clothes? Everyone loved Artemis like a daughter; only one of her contemporaries, who worked in the same department, couldn't stand her, for she knew better than others Artemis' place in the new order of things, the new generation; and she always sniffed scornfully when Andrei engaged Artemis in conversation and listened attentively to what she had to say. This contemporary of Artemis', a splendid hard-working girl from a modest intelligentsia family, had befriended Andrei in good faith, with no ulterior motives. And he, it appeared, had no such motives either, judging from the way he'd steer clear of all the other ladies and pester Artemis alone ... 'Poof!' the other girl would laugh. 'Who do you think you're talking to? You might just as well go and talk to that great empty oak cupboard over there'.

It was beginning to feel cramped and stuffy in the lab because of these two, Artemis and Andrei, especially when he went up to her desk to dictate something to her – his voice would break, it's a documented fact. She wasn't much of a typing pro as it was, and when Andrei was standing there you could hear her mutter 'pestiferous!' every other minute, and the sound of the eraser scratching at the paper.

And suddenly she ceased talking to her artist on the phone. And she'd slip past his Mercedes after work; and he, being somewhat stout, couldn't just take to his heels and leave the car door wide open, and by the time he'd locked it she'd already be down in the metro ...

And finally it got to the point when the artist rang up and asked to speak to Andrei. Andrei, for some reason assuming a rather nasal accent, spoke long and tediously to the distraught artist, saying that everyone here in the lab was concerned only for Artemis' welfare, since she was so young and had her whole life ahead of her and they didn't want her to get dragged through the mud ('Go away', said Andrei, and Artemis left the room) – I wasn't speaking to you, Andrei said down the phone, and in the same diabolical, adenoidal tones continued spinning his demagogical web, without, however, any great enthusiasm; and in conclusion he said reflectively, thinking he was alone – well all right, he said, I'm just an outsider, an impartial observer, so take her if you like, but look after her properly, she deserves it – whereupon the artist, talking off the top of his head, started muttering that he would marry her, he would, although how was he going to marry her when he had a live wife and children and a certain Olya besides? But he would marry her, he definitely would – and, agreed on this, Andrei hung up. But meanwhile, sitting behind the cabinets – not hiding, but simply sitting at her desk – was Alya, Artemis' aforementioned contemporary, the friend-in-good-faith who had no ulterior motives – and she sprang out and declared in a rage: 'What filthy lies, how dare they smear you so! You said exactly what you should have done!' – and out she went and there, in the corridor, stood the young Artemis, leaning against the wall like a schoolgirl outside the staff room when a teachers' meeting is in progress. Alya walked past her without saying a word. And a few minutes later Andrei emerged with his briefcase, for it was the end of the working day and they were locking up the institute, and off went the two of them, Andrei and Artemis, and thus, in a whirl, their witches' sabbath began. Once or twice, surrounded by his students, the stout wealthy artist loomed up on the horizon: he had his studio, and the whole cabal met there and painted, and he gave them food and drink and pocket money. The students, from afar, issued vague threats to Andrei, but since they were mostly unemployed folk of no fixed abode, they stayed put where they were and went no further, fading away like smoke in due course. 'Dear little Artemis' cried one from the outer darkness.

At this point, incidentally, we may appropriately bid a fond farewell to the millionaire artist, who was, as a matter of fact, no artist at all, but merely a brilliant organiser and a terrific host who loved to get a good crowd together and drink, and who did his job with great relish and managed to feed not only his five students but a wife and two children besides and Artemis into the bargain, not to mention his great, unforgettable love – a certain graduate student – and various others from time to time; and he did all this calmly, unhurriedly, pensively, looking out with his colourless gaze from behind gold spectacles, never stepping beyond certain bounds, except perhaps when pushed by Andrei, who'd managed to wrest Artemis away from him, but couldn't or didn't want to take care of her properly. In short, Artemis carried on eating just a sandwich for lunch, and swearing quietly away at the typewriter, but she never set eyes on a Mercedes again, or suits from Italy or fancy dress balls. A secretive creature, she lived on in silence and never complained – only Lidka saw the blood in her boot, and that was in the ladies', where Artemis was examining her losses in the form of a blood-soaked stocking (a gift from the millionaire, fifteen roubles cash). The blood resulted from the fact that Artemis would not permit herself to limp, and merely walked round looking mildly off-colour, an iron spike meanwhile lodged in her flesh, until Lidka rushed off and fetched a bit of cardboard. But there are far greater torments in life than this!

Far greater torments, indeed; and later we'll learn what other nails, besides those visible to all, were to pierce the tender, pliant body of Artemis.

Those visible to all appeared immediately after the May Day holiday. The weather was lovely that year; people took several days off round May Day and three days off round Victory Day a week later, and there were only a few working days left in between; so those in cushy positions fixed proper eleven-day holidays for themselves, headed south or west to the sea, and there was a great hubbub around the Aeroflot offices.

Andrei, too, disappeared and took himself a little break; he was always having little breaks, for as a bachelor with no family ties he was often sent off to do vegetable picking on Saturdays or to help out with the potato harvest in the autumn or haymaking in July, and thus got leave in lieu . . .

(People – just to digress briefly from our story once more – have different ways of fixing holidays for themselves: a certain woman, for instance, donates blood twelve times a year, every blessed month, and gets paid in leave instead of cash, so that every spring, to the helpless fury of her boss, she goes skiing in Dombay, skiing on her own blood; she gets away with murder, in other words, on every count, for of course someone has to fill in for her on those twelve days – work never stands still, after all!)

But Artemis, with a kind of blind, child-like cunning, managed simply not to turn up to work for those few days in between; and when she did come back, reappearing at work on the same day as Andrei and looking just as tanned and fresh as he, she calmly lied that she'd been in Kiev all the while and it had been quite impossible to obtain a return ticket for either the fourth, the fifth or the sixth. And she stuck to this guile-less tale of hers while they dragged her from Personnel to the local Party Committee, and Andrei stayed right out of it, and once again everyone kept their mouths shut in solidarity, not wanting to get their Andrei entwined in Artemis' shameful crown of thorns. Finally V.D, secretly sympathetic to Artemis, dismissed the whole affair in disgust and merely gave her a reprimand for being late at work; though Andrei, it should be made quite clear, didn't lift a finger to prompt this kind-hearted and charitable act. He simply watched events unfold from the sidelines, aloof and even, it seemed, somewhat weary. Right from the start he'd been none too keen on having Artemis come on the trip, and had resigned himself to it only on the grounds that it would have been improper to deposit her back off the plane – unbecoming and impolite (as we recall, this was typical of Andrei: all right, he'd let himself be saddled the first time round, but only that first time, as if just experimenting to see what would come of it).

And then, Andrei hadn't exactly supported Artemis in her assurance that she'd be forgiven those four days' truancy. And the delicacy of the situation was further compounded by the fact that Andrei was Artemis' immediate boss, and it was he who had drafted the order that the reprimand be placed on her work record, and he who authorised Artemis' application, fabricated *post factum*, to have four days' leave without pay. It isn't hard to imagine how repulsive and unworthy he found the whole business, all this covering-up and the general awareness, on everyone's part, that precisely he, for some reason, was obliged to go through with it. But as always he accomplished all the necessary manipulations, and Artemis continued to lead her quiet existence, seated at her typewriter beside the window, an existence interrupted only by a certain feline hissing, a muttered 'pestiferous' and the aforementioned sound of the eraser scratching the paper.

Incidentally, it was Alya who had to take Artemis' place at the typewriter for those four days that Artemis was AWOL – Alya, who detested inequality of any kind, and especially one that involved her being less than the equal of Artemis, whose professorial heredity had been hatched in the course of a single generation, whereas Alya herself was at the very least fifth-generation intelligentsia. And there were no more accurately-typed pages in the world than hers, and no ocean in the world that could be compared in volume to the ocean of scorn that filled Alya's eyes.

We are close now to the finale, and to the moment when the quiet and triumphant scorn that filled Alya's entire being was suddenly replaced by sharp, unqualified, even terrified disgust, by squeamish revulsion and sheer horror in the face of Artemis, who continued to sit at her typewriter by the window with her back to the world and her face to the laboratory, so that only the 'Rhinemetal' ridge – the grey, iron bulge of the typewriter – could screen any part whatsoever of Artemis' being. It wasn't that Artemis looked crushed, exactly, she simply sat looking wan and off-colour; and in this connection we should recall the nail in Artemis' boot, and how at the time Artemis had walked round looking, precisely, off-colour, but not for a moment limping, not at all!

The whole business with Artemis was cleared up unexpectedly quickly: Alya – who was not bad-looking – got to know a certain fellow who was also a contemporary of hers and Artemis', indeed, he'd been born exactly the same year and, as it turned out, had been a classmate of Artemis. Anyway, this fellow simply announced that Artemis was not a professor's daughter at all, but the daughter of a typist, and that she hadn't graduated from the English school, where typing and stenography were taught, but from a perfectly ordinary, regular school, and, yes, the family had been given an apartment at one time or other, but a two-roomer, not a three-roomer, and Artemis' married sister and her family lived in the second room, the thoroughfare – and that was that.

So that was that – utterly shameful and absurd, as it turned out, and Andrei would sometimes throw back his head and shake it in disbelief, as if the world he inhabited were quite beyond his comprehension; and Artemis, meanwhile, continued sitting behind her defensive rampart, her little earthwork, her tiny parapet, virtually undefended, vulnerable to every bullet and nail – but what was to be done with her, the little fibber! As they say of a dead murderer – like it or not, you can't leave them unburied. So it was with Artemis – what on earth was to be done with her? She had punished herself, beat herself like a slave – and just look how long she'd been telling these lies, making the whole thing up, eating just a little sandwich for lunch supposedly because her stomach had shrunk in childhood, had kept shrinking and shrinking, and her famous mother didn't know what on earth to do with her skinny daughter – when in fact what the whole sandwich business boiled down to was purely and simply a question of finance!

And the situation she'd got herself into was so utterly absurd and stupid that no one could even find it in their hearts to pity her – what was there to pity, one might well ask? The only thing there was room for here was laughter and bewilderment and that was it; like Andrei, one just had to shake one's head.

Yet pity, like love, has its own inscrutable ways, and pitying someone – pitying them desperately with your whole soul – turns out, in the end, to be an arbitrary and illogical thing.

Out of the blue Andrei was forced to quit his job and put a distance between himself and the whole business – not specifically the business with Artemis, unendurable though he found it with his austere soul, but simply the whole strange business that brewed up between him and V.D. Something had happened with V.D, who up till then had always considered Andrei the sole hope of science and had behaved towards him like an obstinate but helpless father – helpless in the face of his own paternal love. What could have forced Andrei to leave his job? Surely not just the presence, right there alongside him, of the fallen Artemis? No, something had clearly happened, and obviously a certain situation had developed in the office which in one fell blow put an end to Andrei's prospects of advancement, for V.D kept trying to look straight past Andrei, and Edik, in great alarm, kept ringing Lidka up, and she would answer him monosyllabically, and it was obvious that Edik was fully in the know and had been even more deeply wounded than before, and that it was Lidka who had enlightened him on the whole chain of events and as a result set him absolutely fuming.

Meanwhile V.D, God knows by what impelled, suddenly started yelling at Artemis during a meeting, telling her she just couldn't be bothered going to college and was wasting time on heaven knows what, clothes and other such nonsense.

Artemis, distinctly lacklustre, took leave to do her entrance exams for college – for a college that V.D had recommended her, a place where he was still remembered and could pull a few strings. Lidka alone knew that Artemis didn't take any such exams, but spent a few days in hospital and returned looking wan and wary, telling everyone that she hadn't passed.

200

Andrei by this time had disappeared over the horizon; he was working in a brand new institute, and had started a new life full of hopes of promotion, an apartment and so on; and in due course, indeed, all this came to pass . . .

So that our narrative ends with total victory for our hero.

Some, doubtless, will say that victory's all very well, but who was there to be conquered in any case? – Just a few old folks, women and neurotics? And yet that's precisely what all of us are too.

And there again: what exactly does victory over us mean? Shouldn't we uphold the idea expressed at the very beginning of our narrative – that all such victories are only temporary phenomena, and weaving and dodging are part and parcel of life; after each fresh blow life picks itself up, and goes on growing and goes on expanding.

To get down to particulars: one fine day, a regular working day, a frightened Lidka – let's get back to Lidka – rang Edik and informed him that she'd seen Andrei in town and Andrei had apparently said that he was going to go public with her – Lidka that is – meaning, no doubt, that he was planning to tell her husband the whole thing. But why? In response to this, Edik, by now remote from the scene, gasped automatically but without his customary enthusiasm, as if he were pondering something to himself, as though something else – some bitter thought or other – were distracting him at that particular moment.

But just a week later Lidka rang Edik again and said that everything was in fact all right; it was simply, she'd found out, that Andrei had decided to become a writer and to depict her, Lidka, in his first book.

At which Edik started laughing long and joyfully, just the way he used to do, as if all his strength had suddenly returned to him and he'd become young and healthy once more.

But a joke's a joke and a laugh's a laugh, as one unmarried librarian loves to say; a joke's a joke, yet still the heart bleeds and still it aches, and still it seeks revenge. What for? you might ask – for the grass keeps growing, and life itself, after all, seems indestructible. Ah, but it is destructible, it is destructible. And that's the whole point.

Monologues

Crossing the Field

I never met him again; just once in my whole life we went together on a visit to someone's dacha, a long way out of town on a newly-built estate; you had to walk three miles through a wood and then cross a bare field, which no doubt could have looked beautiful all the year round, but on that day looked dreadful; we were standing at the edge of the wood and couldn't make up our minds to emerge onto open ground, the thunder was terrifying. Lightning struck the clayey track, and the field looked absolutely stark; I remember those ruts of clay, the bare, absolutely bare beaten earth, the downpour and the lightning. Possibly the field had been sown, but nothing had started growing yet; our feet slithered apart, twisted and buckled as the bare field reared up before us; we'd decided to take the shortest route and set off straight across. The track led uphill and we laughed wildly, for some reason both bending double. He was usually quite silent, as far as I remembered him from the various occasions we'd met before, birthday parties and outings of one kind and another. I didn't know the value of silence then, I didn't appreciate it and kept trying to draw Vovik out, especially since we'd spent one and a half hours together on the train, alone among strangers, and it was awkward and somehow shaming to sit there in silence. He would glance at me now and then with his small, kind eyes, smiling to himself and saying virtually nothing. But that would have been all right, perfectly bearable, if it hadn't been for the downpour that greeted us at the station! My newly-washed, newly-curled hair, the mascara I'd put on – it was all for nought, everything, the flimsy little dress and handbag which got all shrunk and grey - the whole bang lot. Vovik smiled foolishly, hunched his head in his shoulders and turned up the collar of his white shirt; a drop immediately gathered at the tip of his thin nose but there was nothing to be done – for some strange reason there we were, wandering about in the clay and the pouring rain; he knew the way and I didn't, and he said it wasn't far if you went straight, and so we emerged onto that dreadful field with the lightning playing, one minute darting out alongside us, the next a bit farther away, and we waded through waves of clayey earth, not even taking our shoes off, perhaps because we felt shy of each other, I don't know.

I was embarrassed in those days by any form of naturalness and above all by my own bare feet, which seemed to me the very incarnation of monstrous ugliness. Since then I've met women who share the same view and would never walk round barefoot, especially in front of their man. One went through such torments when she got married that she thoroughly earned the wigging her husband gave her: 'What ugly feet you turn out to have!' Others didn't give a damn, crooked or hairy or too big or too bald, they couldn't care less, and they turned out to be right. That day we went slithering about on our accursed soles, a hair's breadth from death, and we were happy as Larry. We were both twenty years old. He'd glance round good-naturedly, a little timid, walking a bit apart from me, a yard and a half or so: later I found out that two people at once can be struck by lightning if they're walking side by side. But it wasn't timidity that stopped him taking my hand that day; his fiancée was waiting for us at the dacha, and he wouldn't give me his hand out of youthful zeal in serving his beloved and her alone. But we both laughed like crazy; rolling and pitching on those waves of earth, plastered with mud, we somehow came to terms. Three miles in that clay and that rain took us an amazingly long time; there are times in one's life that are tough to live through and which seem to go on for ever – like forced labour or sudden solitude or a long-distance run. We lived through those three miles together. Right at the end, as we reached the door, he helped me clamber up the front step and, still giggling, we entered the warm house to the astonished laughter of the other guests and strained exclamations from the fiancée. Everything was ruined – his suit, my dress, our shoes, our hair; his nose was still dripping, but there was no one closer to me in the world than him. Vaguely it dawned on me that I'd been lucky in my journey through life to run across such a good, true man, and the treasure of his soul together with the drip on the end of his nose moved me to tears, I was shaken to the core and didn't know what to do. We were taken off to separate rooms in that empty, dusty dacha, not yet made homely by its new residents, and I was given fresh clothes and so was he, and then they brought us back in and gave us each a little glass of vodka – a miracle! At table he glanced in my direction now and then, smiling foolishly and sniffing and warming his hands on a glass of tea. I knew that none of this was mine or would ever be mine, this miracle of kindness and purity and everything, everything, including beauty too. He'd been claimed by a friend of his, and they sat and played chess, and his fiancée was waiting for him, but I wasn't waiting, I was warming my soul after a long, hard stretch of life's journey, knowing that tomorrow, even today perhaps I'd be torn away from this warmth and light and flung out again to walk alone across that field of clay, under the rain, and that's how life is, and you have to be strong, for everyone must do the same, including Vovik and Vovik's poor fiancée, for a person shines once in his lifetime for just one other person, and that's just the way it is.

Nets and Snares

This is what happened to me when I was twenty years old.

Truth to tell, my being twenty was neither here nor there – I might just as well have been seventeen or thirty: what matters was that this was the first time I'd fetched up in that role, the first time ever I'd found myself in that situation. I never landed up in the same situation again; later, I suppose, I sensed instinctively the danger of slipping into the same role again, and at the first whiff of it I'd be off and away, escape right through the nets spread out to snare me. Though there were no nets, in fact; nobody – even on that first and only occasion – had dreamt of trying to trap me; to be honest, there were no evil designs on anyone's part, no nets or snares, neither that first time nor any time since; indeed there was never even the simplest, most minimal interest in me as a person; I personally was of no use or interest at all in this situation, except in being my husband's wife, just that.

So there were absolutely no nets spread out to trap me at the point where my husband, poised to begin his postgraduate studies, was still employed at his place of work; and I, his wife, being in a certain condition, had gone to stay with his mother in another city. My husband was supposed to follow on soon afterwards to get me settled in my new home, register our marriage, celebrate the wedding at last, pass the necessary exams and embark on a whole new life.

Thus the immediate horizon was clear and unclouded, while everything else would be settled in the distant future; and that's indeed how things turned out in the end.

The position I found myself in was absolutely simple, pure and clear; or rather, it would have been simple, pure and clear, if I'd had in my possession a document confirming that I was Georgy's wife. In all other respects everything was normal: as Georgy's wife, I was going, for the time being alone, to have the baby at his mother's house, since for the time being he was unable to get away himself; he wanted me to have the child in his own home, because a birth should take place in calm surroundings, not the sort of atmosphere Georgy and I lived in in our little hole of a room. It's true that I could have gone to my own parents' home to give birth, though they lived a long way away; but I wanted to link my fate as closely as possible to Georgy's, to his family and his mother, whom I'd never yet set eyes on and who knew of my existence only from her son's letters.

So everything appeared to be completely straightforward, aside from the fact that I wasn't yet Georgy's wife. And I wasn't Georgy's wife for the simple reason that he was already married and had a child of five, and his first wife lived right there in the same town where Georgy's mother lived and where he himself had spent the greater part of his life. Georgy had split up with his wife a long time ago, and not just as a result of the long drawn-out estrangement that occurs when the husband works in one city and the wife and child live in another and bit by bit the relationship disintegrates, everyone gets unused to each other and the mutual visits cease, although there's no immediate pretext either for formal

divorce or for having it out with one another definitively. In Georgy's case everything was much more
conclusive: he paid his wife alimony for their son, and
they split up when they were still living in the same
town; Georgy's wife took the child and went to live
with her parents, and after a while Georgy was
assigned work in another town, the place to which I
too moved, from Siberia, when I began my studies.

So that's the story of my acquaintance with Georgy
and at the same time the story of why, one hot summer,
three years after I'd begun my studies, I went off to stay
in a strange town with my future mother-in-law, taking
with me a suitcase, a raincoat and a handbag containing
a letter from Georgy to his mother.

To be honest, Georgy wasn't all that pleased that I
was going to give birth at his mother's house. But
I managed to get my way; or rather, I simply did as I
thought best, having – naturally enough in my condition
– certain fears for the future: if I were to go back to
my parents in Siberia, while Georgy embarked on his
postgraduate studies, there'd be no chance in the fore-
seeable future of our setting up home as a family. Back
in Siberia I'd be well provided for, the child would
receive excellent care, I'd soon be able to find work or
continue my studies, in short, life would be structured
in such a way that Georgy need not be involved at all.
And that was precisely what I feared most: living in
peace and comfort without Georgy, for, as I knew very
well, his natural compunction and nobility of spirit
would never permit him to leave me and the child in
some precarious situation. If any such situation should
arise, I knew, he was bound to come to my aid. In
other words, he would turn up and arrange things as
required.

An unsettled state of affairs would automatically encourage some effort on his part to settle things properly, whereas a convenient set-up of some kind – with me in Siberia with my mother, say, or in the town where Georgy and I lived and where, if necessary, I could have got a room in a student hostel – any set-up of this kind would encourage only maintenance of the status quo, since Georgy would be able to rest assured from the start of my safety and the child's, and could embark with a clear conscience on his new life as a postgraduate, thus making it practically impossible to force him to do anything – file officially for divorce, for instance, and arrange for me and the child to come and live with him.

None of the above, however, explains the state of blind enthusiasm with which I rushed into the embrace of a family of strangers, and specifically into the arms of Nina Nikolaevna, Georgy's mother. She lived in a big, old-fashioned, comfortable house, and what a joy it was to come in off the dusty summer streets and enter the bathroom, with its antique porcelain basin, cracked and patterned in blue, and its cast-iron bathtub whose enamel was long since worn away at the bottom!

No special enthusiasm, however, attended our first encounter. Nina Nikolaevna, it must be said, made no effort to conceal her doubts. She read the letter attentively while I stood ready in the hall, having made up my mind to leave immediately if need be. I had checked my suitcase into the left luggage depot and had even spent half the day (I'd arrived in the morning) finding myself a bed for the night somewhere near the station.

I should point out here that I hadn't counted on receiving any great consideration in Georgy's home.

Indeed I had anticipated everything in that regard, for Georgy, who was ten years older than me and had seen a good deal in life, had drawn a very clear picture for me of his mother and the situation back home. He had said that everything would depend on me and on me alone, on how intelligent and self-reliant I proved to be, self-reliant above all. This term, self-reliant, cropped up in various guises, and he explained its meaning to me – a self-reliant person was one who stood on his own two feet, not relying on anyone else and demanding nothing of anyone. Only such a person, Georgy opined, could hope for success with regard to his mother, only a self-reliant person, not the sort of weak-kneed character who was grateful for the slightest show of sympathy and yielded to everyone else, eagerly offering assistance just to show how kind and decent they were. For this reason Georgy gave me to understand that he didn't like my eagerness to try and please and fit in with everybody, my tendency unquestioningly to show trust in everyone; he didn't like the way I rushed to bare my soul to all and sundry in the hope of receiving their understanding in turn. Georgy wanted me to be much tougher, and he froze inwardly when I tried to entertain guests in the little room where he and I lived after I'd left the hostel. Georgy hated my servility, my readiness to laugh at every joke and take any sign of attention at face value, as a willingness to be friendly and nothing more. After Georgy's friends had left, Georgy was quite capable of not speaking to me for several days, displeased with the fact that all his efforts to educate me had been in vain, that he hadn't succeeded in making me into the sort of tough, self-reliant person who could be counted on to react with dignity to crude jokes and trivial chit-chat. And even the way I reacted to this silence on Georgy's part, the way I wept and tried to get back into his good books – even this he regarded as a departure from the required norm of proud, self-reliant behaviour. 'Try and show just an ounce of pride', was Georgy's only response, and again he'd fall silent.

During the last month of our life together it was quite impossible to get any sense out of Georgy: he kept disappearing, never revealing his plans; nor would he say how the preparation for his exams was going, as if I were trying to worm some special information out of him on this trifling matter, as if I really needed to know such details. He defended himself from such incursions, however, as if I ardently desired the information and couldn't resist showering him with questions about how the day had gone and what he'd been up to. All his files and books and notebooks were jealously guarded from me, along with all his trivial purchases.

And yet he sat down with the utmost straight-forwardness to write his mother a letter when I said that I was going to her house to have the baby, since I couldn't afford to go home to my own parents in Siberia. He wrote this letter not only because I begged him on bended knee to do so, but because, so it seemed to me, he himself wanted me out of the way as soon as possible, just out of the way and never mind where I went. So in that sense I'd of course been over-hasty in going cap in hand and begging him on bended knee, for in any case, as Georgy said – taking the opportunity to teach me yet another lesson – by such means no one had ever succeeded in forcing anyone to do anything. He then started reprimanding me for my failure to understand the mood of the moment and my general inability to see further than the end of my nose; he reproached me for being so lacking in self-reliance and said that my journey to see his mother would come to nothing, since I was such an un-self-reliant person. And at this point he gave me his usual lecture on the theme of how he would like me to be; and this was a rare and noteworthy event, the principal event of that month, since during that period he had virtually ceased paying me any attention at all and was concerned only to safeguard his own private world, limiting as far as possible my incursions into it and gradually extending the boundaries of his forbidden zone, so that I spent virtually the whole time sitting in the kitchen. It was summertime, and I sat and sat in the kitchen because I didn't want to be caught napping at the very moment when Georgy went off to do his exams. Things being as they were he could very simply have failed to leave me the key, and I would have had to go all the way out to the remote suburbs to get a key from the landlady, and the landlady wasn't especially friendly towards me, having quickly diagnosed the particulars of my position and being prone to say that she had rented the room to a solitary engineer, only to find a whole menagerie living there.

So Georgy sat down and wrote the letter, and I didn't say anything in reply, just took the sheet of paper and went back to the kitchen. I had begun by then to try to put into effect my decision to undertake a fundamental restructuring in my relationship with Georgy, and to develop a little pride. So without saying a word I took the letter, waited for Georgy to go out, then quietly gathered up my things and left, not even leaving him a note.

I had reflected on the reasons why Georgy might so

unquestioningly have permitted me to go and see his mother, and had come to no satisfactory conclusion. I knew that his relationship with his mother was a complex one, and that it was first and foremost with her, and only subsequently with Georgy, that his first wife had found herself temperamentally at odds. For some reason, however, this didn't alarm me, I'd thought and thought about it and then stopped thinking, but as the train chugged along, bringing me in due course, after a 24-hour journey, to the station in Georgy's native town, the place where his lawful wife and son resided, where he himself had spent his childhood and so forth – all these considerations became extraordinarily worrying, and upon my arrival I didn't immediately feel able to carry out my plan, and go and find myself a lodging for the night.

Thus if the reception which Georgy's mother accorded me was not altogether amiable, I at least hadn't counted on anything of the kind. Nina Nikolaevna read the letter in the hall, not allowing me into her apartment. My appearance, it must be said, was unexceptionable; I had had a wash at the place where I'd rented a room for the night. There, too, I had sewn a white collar on to my dress, for a pregnant woman's beauty resides above all in neatness and freshness, in the particular charm of cleanliness, rather than in the stylishness of her attire.

Having read the letter, Nina Nikolaevna showed no greater warmth towards me, but invited me to come in.

Her room was enormous and rather dark, with pretty, antique furniture and a parquet floor almost black with age. I immediately fell completely in love with it, my heart was unaccountably filled with joy and with the desire to stay and live there forever.

When asked, however, where I was staying, I replied that I was lodging with acquaintances and that there was no problem in that regard. Asked furthermore whether I had any money I replied that I had and, all in all, had simply come to make her acquaintance, now that I happened to be here. As to the question why I had come in the first place, I replied that I intended to stay here with the baby pending Georgy's arrival. 'And how soon is the baby due?' Nina Nikolaevna asked, and I said I didn't know exactly, since the doctors said one thing but I thought otherwise. Nina Nikolaevna then asked what I calculated myself, and I said it would be roundabout the November holidays. Finally she enquired whether the baby was Georgy's, and I said that it was and promptly burst into tears.

I couldn't hold back those dreadful tears, which no doubt represented an outpouring of all my suffering during the preceding months when I'd laughed rather than wept at all Georgy's scoldings over my lack of self-reliance. This groundless, idiotic laughter, incidentally, was the thing that had driven Georgy mad most of all; but I couldn't do anything about it, it burst out of me quite involuntarily, just as I quite involuntarily burst into tears when Nina Nikolaevna asked whether Georgy was the baby's father.

My weeping made an impression on Nina Nikolaevna. It seemed she understood there and then who she was dealing with, for thenceforward her behaviour towards me was such that her every action evoked in me a feeling of enormous, incomparable gratitude and such happiness, as if I had found myself back in the longed-for home of my childhood – the only difference being that I had no desire to be back in my own childhood home at all. That indeed was the awful thing, that there was nowhere in the world – even the home that Georgy and I would one day have – that drew me so much as Nina Nikolaevna's home, that dear, beautiful place, where nothing at all had been meant for me, and everything existed as if on a higher plane, everything was nobler, more beautiful than I, yet everything was replete for me with such hopes of happiness. With what reverence I gazed at the paintings in their heavy frames, at the lovely cushions on the couch, the carpet on the floor, and the dining-room clock in the corner!

I was filled with tenderness even at the sight of the vulgar little knick-knacks she'd kept for forty-odd years, the souvenir boxes and bootees decorated with cockle-shells, the empty bottles of scent. I'd have loved to be able to give them a dusting and arrange them neatly under the mirror. Later on I tried to do just that, but Nina Nikolaevna nipped all such attempts in the bud; nothing whatsoever was to be touched in her room.

Truth to tell the room wasn't all that beautiful or especially well cared for. But it communicated the special charm of a place long lived-in, the charm of old, enduring things, and immediately arrested my gaze, just as food arrests the gaze of a hungry man, or a quiet haven that of a homeless wanderer.

I repeat that not a single net had been spread out to snare or destroy me. And I myself, moreover, went blindly on with no hope at all that somehow, sometime I'd be caught in the net. For the profound feeling that I sensed in Nina Nikolaevna, her maternal protectiveness (no, not maternal but something loftier, superior!) could hardly be considered a trap! I've expressed it badly – it wasn't maternal, it was something better, something loftier, for a mother can't afford you that kind of protection. And at the same time my heart had been so touched and softened that once, when Nina Nikolaevna was in the bath, I called out to her through the door that I'd like to be able just to call her Mother. She didn't catch what I'd said and asked me to repeat it, but the noise of running water drowned my words, and I made no further attempt to put forward proposals of such far-reaching implications.

I felt I was in paradise. At first I still kept trying to go back to my landlady near the railway station and, just in case, come to some future arrangement over lodgings, but subsequently I didn't even mention the subject to Nina Nikolaevna (and very soon I'd revealed to her all the secret plans I'd made to book a bed there in advance).

That first day Nina Nikolaevna wouldn't allow me to go anywhere, and with every day she grew more and more attached to me. She literally wouldn't let a speck of dust touch me, rushed out of the house before work to buy me fresh vegetables at the market and grated carrots for me to eat each morning.

As I've already mentioned, Nina Nikolaevna wouldn't let me do a thing – she herself prepared the food for the whole day, leaving me only to heat up my dinner. In the evenings I'd sit by the window, waiting to have supper until she came home. When she returned we'd eat together, then take a walk before retiring to bed. I slept between linen sheets on an enormous, roomy couch.

Now and then Nina Nikolaevna would give me presents; once we went shopping together and bought two calico print dresses with enough extra width to allow for growth; she also bought me nightdresses, sandals to accommodate my swelling feet, and all manner of other things.

Absolutely never, before or since, have I felt so completely happy. The total spiritual harmony between us extended even to her liking for jokes; I loved to have a laugh too, and we laughed together long and heartily, glad of any pretext for merriment.

Nina Nikolaevna confessed that her life would feel dull now without me, that the sound of my bright voice had enlivened her quiet, solitary existence. Sometimes she and I sang duets, and we generally brought the evening to a close by watching a TV programme together, after which I'd stretch out, under the green silk coverlet, between the linen sheets.

Meanwhile there was no word at all from Georgy; we had no idea how the preparation was going for his exams or indeed where he was. I wrote him several letters in Nina Nikolaevna's presence, but got no reply; nor were any of my letters returned stamped 'no longer at this address'.

Having no new information to go on, Nina Nikolaevna and I spent hours on end mulling over old stories of Georgy – we'd exchange recollections of his childhood, which I knew just as well as she if not better. Indeed I told Nina Nikolaevna stories she'd never heard – about Georgy falling off the roof when he was ten years old, for instance (he'd concealed this from her at the time), and about his first love, and then about more recent things – Georgy's work, his friends, his habits, his relationship with his boss. Nina Nikolaevna eagerly entered into these conversations, fastening on every titbit I offered and demanding more and more details about our life together, about how our domestic chores were divided between us and how Georgy had reacted to the news of my pregnancy. I told Nina Nikolaevna the story of how we'd met at a college dance one evening, and how two of them, Georgy and a friend of his ('Which friend was that?') had accompanied me all the way back to my hostel, ('And where's that friend of his now?'). I understood everything, I realised that she was comparing dates – she was always asking for dates – and names and incidents to make quite sure that it really was Georgy's son, her grandson, that I was carrying beneath my heart, and not the child of some other admirer of mine who'd seen me home one dark night and promptly vanished, leaving Georgy to sort out the mess. To tell the truth I was rather touched by these guileless interrogations of hers, the doubts she made no effort to conceal – for they only proved more clearly than ever how much she feared to be deceived in her hopes, and how tenderly she cherished those dreams of a grandson!

Once a week Nina Nikolaevna went to see her other, first grandson out at the dacha, taking him this or that little gift, and I liked this custom of hers, the fact that she hadn't forgotten the child, who after all wasn't guilty of anything, but carried on doing her duty by him. Several times, indeed, I asked to go with her, but at this she became uncharacteristically severe and immediately put me in my place with a few simple but ruthless words: she made it clear that she had her own, independent world which had nothing to do with the world she shared with me – she had her own world, just like Georgy had; and this world of hers, to which I had no access, gradually and imperceptibly but inexorably kept growing, and she began jealously guarding it from my incursions; and thus once again, having unburdened my soul, I found myself left with nothing at all. She began making various long-distance phone calls and wouldn't tell me who they were to, and she started going out for entire evenings without leaving me the key. Our conversations in the evening were now conducted on unequal terms; now it was I who asked all the questions and told all the stories, I who praised Nina Nikolaevna's figure and offered her the sour cream; and she'd say, 'This is my house, I do all the cooking, I'll take what I want myself, thank you very much, and you just help yourself.'

How this metamorphosis occurred I really don't know. All of a sudden I got the distinct feeling that she had risen far above me, that she was bearing down on me like a mountain, weighing down my every movement. I found it hard now just to move about her room, hard just to talk to her. Everything got on her nerves now, and sometimes she didn't even answer my questions.

But this situation, which I'd already been through once before, represented a familiar snare, a familiar net – although, I repeat, it was in fact neither net nor snare, it was simply a disastrous situation, one I had no means to avert, and which was even more disastrous in this case than before, because at least with Georgy there was still a gleam of hope in the form of his mother, and the nobility she would surely demonstrate, were I to find myself in some desperate situation.

I continued to drag out my ambiguous existence in Nina Nikolaevna's home, for I had nowhere else to go. The landlady near the railway station advised me to hold on to whatever I had, since no one was going to give me a room once I had the baby.

I started going then to the so-called 'stock exchange', where apartment owners and would-be lodgers regularly met. Summer was turning to autumn, Georgy had long since arrived – I simply sensed, physically sensed, that he was around, although he never showed up at his mother's house, and she was becoming fiercer by the day. All of a sudden, as if simply discarding any sense of obligation, she began talking of some friend of hers who was coming together with her daughters to stay, and afterwards she was going to stay with them and the apartment would be locked up – her neighbours were out of town, it was they who had entrusted the apartment to her, and no one would permit a complete outsider, no relation to anyone, to live there in her absence.

I suggested we should have a proper talk, bring things out into the open. She said things were out in the open quite enough as it was, disgustingly out in the open, she said, and it was improper to go lumbering a man with someone else's child, a man who was innocent in body and spirit, quite improper, what with all this cavorting around at dances and having men seeing you right home to your doorstep.

I burst out laughing, and this put an end to the conversation. My things were put out in the corridor, Nina Nikolaevna locked herself in her room, and I spent the night in the kitchen. In the morning Nina Nikolaevna put my things out on the stairs.

And that was the end of my adventure. The rest is of no great interest – afterwards I lodged with the lady near the station and regularly went to the stock exchange, concealing my expanding waistline beneath my raincoat, and in the end some old codger who'd got himself a job up north let me have his room almost literally for peanuts. It's hardly worth mentioning that there was just a completely bare, iron-framed bedstead in the room and I spent my first night in my new lodgings sleeping on that bare frame with just my raincoat for bedding, quite happy and serene, until the time came in the morning to head for the maternity hospital.

And that brings to a close that first phase of my life, a phase that will never be repeated, thanks to the few simple techniques I've since mastered. Never again will I repeat what I went through then, in the days when I believed so completely in happiness, when I loved so deeply and handed over my entire being so unconditionally, right down to my innards, as if my being were of no worth at all. Never again will that phase of my life be repeated. Since then there've been other times, other people; since then, as well, there's been the life of my daughter, our daughter, whom Georgy and I bring up as best we can, whom Georgy loves devotedly, much more devotedly than he ever loved me. But that hardly troubles me now, for I've entered a different phase of my life now, a completely different phase, completely different.

Grisha

That summer, single and alone, I rented myself a dacha. Or rather, I rented part of a barn – another part served as the owners' storeroom, while hens were kept in the part furthest from me. Sometimes the hens made a great din at night, and a couple of times I ran and asked the owners to have a look and see what was going on. Sima, my landlady, said it was just the weasels making mischief.

My bit of the barn had wallpaper, two windows, a stove, a table, and a dilapidated trestle-bed, and it was to this bed that I returned from Moscow each day, even late at night, running home in the dark from the local station. Numerous dangers lay in wait for a single woman returning down the unlit road from the station to home. Later our landlord, Grisha, was to meet his end right there in our little back lane, but for some strange reason I always believed I was quite safe and that no one was going to touch me. The pitch black night served as just a good a cover for me as for a criminal or anyone else. And I always turned the light on at home, even though I realised that in the pitch darkness my barn would be lit up like an open target, all the way across to the station and down to the end of our lane. But I turned on the light nonetheless, sang to myself and put on the kettle as if I hadn't a worry. The main trouble was that by mid-summer the runner beans had grown along the wires and the whole of the barn was overgrown with leaves, so that it would have been the easiest thing in the world to glance in at my window without attracting attention. My landlords didn't keep a dog, and that in the end played a role in the story too, for Grisha was killed right there by his gate, and if there'd been a dog it couldn't have happened so easily.

In the ocean of darkness that surrounded my little barn anyone could quite easily have come up to my window, and the fact that I lived there, far from the nearest habitation and all alone, was well known to everyone in the neighbouring lanes and even to people who lived on the other side of the railway. Grisha was killed in the winter; I left in October, and when I came back to visit them, the first person I ran into, a total stranger, told me that Grisha had been stabbed to death. The stranger then turned off down the other side of the tracks. So he must have known me, even though he lived on the other side of the line.

But although I was afraid coming home to my barn late at night, though I was afraid to turn on the light, I did it every day, somehow not really believing that I could come to any harm. Sometimes I was haunted by dreadful images, scenes out of gangster films – three men coming into my barn, greasing the bolt and entering without a sound, that sort of thing. But at the same time I never experienced the sort of horror you can feel just watching a movie – the imaginary scenes that passed through my mind were somehow removed from fear, they didn't arouse any particular sensation – they presented themselves just as various hypotheses, like when you're cleaning the window and imagine what would happen if the chair collapsed and you went flying out.

Nothing really scared me, even when the landlords'

son Vladik took to coming in drunk and spending the night on the other side of my wall in the storeroom, deliberately clattering and crashing about just to let me know he was there. Not only did this fail to frighten me, I even found it funny, as if Vladik, languishing in hiding there behind the wall, was courting me in his own way by thundering about. Needless to say, Vladik wasn't courting me at all, he'd simply heard that all solitary women renting dachas were whores, and had decided to meet the danger head on. Sima paid no heed to the fact that Vladik had spent the night in the storeroom; maybe she reckoned that it was high time Vladik broke his fast in any case, but she didn't seem to attach much significance to this either, for the following day she wore her usual air and chatted to me just as she always did – though doubtless she would have gone on chatting in the same way no matter what.

Sometimes I dropped by at the landlords' place to watch television and observed their simple, unpretentious, traditional ways: there was Sima, the head of the household, Vladik the darling boy of the family, Zina, the elder daughter, little Ira the granddaughter and Grisha, a quiet fellow who just muttered away, fetch this, fetch that, don't walk there on the newly-washed floor; a quiet man, fifty-five years old, he worked as a fitter at the local factory. I'd grown fond of the family, the whole bunch of them, I liked them all; I liked the way they always had people in the house, and the neighbours were forever dropping in; I liked Sima, stern but never fierce, and Vladik, so attentive and obedient to his mother, and fat Zina, who in idle moments could always be found nibbling at a loaf of white bread. Zina had a husband, Vasya, who drank too much and seldom came to visit his in-laws; Zina came alone to see her little Ira and to wash the floor and do the laundry on Sundays. Vasya, when he did put in an appearance, was silent for the most part, upset in advance that Zina might speak ill of him – of his behaviour, his mother, their life together. But even Vasya, on closer inspection, turned out to be a loving husband; and when he'd had a drink or two he'd sit and rest his head on Zina's shoulder.

So we had our little idyll together down there. Sometimes the family would interrupt my existence, as when Sima sent Grisha up onto the roof of my barn to tighten a sagging cable. I stood with Sima watching from the yard as Grisha stomped about the roof, completely foxed as to how he was going to get at the cable, let alone fix it. Sima was worried about the barn, afraid that the cable would eventually touch the roof and set it alight, while the thought crossed my mind as I stood watching Grisha stomping about up there that he was going to die when he finally reached the cable – but this thought drifted somewhere above my mind, like my thoughts of gangsters and the sticking plaster they'd used to seal up the victim's mouth. Grisha couldn't reach the cable in the end, and Sima fussed about him getting safely down, meanwhile saying that they'd have to find an electrician and offer him a bottle for his trouble, otherwise the barn was bound to go up in flames.

But I kept remembering Grisha on top of the barn, reaching up to the cable six inches away from death, and Sima down below, fretting like any housewife over her house.

I spoke to Grisha only once in the course of that whole summer – when I asked him to take me mushrooming with him. I'd never once been into the forest, and in fact never went anywhere at all that summer, and it was Grisha's fault I didn't. I'd asked him to wake me at five o'clock in the morning; he woke me with a knock at the door and I dressed and had tea; he was busy attending to this and that in the garden and several times went to and fro past my window, looking preoccupied. But when I emerged Grisha was nowhere to be seen, and when I knocked at their door Zina sleepily appeared and told me that Dad had long since set off to catch the 5.40 train.

God, how I ran to the station! But the 5.40 train was pulling out of the station literally as I arrived; maybe Grisha even saw me standing there by the rails below. Though come to think of it he was pretty unlikely ever to stand staring out of a train window – he was a very quiet man and I don't think he ever just amused himself idly.

That Sunday was completely messed up. I went back to bed and slept till midday; when I awoke it was terribly hot and I had a headache. Grisha returned just as discreetly as he'd left, and the family scolded him for not having waited for the lodger to come too.

I realised then that Grisha had been hanging about on purpose beneath my window that morning but was too shy to tell me it was time to leave, too shy to say anything at all in fact. And it was an odd thing, but the pity I'd felt watching Grisha on the barn roof stretching up to that cable suddenly rose up in me more strongly than ever. Now in addition I felt sorry for Grisha for being so totally tongue-tied, so terribly vulnerable, that he was quite unable to remind me to get a move on even once he'd made the arrangement with me, and had decided it was better just not to make a fuss. It struck me then that he was the sort of timid little worker, always toiling away, that no one – least of all himself – ever bothers to think about. Although perhaps he'd just felt awkward about taking me mushrooming with him in the first place and was simply too shy to say no – what excuse could he find for not taking me? And the fact that he'd set off by himself was not a gesture of despair after all, but the decisive action of a man who, when all's said and done, couldn't care less about common niceties and simply did what suited him. But at that time I interpreted his departure as a sign of his bashfulness.

It's seldom happened that I've felt real pity for someone – beggars and cripples and lonely old men and weeping relatives at funerals have never evoked much pity in me, I don't know why. I've always felt that somewhere out there they've got their own lives to get on with; for a moment, as they flash by, you're aghast at their appearance, but then they vanish again into that other existence of theirs, disappear into their various homes, sit and warm themselves by the radiator or have a bowl of hot soup, in other words live like everyone else, give or take a few minor adjustments. I rarely feel sorry for people. But to this day I can't rid myself of Grisha, the mad pity I feel for him – though not because someone stabbed him in the stomach and he suffered a lot before he died; I'll suffer too on my deathbed, we all will, and that's our private affair. But I keep remembering how he hung about, pacing up and down in the garden, then washed his hands of it and set off alone, running all the way to the station; and I ran after him eight minutes later, but he'd already triumphantly moved off, departed all by himself in the train.

He was killed by some youths when he refused to

give them a cigarette and told them into the bargain to go wipe the snot off their faces. Obviously something had started seething inside that meek man, or maybe he wasn't a meek man at all.

After his death the family fell apart. Vasya abandoned Zina, and the old woman went mad and kept digging her husband out of the grave to prove that his hands had been bitten. But no one could bear witness to the fact, for the body had disintegrated and nothing now remains of Grisha, and only Vladik has stayed with his mother, as timid as ever and still hoping for happiness.

This Little Girl

Now it's as if she'd died for me. And maybe she really has died, although no one from our block has been buried this past month. Ours is an ordinary block – five storeys, no lift, four outside entrances, and exactly the same sort of building opposite. If she really had died, we'd all have got to hear of it straight away. So somehow, somewhere, she must still be alive.

Take a look: I've got a photo, a contact print, stuck to my drawer where I keep the blank filing cards. That's her, Raisa, Ravilya, with the stress on the last syllable; she's a Tatar. You can't really see anything from the picture: face hidden by a curtain of hair; two arms, two legs; the pose like Rodin's *Thinker*.

She always sits like that; not so long ago she was sitting just like that at my birthday party. That was the first time I'd seen her in company; up till then it had always been just us four, two plus two – her with her Seva, and me with my Petrov.

It turned out she couldn't dance either; she just sat there, quiet as a mouse. Petrov dragged her up to dance with him, but after that one dance she went straight home.

Yes, she was no good at dancing. But she was a real professional whore. God knows where Seva got hold of her, what hole he dug her out of. She'd just got out of reform school and gone back on the game, and Seva upped and married her. It was he who told me, all shaken up about it, but I had to promise under terrible oath not to tell a soul. He told me all about her father too, how Raisa from the age of five had had to work sticking pill packets together; she and her mother did it for her father, who'd got the job because he was disabled. Then her mother died in hospital from a heart attack, and the father started openly bringing women back home to their room. All in all it was a dreadful story. Raisa had run away from home and fetched up with a bunch of youths in an empty apartment and for several months – as they found out some time later, when the apartment was discovered – they wouldn't let her out at all. But that's ancient history now, of no concern to anyone; the point is that Raisa's still in the same business now.

Seva went out to work while she stayed at home; she never had a job of any kind. Seva would leave her her dinner all prepared, but when he came home she wouldn't have bothered to heat it up, wouldn't even have been in the kitchen. She'd lie in bed for days on end smoking, or go wandering round the shops. Or weep. She'd suddenly start weeping for no reason at all and cry for four hours on end. So of course the neighbour would come running in looking scared to death – you've got to rescue Raisa, she'd say, hurry up, she's weeping. And I'd rush in with the tranquillisers and valerian drops. Although it happens to me too sometimes – and not just out of the blue, for no reason – I just want to give up and lie down and die. But nobody knows what goes on in my soul, nobody knows what burdens I have to bear. I don't start shrieking and rolling about on the bed with the bedclothes in disarray. Only when my Petrov ditched me for the first time, when he wanted to run off and marry that girl Stanislava and was looking round for a loan to pay for the divorce and the apartment and wanted officially to get custody of Sasha – that was the only time in my life I went to pieces. It's true Raisa defended me like she would her own baby that time, and went for Petrov with her bare hands and nails.

Roughly three or four times a year my Petrov falls in love for evermore and eternity. I know that now. But at the beginning, the first time he left me, I was a hair's breadth from throwing myself out the second floor window. I was literally trembling with impatience to put an end to the whole thing, because the day before he'd told me that he was bringing Stanislava over to introduce her to Sasha. Early that morning I took Sasha off to my mother's on Nagornaya street, then came back and waited for them the entire day. And then I climbed up on the windowsill and started tying up a piece of wire we had left over from when Petrov had fixed up a washing-line in the kitchen, several rows of wire, to dry Sasha's nappies. The wire was strong and insulated with vinyl. I tied this bit of wire to the spike that Petrov had driven into the concrete wall ages ago to strengthen the cornice. We'd only just got the room at that stage, it was before Sasha was born, and I remember Petrov hammering away at that wall for almost an hour. I wound the end of the wire round that spike, but the wire was too smooth and the loop kept slipping off. But I kept on winding it round just the same and made another loop at the other end for my neck, somehow I worked out where to tie what. But at that very moment I heard someone in the hallway turning a key in the front door. And I forgot absolutely everything – I even forgot Sasha, all I remembered was that they wanted to get custody and because of that he'd got somehow defiled in my mind, as if it wasn't me that had given birth to him and fed him from my own breast. I was scared Petrov and Stanislava were coming into the apartment right then, and I gave the window latch such a jerk that the plaster cracked. We'd plastered up all the window frames for the winter.

It was already dark in the room. From the window you could see the block opposite, empty, unlit – no one had moved in yet. There was only a street lamp burning not far below. This time I tugged at the window so hard that even the frame gave way. At this point Raisa rushed into the room and clasped me round the ankles. She's weak and I'm strong and right then I was furious too, but she'd latched on to my legs like a dog and kept saying over and over again, 'Let's do it together, let's do it together, wait for me.' And then I started thinking, how come you're barging in on the act? What have you got to worry about anyway? And I even took it as a kind of personal insult. There I was so to speak with my life in pieces – my husband had ditched me along with my little boy and now he wanted to take the boy away, whereas Raisa – come off it! But Raisa kept thrusting her knee through the open window, even though it would have been a joke just to jump out of a second floor window into deep snow without even putting a noose round your neck. So I shoved her back as hard as I could and my hand landed on her face, which was wet, slippery and icy cold. And then I jumped right down and closed the window, and the plaster had got all scrunched up and there was no way I could smooth it out again; I couldn't keep control of my hands in any case.

And the only thing that resulted from this whole incident was that my mind turned stone cold. I don't know if Raisa really played a role in the whole thing, but I realised it just wasn't me to go flinging myself around like that and acting out every mad impulse. How could someone like me be compared to Raisa?

As it turned out, all that was needed was a bit of intelligence. I took action and very soon Stanislava was confined to history. The whole thing proved extremely easy, because Petrov had been stupid enough to blab about where she worked and what she did, and luckily she had a pretty unusual surname too. Others followed, of course, and I never even learned the names of half of them and they could all go to blazes as far as I was concerned, but I wasn't going to go putting a noose round my neck and jumping. And when he started talking about divorce I just brushed him aside. He could weep as much as he liked and tell me he hated me, it all left me stone cold. I just laughed at him. 'You can't run away from yourself, sweetheart,' I said, 'If you're a schizophrenic, go and get your head shrunk.'

But the truth was he was in a hopeless position anyway: I'd no intention of signing away my claim to our room. I had nowhere else to go. And there was no chance of our exchanging our sixteen square metre room for two separate ones. And there was another thing, too: when Sasha was born, the management at Petrov's work had promised him a two-room apartment. So every time he started having his bit on the side again I knew he'd be back, because whenever a new block was built and they started looking through the applications for apartments he knew he wouldn't stand a chance being on his own, and divorced at that. Whereas once we'd got a two-room apartment we'd be able to exchange it for two individual ones and get ourselves divorced. So every time Petrov stayed put with me, waiting for the two-room apartment. And maybe that wasn't the only reason he came back either. Because I'd always sensed that if Petrov really took it into his head to go he wouldn't think twice about the apartment or anything else, he'd just vanish without a trace.

And when he was done with the latest fling he'd start spending the evenings at home again, watch me flying in and out of the kitchen, lend me a hand with Sasha, even pick him up from kindergarten sometimes and put him to bed when I was on evening shift. And finally he'd bring home a bottle of demi-sec champagne, he knows I'm fond of a drop of champagne. I have to say I always foresaw when the moment was coming, and made my own little preparations too. He'd say with a sigh, 'Won't you have a drink with me?', and I'd fetch the tall Czech wine glasses out of the sideboard. It was always exciting, like on your first date, the only difference being that we both knew how the night would end. These zigzags lent a certain spice to life. And Petrov would whisper that I was the most passionate woman he knew, the most tender, the most fiery.

While Raisa, of course, was a dead loss in that respect. The men we knew, the ones she did her business with – you couldn't say slept with, because it generally took place in daytime, when Seva was out, and they just had to find her on her own in the room to get what they wanted with no trouble at all – they all said she was a complete dud; not just that she behaved like she couldn't care less but she actually seemed to find the whole thing disgusting. And when it was over she never wanted to chat, the way people usually do – people aren't just animals, after all, but thinking beings; they have some curiosity, they want to know a bit about the person lying next to them, who they are and how they live. Sometimes Petrov and I talked the whole night long, especially after those zigzags of his; we were insatiable. He'd tell me about his various women, comparing them all with me, and I couldn't get enough of it – I'd drag every last detail out of him. And we'd have a good laugh together over Raisa – never unkindly, of course. Because every single bloke we knew – but literally every one, right down to the folks from Petrov's home-town that came on a visit from time to time – they'd all been at Raisa's, the whole bang lot of them. And they'd all tell us all about it.

There was a boy called Grant, for instance, that Petrov had known back home. We wrote and told him that if he arrived while we were out he could get the key next door at Raisa's, she was almost always home. We'd been doing this for ages, leaving a key with her. It was so convenient; we kept a key to her apartment too, and that way we didn't have to ring up specially when we were going to be out or involve the other neighbours.

When the two of us got back from work Grant was already sitting there on Sasha's divan bed, red in the face and leafing mournfully through a book on Alfred Sisley. And the set of keys that Raisa kept was lying there on Sasha's little desk. We took the whole thing in at a glance and burst out laughing. 'So, Raisa took a drubbing, did she?' I asked. He gave us a scared look, thoroughly shaken. Then when we explained the whole thing to him he sobered up and calmed down and told us the whole story. When she opened the door to him, he said, he'd even had to ask her, 'Why so scared? I don't bite' – she'd jumped right into the corner. She was wearing just her dressing-gown, that's how she always goes round at home. And he added that it seemed like she went along with it all because she was terrified of something, literally terrified out of her wits. And it left you with a kind of loathsome aftertaste, he said, as if you'd done her a terrible injury, though she never said a thing and didn't resist at all.

But we reassured him and told him not to worry. That's the impression she always created at first. She looked at first just like a tiny, quiet, dark-haired little girl, just a little girl who didn't even know how to dance; when we had guests round she'd sit quiet as a mouse on Sasha's divan and you had to move heaven and earth to get her to dance, because she was scared of a big crowd. And all the men fell for it straight away, she wakened the hunting instinct in them, they'd drag her out of the corner by the hands, and she'd be trembling all over. And then she'd go off home.

She stung me in just the same way when I first got to know her. She was like a new-born animal – new-born, precisely, not just little – who doesn't move you by its prettiness so much as stings you with pity, right in the heart. No amount of love can stifle pity like that, pure pity that takes your breath away.

It all began with her ringing our doorbell at three o'clock in the morning; it didn't seem to have occurred to her that we were total strangers and it was the middle of the night. I opened the door and she was standing there in her little dressing-gown with sodden cheeks, the tears dripping off her chin, her hands in her pockets, trembling all over – and asking for a cigarette. I took her into the kitchen, turned on the light, and found a newly-opened pack of cigarettes in Petrov's coat pocket. We both had a smoke, and I asked her 'Where's your Seva?' And with swollen lips she said, 'He's gone away on business'. I made her some coffee and we sat there a long while till she stopped trembling. Then I sensed Sasha had pushed off the bedclothes in his sleep, went back into the room, tucked him in again – and returned to find her huddled up on the stool again, weeping. 'What's the matter?' I asked. 'I suppose you're missing your husband?' She lifted her head and said: 'I'm frightened of the atom bomb.' She wasn't frightened of death but of the atom bomb, can you imagine? And it was obvious she wasn't play-acting at all – if there's one thing certain, it's that there wasn't an ounce of game-playing in her. She always did what she had to do, she never pretended. That was what was so odd about her – it was as if she had no resistance in her at all. As if something inside her had got spoiled, some instinct of self-preservation. And you could sense it straight away.

Before she left, standing in the doorway, she burst into tears again, and so she went back to her own place, weeping. I didn't try to detain her – morning was breaking already, and I had to be at work by nine. Later on at work I told all the girls about my neighbour – this little girl, the conscience of the world. I was even a little proud of her.

From then on we couldn't get through the day without seeing one another. Either she and Seva would be round at our place, or we'd be round at theirs. 'Sit yourself down,' she'd say if you dropped by for a cigarette, 'Let's have a smoke'. And you'd be there two hours. I'd tell her everything, just like I'm telling you now. I'm that sort of person, it makes me feel better to tell people things. So we'd sit there for a couple of hours discussing the problems of the world – life, other people. I like sitting peacefully, chatting away. I'm a good housewife, everything gets done first thing in the morning, dinner included, and when I'm on second shift I rush off to the institute straight after dinner. Whereas she neither works nor gets anything done – as though she weren't really Seva's wife at all. He goes out to work and does all the shopping and dashes home like a madman as if to rescue a yelling baby. He comes in and tidies everything up, although apart from a full ashtray Raisa leaves no mess at all, not a single dirty dish. Seva leaves her a pot of soup on the stove and a pan with the main course ready – but she doesn't even glance at it, won't take a spoonful.

Seva took her to the doctor, got leave from work to take her. The doctor declared her totally emaciated and even talked of anorexia. She looked as if she'd lived through the seige of Leningrad. He prescribed her injections of aloe.

She bought herself a syringe – and that became her new pastime, injecting herself just above the knee. She had it all sorted out – the cottonwool, the spirit, the sterile pads, and she'd boil up the needle herself. Somewhere or other she'd learned all about it. She'd sit down at the window and say 'Turn away' – and then there'd be a slight, filtering, squeezing sound. I'd shudder inwardly and look at Seva – he'd be standing there white as a sheet, leaning against the door frame. And she'd say: 'There, it's done, you fools' – but the syringe would still be in there, she'd be waiting for the last drop to go through.

We became such friends, I lost count of the times she came to blows with Petrov over me. She didn't really know how to swear; she'd just say: 'You're a real sonofabitch, do you know that?' Probably that's what they said at reform school.

Petrov had recently taken up with another girl, she worked with us in the institute in Antonova's laboratory. You know the one – a dumpy, flabby girl, complete nonentity. And my Petrov was endlessly dropping in on me at work, even if he knew, for instance, that I was on second shift and couldn't go home. 'Will you be coming home now?' he'd ask me just the same. No, I'd answer. 'Then I won't wait for you' – and he'd be straight off to see her in the laboratory. And strangely enough she started dropping in on me too in the catalogue room. And Petrov would just so happen to be there too. We'd all get chatting, and before I'd had time to blink he'd have asked her home. He loves having people round, can't get by without. If we have an empty evening he'll just sit there all morose, then suddenly jump up and go out.

And just around then it had got to the point where he absolutely had to have something to fill those empty evenings. I could feel it coming on physically. I looked about me and made a mental note of all the girls around and asked myself would it be this one or that? We had lots of people coming round at the time. I more or less had Sasha staying permanently with my mother on Nagornaya Street, even though she had her little granddaughter there with her too. We had guests every single evening, our room was like an inn, Petrov and I were in a complete whirl, people would come round with guitars and bottles of wine. I did my standard dishes – nut rolls wrapped in cellophane and onions fried with egg yolk and rye toast. And I had the feeling that it was all wasted effort, everything was caving in, everything was about to shatter in pieces, because despite all the singing and dancing and strumming of guitars and music on the tape recorder, handsome men and pretty girls, those evenings at our house all somehow felt forced and boring.

And I looked at all these young girls – whole clusters of them seemed to have ripened all the time that I'd been giving birth to Sasha and bringing him up and traipsing round the shops and feeding Petrov and doing his washing, all the time that we'd been buying the tape recorder and the furniture for Sasha now that he was bigger. Whole battalions of these girls had gone on the offensive at once – beautiful, stylishly coiffured, skilfully getting by on their meagre grants and wages, they were ready for everything, on the *qui vive*, aggressive. But I knew that they weren't the real danger. I knew my Petrov too well. And I looked at all these girls and knew that the one he needed was Raisa, and not just as a one-off but for the whole of his life.

Meanwhile, oddly enough, relations between them didn't just fail to settle down, they actually got worse. She couldn't bear to see him and appeared at our place more and more seldom. She couldn't forgive him the fact that I was dying of uncertainty – for after all I'd told her everything apart from the thing I suspected most.

And then he went and invited home that fat, flabby Nadezhda from lab no. 3. That's always been an odd habit of his with the girls he fancies – sooner or later he invites each and every one home. I can't imagine what makes him do it. Sometimes I feel he does it because of me, just to spite me, to put me through even greater torments and thus make his zigzags to and fro all the sweeter. But then it occurs to me that maybe I've got nothing to do with it and that Petrov just brings his current girl home for his own peace of mind, so there'd be no cheating, everything would be out in the open and the girl in question would know precisely what her prospects were and what she was in for – while afterwards Petrov himself could keep aloof from the fray, creating a vacuum so the two of us, the other woman and me, would fight it out between us instead of with him. But maybe Petrov wasn't up to these psychological subtleties; perhaps he just lured the other woman into playing the tricky, ambiguous role of family friend before moving on to the next stage and going to bed with her. On the face of it, after all, Petrov's a pretty dull-looking fellow; what all these women saw in him I've no idea.

Anyway, amid the general bedlam this girl Nadezhda suddenly started showing up at our house. I even had the feeling that Petrov wasn't all that interested in her, that she'd be no match for me in bed and that the zigzag wouldn't last long on this occasion. She seemed very submissive and undemanding. There was nothing of the wild creature about her that you'd be frightened of scaring. She was like a domestic animal that you could drive with a flick of the switch. So I felt sorry for her. We became quite friendly. We'd leave the institute together when I'd been working the first shift. And I gradually discovered that she didn't understand a thing in life, hadn't a clue about anything – decent underwear, books, good food. She just felt her way blindly, sensing warmth and kindness through the pores of her skin and heading straight towards them without saying a word, without even changing her expression. At the institute she'd chalked up several inconclusive affairs and even a pregnancy that resulted in a still-born child. I remembered it happening, and remembered some of the women saying it was a blessing really, Nadezhda was better off without.

This triangular friendship lasted some time and would have lasted longer if it hadn't been for one incident. One day, as I was going out of the room to fetch the coffee from the kitchen, I glanced in passing at the hallway mirror. The mirror reflected part of the main room, including the table where Petrov and Nadezhda were sitting. And I saw Petrov cautiously, as he would with a child, stroking Nadezhda's chin with his cupped palm, and Nadezhda taking his hand and placing it on her breast.

I kept a grip on myself, though the thing that tormented me was this: how could I have missed it this time round? Why had I been thinking of Raisa, when the real danger was right here – it had swelled up right alongside me, and was all the more terrible because Nadezhda in herself was such a nobody. Raisa at least was 'this little girl, the conscience of the world' whereas this one was a complete nonentity.

Petrov took Nadezhda home and returned at one in the morning completely exhausted, worn-out, dead beat. I didn't touch him, didn't say a word, because I knew that in this state the only thing Petrov cared about was sleep. If I'd said something to him and thrown him out he would have gone to sleep in the kitchen or on the stairs outside or on the window sill. Or he could have gone back to Nadezhda's and stayed with her. For some reason he'd come home. Which meant that all was not lost. It meant that we hadn't yet reached the final stage; he'd just embarked on a new zigzag, nothing more than his usual protest against the monotony of married life. That was the only thing that made Petrov restless: just the fact that one fine day he felt bored. Sometimes he'd get hold of some illiterately retyped and duplicated copies of medical lectures or advice manuals – pure pornography, in other words. We'd read them aloud to Seva and Raisa, though I must say they didn't seem to make much of an impression on them. They'd listen politely but indifferently, as if for some reason we'd suddenly decided to treat them to a word of advice for sufferers from arteriosclerosis. Whereas Petrov and I laughed till we were crimson. And that would be the start of a little zigzag too, though it didn't last long and completely lacked that sense of real spiritual reconciliation that came about on the evenings Petrov returned to the bosom of the family.

So anyway I was figuring on Petrov coming home of his own accord on this occasion too, leaving out of account all other factors – his coming home so late, and the fact that he'd abandoned all interest in Sasha and had stopped teaching him to read. But a while later one of our neighbours told me that all the previous week, when I'd been working the evening shift, Petrov had been bringing some fat girl or other home and keeping her there till just before I got back. Sasha hadn't been at home that week – my mother had been picking him up at kindergarten and taking him over to her place, so that the room had been entirely free.

I immediately rang Mum and asked her, just for this once, to babysit Sasha at our place – put him to bed at home and wait for me to come back. Mum was reluctant, because she had so much on her plate back home – my older brother had completely saddled her with his daughter Nina. But I talked her into helping me – my brother would just have to manage that one evening without her. I don't remember what aspersions I cast on my brother to flatter my mother into coming over to our place. Mum didn't know anything of Petrov's zigzags, and if she had she would have got us divorced on the spot. So I didn't breathe a word, and she and Petrov were on quite good terms.

Just as I'd calculated, Petrov brought Nadezhda home again that evening, and there they bumped into my mother. Some incident then occurred between her and Nadezhda – because, I repeat, the battle was never fought with Petrov but with Nadezhda herself. And I'd counted on Nadezhda proving weak and beating a retreat as soon as she caught sight of Petrov's infuriated mother-in-law and his weeping child.

And maybe she did back off. But not Petrov. He didn't come home that night, and it looked as if he wasn't planning on returning at all. He did come back a few times – to fetch his razor, his socks and shirts, and finally the tape recorder. He'd gone wild, pulled out completely and suddenly reverted to being just like that dear young boy who'd once upon a time been crazily in love with me.

I didn't say a word to him; without a murmur I handed over the tape recorder and everything else he asked for, yet he was obstinately sullen, as if in his mind I'd already answered all his unspoken questions. But I kept silent, although it was already apparent that no amount of nobility on my part was going to win him back.

And suddenly I understood that I was losing everything, my whole world. The only person who remained on my side of the fence was Raisa; all the rest of the world was on the other side. Mum, alarmed by the unexpected results of her intervention, was angry at me for having plotted this encounter in the first place. As for Sasha – well, I'm a pretty level-headed woman and I know very well that a child's love and affection are not directed towards his parents as concrete individuals.

He could have formed just as strong an attachment to any other combination of features: face, figure, hair, character, mentality. Sasha would love me irrespective of whether I was a murderer or a great violinist or a salesgirl or a prostitute or a saint. But these feelings would last only as long as he needed to suck his life out of me; after that, indifferent as ever to me as a person, he'd up and leave. This consciousness of imminent betrayal disheartened me every time I bent over to give him a hug as he lay, bathed and tucked up, on his divan bed in the semi-darkness. Perhaps I owed this sense to Petrov, who'd taught me to expect betrayal.

Mother too had ceased to love me. Indeed she'd never really loved me as a person, only as her offspring, her flesh and blood. Now in her old age she was painfully attached to Sasha and to her other little grand-child, Nina. But Petrov and I and my older brother and his wife didn't mean much to her these days – we were just relatives, that's all.

I went to Raisa and told her the whole lot. I suppose I'm quite an experienced raconteur. I tell all sorts of things to my girls at the institute, even to women I meet quite by chance, like when you're in hospital for the few days after an abortion. But on this occasion with Raisa it was different. Raisa really understood that she was all I had left in the world. And that I wasn't just talking here about the usual zigzags, but about Sasha and me being left with nowhere to live, our losing all hope of the two-room apartment that I'd longed for so passionately and even dreamt of at nights. I don't know how many times Petrov and I had furnished the place in our imagination, chatting together at night in bed. Petrov wanted to paint a huge fresco on the kitchen wall himself, like Sykaros, he even wanted to paint the fridge and the white enamel round the gas stove. These were all dreams, of course, although Petrov is quite a dab hand with the pen and ink, he copies portraits of famous jazzmen out of magazines, frames them in black and hangs them on the walls. Petrov once played piano in a jazz ensemble; for several years he was involved in a group at the 'Victory' club, until he suddenly felt too old to take part in all these amateur activities, bus trips to benefit performances at collective farms and compulsory sessions accompanying students in the solo singing class. Petrov mastered percussion as well and played bass a bit. And several times he got a jazz quartet – piano, guitar, bass, drums – to back him singing that English song 'Shakeyerhand' or however it was pronounced. But no one properly appreciated his simple, unnuanced, not specially husky voice or his impeccable English accent. He didn't sing the way he spoke – there's something artificial in doing that too. He sang simply, loudly, woodenly, monotonously, but he was so direct, so sincere in his masculine way, so vulnerable. He was taut as a violin string when he sang, straining every nerve and shuddering ever so slightly at the rhythm of the song. I heard him just the one time, when Sasha was two months old. My thoughts weren't really on Petrov that evening, I was flooded with milk, it filled every pore and my breasts felt hard, hewn, rock-solid. I was frantic with nerves, knowing that Sasha was hungry and that Petrov's number – as always – came right at the end of the programme. But at last there he was on stage with the other guys and they rolled on the piano and he was holding a little microphone, brand new. The guy on percussion spent ages setting up his drums, and then they played 'Chamberlain', a gentle little waltz, and finally 'Shakeyerhand'.

Petrov sang, his whole, long body shuddering to the beat, and I was quite captivated despite myself, but the milk was bursting in my breasts and I knew I had to rush back to Sasha, that he was screaming right now and demanding his food. And I stood up, though the song wasn't finished, turned my back on Petrov and dashed out of the hall. I couldn't put Petrov first, just as I can't now, because Sasha takes up every inch of me, just as the milk filled every inch of my breast that day, leaving only the odd landmark visible here and there. And to this day I don't know how Petrov took my flight from the auditorium and whether he got the applause he deserved – I didn't ask him and he didn't tell me. I didn't bother to explain; in those days we never talked much anyway.

I don't know why I related all this to Raisa. I wept before her as if she alone could save me. I didn't know how to get Petrov back. It wasn't just that the apartment – my dream – had collapsed in ruins. I was suddenly confronted by the menacing spectre of Sasha left totally fatherless. That was the most painful thought of all, and perhaps that was the reason I'd clung so hard to Petrov all this time. I would become a single mother, Sasha would pine for the touch of a man's hand and run away from me. He'd run after anything in trousers, hungry for masculine words, masculine behaviour, and he'd wind up in a gang and be sent to reform school.

I wept in front of Raisa, and she sat frozen in her usual pose on the edge of the divan. She didn't even flinch at the words 'reform school'.

But by morning I'd dried out. All of a sudden I got the feeling that Petrov was just going through one of his routine zigzags, because it wasn't Nadezhda he loved and there'd been nothing bad between us, we hadn't quarrelled or had words – it was only my mother that had quarrelled with him, and my mother after all wasn't me. On my way to work the crazy thought occurred to me of going and talking directly to Nadezhda. But I abandoned the idea. Only the prospect of something better, only some kindness, some real concern for her, could succeed in dislodging her, and what good could I offer her? She'd only just set her sights on Petrov – was she going to give him up voluntarily now? She wouldn't even understand what I was talking about.

But that wasn't the main thing – the main thing was to persuade Petrov to come back to us, if only fictitiously. Let him go where he liked, but Sasha had to see him. But how could I even propose this to Petrov – he wouldn't do it of his own accord, and he wasn't going to do it at my request either.

I went to Raisa and asked her to ring Petrov and have a word with him. Just say hello and how are you doing and we haven't seen you for quite a while, you should drop by for a chat one of these days – something like that, straightforward, unassuming. She agreed. But she sounded kind of scared. Though at the time, I must admit, I didn't really notice.

In the evening I dropped in on Raisa. She was lying on the divan smoking. She said she'd had a talk with Petrov. She said he'd be back tomorrow. That was all she said, and then suddenly, in her usual way, she burst into tears. I brought her a glass of water from the kitchen and rushed off to pick Sasha up from kindergarten.

The following day Petrov returned with his briefcase and the tape recorder. In the briefcase were a couple of shirts and some socks, rolled up in a ball and wrapped in newspaper. The room was clean and cosy and the three of us had breakfast together. Sasha kept tugging at Petrov's newspaper and asking him was this the letter B?

True, the end of the zigzag was not yet in sight. Petrov paid no attention to me and was seldom home. But that was already a good deal better than total absence.

What with one thing and another I didn't have time to drop in on Raisa. And I felt no need to either. Home had swallowed up all my energy. The question of the new apartment was about to be resolved. I rushed about, put in an order for a new three-piece suite, stood for hours in queues for furniture.

Petrov had already started giving me interrogative looks and watching with obvious approval as I flew to and from the kitchen to the room and chatted away to Sasha. Just before supper one day Petrov went out without saying a word and came back home with a bottle of demi-sec champagne.

'Won't you have a drink with me?' he said.

I ran into the kitchen to fetch the tall Czech glasses. We clinked glasses. And I said jokingly:

'To Raisa. Our good fairy.'

And Petrov gave me an ironic smile and said a shade maliciously that all the guys had been quite right, she really was a complete dead loss.

It was only then that I guessed the whole thing and felt a pang that Raisa had betrayed me.

And she ceased to exist for me, just as if she had died.

Seryozha

There's just one thing I can't understand: why did he abandon Nadya? He must have known it would finish her off, and indeed she died just a year after his death. Yet he went and ditched her in the most banal, appalling way, as if to maximise the sense of bombing his life to bits. Actually I've known several boys who've opted to leave a woman that way, just when she'd come to depend on them. These kids aim to penetrate right inside a woman's soul, they'll literally interrogate her on everything, her past, her thoughts, they'll get right inside her consciousness and leave no room for anything that's not connected, one way or another, with their present relationship. The fact that their women nevertheless don't trust them makes these boys feel genuinely miserable – for of course the women in question have learned a thing or two about life as well; they no longer believe in the perfect compatibility of souls. But it always turns out that as time goes on, weakening under the pressure of these boys' continual presence inside their hearts, the women after all start believing in kindred souls, believing that their life has stumbled on some peaceful chapel, some safe, quiet harbour of all-enveloping love. And so they open up their granaries and treasure-houses and, under the boys' intent gaze, start unpacking the entire contents, one thing after another, right down to their dreams and their childhood experiences and their most primitive hopes and fears. And all these things, of course, begin to fade and lose their value the minute they're explained and interpreted and sorted out; they vanish for good from the far corners of memory and lose all meaning once spoken out loud. But strangely enough the woman rejoices, finding recompense now in something quite else – in *his* recollections of childhood, the terrible, mystical tragedy of a boy abandoned in London, for instance, while his diplomat stepfather and his mother, a wife and hostess, went off on numerous trips without him. And now the woman stores up, is forced to store up all *his* experiences – the memory of his first prostitute, and his first whisky and soda, and the way he loathed his stepfather when the latter came back home and demanded a detailed financial statement of what the boy had spent, tortured him over every last penny, and forced him to lie and later caught him out in the fibs he'd extracted from him.

And then comes the finale in this tale of kindred souls, a very simple, crude finale with an additional, incomprehensible tinge of gloating and self-destruction: thus, for example, one fine day Nadya learned from her boyfriend that he was getting married.

After his death I questioned everyone, including Nadya, troubled already at the time by the kidney ailment that was soon going to kill her – and Nadya didn't tell me anything in particular, apart from the fact that she'd been simply knocked out by this announcement of his and by his behaviour, and above all had found the whole thing utterly incomprehensible. And she told me how, just like a little boy, he'd meanly slammed the door behind him, as if determined to renounce his own customary politeness; and that, Nadya said, she just couldn't bear. To cap it all, he'd been holding a huge, beautiful box of chocolates and refused to let go of it, slamming the door as if to emphasise that it was precisely the chocolates that prevented him from closing it properly.

He married Ira a month later. Ira was a friend of mine, and I was a witness at their wedding. I remember how, right up to the last minute, she didn't believe it was going to happen; I held her by the arm as she went up to the table to sign, gripping her tightly by the elbow because she was shaking so violently. She carried on being afraid of him for almost a whole year after they got married. She didn't conceal the fact from me. She said that every attempt she made to establish contact with him ended in failure, for most of the time he just sat there, staring fixedly at one spot and refusing to respond to her appeals, even to an appeal to have a cup of tea. For the whole of that first year she was still amazed that he had married her. But the phrase 'she couldn't believe her happiness' wasn't applicable either. She didn't love him, she hadn't had time to fall in love during the few brief encounters they'd had when they got acquainted. They'd met just three or four times, and she recalled how one day he brought her a huge box of chocolates and then proposed to her. She agreed straight away because, for a start, she was very attracted to him, he was so unusual, and then it's rare for a woman to turn down a proposal issuing from so spirited a man. And perhaps too she felt it was simply time she got married.

So they lived like that for their first year together, but at the end of that year Ira recovered her equilibrium and things between them took a turn for the better. He made no attempt to penetrate her inner world and neither did she; she was an extremely clever woman. There was no spiritual intimacy between them, no intuitive grasp of each others' half-spoken thoughts. And yet they were very happy together, constantly surrounded by friends. Ira turned out to have one magnificent quality – one that had always been there, but only now burst splendidly into flower: she had faith in herself. She never allowed herself to doubt her own value as a person, but confidently revealed herself for all to see, maintaining grace and a sense of proportion in everything she did – in the way she ate, in her conversation. She took entirely seriously each aspect of her being, without in any sense imposing herself on others, for it would never even have occurred to her to try to prove her own significance, or to seek confirmation of it in someone else. She never deigned to put on make-up, and it must be said that she was, by nature, quite unusually plain. But not absurdly so: she was plain in a good, natural, thoroughbred way. Quite by chance, in other words, Seryozha had managed to find himself a perfect companion for life; and perhaps, indeed, there was more to it than chance.

All of us revolved about this couple; it was permanent open house at their home, and we found ourselves talking with them about everything under the sun. Seryozha had spoken several languages ever since he was a child; he was extremely erudite and well-read and spent several evenings every week in the library. He was studying the nineteenth-century Populist Movement, studying for the sake of it, not because of his work – by profession he was just a translator. But he was studying the Russian Populists and sometimes told us things about them, though I didn't take in too much of what he said; there were no anecdotes or juicy titbits, just a straightforward, unleavened account of important events – very dull, on the face of it, and strictly chronological.

But at any rate one sensed that he was studying the Populist Movement for its own sake, not because it would serve some special purpose in the future. Certainly not because he wanted to enrich his inner world, let alone because he was planning to write a book about the Populists. It was just a sort of habit of his, like collecting trinkets or bars of soap.

And that was why we were so enamoured with Seryozha – there was nothing in life that he craved for himself. He wasn't the least bit ambitious or vain, indeed he was painfully lacking in vanity. He was so free of vanity, in fact, that we sensed in him the soul of a great general, who had fallen into disfavour and now squeamishly rejected all petty demonstrations of respect, trivial reminiscences or idle dreams.

He seemed to need nothing at all, except now and then to disappear to the dacha down in the country and pass the time with the old folks living there – Ira's parents, though of course he lived separately from them. Ira couldn't bear going down to the dacha herself and never accompanied Seryozha there.

I realise now that of course he had an incredible influence on us. I can't say much else about myself, because in those days I was quite incapable of self-analysis; at the time I was just an amorphous blob. Of course I had my own dreams and recollections of childhood too, which not a soul had yet sought to encroach upon. I didn't attribute any special significance to them. Even then, when I wasn't on the lookout for anyone – anyone of the kind that might later come to scorn the things I held dear – I rejected all that and never came back to it. Instead I was full of thoughts of Seryozha.

None of us was what you'd call creative. There wasn't

a single artist or poet or actor among us. None of us was even specially talented in matters social or domestic. We never brought anyone to Seryozha's house who could embellish our group just by his presence among us. Somehow all of us sensed instinctively that 'creative' people, so-called, can never be self-sufficient; they demand constant attention. We never discussed questions such as whether art can survive without an audience, without a second point of view, without being properly perused and listened to and judged by the crowd. And none of us felt sorry that Seryozha's great resources of spirit and mind had gone to waste, that they had never been used in any creative sphere. I'd even go so far as to say that the greatness of Seryozha's spirit would simply have faded away and evaporated had he set about writing, for instance, a novel. Seryozha was incapable of exposing himself, naked and defenceless, to the judgement of others. Exposure in itself he would have found quite intolerable.

Indeed I'd say that Seryozha and Ira didn't even live together in the generally accepted sense of the term. And to a certain extent – though to what extent exactly I can't say – this too had to do with his views on creativity, however absurd that might sound. For marriage, too, involves a kind of taken-for-granted shamelessness, consecrated in the subsequent appearance of children.

One day I got a phone call from one of Seryozha's neighbours, a young man who lived in the same communal apartment with his wife and little daughter. In a voice choked with tears he said: 'We've had a terrible misfortune – are you there?'

I immediately burst into tears, realising their little girl must have died; the mere thought of it had always filled me with horror; I loved her to distraction, with a kind of animal love; she was the only child in our circle and Seryozha loved her more than his own life; sometimes he'd go and gaze at her while she was asleep, and he'd sit by her bedside for days on end when she was ill and would have happily sat up all night as well.

'Are you there?' the neighbour asked. 'Our Seryozha has hanged himself. We've just come back from the morgue. Some shepherds brought him back from the dacha, they found him in a wood.'

And there and then, that sunny morning at work, I started rolling about, right in front of everyone, among the desks on the office floor, in the full realisation that I was too late, too late, too late . . .

And it was only afterwards that I started going around all his old acquaintances, and found Nadya and had a long talk with her, and later went and visited her in hospital and buried her a year later. I found out everything there was to know about Seryozha, things that Ira had never known or learned since. Yet it wasn't enough, it was nowhere near enough for me. To this day I still feel what I felt then, that day on the office floor – too late, too late, I left it too late . . .

Words

The first thing I heard him say was, look, there's a girl sitting all by herself, let's join her.

There were two of them, him and another, younger guy, and from the face of the young one, who was sitting opposite me, it was clear he reckoned that he was the one I was interested in. So he was all self-conscious, offhand, biding his time. He behaved as if the whole world was looking at him, at his appearance, his haircut, the shirt he was wearing. Maybe the point was that he had various talents – perhaps he played the accordion, for instance, or was an artist who'd designed the packaging for a souvenir factory; or maybe he had other talents that he was keeping under wraps for the moment, all the better to astonish me later.

The other guy, the older one, probably knew all about these various qualities that the young guy always kept hidden till the moment was ripe, and which he'd only later – for the hundredth time – reveal bit by bit. And it was quite evident that the older guy was already bored with the whole business, because the young guy was incapable of keeping his talents a secret and always did reveal them, so they were no secret or surprise to any of his friends any more; and now the older guy was just waiting for the young one to start all over again, opening himself out bit by bit to me. And the older guy was a wee bit jealous over the other one and, as an opening gambit, asked me: 'What do you think, love, which of us is the younger?'

I said I couldn't tell.

My best friend's always scolding me for bothering to reply to drunks and letting myself get dragged into long conversations. But I can't do anything about it, and not because I think that everyone's equally interesting or that drunks are more sincere than anybody else, nor because I'm short of human intercourse and latch on to anyone that shows me the slightest attention. It all just happens in spite of me. People ask me things and I respond automatically. I feel ashamed for not wanting to answer and wishing I could just stand there as if I hadn't heard the question and hadn't noticed that someone was looking me directly in the face. But even before I've had time to think that I'd rather not get involved in a long conversation, I find myself responding to the very first idle words. People don't usually expect to get an answer right off, and stop short, bewildered, at a loss themselves whether to pursue the conversation or not. For a moment they hesitate, but not for long, because all of a sudden the whole world brightens up for them, becomes what it should be, and they suddenly feel all good about themselves as well. So they start explaining at length that of course they'd meant no harm at all to a nice young girl; they twist themselves in knots, trying to explain and understand the sense of something which only a minute ago was quite clear – that you mustn't offend a young girl; but why? For suddenly they're aware of the full enormity of the question, they struggle to answer it, for they've lost track of the basic principle – the common sense principle that forbids you to address a stranger in the street without some easily explicable excuse. And that excuse, precisely, is what they lack; they'd initiated the conversation just like that, to be sociable, and now they have to try and get out of it as best they can. And because of this they feel awfully guilty – for having started up a conversation for no good reason and then, unexpectedly, got a response, so that now they're obliged to justify themselves and apologise and explain why they'd started talking in the first place.

These two, the young guy and the older one, were just slightly tipsy. But the older one didn't feel any need to explain why he'd got talking to me. We'd already struck up an acquaintance, in the easy, straightforward way that travellers do. And while the young guy, fastened with both hands to his seat, his head hunched into his shoulders, stared out of the carriage window, the older one was chatting cheerfully away. I liked him immediately. Liked not in the sense that young girls say: 'I like him as a person', but in a light-hearted, cheerful, untroubled way.

It was obvious that he wasn't the least bit concerned what kind of person I was, but was simply talking straight from the heart. Naturally he observed what I was wearing and how I'd done my hair and how I talked, but none of this mattered to him, just as it's never mattered to me how I look. I've always left my appearance to take care of itself, I don't go thinking of it every other minute. And nor did he, I'm convinced of that. Perhaps because the whole thing was so clearly delineated: we were simply having a light-hearted conversation in a train. And that was all. The difference between us was too great. He told me straight away that he was a carpenter and a joiner and a fully-qualified fitter and that he'd fixed everything in his apartment himself – the kitchen fittings, the standard lamp, the shelves.

262

He told me that he'd been married, but his wife had died of a heart attack in childbirth.

I didn't ask him anything myself. Not because I was afraid that he wouldn't answer. After all, people sometimes fail to answer questions just because they've been asked and they suddenly realise that their secrets, which no one ever needed before, have suddenly become true secrets and need to be kept.

But I wasn't afraid that he wouldn't answer my questions. Everything was so simple and open with him. I didn't ask him questions – I told him all about my daughter, and he told me about his child, who'd got cut in the course of the Caesarian and was never therefore born. I told him how my little girl was staying at a dacha in a village far away, four hours altogether on two different trains, and then a further seven miles on foot or hitching.

I told him how last summer I'd gone to work just one day a week and was therefore able to spend the whole summer with my daughter. And then I'd moved to a different institute, and there I had to be at work two days a week, and now my daughter was living in the country with someone else's granny, from my brother-in-law's family, all alone there at the age of four.

He told me that he'd lived alone ever since then and that his wife had died in his arms: he was present in the labour room when she was giving birth.

And I told him that every time I left my daughter, setting off on foot to catch the three o'clock bus, setting out alone across the field to leave her for four whole days, going the long way round to avoid the ravine that I'm afraid to cross – every time I found myself vividly imagining that when I got back to the city a war would break out and my daughter would be left stranded alone in the country.

It didn't matter in the least that he was lying while I was telling him the truth. I like it when people lie about themselves, I'm perfectly willing to meet them halfway and welcome and accept what they say as pure fact, because after all it could quite easily turn out to be true. It never affects my relationship with a person. It's much easier and much nicer to accept a person in the light they want to present themselves in. I never try to construct things from the fragments of truth that sometimes filter through or suddenly burst out of them. I prefer just to let be.

He told me that lots of twenty-year-old girls latched on to him, but it wasn't the same thing at all, and the fact that he had a two-room apartment had a good deal to do with it anyway. And he never felt the same with any of these girls as he did with his wife.

Meanwhile the young guy kept on getting up and wandering off and sitting down again, and I began to get the feeling that they were travelling with someone else, that there was a whole bunch of them in the carriage. So when another one came along, sat down on the empty seat opposite the young guy and immediately started chatting to me, I got into conversation with him as well. But though I was thoroughly wrapped up in the conversation by then, I couldn't help noticing that his style was completely different from the other guy's, the first's.

He wasn't open and sincere and unimportunate like the first man had been. The first one, the older guy, hadn't asked me anything, he wasn't interested in me in this crude, heavy-handed, pressing way.

But this guy, the one that had just sat down, immediately seized on something I'd said and kept repeating it, shaking his head and saying 'Well I'll be damned'. And then he said: 'I'm looking at you and thinking: what a nice girl, I wonder if she's got anyone back home?' And then the blockhead started saying other things and chuckling. I should have cut him dead straight away and refused to talk.

But he went on and on, and the other two kept quiet and all of a sudden the older one lit up and offered a light to the younger and the two of them started smoking right there in the carriage.

And then something terrible happened. Everyone suddenly turned on them, the whole carriage started shouting. Especially the men. And it was obvious that the smoking was just an excuse, a pretext, that they'd been dying for ages to give them a piece of their mind. And then I went and said to the two of them, 'Maybe they're right, though, you shouldn't be smoking here?'

Whereupon they both got up and went out, and I never saw them again. And that fathead went on bothering me for the whole of the rest of the journey.

Maybe they just went and had a smoke in the gap between carriages, or maybe they moved to a different carriage or got out altogether at one or other of the stations.

But I was left with the feeling that I'd violated some basic law, done something that you should never do.

A Guest

In the end I went ahead and invited this Tolya home, charming Tolya, already getting flabby in the jowls, and I said to him: 'Tolya, why are you looking so old already? Why have you started ageing so soon? Do you remember how enchanting you were when you were young?'

We did everything properly, with music and candle-light, and by morning just a burned-out wick remained in the candlestick. Tolya, as always, tedious to a degree, embarked in great detail on some long-winded tale. He opened the bottle; I brought fried potatoes in from the kitchen. He helped himself leisurely to this and that, pronged a few more mushrooms, sat back in his chair with his hands in his lap, then poured us each a full glass of beer to drink on the side.

The whole enterprise was mad from the start, of course – drinking beer with vodka. But for some reason I paid no great heed to it, I was past caring that evening. Or maybe, on the contrary, that was the thing I paid heed to most. At all events, there we were alone, the neighbours could think what the hell they liked in the morning, especially since the whole thing ended so unbelievably, but that didn't worry me either, and still doesn't.

To cut a long story short, Tolya related his long-winded tale, talking complete drivel in his nice tender voice, although he has extraordinarily fine taste and knows just how to respond to things. But he always goes on and on so long, so tediously, agonising over the same old thing – that he's a lost soul, he's lost the thread of life, nothing really gets to him any more, nothing at all, every now and then he makes up his mind to fling himself into action, accomplish something, experience new things, go to extremes, but he always ends up just as indifferent as before.

'Tolya,' I say to him, 'Haven't you ever wanted simple joy and happiness? Is there really nothing of the pagan in you, the worshipper of earth and sky?'

'No, suffering's what I want, I'd just like to suffer, I'm incapable of enjoying things, honest to God, completely incapable.'

'But Tolya,' I say, 'what about those endless parties you go to, your girlfriends' birthdays and all those other dos? Don't they at least provide some entertainment? Of course I know what you mean. But still you should let the pagan come out in you now and then, bow down to the earth and all its joys, to wine . . .'

'No,' says Tolya, warming to the theme, 'all that happens is I wind up having to get a taxi home, and it's a sheer waste of nervous energy having to ask Mother for the money night after night.'

'But what about your music, your concerts?'

'What about them?' says Tolya pensively. 'Coming home all aglow, like our old Liza? If Mother beats her up, gives her a scolding or chases her out of the kitchen, off she goes to church and comes back all radiant, absolved. That's the reason I'm so weird,' says Tolya. 'That Mother gave birth to me when she was forty years old, and Father fifty.'

'So you mean the point is they loved and spoiled you too much?'

'No,' says Tolya, 'I don't think that's it.'

And he starts explaining at tedious length how dreadfully the secret of a person's birth can weigh on him.

'But Tolya,' I say, after this long, boring account of how a man's fate gets determined even before he's born, 'why do you go on ringing me up? You keep ringing and ringing. Sometimes when I pick up the phone you must sense, don't you, the way I'm talking to you, how uneasy the whole thing makes me? I simply can't work out why you need me. Even when it's me ringing you I can't understand why I'm doing it. Every time I hesitate before I pick up the phone, but every single time I find myself willy-nilly dialling your number without knowing why and then having these forced conversations with no redeeming purpose whatsoever. And you probably have exactly the same feeling, that you don't know why I've gone and phoned you again, and you spend ages ruminating over it, and can't make head or tail of it, but after a while there it is, you find yourself picking up the phone and ringing me again. So why do you do it, Tolya, go on, tell me? I'm sure you've no idea why. But tell me frankly. We've got nothing to hide and no reason to hide things, you and I.'

'I like you. Why do you ring me?'

'I want to understand you. All these words of yours go right past me, somehow, I don't connect them at all with you, with the enchanting image I have of you. Sometimes I have the feeling I've reached out a hand to touch you and it just goes right through you, right through your breast. Do you understand what I mean? You're somehow insubstantial, incorporeal, or maybe that's just my impression, maybe I'm wrong, but I get more and more convinced I'm right.'

'But you seem to dwell in the Elysian fields yourself.'

'In what sense, Tolya? What do you mean, the Elysian fields? You mean I'm a kind of heavenly spirit? Or what? I've got exactly that sensation again, that if I were to reach out and touch you my hand would go in one side and out the other. If I reach out and touch you now all I'll touch is the back of your chair.'

Tolya just shrugs and drinks his beer.

'Listen, Tolya, I'm getting the same feeling that comes over me every time I pick up the telephone to ring you. What's this all about? It's somehow strained and unnatural, don't you feel that too? Why do you ring me up, why have you come here tonight and why have I been making fried potatoes and had my hair done? And why did you go and buy vodka and then beer as well, what was the point of the beer? How can one drink beer with vodka? What for? What have you got to say to that, eh, Tolya? What was the point of the beer?'

'To drink on the side. It's the done thing.'

'And then what?'

'How d'you mean – then what?'

'I mean we'll drink vodka with beer, and eat fried potatoes, and then what? I don't mean what steps ought we to take and what sort of future do the two of us have, but just that: what then? What happens next? OK, all right then, tell me about your work, how things are going – I know nothing about you. How do things stand at work? Don't go all coy on me, for heaven's sake, we can't have any secrets from one another, there's nothing between us. People who have nothing between them, like you and me, or strangers on a train, or patients in a hospital ward, can't have secrets from one another. We've got no vested interest in one another, have we now, Tolya? Come on, agree! If you're going to start sulking on me I'm going to send you straight home. But I'm right, aren't I, we've got no vested interest in one another, have we? Come on, now, have we?'

'Why do you say I'm sulking? I'm listening to you. I'll say it again: I like you. Let's drink to it: what a feast, what vodka, what mushrooms!'

'You are a bit of a pagan, really, aren't you, Tolya, own up! I've sussed you out, you see, haven't I, even though I don't know the first thing about you. Do you enjoy your work? How much do you earn? Do they pay you good money over there at your place?'

'We get between a hundred and a hundred fifty.'

'But you yourself? How much do you get? I want to know all about you!'

'At the moment I just get ninety, but I have two days off. Though when I say off I mean I just take a whole bunch of files home with me and warn the boss I'm going to be working at home. A couple of days later I bring the whole lot back in to work.'

'God almighty, let's drink, Tolya! Pour me some beer as well, what the hell.'

'It's a pretty nice set-up I've got myself there. To all intents and purposes I just have to be there three days a week.'

'Your health, Tolya! I bet you were incredibly charming when you were eighteen. Even a year ago your hair was a completely different colour, you've gone darker now, but your hair was beautiful then, such an unusual colour.'

'When I was eighteen,' says Tolya, throwing back his head and staring at the candle from afar. 'Well, I don't remember anything from when I was eighteen, I've got nothing stored away in my memory, I was wholly absorbed in growing up sexually.'

'This is fascinating, Tolya! A new note's creeping into your conversation, it must be this beer you're so bent on mixing with vodka. Well, never mind. What happened when you were eighteen? Later on, I heard, you got married and then divorced. People shouldn't get divorced, it's so incredibly painful.'

'No, no, there was nothing of the sort in our case. It was just a marriage of convenience. My wife had to get herself properly established here, she needed her little girl to have a surname and all the rest of it.'

'What about you, though, what was in it for you? What was the advantage from your point of view – what was the point of marrying a woman with a child? Did you feel it lent you a certain *gravitas*? I must admit I can't understand you there. Now don't clam up on me, explain yourself, I'm a friend. You conceal everything from me, and that's not good. You used to be so charming, if it weren't for those jowls of yours – you shouldn't drink so much, Tolya! It ages you, and you should be eternally youthful, like Eros!'

'If you'll excuse me, I'll just lie down for a minute', was Tolya's reply to all this, and he lay down on the couch and slept until nine o'clock in the morning. I cleared everything away and sat there by candlelight, like someone out of the nineteenth century, then I fetched my pyjamas from under Tolya's head, from under the pillow, and settled down for the night on the camp bed; luckily I'd put all the bedding away in the cupboard.

Once during the night Tolya jumped up and muttered, quick as a flash, 'There used to be an exit in this room, and now there's no exit.'

'What's up, Tolya?' I asked, 'What's the matter with you?' He sat fully-dressed on the couch, all yellow in the candlelight, and then said: 'Just a second' – and again collapsed, and woke up at nine o'clock in the morning as if nothing untoward had happened at all.

By that time I was already drinking tea in the kitchen – for some reason I felt like a cup of tea – and thinking what an idiotic position this Tolya had put me in *vis-à-vis* the neighbours. Tolya woke up quite unperturbed, had a cup of tea with me and sat there until midday, and again he went on and on, at tedious length, about how, in his consciousness, he'd lost all track of time; and then he related the plot of a film that I hadn't yet seen, and finally he bade me farewell and departed.

And all I got out of it all was a headache.

Weak Bones

'But Ravshan, kindly tell me what I'm to do with her?'

'I promised her. Just five minutes more.'

'Just landing on me like this. What on earth do you want with her?'

'Please, let's just wait five minutes more.'

'A shady customer, no doubt. She's probably a journalist.'

At last she appeared and, as it turned out, she was indeed a journalist in short, wide pantaloons, 'pure cotton', to be precise, as she later explained modestly; pure cotton with mauve flowers on a grey background, unbelievable stuff, the trousers barely reaching her ankles, and then a pair of white shoes like you'd wear in a coffin – but what aplomb! She pranced about on tiptoes like a little she-goat, coming out of the Hotel Intourist to meet her fate and her doom, that's to say, to meet Ravshan and me.

'I was just saying to Ravshan here,' I said, 'why the hell have you gone and landed on us, straight out of the clear blue sky? What are you, a journalist?'

'You've a keen eye,' she said, flustered. 'How could you tell straight off?'

She was quite bowled over. I said:

'Where are you from? What paper?'

'Not a newspaper, a magazine. *Your View*. Is that all right by you?'

'I know the one. On Polevaya Street.'

'You *have* got a keen eye! You got the whole thing in one.'

'I can tell a journalist a mile off. What section do you write for?'

'Foreign.'

'I see,' I said, thinking meanwhile that I hadn't heard of anyone working there and wondering what kind of section 'foreign' might be, but you could imagine the scene – her doing interviews and going round with foreigners, that's why she had a sort of foreign look to her, the sort of air, that is, that foreign females affect when they cast off their chains and cross through the iron curtain, there to represent, beyond the curtain, a picture of gilded youth, laughing uproariously, chatting away, walking round without bras and reacting with indignation when black marketeers waylay them of an evening as they enter their hotels and address them, out of the corner of their mouths, in gross, coarse voices, asking, however, not what you might expect, but:

'Jeans, huh? Huh, jeans?'

'No, non, nein.'

'Nicht,' these unsavoury types repeat. 'Jeans, huh?'

That was just the sort she was. Dozens of enamel bracelets on her arms for a start. And red hair, bright red in places (obviously going grey beneath the henna), plaited into two loose braids that were coming undone, one tied with a bit of red cord, the other with something else. Iridescent, dioptric glasses, tiny little eyes beneath huge lenses, and her face, when she turned her head, all creased into wrinkles at the neck, yet scattered with childish freckles all over. Such a contradiction.

'Redheads,' she said, 'redheads always have this and that,' she explained, 'It's always the way, haven't you noticed? With that keen eye of yours?'

'How should I know that you're a redhead?'

She giggled uneasily, obviously stung that anyone should notice she'd dyed her hair.

You're pretty transparent, my darling, you can tell the lot at first glance.

'And why have you gone and dolled yourself up like that?'

'It's pure cotton,' she explained. 'Not Soviet, of course. I mostly wear non-Soviet stuff.'

Picked up cut-price, no doubt, at discount stores.

There was a pause.

'My dream is to find a proper dressmaker!' she exclaimed. 'A nice girl who could do things just the way I want.'

This ludicrous journalist, with her enormous glasses and her freckles and her plaits and her red hair and her mauve bloomers and her little white shoes looked twenty-five, thirty at most – but her wrinkles! She looked ravaged, exhausted – there's an illness that does that, atrophy of the muscles; obviously that's what she had. Nothing to be done about it! Someone told me once about a similar case, a fellow who looked like an old, old man when he was forty years old, in the prime of manhood. I have a dream-like recollection of seeing this fellow – maybe for real, or perhaps it was a dream. To continue, I pointed out:

'None of your stuff would have a designer label, though, would it, with this little dressmaker of yours. It'd all look homemade.'

'What?'

'I mean, no one wears homemade things these days.'

'Oh, I'd design everything myself, I'd definitely wear my own designs. I'm very fussy about clothes. I've got a friend who makes stuff; she's dear, of course, but then Dior's dear too.'

'You mean you wear Dior?'

'Oh, I've got the odd piece from Dior.'

She's lying. I have the feeling the whole thing's a pack of lies. She hasn't got a stitch from Dior. It doesn't add up – her with her mauve bloomers.

Ravshan meanwhile hasn't said a thing. He joins in only when we pass through the arched gateway to the ancient city of Kaza, over a roadway built with precious stones. Children yell; the street's barely an arm's length wide. And everywhere, pipes; civilisation, in the form of gas, has overlaid the whole lot.

Now that artful little trickster draws Ravshan in as well. She twitters:

'But what about you now, own up, would you really go and kill your wife if she was unfaithful?'

'Me? Of course I would!' says Ravshan stoutly, and I believe him. He never ever lies, he's not that sort of person, it's written all over him.

He and I had spent four hours together; it was arranged that he should accompany me back to the hotel after the lecture. He carried my bouquet around the town, and everyone responded to his traditional greeting: 'How's your health, how's your mother?', shouting back:

'Congratulations!'

Meaning me, of course – his escorting me round with a bouquet of flowers. They all roared with laughter. Ravshan shrugged it off with a joke; he was very tactful.

He'd brought me back to the hotel so that he could take me on a tour round the town afterwards; and it was there, in the vestibule, that this journalist latched on to us. She said her name was Lionella – it had to be something fancy, of course, though she was probably lying about that as well. But you should have seen her! A typical foreigner; she was wearing some other outfit then, not the mauve pantaloons – I don't remember exactly what; not the white shoes at any rate. Jeans, probably. And I had jeans on too. Snap! She kept blinking and nodding in such a friendly way at the two of us as we stood there discussing my trip to Klych the next day.

'Klych? I'm going to Klych too. And Safi, right? Are you going to Safi?'

'Yes, yes, Safi,' I said cordially, taking her for a foreign visitor and responding accordingly – somehow not quite as I would to 'one of ours', but with a touch of servility. I tried to say as little as possible myself; it's an automatic reflex now, something I've learned on my wanderings round hotels – the less you say, the greater the chance of being made 'legitimate', taken as a foreigner by others. Which means the waiters will serve you till eleven o'clock in the morning, along with the other foreigners, and any passing driver will be honoured to give you a free lift, and traders at the bazaar will invite you to try a slice of melon, offering you a knife to cut it yourself.

So 'Safi', I said, automatically declining to expand on the subject further.

My ruse had evidently worked: she seemed over-joyed at having picked up a foreigner for a travelling companion, and she immediately launched freely (since I was a foreigner) into explaining, in Russian, which flight to catch and when you had to get up, and at this point Ravshan promised to get a car at six in the morning to take us to the airport. In short I'd barely uttered two words before she'd latched on to me and arranged to go with me to Safi. Via Klych. Fine. Ravshan would wait for us down here; I ran up to my room to use the bathroom, take a shower and change – and on coming down found Ravshan standing there, steadfast as a donkey, determined to wait a further five minutes for this Adelailina.

'But Ravshan, kindly explain what I'm supposed to do with her. She's just landed on me. She makes me feel quite ill. What did she say her name was, Emerald? I can't stand people like that more than five minutes at a stretch.'

'Just five minutes more,' says Ravshan, smiling firmly. 'I promised her.'

'Bloody journalist. You'll see, I bet she's a journalist.'

Ravshan shakes his head. An impenetrable smile plays about his lips. He's determined to wait. So I wait too. At last she flutters out; she's changed her shoes, and for lack of high heels trips about on tiptoe, evidently meaning to make an impact. She's obviously spent ages thinking what to wear, and eventually settled on this ludicrous pure cotton number. We then embark on the conversation already related, about my powers of observation and her, Iraidina's, work in the foreign section. We walk into town; dusk is already falling above the clay-built cubes and cupolas and walls, the stone roadway beneath which, one senses, yawns a deep, empty vault. The conversation turns to how Moslems bury their dead. Ravshan explains, talking in great detail about the wailing of relatives, about how they wrap the body in a shroud and lower it into the grave, slipping it on its side into a pit that's been specially opened out at the bottom, a sort of cave, where there's plenty of space above the corpse's head.

After explaining all this, Ravshan mildly criticises the old women's wailing, says it's unbearable to listen to when they wail at home. I suddenly recall that Ravshan's father died two years ago, he'd told me so; and the father for them is the holy of holies. The father and the children. Especially the boys.

'But still, Ravshan, you surely wouldn't kill her if you knew that someone could be executed or sentenced to years in prison for murdering his wife?'

'Me? No, I'd kill her,' says Ravshan, who isn't yet married, but already knows his bride and the whole course of his life ahead. 'You know,' says Ravshan, 'When I come home in the evening I just collapse. I fall straight asleep.'

He wants to change the subject abruptly – wants to tell us all about himself, enjoying being indulged and spoiled with attention. He's sensed our trust in him.

'Don't you even eat supper?' I ask.

'No, I eat supper and then I seem to collapse.'

'You don't even get undressed?'

'No, I eat supper and get undressed and then I collapse.'

'Well, and so what?'

'It happens immediately. I fall asleep on the spot. I don't dream at all, not a single dream. That's very bad. I'm on my feet all day never feeling the least bit tired, and then I collapse and don't dream at all.'

'You should ask someone to watch you when you're asleep,' I say, 'to see if your eyeballs move at all. If they do there's nothing wrong with you, it's just that you don't remember your dreams.'

'You're probably right,' says Ravshan, who works for the 'Society of Knowledge'.

End of story. We've exhausted the theme. Adelaida

with her poor skin is shining in the darkness for Ravshan, she wants to take flight, to dance. Now she's walking along the parapet above the canal.

'I always wanted to be a ballerina,' she says, dancing on the parapet. Ravshan's there beside her already, holding her hand. 'If I'd been a ballerina,' she informs us, 'I'd have danced a belly dance in the harem. What d'you think, Ravshan, would I have done all right in a harem?'

Ravshan wants to say something, but I interrupt:

'I was just reading about a young woman, twenty-four years old, who had the highest IQ in the world, something like a hundred and eighty-six. Einstein had an IQ of a hundred and seventy-five, and she had a hundred and eighty-six. She had a doctorate in physics and philosophy, and then she went and chucked it all in and became a belly dancer in a tavern.'

'That's me all over,' says our Semiramida, and Ravshan grips her tightly by the hand. Then he leads us somewhere deep into the town, away from the canal; we climb up onto the roof of the Chor-Minor mosque with its four minarets, lighting our way with torches of newspaper, climbing the dark stairway and revelling in it like kids. Ravshan supports the two of us in turn; he's my companion, but Adelina's unofficial knight in arms. Now he's got me by the elbow as well, he's really letting himself go. He buys us a melon in the bazaar, where everyone's already packing up for the night; we feel like part of the family here. The traders are bedding down in their stalls, and the tower of death stands over the bazaar, half-lit by a lamp in the far corner; and beyond lies darkness, the starlight and the dark silhouette of the tower reaching up to the sky. A chill enters my soul.

'My heart's stopped beating,' says that little aminoacid, devouring everything that rightly belongs to me. 'Is this me or not me? I can't tell any more. What a lovely warm night!'

'Bloody journalist, what a load of crap!' I say. They both laugh, their hearts quite melting.

At this point our Solomonida gives us a whole performance; with her thin little hands and her little white shoes, slapping her thighs, she's inspired, ecstatic. Ravshan's inspired too; he laughs and chatters away; he's completely forgotten about me. He keeps pressing Salome with questions: shouldn't we drop in, he says, at the all-night bar in the hotel? And, suddenly business-like, she replies:

'If you had some foreign currency on you, by all means. Everything's sold for foreign currency there.'

And Ravshan sobers up. Not everything's possible. He understands.

By now we're already heading homewards.

'Let's go, let's go, let's go right up to the top floor, to the roof, to look at the lights of Kaza at night,' says she. I won't go with them, they've no need of me. She's got a room of her own – she's paid double to have it all to herself. Let them sort themselves out together there.

Who is she? She doesn't work on a magazine, that's for sure. We're into a totally different ball game here. Women like that, on magazines, don't deal in this sort of shady business. She's probably just a stray bitch who runs the odd errand. Here she's posing as a foreign tourist, the type who sits at home saving and saving and then, tra-la-la, goes skipping off abroad, astonishing the natives by swanning round in public in her fancy pants and T-shirt with no bra.

She's lying through her teeth; all she does is pick up the odd Ravshan in passing. Home's completely empty, a total void; she hasn't a thing there, no clothes, no children, no man; she's just packed all her belongings into two big suitcases and fixed herself a holiday out of sheer ennui. She keeps talking dates – says she's got to be home by the eighteenth, but for whose sake I wonder? She said she hadn't planned to travel alone, that's why she's got the two cases, someone let her down and failed to come. It would be a crime *not* to stand up a woman like that, she'd force you into it. She's easy game, with her baggy skin and weak bones. She's got her eyes wide open, takes what comes; 'I'll do all right for myself,' she says, 'so long as there are brunettes in the world.' In actual fact she isn't quite as simple as she makes herself out to be; it's just the game she's playing here. Her illness is the only genuine thing about her. Where did she pick it up, this weakness of hers, this atrophied look? She must be thirty, not more, and in fact it's only the skin that makes her look thirty, otherwise she'd be no more than twenty-five. Awful to have a disease like that. When she tilted her head so elegantly that time her chin all crumpled into little folds. Totally done for but still prancing about.

'I can't bear a night without sleep, I'm completely done in. Ravshan was so passionate,' she said afterwards, when we were already in Klych. We'd flown there after a sleepless night, leaving Ravshan behind, and there we were in the main square, not knowing what to do with ourselves; we couldn't get a hotel room. I had no public appearance scheduled here, no one to escort me; I'd gone to Safi just like that – how could you go to Kaza and not visit Safi! The two of us tried to talk the hotel administrator into giving us a room; while I stood in the corridor my Iraida tried to impress her, muttering 'KGB, KGB', whereupon the administrator had shrieked at her to get off staff premises this instant, she still had thirty tourists to find rooms for.

'That's not the way it's done,' I said to Iraiada. 'The administrators can't decide anything themselves. You have to talk to the management.'

'I rang the management but they're all out at lunch. Let's take a stroll and wait a bit.'

We wander round the cold streets of Klych and out there in the open discuss the question of my Adelina's identity. I keep trying to flush her out of hiding, she keeps darting away.

'I can't make the whole thing out. You don't work for a magazine.'

'I'm freelance. I just mentioned the magazine that publishes me most often, that's all.'

So that's how it is. We walk on a bit further.

'And what's all this about the KGB? Do you work for them?'

'You have to know how to make connections. A friend of a friend of mine is an agent here.'

'You mean a KGB man?'

'They call them agents here. You get passed on from one local office to another. From Kazmanda to Kaza and from Kaza to here.'

'But why the KGB?'

'Like I said, you've got to know how to make friends with people from all walks of life. I don't have a regular job. I'm a linguist, I know the lingo. I'm still just a young journalist.'

'But tell me now, do you have an apartment?'

'We've just had one built, a condominium. But it's small, just twenty-seven square metres.'

'Do you live alone?'

'No, with my husband.'

She puts up humbly with my interrogation, I've no idea why. No resistance at all.

'It's not that small for just the two of you.'

'But there's all the books and everything to fit in. And then what if we decided to have ourselves a little baby?'

'Well then it's a different matter, of course.'

She leaves me waiting outside the offices of the local newspaper and in due course returns with a hotel room fixed, in a complete dump, it's true, like a great big stable. Each stall is forty metres high. The sheets smell of clay; they're all grey and crumpled.

'The sheets are dirty, aren't they?' she asks.

'They're clean,' says the old woman with the key, the chambermaid.

'But look, they're dirty, see? Can you change them, please.'

'The matron'll be here after lunch.'

Never mind, our Queen of Sheba has managed to fix something up, though it's all baloney anyway, no way I'm going to stay here in this room.

Later we try and get ourselves a lift to Safi. She fixes a pair of dark glasses over the rainbow ones, stands with one foot in the road, right there on the highway, and snaps her fingers right under the drivers' noses.

They take no notice.

'That's strange,' says she.

The cars whip by – zip, zip. I'm just an observer – an observer only. The drivers don't even see us, they don't so much as look in our direction. An extraordinary spectacle – those red plaits and glasses – and they don't even bother to look. Look, look! She stretches her hand out, clicks her fingers.

'Very strange.'

At last we get our lift to Safi. What with this and that, all our dawdling about at the hotel, it's three o'clock by the time we get there. Safi's completely deserted, there are no buses standing outside the gates of the fortress, the little alleys twist and turn and there's no knowing where to start. I want to go to the bazaar, I'm interested in seeing the plates and vessels and pottery, stuff like that. She starts preaching:

'I prefer the spiritual over the material, if you understand me – the spi-ri-tual. I've always been like that. We should at least go to the museum.'

It's pure torture going round with her. You have to be alone to look at things, alone; then everything belongs to you, you can commune with things, reflect on them, fantasise, but with her alongside you don't even want to look about; everything feels wrong, classically wrong, she keeps self-importantly explaining about mosques and madrasahs, using tons of technical terms, and I can't stand technical terms, I can't stand experts, all those technicalities belong to them, whereas something quite different belongs to me. I have my private world. And I'm jealous over everything with everyone and everyone with everything.

So she and I drag ourselves round the museum, look at a life-size model of a cell with a papier-mâché scholar sitting there inside it, and a similar model of a trader sitting in his life-size shop, except this one's head has somehow got crumpled.

OK, I've had it, enough's enough.

'Kindergarten stuff,' said I, and quietly, quietly, just slipped away. I ran through Safi, turned one corner, then another. And I never saw my Gretchen again. It quickly grew dark in Safi, the clouds hung low, I got out of the fortress and on to the main road, where a taxi-driver immediately stopped and flung open the door. And offered to give me a lift for free. I seated myself in his filthy taxi, we set off, and then he had a new proposal to make – we'd just make a detour for an hour or so. Have a bit of fun, as he put it. Then he'd take me to Klych for nothing. 'I've been in your part of the world, the women there are so lovely, so open,' he said sweetly as the taxi rolled down the deserted highway. 'They'll do anything. Shall we have a bit of fun together?'

I replied that at six roubles – all he'd miss out on by way of a fare – he was asking for some pretty cheap fun, and ordered him to stop. He turned off the meter, refused to take my money, and I jumped out on to the road.

Then a bus turned up. I was alone and free, and the whole way home the passengers, all five of them, engaged in animated conversation. There were two gypsy beauties on board, the sort of gypsies you find in the desert, beggars wearing glass bracelets with magical properties and braids of black ribbon fixed on to their hair; and with the help of a Russian woman they answered my questions about how many children they had; and – again through the translator, who joined in the merriment – they guessed my age to be twenty-five, just like in the good old days. The only thing was, they said, I needed to let my hair grow; it was cut too short. In other words, in Gretchen's absence I passed the time quite happily. My soul was open to the desert all around, to the tiny gypsy baby and his mother, as beautiful as Sophia Loren in her youth – the same serene, dark, heavenly looks – sitting there chewing endlessly on the flat, unleavened bread of the region, *lepeshka*, nibbling bits of it, like a child, not from her fingertips but from her palm, from somewhere near her wrist. I felt in fine spirits, like the great explorer Miklukho-Maklay when he was alone with the natives in New Guinea. I could understand him. My gypsies were very poor, the driver had let them ride for free. They'd been to Safi to collect their *lepeshki*; they'd gathered up a whole kerchief full of dry crusts and bits. The younger gypsy sat and ate in silence, but the other kept on smiling at us, kindly, indulgently, showing her dark teeth and gums, and now and then responded to our questions. What bliss! Everyone loved and respected me, and I loved everyone and treasured each little gem.

I arrived in this caravanserai when it was already getting dark in Klych, and she still wasn't there; I was told that she hadn't yet come back. I spent a long time packing my things, preparing for the night flight back; I wrapped and packed up the brass jugs and earthenware dishes, the books and all the bric-à-brac I'd collected, some tiles and whatnot that were no use to anyone. I turned out to have far too many things, and by the time I'd packed everything night had fallen. She still wasn't back. There were no street lamps outside; fortunately, a passerby helped me to get to the bus and told me on no account to take a taxi, let alone hitch a lift. It was very dangerous. People disappeared.

All around was the deep, silent night. I kept hoping that Aida would somehow catch up with me, but it was very unlikely she would. After all I'd seen her passport. The receptionist at the hotel gave it back to me by mistake instead of mine. I looked in her passport and shuddered, seeing how old she was, even older than me, so that her baggy skin was the result of age, and her journey, it seemed, was on account of her age too; and those two incredibly heavy suitcases, no doubt, contained all she had; it wasn't accidental that she was dragging them round with her; it wasn't accidental that she had talked of a baby, about some future child that she could no longer have. And all her hotel rooms, and her little tricks, and her sleepless night with Ravshan, after which even passing drivers recoiled from her – all these too were the result of age. Or maybe not just her age. There are, no doubt, many reasons why a person may end up trailing round the wide world, latching on to everyone, adapting to everyone, expecting friendship and love from everyone, always hoping for something. But so long as there were brunettes on this earth, my Gretchen would survive; I do believe that; she couldn't just perish for so trivial a reason as that I'd abandoned her alone in some sinister little town. She would have to find a way out. True, her swindler's enthusiasm could let her down; and so, especially, could her weak bones. So that I could very well turn out to be the very last stone on her road, the one from which she set sail to eternity. But why me after all? It could have been anyone, literally anyone . . .

Night

From the outside it might have seemed there was no night at all – none of those wonderful night-time hours when everything gets going, unfolding so slowly, smoothly and majestically, with great expectations and premonitions of something supreme, and the longest, most total darkness in the world – precisely that sort of night, it might have seemed, didn't happen at all; everything was so compressed and confused and consisted of constantly changing periods of waiting and preparations for the main thing to come – and, in that sense, those precious hours of night just came and went, until in due course the revellers, expelled from someone's house, set forth in three taxis to someone else's; thence to scatter as well, as if scared away, and fly off ahead of time to their respective homes, before day had yet dawned, with the one and only thought of catching some sleep before they had to go to work, before they had to get up at seven. And it was that argument, the argument that they had to be up at seven, which after all proved decisive in the general uproar accompanying the expulsion of the revellers from house number one, where they'd gathered together from eight in the evening onwards to celebrate a great event – the successful defence of a doctoral dissertation by Ramazan, he being the oppressed father of two small children.

In that sense it wasn't entirely true that what dispersed the party was merely people's wish to get some sleep before they had to rise at seven – that consideration, recurring frequently in the general uproar raised by Ramazan's relatives, touched no one at all; nor did it lodge in people's subconscious, later to emerge from the depths and dispel the cosy crowd, who all night long had stuck together so valiantly, setting off in three taxis to find shelter elsewhere when they were expelled from the first respectable home; no, this consideration about getting up at seven would not have stopped any of them, especially since at that particular moment, when Ramazan's relatives kept repeating it over and over, it sounded hilarious, ridiculous and hopeless; it smacked of old age and approaching death, the desire above all to go to sleep and rest; and all the revellers were full of hope and a childish eagerness to go storming about and whooping it up all night, talking and dancing and drinking till dawn at least.

It was this desire of theirs that, naturally enough, aroused some opposition on the part of Ramazan's relatives, forced to receive the dreadful rabble in their home, among them several drunken individuals whom they had never set eyes on before, so that the head of the household was obliged to limit the quantity of spirits offered at the table, and keep personal guard over several bottles of especially powerful stuff, offering just a glassful here and there to selected guests who had not yet managed to get themselves drunk.

Meanwhile Ramazan kept swearing helplessly and wailing about one Pankov who, just the day before, had gone on a bender all night long and done what the hell he wanted to celebrate *his* dissertation, and no one had said a word to him, because it was *his* night, see? His night. And Ramazan's wife, the quiet and doleful Ira, sat there meanwhile pale with humiliation, with shame at having any part at all in the fuss made by

Ramazan's relatives and by Ramazan himself, with the shame of being put on exhibition in front of all these people, in full sight of whom the pale Ramazan kept helplessly shouting that he loved his Ira, shouting from the far end of the table that all his relatives could f . . . g well go to hell for bullying him like this on *his* night, f . . . g well go to hell.

While this was happening one of Ramazan's guests, the loudest and drunkest of the lot, had already been kicked downstairs and had set off goodness knows where, leaving his velvet jacket behind on the coat rack, for his overcoat had been forcibly shoved on directly over his best white shirt; and evidently failing to understand a thing that was happening to him, he had said not a word about having another jacket somewhere there inside. This guest became a further cause of grief in Ramazan's great lamentation, in which, periodically, he returned to the theme of how the whole lot of them could f . . . g well go to hell.

Incidentally, Ramazan alone held forth on this subject, seated at the table amidst a row of silent guests. None of the guests themselves, the same merry band that would later set off, in three taxis, to prolong the fun elsewhere, felt especially injured or insulted, since the scene unfolding before their eyes was familiar to them since student days, when every party at Ramazan's would come to a head with Ramazan throwing a terrible tantrum, yelling his head off in the kitchen surrounded by alarmed relatives, and end with all the guests departing at once – reckless students, all of them, in those days, who had the impudence to start rowing with Ramazan's father, right there at the table among the cakes and salads, rowing with him over every lofty subject imaginable, and then depart, leaving Ramazan's

parents in a state of shock, the whole foundation of
their existence shaken.

On this occasion Ramazan alone was left to wage
lofty battle for the rights of men; all the other guests sat
in silence on their chairs and stools and on the couch,
leaning against the wall and exchanging glances. Finally
Ramazan all of a sudden recalled yet another incident
from his blighted youth, and, right in front of his parents
and Ira, embarked on his old lament about Anya, Anya
who wouldn't even descend the six flights of stairs
to see him, not even Anya, and he'd stood there and
waited for her, and she despised him and wouldn't
come out and see him and so on and so forth. It looked
as if Ramazan was planning to bring up every single
grievance from his bitter past, every single failure,
although, thank God, he missed out the incident with
Lyuda – no doubt there was some method to these
mad tirades of his, and he left out the things he simply
couldn't bear to recall, like Lyuda, for instance, who'd
actually lived with them, proud, vain Lyuda who'd been
brought to stay with the family from somewhere down
south and then simply disappeared, gathered up her
two dresses and vanished into thin air, because Ramazan
kept endlessly showing her off to his numerous friends,
and these displays and discussions of his bride-to-be
went on forever, and then the gang gave Lyuda the
thumbs down, even though Ramazan's parents had set
their hearts on just such an independent girl as Lyuda.
But Ramazan had let slip the crucial moment, quite
possibly on purpose, and Lyuda vanished into the unknown with her smooth black hair and the simple
orange knitted dress that she wore for best.

And now Ramazan was married to Ira, who silently
despised him, and had two children, both destined to

inherit their mother's bitter, impatient scorn for Ramazan, for his eternal fear of losing his home and children because Ira might one day make up her mind and say 'Go away and never come back'. Ira had once related something of the kind about a friend of hers who'd simply upped and put her husband, a father of three, straight out of the door, simply got rid of him, saying that she'd be much better off without him, absolutely fine, and she didn't want any money from him either. This was the sole occasion on which Ira had told him anything with any animation, and Ramazan, who also knew the bitter lot that had befallen this friend's husband, the father of three, vividly recalled the whole thing, so it seemed, to this day, because in the course of his endless diatribe at the silent table he didn't once bring the subject up or even touch on it obliquely, but kept railing on about this character Pankov and about his vodka and about those six flights of stairs which had once stood between him and Anya's bed and which he, Ramazan, had lacked the strength to overcome; and all this was said right in front of his honourable parents and that very same Anya, herself long since a mother, who meanwhile sat calmly smiling at the table; it was even said in the presence of his wife Ira, who'd attended the occasion only with a sense of utmost martyrdom at having to suffer and put up with this vulgar ritual of congratulation, and was now forced to suffer and put up with something ten times more vulgar and loathsome – the revelations of Ramazan, all pale and sweaty with his shirt undone.

As a result, when Ira hastily departed, Ramazan made no attempt to entice her into staying by promises of the entertainments awaiting them once they departed from his father's house, and by the time it struck midnight Ira was gone. Meanwhile, however, a new face had appeared, a certain Dina, who had to be reckoned with in the scramble for seats in taxis; indeed during the seating procedure certain minor incidents occurred, for no one wanted to share their taxi with this person who'd materialised out of nowhere, out of the darkness, so suddenly, naïvely and openly. Her appearance was the work of a certain Fyodor, the result of his own *naïveté* and openness. It was he who, out in the street in the middle of the night, had suddenly stretched out his arms beneath a street lamp and launched himself with a cry into the darkness, and in the wake of this cry some lightning negotiations had evidently taken place, for a moment later there was Fyodor, triumphant, with a girl in an orange coat under his wing, sumptuous-looking and completely drunk, who, once in a taxi, immediately began conversing in English, singing non-stop and generally entertaining the crowd.

Ramazan, pale with drink, shouted after them as they got into the taxi that Fyodor was a good healthy lad and didn't have the clap. Subsequently, it's true, Ramazan fell silent and was as good as dead for the rest of the journey, but on arrival at their destination he came to and began repeating, like a parrot, the same thing over and over: that our Fyodor was a good healthy lad and they weren't going to yield him up for anything.

Everyone was already seated at the table and all the lights were ablaze, there in the silent room in the depths of night; after their merry chase through the streets everyone seemed to have woken up, to find themselves sitting face to face over a clean, empty table, with three bottles to drink, and the bright orange

Dina, who kept reaching up with both hands to adjust her hairdo, and finally the scowling Fyodor.

'Those parents of mine!' shouted Ramazan in a voice full of hurt. 'Do you know what my mother went and said on the stairs? She said she'd been a kind and stupid mother the whole of her life, and she wasn't going to be stupid any more. Fyodor, you're a good healthy lad, remember that.'

'Either you shut up,' said Fyodor furiously, from down by Dina's knees, 'or I'm going to chuck you out.'

Thus began the second half of the night, played out beneath a quite different emblem now, for all eyes now were trained on Dina, her behaviour, her gestures, and especially her touching sense of being somehow at fault, so that she kept clasping her hands to her breast and saying 'I'm so sorry!' Every five minutes or so she burst out with it, dropping everything else to apologise once again, whereupon all the others would respond in chorus 'No problem', and so the night proceeded.

At first Fyodor performed all his usual ceremonies with her – called her his 'little one' and accompanied her into the hall to ring her parents, standing behind her while she went into long, muddled explanations over the phone. Her parents appeared to have told her she could stay out all night for all they cared, judging at least from what happened afterwards, for she never went home at all that night, despite being offered ample opportunity to do so.

Fyodor gave his Dina first-class treatment, squatting on the floor before her and defending her ardently from the ravings of the injured Ramazan, who on top of everything else kept shouting to no one in particular, 'Aren't you sorry, girls, to miss out on your kind giant Fyodor with his lovely big hands!'

And Fyodor, huddled up with Dina, kept whispering to her feverishly: 'Don't say anything, don't answer back! Don't talk to any of them.' While to Ramazan he yelled:

'I don't like you!'

But now the true outline of Dina herself was slowly taking form, emerging through the mass of orange and all the other hues of youth; for she grew stubborn and began resisting Fyodor – 'I'm not a baby, I'm twenty years old' – and obstinately started conversing with everyone at once, addressing the whole table as a collective entity, raising her glass to them and saying, in a voice laden with significance, 'Hey, boys! Cuckoo!' – and Ramazan, meanwhile, droned on and on about Fyodor, that healthy lad, and Fyodor, scrunched up at Dina's feet, was getting madder and madder, but Dina herself kept chatting away, quite unperturbed, to everyone at once, and only from time to time fell silent, surveyed the company, and said in heartfelt tones 'I'm sorry!'

Evidently she was still bothered by the shameful weakness she'd shown, out there in the street in the middle of the night, letting the gigantic all-powerful Fyodor take her under his wing and remove her, under his protection, from her own gang of friends, who no doubt were just setting off somewhere too and had their own independent plans for the night.

Dina thus became sharper and sharper with Fyodor, by now quite limp and totally done for, cutting him short and once even declaring out loud that she wasn't just to be had for the asking, she set proper store by herself, no one befriended her just like that. This provoked a fresh torrent of words from Ramazan and a new outburst of fury from Fyodor, who simply got up and launched straight into the distraught Ramazan, sitting in front of his vodka in a state of utter desolation.

And Dina like a stuck record kept on and on repeating: 'I'm drunk. I'm sorry. Because you shouldn't. Never ever!'

She considered it her sacred duty to put everything in its place, to explain in detail precisely what had happened, but instead of a coherent defence of her actions she kept saying something about a certain man on whom her continued attendance at college depended, and she said a good deal about the college as well, where she was allowed to go only because of her voice, her singing, because she apparently had no brains at all.

'Stop it now!' Fyodor kept urging her in a heated whisper. 'Look who you're talking to!'

So on and on it went, until Fyodor at last gave up and walked out just as he was into the freezing night. Meanwhile dancing had got into full swing, and Dina was prancing about like a wind-up toy, somehow failing to notice that everyone had started to leave already; the first to set off back home to his warm nest being the devastated Ramazan, with all the others following on behind, conversing loudly in the entrance hall, while Dina meanwhile kept dancing on and on, always keeping the mirror in view so she could adjust her hairdo with both hands. As if on purpose she seemed not to see that one of their hosts, the wife, had gone to bed in the other room, and all the other guests were already outside or descending the stairs. Fyodor, who turned up in the street outside, kept asking everyone who emerged: 'What, hasn't she left yet? What's she doing in there? Has she gone and moved in or something?'

Thus ended the night's long vigil, although, of course, it couldn't just end with Fyodor's questions; Fyodor and the owner of the apartment were obliged to go back into the empty room, where the music was still blaring and Dina still dancing, and while away with empty chit-chat the two hours remaining before work, although subsequently the owner said that in the whole of the last three or four years that Dina girl, as far as he remembered, was the only human specimen he'd come across that was of any interest or deserved any attention whatsoever.

N

Everyone had a good laugh over the incident, but after Shura started relating it, not just within his own little circle, but to all and sundry, the laughter over it lost all sense; what Shura had recounted, to his intimate circle, as the most extraordinary incident, had soon become known through various channels to everyone; so that when Shura, not realising this, started relating the same tale to all and sundry, he began, quite unawares, to repeat himself, and every time people were forced to pretend that they hadn't known a thing, and to feign astonishment and laughter, as if Shura's tale were a revelation to them. This in itself was tiresome enough – hearing the same story twice over, but especially so since the second time round it was presented not just in a cut-and-dried version, with the main points highlighted, but in a detailed, unnecessarily embroidered rendition, with the author adding his own special nuances of feigned mortification and genuine indignation.

And the same story that, when first told backstage, had seemed so intriguing, so profoundly telling, appeared, in its second, more literary rendition, when the author presented it to the public at large, to express only a determination on his part to ridicule and vilify and expose another's sins to shame; which in turn looked like a pathetic, inappropriate and rather revealing attempt on the part of the author to justify himself; for as everyone knows, casting shame on someone else is just another way of confirming one's own self-esteem, or, to put it another way, every action is a form of counteraction.

So that on the second and subsequent occasions that Shura repeated his story – and he repeated it in every possible guise, as if seeking, in the last analysis, some quite other meaning in it from that which was evident on the surface – he no longer evoked such interest as he had done at first; yet he pressed on regardless, quite undeterred.

It was as if this endlessly-repeated story demanded some outlet, as if he couldn't bear to keep it to himself – it was so terribly funny, so unexpected psychologically, and no one had yet been able to explain it. In his wildest dreams, Shura would say, he'd never come near to wanting to touch this woman – 'Let's call her N', he'd say, already aware that everyone knew perfectly well whom he was talking about, but pretending nevertheless that he'd never dream of revealing more, that he alone would withstand the pressure of the avid crowd, that nothing, under any circumstances, could induce him to blacken a woman's good name.

And it seemed that Shura was bent on treasuring this story his whole life long, as testament to his strength, his youth and the glory he'd achieved. For everyone, of course, understood why N should have set her sights on Shura, it wasn't hard to explain – for Shura was a sportsman in his way, a champion indeed, permanently on the lookout for fresh adventure, his appetite for excitement boundless and insatiable.

It was another matter, of course, that the story ceased after a while to trouble anyone, and lost all its savour; and here it was significant that the woman in question, the second protagonist in the whole affair, never attempted to refute the facts or put her own case forward, although in the first instance, when the story was first being passed around, with no one yet knowing who N might be, her own behaviour was such as to give the game away immediately. Yet she needn't have given herself away at all, for lots of other women had gone on the same trip and there were plenty of potential suspects; all of them had had single rooms in the hotel, after all, and all of them had consumed a fair number of intoxicating drinks at the banquet; and they'd all taken part in the conversation round the table, indeed in everything that had led to this so very unexpected outcome.

But of all those who'd been there, she alone had got somewhat upset, looking quite plainly grieved and saddened as soon as the story was told; and there was a certain weariness and resignation in her look as well, though she could perfectly well have assumed the same expression as everyone else – an expression of eager interest, mild indignation and embarrassment, mixed of course with an involuntary smile.

But this same N, immediately identified by all the others, made no attempt even to hear the story out, to suffer it to the bitter end; she simply shrugged her shoulders and went back to her desk while all the others, huddled together, went over the details revealed the day before, at that stage only to Shura's immediate circle.

N could perfectly well have disguised her feelings, instead of getting up and walking away from the group in a patent demonstration of the fact that their discussions were of no interest to her at all. She couldn't have failed to find them interesting, if she'd remained as she was, just like all the other women; but as a result of this incident she'd become a quite different person. The incident had put her in the extraordinary position of a person disgraced, but not obviously so, not to her face, so that her misery, too, could not be openly proclaimed.

That N was miserable was clear to everyone. Outwardly her misery was manifested in an expression of apparent boredom, absent-mindedness, weariness and indifference. Normally such a lively woman, still young and full of fire and *joie de vivre*, N grew wan before everyone's eyes. And this condition set in just as Shura's activities were at their height. Shura, incidentally, worked in the same office as N. In a state of mad hilarity he kept bursting out laughing, and now and then this laughter of his – somehow rapturous and inspired – resounded incongruously amid the general workaday hum of the office, leaving everyone in the room quite bewildered.

Predictably enough, however, the whole story palled with time and lost its sense of immediacy. It was superseded by others – not as piquant, it's true, as Shura's tale, but worthy of attention nonetheless. And Shura's story was put on the back burner, and nothing could be done to revive it. Shura even went so far as to broadcast N's name, several times letting the cat out of the bag quite deliberately, but even this didn't help.

And N's expression remained unchanged, suggesting, as before, that she was tired of sitting at her desk and tired of working at her job. Her weariness was not a hidden, disguised expression of grief or injury, but a quite genuine, unconcealed, natural, perhaps even insurmountable boredom. And Shura, among his various acquaintances, meanwhile kept on and on exclaiming:

'It's not that I set such store by feminine pride or modesty or purity or all the rest of it, not a bit of it! The only thing I insist on – my sole reason for yelling "Help!" – is that I won't be raped, I won't be the blind instrument of another's pleasure. At the end of the day I didn't even want to touch this N, that's all there is to it. It's not my fault' – and he'd start to philosophise on the theme, using this pretext to re-tell the whole tale: 'It's not my fault that N got so fired up by the atmosphere of the banquet and the whole occasion; it's not my fault that she went and dolled herself up in her room, put on her make-up and fixed up her hair there in front of the mirror, as if she were preparing for some great event. There was the cognac, of course, but everyone drank the same amount, so why did she alone behave like that? It's always dangerous to go making preparations just in case something happens. In any case, was she going out on a spree with friends? No, she was going to a conference and a banquet, a banquet where all her office colleagues and part of the branch management would be present. Of course all the flirtatious dancing and sparkling glasses and toasts and jokes and the entire atmosphere could throw anyone off balance, but still, why did I have to fall victim to the whole thing? Notwithstanding all my experience in this sphere, I've never,' Shura went on, 'repeat never, in my worst nightmares, ever wanted to touch her. I understand, of course, she's fed up with the usual formalities, I perfectly understand. And just as I always want to preserve a certain mystery in the whole business, a certain naturalness in the way things unfold, a certain unspoken element, an element of chance, of romance if you like, so she, I assume, has got fed up with it all. Fair enough, she's tired of going through the, so to speak, incubation period, the period when one injudicious word can destroy everything, the period of first words and walks in the woods and all the rest of it. Fair enough, I'm getting to feel that way myself. If it's yes, then yes, if it's no, then no, and what's the point of all the reconnoitring and pretending and gradual acclimatisation and all the rest of it. I can't marry her after all, I'm married already and so is she. The whole thing's clear-cut. And yet,' here Shura would pause for a moment, 'what we're speaking of here is what I'd call the principle of the chase.'

Shura could talk for ages in this vein, analysing, chewing over, spinning out, explaining. It was clear that he was still bothered by the strange situation that he'd found himself in that night in the hotel, when everyone had dispersed to their various rooms and N had suddenly invited him, Shura, to come to her, offering herself straight out in the most unambiguous terms.

But this was no longer of any interest even to those who'd been present on the occasion, when all the participants had been obliged to spend the night following the banquet in a completely empty, newly-built hotel.

People said afterwards that Shura had spent the whole night knocking on people's doors and bursting into various rooms and had even gone so far as to steal a bouquet of flowers from a vase on the little table in the vestibule, placing them with great ceremony in the bowl of the lavatory in one of the rooms, after knocking on the door the whole night long, only to discover that the room was empty.

Who Will Answer?

But who will answer for the innocent tears of Vera Petrovna, the innocent, helpless, old woman's tears that Vera Petrovna wept, there in her hospital bed before she died?

Who'll avenge the blood of Vera Petrovna – not literally her blood, for her blood congealed in her veins and was never shed – but that's what people say: who'll avenge her blood? Who'll avenge the fact that Vera Petrovna, towards the end of her life, as a result of the various drugs she'd been given, went quite mad, became tormented by various strange, innocent, incomprehensible torments and would say to the girls, her colleagues at work: 'Show me your knickers, girls!' And the girls whirled round in their little skirts, grasping nothing with their little minds, not wanting to grasp anything, for women think nothing of revealing these things to each other – showing bras and pants, asking who bought what for how much. But this insistent, mournful 'show me your knickers', uttered in the twilight of life, when everyone knew that V.P was dying and would die in great torment very soon – it rang in the ears long after V.P had died, lying festering in her pus on a stretcher in the corridor of some stinking little hospital for the chronically ill, for the hopeless cases and all those who were on their own, who had no one to intervene for them, no one to get them transferred to a better place and make sure they weren't chucked out to die in a sodden bed, surrounded by draughts, with groans and stench all around.

The memory of all this stuck in the girls' minds too, for they went several times to visit V.P in this hospital on the outskirts of town. Timidly they placed the food they'd brought on V.P's bed, and V.P, fully conscious, cursed and wept, cursed her entire life and the fact that she hadn't gone soon enough to the doctors about her illness, but had let it slide. 'Don't let it slide, girls,' V.P said, weeping, as if something had already got into these girls and they were doomed to travel the exact same path that V.P had travelled, from being a middle-aged but bold, showy woman, to becoming this bearded and bewhiskered creature, left to die in a corridor lying on God knows what.

And it was left to them, too, these girls, to bury V.P, but that was the end of the matter; no monument was erected to her, nor did anyone plan to visit her grave to pay annual respects on Easter Sunday. And after all, other gravestones, not yet so overgrown with grass, have since sprung up around V.P, and on certain days the relatives come to the spot with their traditional food and drink, and the birds fly overhead and settle on V.P's humble place of abode, and the trees after all keep growing all around, and the girls, those former girls, have long since grown up and matured and are quietly ageing, still keeping in their hearts the feeling that used to come over them when V.P would say 'show me your knickers, girls', and they'd swallow their fear and cheerily whirl round, for God forbid they should reveal their misgivings or hurt the feelings of an old woman whose cheeks were already in regular need of a razor, but who was in herself entirely innocent. Innocent, we may add, as all of us are too.

A Strange Man

Not so long ago a man I met took me to be just twenty-three. I'm not the sort of person who tries to dispel other people's impressions of me, and in any case what does it mean that someone might take me to be just x years old? For the time being, thank God, I'm still young enough not to have to conceal my real age. He told me that when he first saw me he'd said to himself, 'There goes a girl who must be twenty-three at most' – and that he'd felt sad at the realisation that he himself was already forty-five.

I told him, admittedly not straight away, that I wasn't twenty-three at all, I was already thirty. This happened towards the end of our evening in the restaurant, and he told me that it already made him feel a lot better, knowing that I wasn't just twenty-three but thirty years old. As if this had changed something inside me and I was no longer the same person that I'd been a minute before; as if, as a result, I'd shifted towards him, become closer, and everything was now much simpler. As if, indeed, life was as good as over by thirty.

In fact he spent the whole evening paying me compliments, although I kept him at arm's length and hardly spoke to him, talking instead mainly to Razzak. I found it strange that Razzak had brought this man, this Misha, along, and had even forewarned me over the telephone that he wouldn't be alone, but was bringing a good friend of his. I told him that I didn't want any strangers with us, he knew very well that I got flustered with strangers. But Razzak, without bothering to reply, just said goodbye and hung up.

That's the way he is, Razzak; he never seems to get hooked on some disagreement but glides smoothly on as if nothing had happened. It gives him an air of absent-mindedness, even indifference to what's being discussed, almost as if he's waiting for someone else to turn up; he doesn't look round, but quite often straightens up and surveys the surrounding scene, talking all the while. And at the same time he's quite capable of asking one and the same question twenty times over in the course of a single evening, as happened the last time, almost exactly a year ago, when I was with him in the restaurant.

He asked me, for example, which I preferred, blondes or brunettes, and meanwhile – though he was clearly very interested in the question – kept looking somehow absent and distracted; he kept scanning the tables in front of us, and probably didn't listen to me giving the same answer every time; what did he take me for, I asked, why did he keep approaching me from this angle? A little later he asked me exactly the same question – which in the end did I really prefer, blondes or brunettes, and I gave just the same answer or words to that effect.

That's not to say that on that last occasion, our first meeting in the restaurant, he'd talked to me only about blondes and brunettes. He also said that I shouldn't be so shy and get so flustered by strangers, that I should regard him as a good friend and not be so scared of him, and indeed, by the end of that first session of ours in the restaurant, a year ago, I'd come to feel quite at home with him, had begun to think of him as my good friend and comrade, and completely forgotten all my doubts as to why he wanted to ask me such things.

I don't really know how it all came about – maybe it was because I suddenly started taking his idiotic questions not as idiotic questions but as a kind of joke, a way of pulling my leg, pretending to play the foolish suitor or something. I started responding to him in the same vein, saying I liked blondes for their delicacy and tact, and brunettes for having loads of money, that sort of thing. By the end of our first meeting in the restaurant, without saying anything at all to each other or giving each other the slightest information about ourselves, about our tastes or requirements, we suddenly felt a genuine bond between us, a kind of mute kinship, and on the way back in the taxi, as I sat in front and he behind, I suddenly felt that he was almost imperceptibly blowing into my collar, somehow amusing himself with this collar of mine, but I didn't turn round and gave no hint that I'd noticed his tiny puffs of breath.

He escorted me to the door and said that next time round, next time he came to the capital, we should definitely go to a restaurant again and spend another delightful evening together.

A year passed, and he rang me, adding that he wouldn't be alone but would be bringing along a good friend of his. I protested, saying he knew very well that I got flustered with strangers, but, just as before, he took no notice of my answer, as if I really hadn't answered at all or else had said 'yes', and on this note he said goodbye and hung up.

Just as I'd done the year before I put on my little sky-blue suit and Razzak and I went to the restaurant, where his friend the greying Misha, wearing a suede jacket, was already waiting for us at the table. 'She's afraid of me,' this Misha began, 'My dear girl, is it really possible to be frightened of me? No girl I've ever known has been scared of me, I don't bite.'

I talked mostly with Razzak, though he and I had no real grounds for conversation. Anything that might have served as a subject, anything that one might have enquired about, asking how things had gone over the preceding year – we had nothing of that kind between us. Neither he nor I knew anything about the other to serve as a basis for asking how things were going.

And cramping our style, on top of this, was the famous Misha, who'd turned up God knows why at our second meeting. Misha was giving a very funny account of his recent visit to Paris, where he'd gone on some conference to do with architecture; he told us how fabulously cheap everything was there, and how much his suede jacket had cost, and how it would have cost him x times more over here, not to mention the fact that he couldn't have got hold of one here at any price; he was the soul of worldliness, this Misha, proposed marvellous toasts and was endlessly topping up my glass, while Razzak for the most part was silent, only now and then straightening himself up and scanning the tables in front of him, behind my back, and every time I was vividly reminded of our meeting last year, of that indefinable spirit of comradeship and spiritual connection which had arisen between us, and of how Razzak, seated behind me in the taxi, had ever so cautiously blown into my collar.

I imagined how this sense of discovered kinship would come over us again when Misha finally got up and left. But Misha, on the contrary, seemed to have no intention of leaving, he kept paying me compliments and asking Razzak whether I was always so shy or only in company, to which Razzak merely smiled in reply.

So the three of us sat there at the table till the restaurant was closing, and Misha had already asked me
for my telephone number and I was telling him that I
had no telephone, when Razzak, taking pity on the
chagrined Misha, took a neat little notebook out of his
jacket pocket and dictated my telephone number out
loud straight to him.

This was a strange thing to do, but I'd already come
to take Razzak's strangeness for granted and didn't
protest in any way, and indeed I was powerless to do
so, for what on earth could I say, sitting in front of
these two men as they so strangely, freely and simply
exchanged my telephone number.

I sat there in silence while Misha said that he'd be
here again only in three months' time, once more on
his way to Paris for a conference, and that he'd phone
me then.

Then the restaurant began to close up for the night,
and they both accompanied me in a taxi home, and
both escorted me right to the door, and I entered the
apartment on tiptoe, locking the door thrice over and
removing the little notice hung up with a piece of string
saying 'Please don't bolt' which we usually put up
when we're going to be out late. But no one had yet
gone to bed in the apartment, because I'd returned at
a quarter past eleven, quite early for a Saturday night,
so that the notice had served no purpose at all.

Our Circle

I'm a tough, ruthless character, full of mockery towards everyone, always with a smile on my full, red lips. For instance, we'd be sitting at Marisha's. Marisha always has a get-together at her place on Fridays, every one of us turns up, or if someone doesn't it's either because they've been prevented by family or family circumstances, or they've specifically been banned from coming here – either by Marisha herself or by the whole indignant crowd of us: as Andrei, for instance, was banned for a long while after giving our Serge a black eye once when he was drunk, Serge being sacrosanct among us, our pride and glory. Long ago, for example, he worked out the aeronautical principle of flying saucers. He worked it out right here on the back of a drawing pad belonging to his genius of a daughter. I saw these calculations later and cheekily took a look at them, right in front of everyone. I couldn't understand a thing, it was all complete gobbledegook – artificial constructions from a completely arbitrary point of origin. Quite beyond me, in other words, and I'm extremely intelligent. If there's something I don't understand then it doesn't exist. So Serge must have made a mistake with his point of origin. And the fact is it's a long time since he's read anything, he relies just on intuition, but you can't get by without reading. He also discovered a new principle for the working of a locomotive with a seventy per cent Efficiency Factor, once again a completely outlandish thing. After he'd made this discovery he was brought out of the woodwork and paraded all over the place, taken to Professors Fram and Livanovich and shown off at various symposia. It was Livanovich who came to his senses first and pointed out his primary source – the principle had been discovered a hundred years ago and described for the popular reader in a foot-note on page such-and-such of a textbook for college students, and the Efficiency Factor in fact turned out to be no more than thirty-six per cent, so the result in the end was nil. All the same there was a terrific hullabaloo, a whole new department was formed under Livanovich and Serge was going to be made the head of it without even having a degree. Not surprisingly, there was great rejoicing among the gang. Serge had a thorough re-think of his whole life, thought over the values he really cared about and decided it wasn't those. He decided it would be better to stay put at the Oceanic and everyone went into shock again; he'd chucked in a career for the sake of freedom and liberty. At the Oceanic he was just a regular junior researcher, with complete freedom to do as he liked and the prospect any time now of a long-planned expedition round the Atlantic, with stop-offs at Vancouver, Boston, Hong Kong and Montreal. Six months' worth of sea and sunshine. So fine, he chose freedom; and over there, in his thirty-six per cent Efficiency department – his own flesh and blood creation – they'd already acquired staff and appointed some complete nonentity with a PhD to run the thing. So that was it, every place was filled, and they started working at a nice leisurely pace, waddling about, sitting in the buffet, taking business trips, and smoke-breaks. They'd come and consult Serge from time to time; or rather, at first they used to consult him, they came a couple of times; Marisha joked that over at the Oceanic they'd lost track of who was who – a certain Serge, just a junior researcher, kept on being hauled off right under their noses for special consultations. But all this came to an end pretty quickly; the Efficiency people soon settled into a rut, and after all it wasn't just a simple matter, it wasn't just a matter of principle but of a whole new technology, entailing the disruption of all existing production: there'd be no need for electricity any more, everything would return to the steam age, the whole caboodle would be scrapped and wasted. Instead of progress, in other words, everything, as always, would just go to blazes. And all this was to be accomplished by just one little department consisting of five souls. Someone we knew, Lenka Marchukaite, got a job as a lab assistant there, and she'd bring us reassuring news from time to time, for instance that the guy with the PhD was about to father a child on the side, and the parents concerned were concocting a letter denouncing him; and he'd completely switched off from work, and kept yelling down the telephone, and there was just the one office, and no one so much as mentioned Energetics. Meanwhile they were preparing a draft resolution on acquiring the use of a workbench in the basement of the institute for three hours a night for experiments. But Serge's freedom-and-liberty option worked out much worse; the time came to fill in the forms to go on the expedition, and on the forms he wrote that he wasn't a Party member, but at the same time said that he'd been a member of the Young Communist League when he first joined the Oceanic. The two statements were compared, and it emerged that he'd left the YCL off his own bat, he wasn't even registered as a member of the Oceanic's YCL branch, and altogether hadn't paid his membership dues for years; and it turned out there was no way this could be corrected, not with dues or anything else; so the commission wouldn't let him go off to the ocean. All this was related to us by the aforementioned renegade Andrei, who turned up and was allowed to stay and drink vodka with everyone else; and he told us all in a rush that none of us was to say a thing, but he'd agreed to be an informer just to get on the expedition; however he'd only be obliged to snitch on board the boat itself, on dry land he'd be off duty. And Andrei indeed went out on the ocean, and in due course returned bearing a little plastic penis from Japan – the reason it was tiny was just because he was so short of dollars, but I said he must have brought it back for his daughter. And Serge sat there looking mournful, although he'd got his total freedom the meantime; the whole Oceanic Institute had gone to the ocean, while he and a small group of lab assistants were left to take care of the loading and send-off and the correspondence and reception of the expedition in Leningrad.

But all this is ancient history now, those days are over – the days when Serge and Marisha jointly grieved for Serge and stuck together steadfastly through thick and thin; all those days of great mutual understanding are over, and God knows what's replaced them now; but every Friday we turn up regular as ever, as if magnetised by the little house on Stulina Street, and drink the whole night through. 'We' means Serge and Marisha, proprietors of the establishment, two rooms in all. Behind the wall, to the sound of music from the tape recorder and bursts of laughter, sleeps their daughter Sonya, brought up a stalwart child, talented, a real young beauty in her way; now she's in fact a relative of mine, can you imagine, but of that more anon. And Marisha's my relative too, and Serge himself; that's one comic side-effect of our lifestyle together, a straightforward case of incest, as Tanya put it, when she attended the marriage between my husband Kolya and Serge's wife Marisha – but we'll come to that later.

So anyway at the start this is how it was: Serge and Marisha, their daughter behind the wall, with me as fifth wheel and my husband Kolya – a true, devoted friend of Serge's; then there was Andrei-the-snitch, first of all with his wife Anyuta, later on with various other women, and thereafter on a permanent basis with Nadya; then Zhora – half-Jewish on his mother's side, which no one apart from me ever so much as mentioned, as if it were some awful flaw in him; once our idol Marisha decided to praise the ill-favoured Zhora and said that he had huge eyes – but what colour were they? Everyone said either they were yellow or light hazel, but I said they were Jewish, and everyone for some reason got embarrassed, and Andrei, my eternal enemy, growled at me. And Kolya even patted Zhora on the shoulder. But what had I actually said? I'd spoken the truth. To continue: another permanent fixture among us was Tanya, a Valkyrie, over six feet tall, with long, blonde hair, very white teeth, which she cleaned like a maniac three times a day for twenty minutes at a stretch (a whole hour a day and your teeth would be snow-white too) and also very big grey-blue eyes; she was a beauty, a favourite of Serge's, who sometimes used to stroke her hair when he'd really drunk himself silly, and none of us knew what was going on; and Marisha would be sitting right there not the least put out, and I'd be sitting there too and saying to Lenka Marchukaite: 'Why don't you have a dance? Go and dance with my husband Kolya' – at which point everyone would burst into crude laughter, but that was already at the very twilight of our life together.

Lenka Marchukaite would be there too, a real beauty of a girl, with a gigantic bust and long, light brown hair, export material, twenty years old. Lenka at the beginning behaved like a shady dealer, which indeed she was – she worked in a record shop. She wormed her way into Marisha's confidence, telling her all about her hard life, then grabbed twenty roubles off her and walked about with this loan as if it were the most natural thing in the world; then she disappeared, returned some time later with four front teeth missing, gave back the twenty roubles ('You see?' said Marisha triumphantly) and announced that she'd been in hospital where they'd passed sentence on her, telling her she could never have children. Marisha loved her all the more after that; Lenka all but slept at their place; but of course she was a different proposition now without her teeth, no longer export material. With Serge's help Lenka got a job as a lab assistant in his thirty-six per cent department, acquired some new teeth, got married to a Jewish dissident kid called Oleg, who turned out to be the son of the famous beautician Marie Lazarevna; and for a while Lenka acted as our spy in this wealthy family, telling us with great amusement what an amazing bedroom Marie had, what incredible wardrobes, each worth enough dollars to last you a lifetime, and what was the latest thing Marie had given her. Marie spoiled Lenka and said that her skin was a real natural treasure. Lenka indeed had unusually delicate natural skin; her white flesh and red blood made a quite fantastic combination at any hour of the day, no matter whether at sunset or dawn; and her lips were truly as red as blood. All children of course have skin like this – take my Alyosha, for example. But Lenka treated herself with contempt; she ran from one shady dive to the next like a cheap little minx, setting no store by herself at all, and finally announced that her Oleg was setting off to America, via Vienna, with his entire family, and she wasn't going – and she didn't go, she divorced Oleg, and it became her trademark, whenever she came to the house, to sit down straight away in one or other of the men's laps; she was in her element, while our poor lads, be it my Kolya or that snitch Andrei, would just grin crookedly by way of response. Serge was the only one she wouldn't risk it with; Serge was untouchable, and anyway there was Marisha right alongside, and Lenka absolutely adored Marisha and wouldn't have dreamt of making fun of her as she made fun of all the rest of us, including Andrei-the-snitch's young wife, who flushed and went out to the kitchen when Lenka, without meaning a thing, plonked herself down in Andrei's lap. This wife of his, Nadya, was even younger than Lenka, she can't have been more than eighteen, and you could have taken her for fifteen – a skinny, delicate, red-headed, depraved looking schoolgirl, the likes of which only Andrei could have latched onto – Andrei who was totally impotent and didn't require a thing, as everyone had long since found out thanks to his garrulous official wife Anyuta. Depraved this Nadya may well have been, but she got herself a husband and became a Russian *baba* to end them all: she'd open those little jaws of hers, the little nymphet, and start crooning away about what dish she'd just made and what they'd just bought and what Andrei had drunk and how she wouldn't allow him to drink any more. The only thing that remained of her former vice and depravity was her unhinged eye, which whenever she made certain awkward movements would slip out of its orbit and slither down her cheek like a soft-boiled egg. It must have been a dreadful sight to behold, but

Andrei got used to it, and with her holding the eye in the palm of her hand he'd take her off to hospital, where they got it fixed; on these nights, I imagine, Andrei rose to the occasion. And with his previous wife, Anyuta, Andrei just lived for the thrilling moments when she had her attacks and he'd have to take her in the ambulance, wrapped in a blanket, from hospital to hospital, until it was finally established that she had a so-called toxic womb. The toxicity of Anyuta's womb made quite an impact in our circle, and both Anyuta and Andrei seemed stamped with the mark of doom. All the rest of us already had children: Zhora had three, I had my Alyosha, and I only had to be absent a couple of weeks from Serge and Marisha's for news to circulate through the ranks that I'd been taken off to the maternity hospital: that was their way of poking fun at my figure. Tanya had a son, famous for the fact that when he was very little he used to crawl up on his mother and suck alternately from each breast; that was how they amused themselves. Andrei and Anyuta weren't able to have children, and we felt sorry for them; for there's something absurd about not having children around, and among us it just wasn't done; the whole effect consisted in having children and messing about with puddings and mash and kinder-gartens, and then on Friday nights feeling human again and going on a bender at full throttle, to the point where the police were sometimes even called in by one or other of the neighbours in Stulina Street. Anyuta and Andrei wore this air of doom about them until one fine day, completely out of the blue, Anyuta suddenly gave birth to a daughter, virtually without changing her appearance at all! There was great rejoicing all round; on the night of the birth Andrei brought two bottles of vodka round to Serge and summoned my Kolya to come over, and they spent the night drinking; and Andrei said he'd call his daughter Marisha in honour of Marisha, and Marisha was rather upset by this homage. But there was nothing to be done, she couldn't forbid them, and so that parasite Andrei called his daughter Marisha. But that was the last of their rejoicing and their family romance, and Andrei, one assumes, must thenceforth have abandoned his conjugal duties, while Anyuta, on the contrary, became aware of her own ordinariness: she'd become like any other woman, free of attacks, and in consequence she began, during her year's maternity leave, to invite home a whole string of new friends, and at this point Andrei set sail on the ocean in his capacity as snitch, and upon his return found a veritable swarm of friends at his house, attracted, no doubt, by the widowed state of Anyuta's formally toxic womb. Andrei then discovered a new romance in the role of abandoned husband, and began romantically bringing selected girlfriends to Serge and Marisha's, and Lenka Marchukaite would brazenly sit in his lap, as if setting her seal on his child-bearing organs, now they were exhausted and done with their business. That was just a little joke and taunt of hers.

One time she sat in my Kolya's lap too, kind, skinny Kolya, who was literally crushed, both physically and morally, by the sheer weight of Lenka; he hadn't anticipated this turn of events and simply kept his hands as far away as possible and kept exchanging glances with Marisha; but Marisha turned away sharply and got into conversation with Zhora; and that was when I began to see what was going on. I realised then that Lenka had blundered, and said:

'Lenka, you've blundered. Marisha's feeling jealous over my husband.'

Lenka, quite unconcerned, just pulled a face and

carried on sitting on Kolya's knees, Kolya meanwhile drooping like a plucked weed. That, I think was the start of Marisha's cooling-off towards Lenka, which led in due course to Lenka's gradual disappearance from the scene, especially when the latter eventually gave birth to a still-born child; but more of that anon. At that particular moment everyone responded with an exaggerated surge of activity; Tanya clinked glasses with Serge, Zhora topped up everyone's glasses and served fresh helpings to the overloaded Kolya and the chilly Marisha; and Andrei gallantly struck up a conversation with his silly little Nadya, who kept triumphantly glancing at me, the wife of the crushed husband.

Lenka never risked sitting on Zhora's lap, however; that would have been too dangerous an undertaking, since Zhora exhibited, like many small men, a state of permanent sexual arousal, and he adored the lot of them – Marisha, Tanya, even Lenka. Lenka, a completely cold creature, risked inciting Zhora to attempted rape right there in front of everyone, as had already happened on one occasion with a lady-friend of Andrei's who'd pretended to terrific passion when dancing with Zhora; but that was something you couldn't permit yourself with him, and when the music was over Zhora, seemingly beside himself, simply grabbed hold of the strapping great lass by the armpits and dragged her into the next room, which as everyone knew was empty, Marisha and Serge's daughter having been sent that night to stay with her grandmother. Zhora succeeded in dumping the half-crazed lady on Sonya's little bed, but at this point Serge and Andrei, laughing despite themselves, entered and dragged Zhora away, while the alarmed lady adjusted her dress, which had ridden up amidst the fray. This incident provoked dreadful hilarity the whole night long; but in fact everyone, apart from the lady herself, a stranger to our circle, knew that the whole thing was just a game; Zhora had been playing the *bon viveur* and libertine ever since student days, when in fact he sat up nights writing his wife's doctoral dissertation and got up when needed to attend to his three children, and it was only on Fridays that he'd put on his lionskin and go a-courting the whole night long.

But the cautious Lenka Marchukaite, who likewise played her sexual games with amazing *sang froid*, wouldn't risk inciting Zhora to perform his usual role; two performances at once would have been too much, it would have forced them to some kind of conclusion: Lenka would have seated herself, Zhora would straight away have started pawing her and what have you, and Lenka didn't really like all that, just as Zhora, when all was said and done, didn't really care for it either. However, Lenka Marchukaite came and went, just as Marisha wanted; one moment she was there and the next she'd disappeared, and when I mention her name out loud now in front of everyone it sounds like the usual crass tactlessness on my part.

Somehow everything's got muddled up in my memory as a result of recent events in my life, specifically the fact that I've started going blind. Did ten years pass with those Friday gatherings, or was it fifteen? Various great events rolled by – the Czech, the Polish, the Chinese, the Romanian, or was it the Yugoslav events, and there were various trials, and then trials of the people who'd protested against the first trials, and then trials of the people who'd collected money to help the families of those sent to the camps – all these happenings flew by in the meantime. Sometimes stray birds from other, adjacent fields of human activity would fly in; thus, for example, a certain district policeman took to dropping in on our Fridays, a stubborn, arrogant fellow called Valera, a sambo-wrestler. The door to the apartment was left open on Fridays, and it was just three steps up from the pavement to the door; he came the first time and asked for everyone's documents, in connection with a complaint from the residents of the house opposite on Stulina Street, concerning excessive noise after eleven o'clock at night and continuing right up to five in the morning. Valera conscientiously checked everyone's documents, or rather, checked who had their documents, because none of our lads turned out to have their passports on them. He didn't check the girls, and subsequently this led us to suspect that Valera was looking for someone in particular. All the following week everyone kept ringing each other up in a state of great agitation and nerves; we were all very troubled and frightened, feverishly excited. For a real danger had suddenly entered our quiet little abode, where the only noise usually was the music from the tape recorder; because of Valera and his document inspection, we'd been flung right into the centre of events. By the following Friday we were all dead certain that Valera was searching for a Russo-American, Levka, who'd been living a whole year in the country with an expired visa, wandering from haunt to haunt, from one private apartment to another – not because he didn't want to go back to the States, but simply because he'd outstayed his visa, which, he'd been told, could land him a term in jail according to our laws; so he'd started hiding out, and everyone stowed him away with great excitement and laughter, but I'd never seen him at Marisha's place, though Levka-the-American sometimes stayed the night on the floor in the apartment of Marisha's next-door neighbours in the house, a rather shady bunch consisting of two girls, eternal students with no permanent Moscow residence permit, and assorted tribes of cohabitees; and once, by chance, the students told us, Levka had dropped by to borrow a rouble and ended up deflowering a certain Nina, a second-year journalism student and a minister's daughter; Nina lost her cherry and woke up covered in blood, and in a panic dragged the mattress into the kitchen to wash it out, since there was no bathroom in the apartment. Levka-the-American vanished without trace, and Nina bore him no grudge and now, apparently, had started in turn wandering from one low dive to another, searching for Levka to whom, in the Russian sense of the term, she had given her all. Ever since then, apparently, Levka had stopped spending the night on Stulina Street, and so, in this sense, Valera's visits were quite fruitless.

However, he turned up again at five past eleven – turned up to turn off the tape recorder, and the tape recorder was duly turned off and we sat and drank in silence, and Valera, for purposes quite unclear to us, sat there as well; perhaps he'd decided nonetheless just to sit it out and wait for Levka, or maybe he absolutely had to get rid of our harmless little crowd once and for all; at any rate he sat there and wouldn't go away. Marisha, who'd convinced us all, with her passionate argument, that everyone's interesting in their way (she always had various stray folk, picked up at railway stations, staying the night, and once she had a woman staying a whole month with her paralysed year-old daughter; the woman had come for an appointment at the Paediatrics Institute, strictly on a no-treatment, consultation-only basis) – Marisha it was who first

324

found the right key and began to treat Valera as an unfortunate, lonely fellow; and after all no stranger was denied a welcome in this house; it was simply unusual for someone to try and foist themselves on us like that. Marisha, and then Serge, began animatedly conversing with Valera on various themes; they gave him a glass of wine, offered him black bread and cheese – the only things on the table – and Valera didn't evade any of their questions and didn't once seem to feel wounded in his self-esteem. So, for instance, Serge asked him:

'Did you join the police just so as to get a residence permit, then?'

'No, I had a permit already,' Valera answered.

'So what did you do it for?'

'Mine's a difficult district,' Valera answered, 'and I'm a sambo-wrestler, though because of a shoulder injury I didn't make it to second grade back in the army. In sambo if your arm gets twisted you're meant to give some sort of sound signal.'

'What d'you mean, sound signal?' I asked.

'Well if you'll excuse the expression you're meant at least to cough or fart so they don't break your arm.'

I immediately asked how it was possible to fart to order.

Valera said that he hadn't managed to give a sound signal in time and that his arm had been wrenched out of joint at the shoulder, but at any rate he'd got to third grade. Then, without pausing for breath, he set out his point or view on the existing state of affairs in the country and on the fact that everything was going to change and everything would be like it was in Stalin's day and in Stalin's day there was law and order.

In short, the whole of that evening was spent on a sociological investigation of Valera's type, and in the end, perhaps because he was really quite shrewd, or because we had all taken a passive role, but at any rate instead of our usual questionnaire, which we'd tried on more than one occasion with various stray creatures, such as the prostitutes brought in by Andrei or the music lovers that sometimes stopped under our window on quiet Stulina Street and engaged us in conversation over the window sill and finally, by the same route, climbed into the room and were then obliged to answer a whole series of questions – on this occasion things proceeded quite differently, and Valera, without touching concretely on any of his professional duties, lectured us loudly for an entire hour on how things were under Stalin, and nobody tried particularly to contradict him; everyone was afraid, I suppose, that this was a provocation, they were nervous of expressing their views in front of a representative of authority, and in any case it wasn't the done thing among us to go expressing our views, we thought it puerile to go yelling about our views on things, let alone doing so in front of that idiot Valera, a slippery character and a dark horse who'd come and sat down, at our humble round table, in Marisha and Serge's meagre room, for purposes that were quite unclear.

At midnight all of us, feeling thoroughly humiliated, got up and left – all except Valera. Perhaps Valera had nowhere else to spend his night on duty, or maybe he'd been given some clear-cut task, but at any rate he sat there at Marisha and Serge's until morning, and Serge subsequently ventured the opinion – in due course relayed to the masses via Marisha over the telephone – that Valera was the most interesting fellow he'd come across over the last four years, but this was no more than defensive formula on Serge's part. Serge had taken

Valera entirely on himself, as Marisha had gone and
slept on the floor in Sonya's room, while Serge, as the
man of the house, stayed and drank tea with Valera, a
special tea brewed from St. John's wort; they drank a
whole teapotful of this diuretic, and Valera, moreover,
didn't once go to the lavatory and left only when his
night-duty was over. Evidently Valera hadn't wanted to
leave his post for a second and therefore accomplished
a veritable feat of urine-retention. Serge, for his part,
didn't leave the room either, fearing a search in his
absence.

Be that as it may, that Friday was a Friday of torments,
and we all felt like fish out of water. Lenka Marchukaite
didn't once sit in anyone's lap, let alone Valera's,
and Zhora didn't once yell 'virgins!' through the window
to passing schoolgirls, and only I kept asking how
sambo-wrestlers learn to fart: was it by sheer force of
will or through eating some special diet? This theme
kept me going the whole evening, since precisely this
was the only theme Valera kept avoiding. He'd knit his
brows and somehow side-step the subject, didn't once
pronounce the word 'fart' out loud again and took a great
dislike to me, as everyone does at first glance and for
evermore. But there was no getting out of it; the word
in question does not, it would seem, appear in the
unpublished list of words that can earn you fifteen days'
imprisonment if spoken out loud in a public place, and
in any case it was Valera who'd gone and uttered it in
the first place! So I alone kept sticking my oar in, interrupting the intellectual conversation which Serge had
set going with a few leading questions, still hoping to
elevate himself by playing the role of mocking observer
of life's strange phenomena, Valera serving potentially as
one such phenomenon. But Valera couldn't care less

about Serge's patronising questions, and forged straight ahead, saying a number of things that could well have endangered his professional position, regarding the fact that they understood what's what in the army and you lot won't be monkeying round much longer and a big boss will come along and set things to rights.

'But do tell me,' I interrupted, 'is it in the army that they teach you to fart? But you failed to learn, I see, because you weren't able to fart in time and didn't get your second grade.'

'You should see the guys we've got in the army, the techno-men,' Valera went on, 'they've got all the know-how they need, all the technology at their fingertips. They know what's what, those guys, they've got their heads screwed on the right way.'

Serge asked, for example, whether Valera often did night-duty and where was the room he'd been given. Marisha asked, in her usual kindly, sympathetic tone whether Valera was married and had children. Tanya, our beautiful Valkyrie, just snorted away quietly to herself and muttered a running commentary, hunched over her glass, on Valera's most scintillating statements, always addressing herself to Zhora, as if to support him in this difficult situation where he, a half-Jew, but pure Jewish in appearance, had had to present his passport to Valera (he was the only one who had his passport on him on that occasion) and Valera had read it out loud: Georgy (Zhora) Aleksandrovich Perevoshchikov, Russian!

Yes, on this second visit of his Valera again asked for people's passports and again checked Serge's and again got nothing from Andrei or Kolya or from an outsider who'd by chance wandered in on this dangerous party – an Orthodox Christian called Zilberman who seldom came to Moscow; he was terribly scared, and instead of his passport presented his old student card, which he always used to get reduced train fares. Valera took Zilberman's card off him, simply put it in his pocket, and Zilberman disappeared, asking loudly where the toilet was. Valera, though he'd threatened at first to take Zilberman along with him for proper identification, didn't make a move to follow him, and we all stood there suffering at the thought of how terrified and shaky poor Zilberman would be, having, on top of everything else, been caught on the hook now. But apparently Valera had no use for Zilberman.

I was interested to see how that snitch Andrei would comport himself, but Andrei's behaviour was also cautious and reserved. As soon as the tape-recorder was turned off, Andrei lost the chance of dancing with whom-ever he pleased; he was a capricious dancer, sometimes didn't dance at all, and his wife Nadya, who'd turned herself into such a thoroughgoing Russian *baba*, despite her depraved adolescent look, sat like a statue through-out, belatedly feeling jealous; so there it was, Andrei just sat with his Nadya. Nadya's father was a colonel on the up-and-up, and all Valera's speeches, as a man of junior rank, Nadya absorbed only through the prism of the fact that, when Serge asked him what rank had in fact been conferred on him, Valera said that, albeit against many people's wishes, he'd immediately been made a lieutenant. Nadya, alone of all of us, digested the whole situation immediately, started wandering about, took Andrei off to ring up a certain Ira and then took him away altogether, and Valera didn't react at all. Quite possibly even if all of us had left he would have stayed just the same, this was his 'target'; or maybe not, after all.

Kolya and I on this occasion didn't waste money on a taxi, but managed to catch a bus from the metro station and arrived home at a human hour, to discover Alyosha still up at half past one in the morning, dozing in front of the television, whose screen was ablaze to no purpose. This was the first time we'd returned home at night – instead of in the morning – from one of our Fridays, and we saw that in his own way Alyosha also celebrated this night; but when I was putting him to bed he said that he was afraid to sleep alone and afraid to turn out the light. And indeed every light in the place was on, though Alyosha didn't use to be afraid; of course he used to have his grandfather there, but his grandfather, my father, had died not long before, and my mother had died three months before that; in the course of a single winter I'd lost both my parents; moreover my mother had died of the same kidney disease which, during the last while, had shown signs of developing in me as well, and which begins with blindness. Be that as it may, I discovered that Alyosha was afraid to go to sleep when there was nobody home. Obviously the shades of his grandparents still haunted him; my father and mother had raised him, spoiled him and generally brought him up, and now Alyosha would be totally alone, bearing in mind that I too was going to die soon, and my kind husband Kolya, always so quiet in company, who moped about at home or quite improperly started yelling at Alyosha whenever the boy ate with us – Kolya, it seemed, was planning to leave me, and planning to leave me for none other than Marisha.

As I say, many years flew by above that peaceful little Friday nest of ours; Andrei, from the golden-haired Paris he was in his youth, became by turns a father, an abandoned husband, a snitch on board an expeditionary boat, then a lawful spouse again and the owner of a fine apartment, bought by the colonel for his little Nadya, and finally an alcoholic; he still loved Marisha alone, as he had done all his life, ever since student days, and Marisha knew this and valued it; and all the other ladies in his life were simply a replacement for her. And the crowning item on Andrei's agenda were his dances with Marisha, one or two sacred dances a year.

Zhora had also grown up, turning from a bumptious student, full of pranks, into a modest, impoverished, senior scientist, attired in the cheapest shirts and dark grey trousers, a father of three, a budding professor and future prize-winner with no pretensions at all; but lodged in the very core of him there'd always been just that one thing: his love for Marisha, who'd always loved Serge and nobody else.

My Kolya, too, loved and worshipped Marisha; right from the start, in their first year at college, they'd all gone beserk about Marisha, and the game had gone on right up to this moment, when Serge, to whose lot the lovely Marisha had fallen, and who'd gone on living with her all those years, suddenly went and found himself a new beloved, a woman he'd known from way back in high school; and one night, on New Year's Eve, when we'd all been drinking and were playing charades, Serge said 'I'm going to go and ring my beloved' – and we were all thunderstruck, for if the men all loved Marisha and regarded Serge as the only human amongst us, we all loved Marisha and Serge above all; Serge's name was on everyone's lips, although he himself said little – it was Marisha who had elevated him so, Marisha who worshipped him on her knees, worshipped him as her fellow-fighter in life; she revered his every word and gesture, because once upon a time, way back in their first year, when Serge had fallen in love with her along with everyone else and proposed to her and slept with her, she'd gone and left him, given in to her erotic inclinations and rented a room with a certain Jean, renouncing her first and pure love for Serge; and then Jean had abandoned her, and she herself, on her own initiative, came back to Serge and proposed to him herself, once and for all giving up the notion of getting erotic love on the side; and they got married, and Marisha would sometimes say with a kind of holy radiance that Serge was her crystal goblet. To which I'd say these days that you should never try sleeping with a crystal goblet, it just won't work, or if it does work you'll get yourself cut in pieces.

But in those days our whole lives revolved around walking holidays and camp fires, we drank dry wine and scoffed at everything and didn't touch on anything to do with sex, because we were still too young and didn't know what awaited us in the future; the only thing from the sexual arena that bothered the company at all was that I had a white bathing suit which turned out to be completely see-through, and everyone did their best to make fun of me; this was when we were all living in tents by the seaside, and something of the sexual sphere obtruded here too in the sense that Zhora complained of there being no lavatory; the shit just wouldn't float away in the sea. And this same Zhora kept shouting as well that what the other female tourists needed was a first class abortionist; Andrei, meanwhile, kept romantically going to dances with girls from the TB clinic four miles away in the town of

Simeiz, and Serge stubbornly carried on fishing with the help of some underwater fishing tackle, choosing to prove his manhood this way, and at nights I kept listening to the regular thump thump emanating from their tent; but her whole life long Marisha stayed a restless creature with fire in her eyes, and this spoke ill of Serge's abilities, and the boys were all on their marks and raring to go, ready, it seemed, collectively to fill in the gaps for her; but their path was blocked. And together with her inaccessibility, this sexual fire that consumed Marisha, our high priestess of love, was really the thing that allowed our circle to stay together so long, because other people's love is infectious, it's a proven fact. We girls loved Serge and loved Marisha at the same time, we suffered on her behalf and, like her, were torn to bits, but in our own way – on the one hand, we loved Serge and dreamt of replacing Marisha; on the other we couldn't possibly have done it, out of sympathy for Marisha, out of love and pity for her. In short, everything was filled to the brim with this indivisible love of Marisha and Serge, the unrealisability of their love; everyone was enthralled by it, and it drove Serge mad – he being the only one who had full rights in the matter. Once the ulcer burst, although not entirely, when during some harmless sexual chit-chat round the table – the chit-chat of pure people who for that very reason can talk about whatever they like – the conversation turned to a book by a Polish author on sexopathology. This was something new for our circle, for until then all of us had lived as if his or her case were completely unique, not something to examine ourselves or reveal to others. But the new wave of enlightenment touched our little circle too, and I said:

'I've been told about this book *Sexopathology*, where

apparently the sexual act is divided into various different stages; apparently, Serge, the husband and wife have to arouse one another first, and what you have to do to begin with, I gather, is stroke your partner's earlobe! Apparently the earlobe's an erogenous zone!'

Everyone froze, and Serge said straight out that he took an extremely negative view of me; he began to splutter and shout, but what did I care, I sat there as if made of stone, for I'd clearly hit the nail on the head.

But this was before Serge found the love of his life, the girl next door from the street of his childhood; before he met the erotic dream of his youth, who was now – as various well-informed people reported – a plump brunette; and before the policeman Valera began regularly coming to the apartment on Stulina Street and fighting his battle for the right to silence, from eleven at night through till seven in the morning; and it took place, too, before I started gradually discovering that I was going blind, let alone discovered that Marisha was jealous of Lenka Marchukaite over my Kolya.

Thus in the twinkling of an eye all the knots came undone: Serge stopped spending his nights at home; the Fridays at their place faded out and a new series was instituted in a safer place, in the room of the Valkyrie Tanya, albeit in the presence of her adolescent son, who guarded his mother jealously from everyone. Later the adolescent was put in isolation, sent off to Stulina Street to spend Fridays with the girl Sonya, apropos of which I remarked that it was useful for children to sleep with one another, but they paid no attention to me, as always, even though I'd spoken the truth.

But meanwhile a great wave of tumultuous events rolled by in the intervals between our Fridays: Marisha's father died after paying them a visit at Stulina Street; on that very evening, on that very street, he was run over by a car in an unauthorised place, and moreover, as the post-mortem revealed, in a state of inebriation, since before setting off home he'd got thoroughly drunk with Serge. Everything was tangled up in this horribly unfortunate incident: the fact that Marisha's father had wanted to have a man-to-man talk with Serge about why he was leaving Marisha, and the fact that this conversation took place in the evening, when Sonya had not yet gone to bed; and Marisha and Serge were concealing from Sonya the fact that Serge wasn't sleeping at home; Serge would tenderly put Sonya to bed and only afterwards set off to his other woman, and in the morning in any case Sonya woke up only just in time for school, when Serge was already on his way to work; and after work, from six until nine, Serge would be on duty again with his daughter, they'd work on her music and make up stories together; and it was during this balmy interval that Marisha's distressed father struck the household, he himself, incidentally, having lived for many years now with another family, and having experienced his fair share of sorrow and had a further son, now twenty years old. Marisha's father drank and talked a great deal, saying God knows what to no purpose whatsoever, and for no purpose whatsoever was run over by a car on the doorstep of his daughter's house right there on Stulina Street, at the quiet hour of 9.30 in the evening.

During the same period my mother quietly burned out, dwindling from over twelve stone to less than five, and she died with great bravery, kept cheering everyone else up, including me; and right at the end the doctors took it upon themselves to find a non-existent abscess in her, opened it up, accidentally sewed her intestine to her peritoneum and left her to die with an open wound the size of a fist, and when she was rolled out to us dead, disembowelled and sewn up any old how right up to her chin with a great hole in her belly, I couldn't believe such things could befall a human being, and for a moment imagined this wasn't my mother, and that my mother must be somewhere else. Kolya took no part in all these goings on; the two of us had formally separated five years before, only neither of us had paid for the divorce, both having settled down to simple coexistence, like a husband and wife who make no claims on each other, or just live together like everyone else; but at this point it turned out that he'd gone and paid for the divorce after all, and after the funeral he suggested to me in all serious- ness that I should pay too, and I paid. Then my father, fatally struck down by grief, passed away too, dying of a heart attack, easily and happily, in his sleep: one night, getting up to tuck Alyosha in, I simply noticed my father wasn't breathing; so I went back to bed, lay there until morning, took Alyosha to school, and then took my father to the hospital morgue.

But all this took place in the intervals between Fridays; I missed a few of them, and then a month later it was Easter, and once again I invited everyone to come round to our place as they did every year. Once a year, at Easter, we all gathered at my and Kolya's place, and with Mum and Dad's help I made lots of food, and then my parents took Alyosha off with them to our dacha in the country, an hour and a half's ride out of town, to burn all the dead leaves, put the little house in order and plant this and that – and there, in the unheated hut, the three of them slept, allowing my guests the chance to eat, drink and be merry the whole night long. And it was all just the same on this occasion; and in order that it should all be just the same, I told Alyosha that he was to go alone to the dacha and spend the night there. There was no other solution, he was already grown up, seven years old, he knew the way there perfectly well, and in addition I'd warned him that he was on no account to come back and ring the doorbell. And so he set off, a solitary waif. That Sunday morning he and I had visited the graves of his grandfather and grandmother; it was the first time he'd been to a cemetery, and he carted the water for me to and fro in the pail, and we planted daisies round the graves. He was supposed to embark on a new life from that point on; we ate a hasty meal there, bread, sausage, cheese and tea – taken from the supplies for out festive meal that night – and Alyosha then set off, without pausing to rest, for the next leg of the journey to the dacha, while I, back home, set about preparing the dough for the cabbage pies. My resources by this time were pretty slender; a cabbage pie, a pie made with mother's jam, potato salad, eggs with onion, grated beetroot with mayonnaise, a bit of cheese and sausage – they'd gobble it all up no matter what. And a bottle of vodka. The fact was I didn't earn much, and there was no point expecting anything much from Kolya, he'd almost totally moved out to live with his parents by this time, and on the rare occasions that he visited he kept shouting at Alyosha for eating all wrong and hiccoughing all wrong and dropping crumbs on the floor, and finally he yelled that the boy spent the whole time watching television and God knows what he'd grow up to be, he didn't read, didn't draw. This helpless cry was a cry of jealousy in relation to Sonya, who sang, composed music, attended a prestigious music school where there were three hundred applicants for every place, had been a bookworm from the age of two and wrote poetry and stories herself. In the final analysis Kolya loved Alyosha, but he would have loved him a great deal more if the child had been talented and good-looking, brilliant at school and strong amongst his schoolfellows. Then Kolya would have loved him a great deal more, but as it was he saw himself in the boy and it made him mad, and especially mad when Alyosha was eating. Alyosha had bad teeth, at the age of seven they hadn't grown properly at the front, and Alyosha hadn't yet adapted to his orphaned state since the death of his grandparents, and he ate distractedly, swallowing great lumps without chewing properly, dropping crumbs and bits and pieces all over his trousers and endlessly spilling things; and to cap it all he'd started wetting his bed. I think Kolya popped like a cork straight out of our family nest just in order not to have to see his urine-soaked son, trembling in his wet pants on his skinny little legs. When Kolya, woken by Alyosha's weeping, first came upon this disgrace, he went for Alyosha, slapping him straight on the cheek, and Alyosha swiftly ran back to his sodden, sour-smelling bed, but he didn't cry much, he even felt relieved at having been punished. I just smiled ironically, left the room and set off to work, leaving them to sort out the mess between them. On that day I was due to have my eyes examined; they were already showing signs of the hereditary disease my mother had died from. Or rather, the doctor hadn't given me a final diagnosis, but the drops she prescribed were the same as those prescribed for my mother, and I was due to undergo the same tests. I was in for it now, that was how things stood, and what could I care if Alyosha wet the bed or Kolya hit him? New horizons had opened out before me. I won't say what sort of horizons, but I started to take measures. Kolya left. I returned home and found that Kolya's wearable items had disappeared – everything else, to do him justice, he had graciously left me. And now it was Easter and I baked the pies and pulled out the table, covered it with a tablecloth and set out the plates and glasses and salads, the sausage and cheese and bread; there were even a few apples that a friend of my mother's had given me, she'd brought a whole bag of them, a rare find in springtime, along with some painted eggs, and I took a few along to the cemetery, scattered some food for the birds on the little planks, and Alyosha and I ate a bit too. There were lots of people around, I remember, standing around the other fenced-in graves, chatting animatedly, drinking and having a snack in the fresh air; we've still kept up this tradition of Easter picnics in graveyards; they make you feel that everything, in the end, has worked out all right, the deceased are lying there in peace, and people come and drink to them, and the graves are tended, and the air is fresh, and there are birds about and no one and nothing has been forgotten; and it will be just the same for every one of us, everything will pass and come to an end just as peacefully and happily, with paper flowers and photographs in ceramic frames, and birdies in the air and painted eggs lying right there on the earth. Alyosha, I think, overcame his fear; he grew gradually bolder, planting a bed of daisies with me in the earth; the soil there is clean and sandy, and I'd had my parents cremated, so there were just little boxes of ash buried there, nothing too dreadful; and everything was behind us now, and Alyosha ran to and fro watering the bed, and then we went and washed our hands and ate our eggs, bread and apples, and scattered and crumbled up the rest, as did the numerous visitors to other, neighbouring graves. And on our way home in the bus and on the metro everyone was tipsy but friendly and full of goodwill, as if they'd glanced in at the world beyond the grave and found fresh air there and plastic flowers, and they'd drunk to it all in a spirit of friendship.

So that day, in the evening, alone and free, I awaited the arrival of my slightly embarrassed annual guests, who showed up to a man, because Marisha couldn't not come, she's a forthright woman of noble blood, and all the rest came thanks to her, and Serge was there, and my by now former husband Kolya, who has exactly the same rotten teeth as Alyosha – Kolya came and went straight to the kitchen to unpack everything they'd brought, ready-boiled potatoes with dill and cucumber, and lots of wine in anticipation of a whole night's drinking. And why shouldn't they make merry, after all, when there was someone else's empty apartment available and there was the additional interest of my delicate situation: how, in other words, I was going to react to the arrival of my newly-wedded relations Kolya and Marisha, who'd officially registered their marriage just the day before? So that was how things stood, and there was Serge too, a bit more impatient than usual to get down to drinking; he and Zhora immediately embarked on washing away all the recent events. There'd been no trace of Lenka Marchukaite for ages; we'd heard that she was wandering round with her bosom tied up with a warm scarf, someone had seen her in the metro after she'd given birth to the still-born child; she hadn't moaned about it, but only complained that her milk had come. So Andrei-the-snitch put on a record and Nadya, his underage girl, started playing the proper Russian *baba* again and telling me how much alimony Andrei paid and that it was useless for him even to get a PhD, everything would go on the alimony anyway, and when would it all end? In fourteen years, when Nadya would be hitting thirty three; only then could she consider having a child of her own. Tanya the Valkyrie came in, joyfully flashing her teeth and eyes, and I asked her whether they'd put Sonya and her boy to sleep together, it would be cosier like that, and Tanya in reply, as always, just snorted quietly, showing even more of her enormous teeth, whereas Marisha, on the contrary, quite unlike her old self, got mad at me when I asked:

'What do they get up to there?'

'They get up to precisely that,' the joyful Tanya replied.

'It's all very well for you, you've got a boy, but it's not so good for Marisha; Marisha, have you taught Sonya how to protect herself?'

'Don't worry, I've taught her,' answered Marisha and went to join the quietly snorting Tanya, although I, as usual, had spoken the pure truth.

'What's going on?' asked Nadya, whose eye was just about to pop out of its orbit.

'Nadya,' I said, 'is it true you've got one false eye?'

'She's always like that,' said the radiant Tanya to poor Nadya, and at this point Andrei-the-snitch had his say:

'I take an extremely negative view of you,' he announced, recalling Serge's formula; but I paid no attention to Andrei-the- snitch.

Serge and Zhora emerged from the kitchen, already the worse for wear, and my Kolya came out of our former bedroom, and I knew very well what he'd been up to in there.

'So, Kolya, have you already helped yourself to the best sheets?' I asked, and realised that I'd hit the nail on the head. Kolya shook his head and twisted a finger at his temple to indicate a screw loose; but as a result, thanks to my perspicacity, he didn't take a single item of bed linen during this visit.

'Marisha, do you and my husband have something to sleep on? I realise you must have had to allocate a share of the sheets to Serge. And all my sheets have been ruined in the wash; on his last visit Kolya for the first time in his life undertook to wash all the sheets and threw the whole lot into boiling water, and all the various stains, all the protein in them got nicely brewed up, and now they show up in the form of clouds.'

Whereupon they all burst out laughing with a friendly, satisfied laugh and sat down to table. I'd played my role, and now it was Serge's turn to play his, and he in his vague, inarticulate way, with his nasal voice, started arguing with Zhora about a certain Ryabikin's general theory of fields; in the course of this Serge furiously attacked Ryabikin, and Zhora condescendingly defended him, and then appeared reluctantly to give in and agree, and for the first time one caught a glimpse, in Serge, of the unsuccessful scientist, the one who hadn't made it, whereas in the downtrodden Zhora one saw, for the first time, a rising star in the field of science, for nothing so betrays personal success as condescension towards one's peers.

'So when are you defending your PhD, Zhora?' I asked him, hazarding a guess, and Zhora took the bait and immediately answered that the pre-defence examination was due to take place on Tuesday, and the defence itself whenever it came to his turn.

Everyone fell silent for a moment, and then they started drinking. Everyone drank to the point of total eclipse. Andrei-the-snitch suddenly started complaining about the local council, which wouldn't allow them as a couple to have a three-room apartment, and Nadya's papa had been made a general and was creating an uproar over it all, he kept heaping present after present on Nadya, and there was already a car there waiting for her, and a three-room private apartment, if only Nadya would go to college instead of having a baby.

'But I want to have a baby,' said Nadya stubbornly; no one, however, pursued this theme.

In short, the conversation round the table failed to gel. Kolya and Marisha were engaged in quiet nego-tiations, and I knew very well that they were discussing the fact that he should take all his remaining things right now and store them away somewhere, until they'd successfully completed the exchange of Marisha's apartment for a room for Serge and a tiny two-room apartment for themselves, so that Sonya would have somewhere separate to practise her violin, and Serge would have somewhere to live with his brunette, and my husband would have somewhere to live with Marisha. Or maybe they were whispering that it would be better to give me their two-room apartment and settle themselves in my three-room apartment and begin the exchange from there.

'Do you like it here in my apartment, Marisha?' I asked. 'Maybe you'd like to move in here, and Alyosha and I will move out wherever you say? Alyosha and I don't need much, you can take our things.'

'Fool,' said Andrei loudly. 'Complete idiot! All

Marisha's thinking is that they shouldn't take anything away from you, you idiot!'

'But why on earth, help yourselves!' I said. 'I don't need much myself, and Alyosha after all is leaving altogether, he's going to a children's home. I'm already busy making the arrangements. It's in Borovsk.'

'Really,' said Kolya. 'Whatever next.'

'Let's get out of here, this show is beyond . . .' said Andrei-the-snitch, and he even made a decisive move to stand up together with his Nadya, but the others didn't stir, it was important to them to see the trial to its conclusion.

'I'm arranging to have him put in a children's home. Here are the application forms,' I said and, without getting up, reached up for the already completed forms from behind the glass of the book case.

Kolya took one look at them and tore them up.

'Brazen idiot,' said Andrei.

I leaned back in my chair:

'Have a drink, eat up, I'm about to serve pies with cabbage and jam.'

'All right,' said Serge, and they began drinking again. Andrei put on a record, and Serge went up to his estranged wife Marisha and invited her to dance. Marisha blushed; it was such a delight to see her furtive glance, directed at me, for some reason straight at me. I've become the yardstick of conscience here, I muttered to myself, setting the cabbage pie on the table.

At this point everything began to whirl, the celebration of their great love had begun, everyone was singing and yelling what a terrific time they were having, when suddenly Kolya, left out of things, came up to me and asked: but where's Alyosha?

'I don't know, playing around somewhere,' I said.

'But it's past midnight,' said Kolya and went out to the hall.

I didn't stop him, but he didn't put on his coat; on the way out he disappeared into the lavatory and stayed there, in silence, for an eternity, and meanwhile Marisha started feeling sick, she'd drunk too much and in the end was reduced to hanging out of the kitchen window and throwing up all her beetroot straight onto the wall – as I gathered later, from the caretaker of the block who turned up the next day.

Pies, cigarette butts, ravaged salads, half-eaten apples and apple cores, bottles under the sofa, Nadya sobbing violently and clutching her eye, and Andrei, who had Marisha in his arms and was dancing with her – this was their one celebrated act of the year, accomplished this time after Marisha had splattered the evening's menu all over the front of the house, and Nadya was witnessing it for the first time in her life and was so terrified by the whole business that she'd lost her eye.

Then Andrei gathered himself and sternly gathered up Nadya; we'd got to closing time on the metro, Serge and Zhora amiably put on their coats, Kolya emerged from the lavatory and absent-mindedly lay down on the sofa, but Zhora picked him up and led him out, and the joyful Tanya brought up the rear, and at last I opened the door for all of them, and they all saw Alyosha, who'd fallen asleep out there on the stairs.

I jumped out, lifted him up and with a wild cry: 'What the hell are you doing here!' and slapped him in the face, so hard that the child, not yet awake, started bleeding and choking. I started thrashing him all over, whereupon they all fell upon me, twisted me round, thrust me through the door and slammed it shut, and someone went on holding the door for a long time

345

afterwards while I went on thumping away at it, and from the other side I could hear someone sobbing and Nadya shouting:

'. . . with my bare hands! My God! Of all the vile things!'

And Kolya, descending the stairs, kept shouting:

'My Alyosha! Little Alyosha! That's it! I'm taking you with me! That's it! I don't care where the fuck we go, but you're not staying here! The bitch!'

I bolted the door. My calculations had been correct. One and all of them were unable to bear the sight of a child's blood; they were quite capable of tearing each other to pieces, but children were the holy of holies for them.

I rolled into the kitchen and looked out of the window, over Marisha's by now half-erased vomit. I didn't have long to wait. The whole company tumbled out the front door. Kolya was carrying Alyosha! Altogether it was a triumphant procession. Everyone was talking excitedly, still waiting for someone. Andrei was the last to come out, so it must have been he who'd been holding the door. When he emerged to protect the rear flank, Nadya greeted him by shrieking 'Deprive her of her maternal rights, that's what!' Everyone was in top form. Marisha was fussing with a handkerchief over Alyosha. Drunken voices carried far and wide round the neighbourhood. They'd even got a taxi! Kolya and Alyosha, with Marisha supporting them, staggered into the back seat; Zhora sat in front. Zhora was obviously – as always – going to pay, that's definite, I thought, it was on the way to Zhora's anyway and Zhora always took a taxi in any case. What did it matter, the point was they'd get there.

And they wouldn't take me to court, they weren't

that sort. They'd hide Alyosha from me. They'd surround him with attention. And even longer than everyone else, Andrei-the-snitch and his childless wife Nadya would go on romantically loving Alyosha. Tanya would take him to the sea for the summer. And the Kolya that had taken Alyosha in his arms was no longer the same Kolya that had slapped a seven-year-old child in the face just because he'd wet his bed. Marisha would also love and pity my little, rotten-toothed boy, who'd shown not the slightest talent in any sphere. And Zhora, who was going to be rich, would fork out and toss a bit of bounty his way, just you wait and see, he'd get Alyosha into college. It was a different matter with Serge, who was, on the whole, an unromantic character, dry, cynical and mistrustful – he'd end up living with the only being he genuinely loved, with Sonya, his daughter, and his crazed love for her would lead him round every corner and down every back street and into all the dark cellars of life until he finally acknowledged it fully and abandoned all other women and lived for her sake alone, the girl whom he'd fathered from his own loins. There've been other such cases, now and in the past. That would give my little crowd of friends a surprise, something to worry about and puzzle over in the future, but not straight away, not for another eight years, and during those years Alyosha would have time to gather his strength and intelligence and everything he needed. I'd thus settled his fate at very small cost. Had I not done so, he would have wandered from one orphanage to another after my death and would have been an unwelcome guest in his own father's home. But I'd simply sent him out to the dacha and failed on purpose to give him the key, and thus he was forced to return, and I'd forbidden him to knock on the door, and by that time I'd already taught him to understand the word 'forbidden'. And thus the scene of child abuse I'd staged, at such minimal cost, would provide the necessary first jolt to set in motion a new, long-lasting, romantic tradition in the life of my orphaned Alyosha, with his new, noble-spirited adoptive parents, who'd forget their own interests and instead protect his.

That's what I'd calculated, and that's how it's going to be. And it's also good that the whole mixed family will be living right here in Alyosha's own apartment, in his own home, rather than he in theirs; that's just perfect too, for very soon I'll be departing the way of my ancestors. Alyosha, I think, will come and visit me on Easter Sundays, mentally I made that pact with him, pointing out the way there and the day; I believe he'll guess, he's a very bright boy, and there, among the painted eggs and the plastic wreaths and the dishevelled, drunk and kindly crowd, he'll forgive me the fact that I didn't allow him to say goodbye, but gave him a slap in the face instead of a blessing. But it's better that way – for everyone. I'm an intelligent woman, I understand these things.

About the author

Ludmilla Petrushevskaya is one of Russia's most prestigious contemporary writers. She has been awarded the Pushkin Prize, and *The Time: Night* was shortlisted for the first Russian Booker Prize in 1992. Her plays, stories, and novels have been translated into French, German, Italian, and English. She lives in Moscow.